Flight of

A scream sliced th
far removed from a hu
of tortured metal. It was a sound that went on and on as we hurried toward the RV. Mooncloud yanked the passenger door open and then ran around to the driver's side as I climbed up onto the bench seat. As she slid behind the wheel the other woman leapt from the building's rear doorway, sailing over the stairs and landing on the ground below. As she crouched on the asphalt, there was a shattering roar that canceled out the screaming. A ball of flame rolled out from the doorway like an orange party favor, licking the air just a few feet above her head.

Mooncloud threw the van in gear and brought it skidding around as the blaze snapped back through the opening.

Before I could reach for the door handle the woman was springing through the open window to land across my lap.

"Go!" she shouted, but Mooncloud was already whipping the vehicle in a tight turn and accelerating toward the parking lot's north exit. The speed bump smacked my head against the roof of the cab and, by the time my vision cleared, we were driving more sedately down a side street, the woman with the crossbow sitting between me and the passenger door. In the rear-view mirror a pillar of flame was climbing from the roof of the old dormitory that housed the radio station.

I shook my head to clear away the last of the planetarium show and gripped the dashboard. "Will somebody please tell me what's going on?"

"It's very simple, Mr. Csejthe," Dr. Mooncloud said, pressing a button that locked the cab doors. "You are a dead man."

WM. MARK SIMMONS

ONE FOOT IN THE GRAVE

A Baen Books Original

Baen Publishing Enterprises
P.O. Box 1403
Riverdale, NY 10471
www.baen.com

ISBN: 0-671-87721-6

Cover art by Bob Eggleton

First printing, May 1996
Second printing, April 2005

Distributed by Simon & Schuster
1230 Avenue of the Americas
New York, NY 10020

Production & type design by Windhaven Press (www.windhaven.com)
Printed in the United States of America

For Tish,
Her Father's house has many mansions

Such men as come Proud, open-eyed
and laughing to the tomb.

—William Butler Yeats

Chapter One

"Doo-do-n'doo—doo-n'doo-doo—"

"*—Run-run—*"

I cracked an eyelid and peered blearily at the offending clock-radio. Snippets of thought began to daisy-chain into coherent memory.

Eight twenty-two.

Sundown.

Time to rise and shine.

The music became more insistent: Sedaka, Elton John; duet. I moaned, lifting a sleep-numbed arm as they chorused: " . . . *Bad blood! Talkin' 'bout bad blood. . . .*"

My hand closed on the clock's plastic case, ignoring the *off* and *snooze* buttons.

Neil Sedaka belted: *"Bad!"*

"Ba-ad!" echoed Elton John.

"Blood!" wailed Neil.

Elton never got the chance to follow through as the clock-radio arced across the bedroom to a termination point against the far wall. Whatever course the disease might be taking, it had yet to affect my reflexes. I groaned out of bed, shrugged into my robe, and began the evening rounds and rituals.

The house was a split-level arrangement with the downstairs rec room serving as my present sleeping quarters. After opening the heavy curtains to the pale remnants of fading sunlight, I started up the stairs for the kitchen.

Halfway up, I did postal calisthenics, retrieving a spill of mail beneath the brass-flapped slot in the front door. Out of a dozen pieces only three were properly addressed to Mr. Christopher L. Csejthe. One was from the insurance company, and the name was probably the only detail they'd managed to get right in the past year. The rest employed a variety of creative misspellings including one designated for "ocupant" on a dot-matrixed label. So much for computerized spell-checking.

I resisted the urge to lay the envelopes out on the dining room table like a tarot reading—*I see a tall, dark bill collector in your future*—tossed the junk mail aside, and carried the rest into the kitchen. Turned on the radio and began filling the teakettle with tap water.

The graveyard shift makes it easy to disconnect. You sleep while the rest of the world works, plays, lives. Then you rise and go forth while everyone else is in bed, dead to the world. The nightly newscast was my daily ritual for reconnecting. Plus, keeping tabs on the competition is *de rigueur*, when you work in radio.

I set the kettle on the stove to boil, thumbed through the envelopes that obviously contained bills and then, believing you start with the bad news first, opened the one from the insurance company. I expected an argument over last month's billing for lab tests and blood work. Instead, there were two checks inside, both made payable to me: one for twenty-five thousand dollars, the other for ten thousand.

It had taken almost a full year, but they had finally gotten around to rewarding me for killing my wife and daughter.

The tiled bathroom walls amplified the rattlesnake clatter of the shower, smothering the best efforts of the radio just outside the bathroom door. Muffled music gave way to mumbled talk. By the time I reached for my towel, the newscast was five minutes along.

I hadn't missed much; the lead story was the national economy. Again. Congress still hadn't figured out that it was fiscal madness to spend more money than it was taking in every year.

I brushed my teeth as world and national events gave way to regional and local news.

New reports of cattle mutilations a couple of counties to the north. And, between there and here, a couple of people had disappeared in Linn and Bourbon counties. Any day now the local news outlets would start running a short series on UFOs or Satanists. Oboy.

Tonight's icing on the cake: a mysterious murder just across the Missouri state line but considerably closer to home. An orderly had turned up murdered on the nightshift at St. Peter's Regional Medical Center. The Joplin copshop was tight-lipped (as usual) but rumors were circulating that the remains were found "filed" in various parts of the hospital records room.

The news ended with the announcer observing that while no motive or suspects had been established, yet, last night was the first night of the full moon.

Nyuck, nyuck.

Well, actually, it wasn't that facetious a sign-off. The Midwest seems relatively benign to most of the big-city Coasters, but we make up for our lack of urban angst and high crime rates by occasionally producing monsters that make Dave Berkowitz and Jeff Dahmer look like the Hardy Boys. Come to think of it, Dahmer was one of ours as well.

Southeast Kansas has a particularly ghoulish history with more than its share of bloodbaths, hauntings, and just plain weirdness. They run the gamut from the *Marais des Cygnes* massacre to the Bloody Benders of the pioneer days to the purported hauntings of the Lightning Creek bridge, the ghost in Pitt State's McCray Hall, and the stories that linger amid the crumbled remains of the old Greenbush church. Even today those big, empty fields by day aren't always so empty by night. Nope, when the news ends with unusual and unexplained death, the observation of lunar phenomena, and the exhortation to lock your doors and windows, you'd better listen up, friends and neighbors; it's a good night to stay indoors and clean and oil your guns. And listen to Yours Truly on the radio.

Shaving was never the high point of my evening ablutions and, lately, it had become a major nuisance. In spite of slamming 150 watters into the bathroom fixtures, it was getting harder and harder to see what I was doing with the razor. I'd heard of the wasting effect of certain illnesses but, with each passing day, my own reflection seemed to fade before my own eyes.

"To be or not to be," I murmured, peering into the uncooperative mirror. What else had the Bard penned? *O! that this too too solid flesh would melt, thaw and resolve itself into a dew. . . .*

Hamlet was a butthead.

Tonight I decided "hell with it" and made the three-day-old beard official. Additional UV protection, I figured. I wouldn't miss my face in the mirror. Dark hair, dark eyes, a slight Slavic caste to otherwise bland features: it was not the kind of face that distinguished its owner in any definable way. *Why Jenny had ever given me a second look—*

I threw my razor across the bathroom and stalked back into the bedroom. It was shaping up into a good night for throwing things.

Questions, I coached myself, staggering into a pair of white chinos and a tan short sleeve shirt: *Is my eyesight affected? Will I eventually go blind? Is it treatable?*

Is it terminal?

I pulled on a pair of white canvas deck shoes.

Oh hell, let's cut to the chase: have I got AIDS, Doc?

The mirror might play tricks on me, but there was no problem in reading the bathroom scales: I was still losing weight. Which wasn't hard to figure. Since my appetite had deserted me, I'd managed a dozen meals over the past two weeks.

What are you hungry for when you don't know what you're hungry for?

Nothing on a Ritz.

After dark it's only a fifteen-minute drive from one end of Pittsburg, Kansas, to the other.

The population sign boasts 30,000, but the downtown area is condensed into a couple of miles of main street that fronts about eighty percent of the city's shops and stores. The old façades reflect the central European culture from the boomtown coal mining days of nearly a century ago. Today, aside from some manufacturing and a dog track north of town, most of the local economy is tied to agriculture and Pittsburg State University. The mines have long since played out.

The main drag runs north and south. Homes sprawl for miles in all directions but, once you've gone more than four blocks, either east or west, the houses disperse like boxy children in a wide-ranging game of rural hide-and-seek.

So getting from one end of the town proper to the other is relatively quick and simple. Especially after eight P.M. when they roll up the sidewalks.

This particular night, however, the trip to the hospital seemed interminable. Marsh's voice on my answering machine had promised "some answers," but his tone sounded just as bewildered as when he had run the first batch of tests nearly three months ago.

I glanced over at the three books stacked beside me on the passenger seat: Whitman's *Leaves of Grass*, Tuchman's *A Distant Mirror*, and Jung's *Man and His Symbols*.

How much time, Doc?

Maybe I should have picked up something from the Reader's Digest Book Club, instead.

I checked my watch in the Mount Horeb Hospital parking lot: close to an hour before I was due at the radio station. Time enough for "some answers."

But enough time for the answer I dreaded most? And the one that loomed right behind it: will my insurance cover the treatments?

Tough call.

Total your car and your insurance agent consults the Blue Book like it was holy writ. Not so simple when you total a seven-year-old girl and her mother. Some asshole behind a desk at the home office wanted to dither over revised actuarial tables and adjust the compensatory payout schedule. Did he think I was going to cut a special deal with the coroner? Maybe fake a funeral while I took them down to some arcane body shop and got them up and running, again? *Jesus.*

So what kind of investment are they going to see in spending tens of thousands of dollars on dead-end treatments for *moi* that would probably just delay the inevitable for a few more months?

I walked across the parking lot, empty and empty-handed; nothing left to throw.

The emergency room was as silent as a tomb.

Whoa, scratch that allusion. . . .

Besides, there was a faint whisper of background noise, muffled sounds that put one in mind of a high-tech fish tank. Aging fluorescents added to the aquarium effect, but the waiting room was empty, as if some giant ichthyologist had netted it out preemptory to a water change. The lone receptionist surfaced from her computer terminal just long enough to direct me down the corridor with a desultory wave, then submerged again without a single word being spoken. I walked the length of the corridor, feeling my feet drag as if encased in a deep-sea diver's leaden boots.

Dr. Donald Marsh, third-year resident, was waiting for me at the second treatment station. Fair of skin, the only contrast to his green-bleached-to-white surgical scrubs was his buzz-cut orange hair and a dusting of freckles. Picture the Pillsbury Doughboy sprinkled with cinnamon.

I didn't recognize the short, broad-faced woman standing on the other side of the treatment table. Her white lab coat was a sharper contrast to her nut-brown face and hands. Her black hair was braided, curving around and dropping down across her right shoulder like spun obsidian.

Don smiled as I approached. The woman didn't, glanced down at a clipboard. Looked back up at me.

"Chris . . ." Marsh's firm hand enveloped mine, didn't squeeze. " . . . how're you feeling?"

"Like I've got one foot in the grave and the other on a banana peel," I said, trying for the light touch. It almost came off.

Marsh looked uncomfortable. With each examination I had watched that look move across his features like lengthening shadows on an old sundial. Now I studied his face for new shadings but saw nothing beyond fresh uncertainty in his eyes.

"You still don't know." Logic followed on the heels of disappointment: "It's not AIDS, then?"

Marsh shook his head. "We know that much."

"So what else do we know?"

"We know you haven't been taking sulfanilamide or any other drugs known to produce photosensitivity as a side effect," he said. "The blood tests have ruled out eosin, rose bengal, hematoporphyrin, phylloerythrin, and other known photodynamic substances in your bloodstream. And I'm pretty damn sure you haven't been ingesting plants with photoreactive pigments like Hypericum, geeldikkop, and buckwheat."

"Buckwheat?"

"In extreme situations it can cause fagopyrism. But I've never heard of a case in humans and what you have is nothing like fagopyrism."

I'd grown weary of asking Marsh to stop speaking in tongues. "So what *is* it like?"

"Porphyria," the woman answered unexpectedly.

"Excuse me?"

Marsh cleared his throat. "I promised you results on the last batch of tests we ran. Well. I guess you might say the main result is Dr. Mooncloud."

She smiled suddenly and extended a small, brown hand. "Taj Mooncloud, Mr. Csejthe." My surname came out sounding like a sneeze.

Taj?

"My father was a Native American," she explained as if I'd voiced the question, "my mother, East Indian."

Interesting. I took her hand across the gurney. "Pleased," I said. "My great-great grandfather was Rumanian: it's pronounced 'Chey-tay.' "

"Do forgive me."

"No offense taken," I said, patiently two-stepping the dance of etiquette. "You were saying something about my condition?"

"Ah, yes." The businesslike demeanor was back. "I have an interest in certain types of blood disorders and I've arranged for most of the major labs to flag my computer when something unusual comes in for testing. Your blood samples hold a particular interest for me."

"How nice."

"Let's see. Christopher L. Csejthe: Caucasian, male, thirty-two years of age," she read from the clipboard. "No significant history of disease in either personal or family medical records. Military records are curiously incomplete. . . ."

Which meant that she had the edited version. And she shouldn't have had even that.

"Marital blood tests registered no anomalies as of nine years ago."

I glanced down at the white band of flesh circling the base of my ring finger. Almost a year, now, and still refusing to tan. . . .

"Could I have picked something up while I was in the service? Some exotic bug or exposure to chemical—"

Marsh glanced over Mooncloud's shoulder and shook his head. "That was over a decade ago, wasn't it? Even such diverse hazards as malaria or sand flies or Agent Orange have warning symptoms that kick in much sooner."

"How long have you been working in radio?" Mooncloud asked.

It was my turn to shake my head. "If you're wondering about exposure to RF radiation, Doc, it's a dead end. I didn't start my current profession until this thing—whatever it is—necessitated my taking night work. Before that I taught English Lit. Eight years. Exposure to radical ideas comes with the territory but I doubt that's the causative agent here."

Mooncloud consulted the second page on her clipboard: "Patient first complained of sensitivity to light eight months ago. Shortly thereafter the formation of epidermal carcinomas necessitated avoidance of all exposure to ultravi—"

"I am familiar with my own medical history, Doctor; the treatments for skin cancer and subsequent diagnosis of pernicious anemia." My temper was frayed like an old rope that had been stretched too far, too long. "A moment ago you used a word I haven't heard before."

"Porphyria."

"That's the one."

"It's a genetic disorder," Marsh explained, "a hereditary disease that affects the blood. Porphyria causes the body to fail to produce one of the enzymes necessary to make *heme*, the red pigment in your hemoglobin. You're gonna love this—" he grinned wryly "— it's the vampire disease."

I must have goggled a bit. "The what?"

"The vampire disease. At least that's what the tabloids have dubbed it."

I scowled: I was not amused by the idea of a "vampire disease" and any connection to the tabloids was something I liked even less.

Marsh looked to Mooncloud for help, but she was preoccupied with her clipboard. "There was a paper done back in eighty-five by a Canadian chemist named David Dolphin," he said. "He hypothesized that porphyria could have been the basis for some of the medieval legends of vampires and werewolves." He held up a finger. "Extreme sensitivity to light: the most common symptom."

I shook my head. "And vampires can't stand sunlight, right? Give me a br—"

"It's more than that, Chris. Some porphyria victims are so sensitive to sunlight that their skin becomes damaged and, in extreme cases, lose their noses and ears—fingers, too. In other cases, hair may grow on the exposed skin."

"Werewolves," I muttered.

Marsh added a second finger to the first. "Another symptom is the shriveling of the gums and the lips may be drawn tautly, as well, giving the teeth a fanglike appearance."

"Great. Anything else?"

"Well, although it remains incurable, we have a few options in terms of treatment, now. But back in the Middle Ages there was just one way to survive. To fulfill your body's requirements for *heme*, you had to ingest—drink—large quantities of blood."

I stared at Marsh. "Nice. How about garlic and crosses?"

He shrugged. "I don't know anything about the religious angle, but garlic is a definite no-no."

"Really."

"Stimulates *heme* production. Which can turn a mild case of porphyria into an extremely painful one."

"And you're telling me I have this 'porphyria disease'?"

"No," Mooncloud said. "You asked what your symptoms were like. I said 'porphyria'—which they are. Like. But porphyria is a genetic disorder and tends to be hereditary."

"Which is why all that inbreeding during the Middle Ages produced pockets of it," Marsh said.

"But since there's no record of it in your family history," Mooncloud continued, "it seems unlikely. Particularly since it's shown up rather late in life for a genetic condition. Which also rules out hydroa and xeroderma pigmentosum. But I won't rule it out until we've run a full spectrum of genetic tests. Maybe they can tell us what the blood tests didn't."

"Okay." I felt my temper ease back a couple of notches. "Let's get started."

"Not here," Mooncloud said.

"Then where?"

"Washington."

"D.C.?"

She shook her head. "Seattle."

"Tomorrow should see mostly sunny skies with highs in the upper eighties. Currently, it's seventy-three degrees under mostly cloudy skies and although the lunar signs are less than auspicious, I'd give little *credence* to them. . . ." I tapped a button and then closed the microphone as Creedence Clearwater Revival launched into "Bad Moon Rising."

"Clever." Mooncloud had doffed her lab coat and was wearing a sleeveless shirt of blue cotton and tan slacks. Beaded moccasins completed the ensemble.

I shrugged. "Radio—it's what the teeming millions demand and expect."

"Teeming millions? In southeast Kansas?"

"Teeming thousands," I corrected.

"At one o'clock in the morning?"

"Hundreds. Teeming hundreds."

She arched an eyebrow. "How about teeming dozens. . . ." It wasn't a question.

"Hey, it's a job—with benefits and insurance. Something I can't afford to walk away from with a preexisting condition like this." I sorted through stacks of compact disks for my next piece of music.

"All the insurance in the world isn't going to help you if the doctors don't understand what they're treating."

I stopped and leaned across a pair of dusty turntables. "Dr. Mooncloud . . . I appreciate the fact that you traveled all the way to Pittsburg, Kansas, to meet me and review my case. I suppose I should be flattered as hell that you've followed me to work and are sitting here in an empty building in the wee hours of the morning to try to offer me a special treatment program. Most doctors won't even make house calls."

"I am not most doctors, Mr. Csejthe." Her smile was pure Mona Lisa. "And you are not most patients."

"Patience and I seem to be mutually exclusive these days," I said. "Can you guarantee me a cure if I come to Seattle?"

"A cure? Only God guarantees cures and He's a notoriously reluctant prognosticator. I can guarantee you a medical research team with experience in your kind of malady and a strong interest in your particular case. It won't cost you a thing and I can guarantee you a job in the Seattle area—"

"I've already got a job right here. And working the night shift is perfect when your skin suddenly develops an allergy to sunlight."

There was a muffled thump and the lights suddenly went out. The studio was an interior room with no windows to the outside: the darkness was sudden and complete. As was the silence. C.C.R. had gotten as far as "don't go out tonight," quitting as if someone had yanked amp and mike cords in perfect unison.

Then the emergency lighting kicked in like flashlights of the gods, amplifying the shadows in Mooncloud's frown to intimidating proportions. "What's wrong? What happened?"

"Gremlins." Surprise eclipsed annoyance as I watched this professional woman—who had just spent the last forty minutes speaking of medical matters that bordered on twenty-first century science—make the same gesture my grandmother had used to ward off the "evil eye."

"A bird, actually," I said, pulling the phone over and flipping through the pad of emergency numbers. "There's a place on the utility pole, just thirty feet from the building, where the power lines junction with a transformer. When a bird picks that particular spot to roost: zap! One fried feathered friend and one powerless public radio station."

"You don't have a backup generator?"

"Darlin'," I drawled, "this is Kansas and we're public radio." I fumbled the receiver to my ear and began punching out a series of numbers on the keypad. "We just call the power company and they send a guy over with a long pole who resets the circuit breaker—" I stopped, listening to the silence as I pushed the buttons. Breaking the assumed connection, I listened for a dial tone.

"What sort of bird would roost at one in the morning?" she asked, making the gesture again.

I smacked the receiver back into the cradle with a sigh. "Phone's dead."

The emergency lights flickered. And, inexplicably, went out.

"Um, they can't do that," I announced to no one in particular. The emergency lights were on individual battery sources: even if it were remotely possible for one to go out that quickly, they all wouldn't fail at the same time.

Ignoring the rules of probability, the emergency lights remained off-line, preferring some variant of the chaos theory, instead.

"From ghosties and ghoulies and long-leggity beasties," Mooncloud whispered.

"Nocturnal volleyball teams." I groped my way across the room in the darkness.

"I beg your pardon?" I would have sworn that the disoriented quality in her voice was not entirely due to the sudden blackout.

"Things that go 'bump' in the night."

"Marsh warned me about you," she said.

"Yeah? What did he say?"

"That I could look up 'attitude' in the dictionary and find your picture."

I bit back a curse as I barked my shin on a tape console that had been moved out of its place for servicing.

"That you?"

"Of course it's me!" I was trying to keep my temper from erasing my mental map of the studio's layout. "The building's locked up tighter than a drum. Who else would it be?"

There was another sound, then, from the other end of the building. It took a moment to place it: the rattling of a metal security grate. "I stand corrected—someone must have left a door unlocked."

"Is there a back door?" Mooncloud's voice was decidedly unsteady.

"Doctor, there's no need to panic. It's probably one of the campus security guards checking the building. We'll just sit here until the power is restored—"

The security grating rattled again.

And then it screamed.

The sound of rending metal groaned and shrieked, echoing down the hallway like a slow-motion freight train braking in a tunnel. I fumbled for Mooncloud's hand in the darkness, aiming for the luminous dial of her watch. "The back door's this way, Doc. Last one out's—"

"I know," she said grimly. "Far better than you, in fact."

I led her around the consoles and fumbled open the sliding glass door that led to the engineering section. Groping across a bank of demodulators and telemetry panels, we maneuvered through the stacks of equipment toward the back door. A workbench caught my hip, bruising it and turning us around so that I was disoriented for a moment.

"Hurry," she whispered.

"A moment," I hissed, waving my free arm around in search of a blind man's landmark. I suddenly realized that the exit door was before me, a vague, grey rectangle in the deeper blackness. Glancing back over my shoulder, I saw a dim glow through the tiny window inset in the main studio's outer door.

"Don't look back!" Mooncloud shouted, pushing at my shoulder. "Go! *Go!*"

The glow was mesmerizing, intensifying, but I turned my attention to the fire door in front of us. I slapped the crash-bar but the door would not budge.

"Break it down."

"What?"

"Break it down!" she insisted.

I was going to say something about the weight and immovability of a fire door, but the sound of exploding glass from the main studio derailed that train of thought. I whirled and kicked the door just above the bar: the metal panel buckled and the door erupted out of its frame, sailed over the concrete porch and steps, and went surfing across the rear parking lot.

Outside, the night seemed preternaturally bright despite the fact that the streetlights that normally illuminated the north end of the campus were dark. A van—no, one of those mobile homes on wheels—was swinging around a concrete median and heading right for us. It didn't seem to be traveling all that fast, which was fortunate as the driver had neglected to switch on his headlamps.

Dr. Mooncloud was also moving in slow motion, looking somewhat like Lindsay Wagner in a grainy rerun of *The Bionic Woman*. It felt as if Time, itself, had perceptibly tapped its own fourth-dimensional brakes. I had to make a conscious effort to linger, just to keep from leaving her behind.

As I slowed, Dr. Mooncloud seemed to speed up, her left hand withdrawing a hip flask from the pocket of her windbreaker. The RV was braking to a stop just ten feet away and, as she began a slow turn on the ball of her foot, another woman jumped out of the driver's side of the vehicle. The driver closed the distance between us at an amazing speed and I was only able to catch random impressions: long, dark hair, though not as black as Dr. Mooncloud's. Tall, athletic; she wore Nikes, blue jeans, and a tank-top that revealed arms like carved cherry wood. As she reached the foot of the steps, I could see that she was carrying a crossbow. . . .

And suddenly everything seemed to snap back into realtime.

"How many?" the driver bellowed, bounding up the stairs.

"One." Mooncloud turned back to face the doorway we had just passed through. "I only detected one."

"Get in the van," the driver ordered, shouldering her way between us. "Give me fifty and then haul ass whether I'm back or not."

"Soon as I seal the door." Mooncloud unstopped the flask and, as the newcomer disappeared through the doorway, poured the contents across the threshold. She took special care to form a solid, unbroken stream from post to post and then stuffed it back in her jacket. "Come on!" She took me by the arm.

"What?"

"Get in the camper!"

"Camper?" I was still thinking in slow motion.

She yanked me down the stairs and shoved me toward the recreational vehicle. "Now!"

"I can't abandon the station! The FCC—"

A scream sliced the night air—an animal sound as far removed from a human voice as the previous scream of tortured metal. It was a sound that went on and on as we hurried toward the RV. Mooncloud yanked the passenger door open and then ran around to the driver's side as I climbed up onto the bench seat. As she slid behind the wheel the other woman leapt from the building's rear doorway, sailing over the stairs and landing on the ground below. As she crouched on the asphalt, there was a shattering roar that canceled out the screaming. A ball of flame rolled out from the doorway like an orange party favor, licking the air just a few feet above her head.

Mooncloud threw the van in gear and brought it

skidding around as the blaze snapped back through the opening.

Before I could reach for the door handle the woman was springing through the open window to land across my lap.

"Go!" she shouted, but Mooncloud was already whipping the vehicle in a tight turn and accelerating toward the parking lot's north exit. The speed bump smacked my head against the roof of the cab. By the time my vision cleared, we were driving more sedately down a side street, the woman with the crossbow sitting between me and the passenger door. In the rearview mirror a pillar of flame was climbing from the roof of the old dormitory that housed the radio station.

I shook my head to clear away the last of the planetarium show and gripped the dashboard. "Will somebody please tell me what's going on?"

"It's very simple, Mr. Csejthe," Dr. Mooncloud said, pressing a button that locked the cab doors. "You are a dead man."

Chapter Two

"This is kidnapping." I was doing surprisingly well at keeping a reasonable tone to my voice. "Federal offense."

Not that I wasn't grateful: I had apparently been rescued from . . . well . . . *something*. But now my so-called rescuers refused to stop the vehicle or return me to town.

"I mean we are talking *way* beyond vandalism, destruction of property, assault—" I looked at Mooncloud "—impersonating a doctor."

"Obviously, you haven't been listening." This from the woman with the crossbow who had by now introduced herself as Lupé Garou. A slight French-Canadian accent seemed to authenticate her last name while the cloud of smokey, brown-black hair and coffee-with-cream complexion made sense of her first.

"Oh, I've been listening," I said. "I've heard every word you've said since we left town. The problem is I'm just not buying!"

"What part are you having difficulty with?" Garou asked.

I sighed and leaned my forehead against the dashboard.

"Be patient, dear," I heard Mooncloud murmur. "This is all rather new to him."

"Okay, let's start with me." I sat back up, turning to Mooncloud. "You say that I'm a vampire. I'll play along for a moment and pretend that there really are such things." I opened my mouth wider and ran a finger around my incisors. "'Ook, ma; nah fahgs." I withdrew the finger. "Can't bite necks and suck blood without fangs."

Mooncloud was unfazed. "Mr. Csejthe, I did not say that you are a vampire. I was explaining that you appear to be in the transitional phase. A rather long and uncharacteristically drawn out phase, I might add."

Hoo boy.

"Yeah? Well, *how* did I get started on this so-called phase? Where's the bloodsucker who's supposed to have bitten me?"

"That's what we're in the process of trying to determine."

"But you are not being very cooperative," Garou added.

"*I'm* not being cooperative? *I'm* not being cooperative? I want to go home! Or back to the radio station. A crime has been committed, property destroyed—the authorities have to be contacted. Good God! They'll think I was responsible!"

Mooncloud shook her head. "You can't go back."

Garou chimed in. "You're going to have to face the fact that you are a dead man—both figuratively and literally."

"Look, lady, don't threaten me! I've had it up to here and if you keep pushing—"

"You'll what?" she asked coolly.

I stared back, holding her gaze for a long moment while I tried to think. "Wet my pants."

"What?"

"I gotta go." I turned to Mooncloud. "Or are you planning on driving all the way to Seattle without bathroom breaks?" The two women exchanged looks. "Oh great! You were! You really haven't planned this out, have you?"

"We planned on having more time to convince you."

"We hadn't counted on one of Bassarab's hounds showing up so soon," Garou said.

"Whatever," I said, waving my hand. I had no intention of being sidetracked now. "Pull over."

"Lupé and I will decide when and where to stop, Mr. Csejthe."

"What is the big deal here?" I gestured toward the windshield. "We're in the middle of nowhere. Kansas back roads at three A.M. No traffic. Nothing but cornfields in every direction for miles. Where am I gonna go?" My captors exchanged a look. "Except behind a bush."

Mooncloud nodded and began slowing the Winnebago.

"Find me a spot with some bushes. I'm modest."

"I don't like this," Garou muttered.

"It will be all right, dear," her companion said. "I think once we're done here, Mr. Csejthe will be a little more trusting."

Garou scowled but nodded. "And, perhaps, a little less testy."

Gravel crunched as the RV eased over on the road's shoulder and coasted to a stop. Mooncloud killed the lights. Garou opened the door and swung down. Brandishing the crossbow, she gestured to a clump of bushes straddling a barbed-wire fence. "Two minutes, no more. You run and I'll shoot. I can put a bolt through your leg at thirty feet."

I forced a smile as I stepped down, noting that the shrubbery was no more than twenty feet away. The crossbow came up and tracked me all the way across the ditch and over to the fence. "Where are you going?" she demanded as I spread the strands of fence wire.

"Behind the bushes, madam. Or would you prefer an 'I'll show you mine if you show me yours' arrangement?"

Garou looked back at Mooncloud who nodded. I eased my body through to the other side of the fence.

I had already decided to make a break for it in spite of the crossbow. The odds had to be better than getting back in the vehicle with two escaped lunatics. Now that I was behind the bushes, on the other side of the fence with a cornfield maybe thirty feet beyond, it almost looked too good to be true.

The real danger would be those first ten yards without cover.

"Hurry up," Garou called.

"Hey, sweetheart," I called back, "I need to relax for the plumbing to work, and you're not helping any. These things take time, so shut up and let me concentrate!" I crouched down, hoping that would end any dialogue for the next couple of minutes.

"Lupé, we might as well give Mr. Csejthe some slack right here," Mooncloud was saying, "or else how are we going to convince him of the truth?"

A dark shape glided overhead, an owl hooted, and I missed her reply.

"Here, give me the crossbow," Mooncloud said. "You can climb into the back and change now. It will save us all time."

I parted the foliage and peeked back at the road, surprised at how well my night vision was operating, especially with so little moonlight escaping the barricade of clouds. Garou scowled but finally acquiesced, handing the medieval weapon to Mooncloud. I didn't wait to see any more but dropped to my hands and knees and began crawling toward the perimeter of the cornfield.

"Mr. Csejthe," Mooncloud called, as I left the hiss and crackle of dry grass and began creeping across the quiet dirt, "this is to prove to you two very important points. One: you cannot escape. And two: that we are not mad but know very well of that which we speak."

That did it. It's the crazy ones that make just that kind of speech.

I slipped between the cornstalks with nary a rustle and rose halfway to my feet. Rogers & Hammerstein wrote a little ditty in which "the corn is as high as an elephant's eye" but, by midsummer in Southeast Kansas, it was only as high as a man's shoulders. I hunched over and made like Victor Hugo's bellboy of Notre Dame, hoping I was far enough in to prevent any rustling stalks from targeting me.

"Don't hurt him, Lupé," Mooncloud called as I moved deeper into the field. Another thirty feet and I dropped to my belly and began crawling at a right angle to the rows, working my way through columns of cornstalks. Suddenly, I stopped crawling and pressed my cheek to the dirt, listening. There was a susurrus of leaves as something else entered the rows of greenery. And the patter of feet.

Two pairs of feet.

Very light, somewhat small feet.

A dog running loose, I thought, following the trail I had made into the heart of the corn. *Did these women keep bloodhounds in the back of the camper for such exigencies?*

I raised my head and reached out to crawl through the next row.

My hand encountered a shoe.

Empty?

Groping upward, I encountered an ankle, a leg.

Looking up, I saw a giant white spider dropping toward my face: a hand. Cold, implacable fingers closed on my collar and I found myself suddenly ascending, rising into the night sky to hover with my feet off the ground, the tops of the cornstalks now just barely reaching my waist.

"*Urk!*" I said defiantly, staring back at the red-eyed man who was holding me off the ground with just one arm.

"So," hissed the holdup artist, "yer da one dat's put us ta all dis trouble." Then he smiled.

Imagine Jack Palance.

Doing a Jack Nicholson grin.

Displaying Bela Lugosi's eyeteeth.

With Arnold Schwarzenegger's accent it would have been a certified Ex-Lax moment. Somehow the Brooklynese made my assailant sound like Cliff Claven on old *Cheers* reruns; I might have snickered had I not just entered the second stage of asphyxiation.

The roaring in my ears became a growl and a dark grey shape hurtled across my shrinking field of vision. The next thing I knew I was lying in a tangle of broken cornstalks, gasping for air.

"I command you!" the man shrieked as the silver-and-grey furred beast bore him to the ground. "I *command* you!" The wolf snarled and redoubled its efforts to tear out the man's throat. It almost succeeded. Then an ivory fist connected a roundhouse swing and the animal went flying past my shoulder.

"Unnatural bitch!" the man hissed, rising to one knee. "Abomination! I will teach you your place! I will show you who's master! I will—"

He stopped suddenly, looking down at the wooden shaft that had just planted itself in his chest. Mooncloud stepped through a row of cornstalks, reloading the crossbow with another sharpened dowel. It wasn't necessary; the man fell backward, pale fingers wriggling about but not quite touching the bolt in his chest. His body writhed, smoked, then crumbled to dust, leaving an empty set of clothes behind.

Porphyria, my ass!

Maybe Spielberg or Lucas could've topped it, but it was better than any Hammer flick I'd ever seen and the Brits had set the standard.

"You okay?"

I fumbled for an answer before realizing that Mooncloud had addressed the wolf. It whined a bit, limping over to sniff at the ashy remains of our assailant.

Time to leave: I tried to ease backwards, through an adjacent row of corn, but the crackle of crushed stalks betrayed me: the wolf turned its head, growled, and trotted toward me.

"Lupé. . ." Mooncloud warned.

The wolf placed its paws on my shoulders and stared down at me with green eyes, its breath like a furnace on my face. Then the muzzle changed—withdrawing, absorbing back into the creature's face. Eyes migrated.

Fur retracted. Ears slid downward, revising their shape and configuration. Forget Spielberg and Lucas! Close up this was way beyond any ILM computerized morphing. I was now looking up at the face of Lupé Garou. Looking down at a body that was undeniably human and definitely feminine. Not to mention unclothed.

Oh my.

"We'd better get moving," Mooncloud said, breaking the spell. "Mr. Csejthe, do you still need a bathroom break?"

Lupé was already up and disappearing in the direction of the road as I looked down again—this time rather ruefully.

"Not anymore."

I emerged from the RV's closet bathroom with a towel wrapped around my waist. "You didn't tell me that there were facilities on board." I clutched at the doorframe as the rear suspension compensated for a pothole. "We could have avoided the whole bush and cornfield routine."

Mooncloud stood over the propane stove and stirred the contents of a small saucepan. "You needed to make the attempt and we needed to prove to you that escape was not possible. I needed Lupé to retrieve you so that you would believe our credentials."

Ah.

"That guy—"

"The vampire," she coached gently.

"The vampire," I conceded reluctantly. "That was a nice touch. Most convincing. The frosting on the cake, as it were."

"We didn't expect him. We should have: Bassarab's enforcers usually travel in pairs and he wouldn't have sent just one for an intercept so far from home."

"Whoa, whoa; you're losing me here. I'm just getting used to the idea of vampires and werewolves being for real." I staggered the length of the camper shell and sat on a padded bench beside the fold-down table. "Uh, Ms. Garou *is* a werewolf . . . right?"

Mooncloud nodded.

"Well, you've mentioned this Bassarab guy twice now. Who is he and why does his hired muscle sport fangs? And why are they after me?" I arranged the towel for comfort and modesty as I stretched out my legs. "For that matter, why are you two after me?"

She sighed. "I'm afraid, Mr. Csejthe, the answers to your questions are a bit complicated."

No shit. I didn't say that, however; I just looked at her.

"Let's start with vampires. For the sake of argument, you will admit in the possibility of their existence?"

I nodded. I could do that—admit to *their* possibility—without buying a membership in the club for myself.

"There is ample reason for your skepticism, Mr. Csejthe. First, most human beings do not have a close encounter with the undead and live to tell about it. Second, the *wampyr* have a vested interest in keeping their existence a secret.

"While the Children of Bassarab tend to be solitary predators, they have learned that they must cooperate to preserve their anonymity. If any of them threatens the secret of the *wampyr*, that one is hunted down by agents of its own kind—enforcers—and destroyed lest it betray all others of its bloodline."

"These enforcers, they were after *me*."

Mooncloud nodded, adjusting the heat under the saucepan. "Agents of the New York enclave. Their ruler is supposed to be a direct descendant of the original Bassarab and has taken his name. That is as much as we know. Beyond that it is not hard to guess at basic motivations. Your existence is more than a scientific curiosity, Mr. Csejthe. Your medical documentation is a threat to the unmasking of enclaves everywhere."

"Enclaves?"

Garou's voice crackled from the intercom: "*Merde!*

Must you explain everything to this pup? Let the Doman tell him what he will. No more."

"The Doman?"

Mooncloud sighed. "Lupé, you are only adding to our guest's curiosity—"

"Guest!"

"—and making my attempts to reassure Mr. Csejthe that much more complicated. You drive and let me worry about the explanations."

The intercom grunted.

"Or I shall send our guest up to sit in the cab with you and let you answer all his questions."

Oh, great.

There was a tinny growl from the tiny speaker but no further comments.

"Enclaves, Mr. Csejthe, are population centers where vampires gather and agree to live under a set of laws that insure food and safety for all. The leader of this social underground adjudicates the laws, settles disputes, and looks after his own. He—or she—is known as the Doman for that particular enclave. New York is the largest, but Seattle, where we are taking you, has a fairly strong enclave as well."

"What if a vampire does not wish to retain membership in an enclave?" A tangy aroma was beginning to fill the air and my stomach rumbled, reminding me that I hadn't eaten for the past two days.

"Most enclaves will permit members to apply to other demesnes. Both groups must agree to the transfer and that can be complicated by issues such as resources, competition, questions of loyalty—"

"I mean, what if a—" I hesitated over the word "—um, vampire—didn't want to be a member of any enclave?"

"Then he or she would be considered rogue. And nearly every rogue is hunted down and destroyed for the safety of the enclaves."

Swell: no undead is an island. John Donne would have approved. I tried to concentrate past my growing hunger pangs. "Why is one vampire more likely to expose himself than a whole colony?"

"Think, Mr. Csejthe." She turned off the burner and moved the saucepan to the sink. "Vampires tend to beget two things: bloodless corpses and other vampires, either of which threatens to take bloodsucking monsters out of the tabloids and put them in *Time* and *Newsweek*. The enclaves have developed systems for undead population control, ample but safe food supplies, and the means of disposing of corpses and covering up such faux pas if such should occasionally occur."

"Sounds like a bloodless society."

"*Mon Dieu!*" the intercom squawked. "He thinks he has a sense of humor!"

Mooncloud hit the OFF button on the intercom. "Would you like something to eat?"

I nodded and watched her ladle the soup into a bowl. "So what's to become of me? That—um—"

"Vampire."

"Okay, okay: *vampire!* Seemed more inclined to take me back dead than alive. Or should I say 'undead'?"

"I cannot speak for the Doman of New York. I am here at the will of Stefan Pagelovitch."

"So what does he want?"

Mooncloud put the ladle aside and turned to face me. "I have lived among the *wampyr* for most of my life and I have devoted years—decades—to their study. I know everything that they know about their existence, their history. More, in fact, than most." Her eyes narrowed. "But all that I know—all that is known—pales into insignificance beside the questions that remain unanswered to this day. There is still so much that we do not know. For example, why do some victims rest quietly in their graves while others come back as the Children of Bassarab? We know that a two-way exchange of blood between the vampire and victim is significant . . . but not conclusive. You, Mr. Csejthe, may be the missing link in our research."

She turned and picked up the bowl of soup. "Our Doman has sent for you, Mr. Csejthe, and offers you his protection." She set it on the table before me. "What we have done this night may set us at war with the New York enclave, with Bassarab, himself." She handed me a spoon and napkin.

"When Lupé said that you were a dead man, she meant that there was no going back to the life you have known. Whatever has altered your blood and metabolism may eventually lead to your death. Or your undeath. But the process has begun and you have entered a state of Becoming. Bassarab will not permit you to run free. And, frankly, neither can we. We offer you sanctuary. A chance to make a new life that will accommodate the changes you are going through."

I lifted the first spoonful of soup to my mouth. "And this Bassarab? Just who is this guy?" I swallowed, feeling saliva flood my mouth and throat.

"As I said, we don't really know for sure." Mooncloud came and sat down across from me. "The Bassarabs were a great dynasty of the Vlachs, ruling Walachia and fighting off invasions by the Mongols, Turks, and Hungarians back in the fourteenth and fifteenth centuries. Various princes ruled under the names Vlad I through Vlad IV. One of them was so bloody and evil that he was known as Vlad Drakul—which means Vlad the Dragon or Vlad the Devil. His successors, according to legend, were as bad or worse: Vlad Tepes is known to this day as Vlad the Impaler and Vlad Tsepesh was called the Son of the Devil—Drakul, with the diminutive 'a' added to the end."

I looked down at my bowl, which was nearly empty. "You're saying that this Bassarab is Count Dracula?"

She shook her head. "We don't know anything beyond the fact that he claims to be a Bassarab. News from the East Coast has become unreliable these past several years and all we have to go on is rumor and innuendo. But, as you said, his enforcers did seem more inclined to bring you in dead rather than alive. In fact, I'm sure they had something to do with last night's murder in that Joplin hospital."

"Why?"

"I believe Dr. Marsh relayed some of your blood samples through the Missouri labs and the New York team was backtracking your records to find you and destroy all existing evidence. The fact that a hospital employee was killed means that they were either desperate or sloppy. But still very, very deadly. You're lucky that we found you first."

I digested these words with the remainder of my soup. "Thank you," I said finally. "For everything, I guess, if I'm to believe even half of what you've told me." I pushed the bowl across the table. "The soup, too. My appetite hasn't been too normal, lately. I'd forgotten how good tomato soup could taste."

"Tomato soup?" Mooncloud smiled.

I frowned. "There was something else in it—kind of tangy, like V-8 juice. Secret herbs and spices?" I asked hopefully.

Her smile grew broader.

I considered the coppery aftertaste in my mouth and suddenly felt my legs go rubbery. "You're not going to tell me . . . to tell me. . ." Fortunately I was sitting down.

"Some of it was tomato soup, Chris. And, yes, I did add some V-8 juice and a dash of salsa to the mix. But . . ." Her smile grew terribly wide.

I looked down at the remnants of my meal coagulating at the bottom of the bowl.

The worst part was that I had actually enjoyed it.

Chapter Three

Give me monsters. . . .

Crazy-quilt renderings of mismatched flesh with bolted necks stalking through mazed corridors. Demonic beasts of hunched fur and poisoned talons slavering in steaming pits and crawling forth, unhindered by pentagrams and mystic seals. Lunatic shapes that caper and gibber and reach out for you in ways that suggest that there are worse things than death and you can take a long time in getting there. . . .

I'll take monsters any day. Or night.

Because monsters can be run from. Or fought.

But how do you escape when that monstrous, stalking doom is part and parcel of your own anatomy? When it pursues you through the looping corridors of veins and arteries, and nests in the four bedroom chambers of your own heart?

For months my dreams had been scored to background threnodies and funereal winds moaning like a macabre Greek chorus. In time the wailing had changed and I recognized the voices as they took on new tonal qualities.

The sound of my own blood.

Singing.

A vast, choral paean of the *Dies Irae* reverberating through my body: Day of Wrath. . .

There had been no solace in waking up. In time I had discovered the nightmare requiem was but a reflection of my waking reality: shadows were gliding through my bloodstream like sharks turned loose to hunt in a watery theme park. . . .

But now I awoke feeling somewhat rested for the first time in months. Lying in the dark confines of the makeshift bed, I listened to the drone of tires on pavement and then reached out to feel the wooden walls that enclosed me like a coffin. Surprisingly, the panic signs of claustrophobia were absent and I felt rested—a sensation that had eluded me for the better part of a year, now. The sun, I could tell through some arcane faculty, had set nearly an hour before.

There was a knock on the wooden barrier to my side.

"Yes?"

The ceiling lifted up, swung away on side hinges like a casket lid. Dr. Mooncloud reached down, offering her hand. "We're almost there."

She helped me climb out of the rectangular storage space that had been adapted for my sleeping facilities, then closed the cushioned lid that converted the area back into a padded bench seat. The storage area had served as sleeping space for a dozen such recovery missions, she had explained just before sunrise.

"Hungry?" she asked now.

I groaned.

"Admit it, now. You are feeling much better since we introduced hemoglobin into your diet."

I had no ready-made answer to that.

"Well, you're still in transition so we're not exactly sure of your needs and tolerances. If you had completed the transformation, you could go for days—weeks even—between feedings. As it is, we'll have to trust you to be honest about your hunger pangs."

"Please—you make me sound like a—a—" I fumbled to fit a word to the feeling.

"Predator?"

"Specimen. It's all been animal blood, so far. Hasn't it?"

She nodded. "And diluted."

"Just don't switch me over to—to—"

"The human stuff?" The thought seemed to horrify her. "Certainly not before I get you into the lab!"

So much for the subtler nuances of the Hippocratic oath.

The Winnebago coasted to a standstill, backed up and came to a dead stop.

"We're here," Garou's voice crackled from the intercom.

It looked like a castle.

Especially if you'd never seen a real one.

The building across the street looked more like a scaled down fairytale palace that had been airlifted out of Disneyworld and dropped into the far end of Seattle's business district. The crenelated walls rose two stories above street level with twin gate house towers. A recessed keeplike structure rose another two and four stories, respectively. There was even a water-filled moat between the sidewalk and the castle proper, overshot by a wooden drawbridge that looked fully capable of supporting a Sherman tank. The word "*Fantasies*" in blue neon calligraphy was hung above the portcullis in the main archway and strobed off and on like a torpid firefly.

Additional contrast to the weathered stone was provided by expensive, late-model automobiles that lined the street and studded the parking lot like colorful gems.

"Parts of it are real," Mooncloud remarked as she took my arm and started for the crosswalk at the corner. "A good portion of the stonework was recovered from an ancient ruin and shipped over from the old country, stone by stone, and reassembled here."

I smirked. "The *old* country?"

"Of course, some adjustments were made in reconstruction," Garou said, hanging back to activate the vehicle alarm system. The RV chirped and she hurried to catch up. "Front door or back?" The light changed and we started across the street.

My attention was momentarily caught by a flash of white: a face at the rear window of what looked like, by God, an authentic black and white 1931 Duesenberg parked halfway down the block.

"Back," Mooncloud decided. "Not that it makes any real difference, I suppose."

We were halfway through the crosswalk when another car came out of nowhere, bearing down on us at better than sixty miles an hour. There was just enough time for us to dodge left, see the headlights track our escape route, change direction, see the car adjust to follow, and then I found myself being flung across the road with inhuman strength. A red GTO careened past, narrowly missing Mooncloud and myself. Garou was not so fortunate, having lost her advantage in throwing me out of harm's way: the grille caught her with a dull, smacking sound.

Once again time seemed to slow perceptibly and I stared in horror as she tumbled across the hood like a broken rag doll, striking the windshield and rebounding in a starburst of shattered glass. Her body was tossed off to the side where a parked car broke her fall back onto the street.

I stumbled to my feet, barely aware of the strips of abraded skin that flapped from my tattered hands, elbows, and knees. There was no pain, yet; just a disturbing sense of disorientation—that time was out of sync. And a feeling of rage that flashed white hot as I saw her bloodied corpse crumpled between a green Lotus and a grey Mercedes-Benz.

Mooncloud wobbled to her knees, looking slow and stunned. I turned and saw the GTO brake, performing a skidding turn in balletic slo-mo. It was coming about, the driver preparing to make another pass.

Hazed by fury, I ran toward it, sprinting across the asphalt like a noseguard locked in on the opposition quarterback. An old joke flitted through the back of my mind—something about dogs chasing cars and what would they do if they ever caught one? I shook my head, hands balling into fists.

The muscle car was fully turned now and beginning to accelerate, but it still seemed to be jerking through successive frames of sluggish film. It must have been a trick of perspective for I seemed to be moving twice as fast as the automobile. In ten subjective seconds we would meet.

And then what?

In my fury I had insane visions of plowing through the car's front end like it was so much breakaway cardboard or vaulting the hood to smash feet-first through the windshield like in an old Chuck Norris movie. . . .

The headlights were just a few feet away when sanity finally prevailed. There was more than enough time to pirouette and sidestep, the fender caressing my pants leg as the car motored past—plenty of time remaining to reach through the driver's side window. I tore the lap belt and shoulder harness apart like crepe paper and yanked the driver out through the open window.

The car continued to meander down the street as I spun the man around to face me. He reached for something—a weapon, most likely. Time was still dragging so there was plenty of time to intercept his wrist. But I didn't do that. I gave in to the rage, instead. I slammed my fist into his face, distantly surprised at how easily bone and cartilage gave way before my knuckles. The man went limp in my grasp, blood literally bursting from ears, eyes, mouth, and the cratered remains of a nose.

Now the car snapped into high speed, veering off to the right and smashing into a Coupe de Ville parked near the corner of the intersection. The madness was fading and I tossed the driver's corpse aside without even looking at his face. There was no point, anyway: not even his own mother could recognize him now.

"Taj?" I called, like a man waking from an uncertain sleep.

"Over here." She was kneeling beside Garou's body. "Come help me."

I walked over in a daze, the adrenaline rush suddenly gone. I knelt beside her, feeling all dead inside, again.

Was this part of the transformation? I wondered. This past year I had felt my emotions flicker and die, one by one, until anger, alone, remained. It was the one true passion that I still recognized; everything else seemed like so much window dressing.

Mooncloud had turned the body over onto its back. Garou's face was bloody, her eyes disturbingly open and staring. Gently, I reached down and drew her eyelids closed with my fingertips.

"Get your grimy fingers out of my eyes!" Garou snarled. I fell over backwards and landed on my rear. Undignified maybe, but I had some consolation in the fact that my jeans were still dry.

"She's alive," Mooncloud explained gently.

Duh.

"As if it's not enough to get both legs broken along with crushed ribs and multiple skull fractures," Garou's "corpse" groused, "I have to suffer the indignity of this cub trying to poke my eyes out like some kind of Three Stooges routine." She turned her head and spat out a mouthful of blood. "Where's the perp?"

I was trying to get my legs back under me. "I guess I killed him."

"Great!" Her voice dripped with sarcasm.

"It would have been better if we could have interrogated him." Mooncloud looked around. "We need to get her inside."

I was dubious. "Should we move her? Internal injuries—"

Garou clutched my arm in a weak grip, her own arm sagging at a funny angle. "I'm a lycanthrope, you idiot. I'm already starting to regenerate." She coughed, a wet ragged sound. "But I'll be more comfortable inside, in bed, and off the street."

"Plus we'll need to make a few alterations in the evidence of tonight's events before the authorities arrive." Mooncloud turned to a child who had just appeared from behind the Mercedes. "Mordecai, the driver is over there." She pointed at the crumpled body back down the street. "You know what to do."

As Mordecai passed by I saw that my first impression was wrong: this was no child but an old dwarf dressed in livery and a fool's cap. The little man placed a couple of stubby fingers in his mouth and blew a shrill and complicated whistle as he hurried toward the corpse.

I gathered Lupé Garou into my arms as if she were some oversized rag doll. As I stood, I saw the cover of a manhole rise from the street and several more diminutive figures emerge. I turned to Mooncloud. "What—?"

"Knockers," she answered curtly. "Let's go."

"Yeah. . . ." Garou's voice was weak and I had to bow my head to listen. "The mines below the sewers are full of 'em. The Doman almost named the place after 'em. Can you imagine?" Her smile was cut short by another cough and Mooncloud's announcement that we were going in the front door. I nearly dropped her as her body squirmed, shifting in my arms, reassigning mass and shape and flowing into the form of a great, bloodied wolf. Now her clothing hung loosely from her lupine form and Mooncloud quickly pulled it off, stuffing the tattered material in her purse.

"Come on, don't dawdle!" She tugged at my elbow as the great wooden doors, strapped and bound with iron bands and large oval rings, began to swing open. "Make way!" she yelled, pushing through the gathering crowd. "Had a little accident out here! Coming through. Some guy just hit a dog and lost control of his car!"

"My Caddy!" a new voice shrilled. As the man pushed past, I looked back and saw that the body of the driver was already back behind the wheel of the GTO. There was no sign of the knockers and Mordecai was standing on the sidewalk, looking like nothing more than a curious spectator. Mooncloud was moving deeper into the castle's interior and I had to hurry to keep up.

The entry hall split three ways, opening up into a dark,

cavernous room between two outer passages. As we passed the inner portal and started down the left corridor I glanced in at what might have once served as a king's great hall. The darkness was studded with pinpoints of candlelight denoting constellations of tables. At the center of the great room was a nucleus of light, revealing a stage bordered by a vast, circular bar. I caught a glimpse of the dancers on the stage and suddenly understood Garou's sardonic comment regarding the knockers. Then I was past the portal, trying to keep up with Mooncloud as she continued down the outer hallway.

Antique elevator doors opened at the end of the corridor. Inside the filigreed iron cage was a tiny apparition perched atop a high stool. The man couldn't have topped three feet if standing erect and looked even smaller folded in on himself as he sat. His red hair, beard, hat, and spats formed a Christmasy contrast to his green frock coat and breeches. Tiny dark glasses bridged his face, delicately spanned between oversized ears and nose. He cocked his head as they stepped aboard and sniffed delicately. "Fräulein Mooncloud?"

"Yes, Hinzelmann. We need to go down straightaway."

He pulled a lever that closed the doors, then pulled another and the cage started a smooth descent. "It is Fräulein Garou, is it not?" he asked, continuing to stare straight ahead. "Is she hurt badly?" Genuine concern leaked through the formality.

"Not so badly that I won't be taking the stairs in a couple of days," the wolf growled. I nearly dropped her, again.

"Hinzelmann, this is Mr. Csejthe."

The little man nodded gravely without turning. "Herr Csejthe, *guten Tag*."

"Mr. Hinzelmann, *sehr angenehm*," I managed.

"Ach, it is nice to meet a young person with manners these days. Csejthe . . ." he ruminated, ". . . from Hungary?"

I shook my head. "Frontenac."

"Frontenac?"

"Kansas," I elaborated. "Just next to Pittsburg, no 'H'."

"Pittsburgh-no-'H'?"

"Pittsburg, Kansas—with no 'H' on the end of Pittsburg. It's right next door to Frontenac." He looked blank so I added, "It's where I'm from."

"Ah!" A light dawned in his eyes. "*Ich bitte um Entschuldigung*—I mean originally."

"Oh. Originally, Kansas City. Missouri not Kansas."

The light dimmed, nearly going out and the little man grunted as the elevator came to a stop. "But your family—of the Nadasays, perhaps?"

"Perhaps," Mooncloud agreed as the doors opened. "There is much that Mr. Csejthe doesn't know, yet—particularly about himself."

"Another knocker?" I inquired as the doors closed behind us and we continued down a corridor hollowed out of solid stone.

"A *hütchen*."

"A what?"

"A German home sprite."

"Oh. Of course."

"Do I detect a note of sarcasm, Mr. Csejthe?"

"More like sixteen bars with coda." The rattle of small-wheeled casters drew my attention up the corridor. A young woman dressed in a samite gown was pushing a gurney toward us. A textbook Nordic beauty, she had pale blue eyes and wore her white-blond hair piled in coils upon her head. "Human?"

Mooncloud shook her head.

I sighed. "Of course not."

"*Weisse Frauen*."

"*Weisse* or *weise*?"

"One of the White Ladies," said the wolf.

"Hush," Mooncloud scolded. "No unnecessary talk or movement till you're more regenerated." She turned to me as the gurney arrived. " 'White' or 'wise' serve equally when dealing with the *Fainen* women. Where did you learn German?"

"My great grandfather. I picked up a smattering when I was a toddler."

"You seem to have kept up."

"I live in what used to be called the 'Little Balkans' area of Kansas." I shrugged. "Or did live, anyway. . . ."

"They called down and warned us," the pale woman said as I gently laid Garou's lupine form on the gurney. "Surgery is prepared and ready."

"Thank you, Magda." Mooncloud took my arm. "Take her on down. Tell Dr. Burton that I'll be along in a moment." She led me off down a side corridor. "I've got to go tend to Lupé, but we must get you settled, first." We came to a cross corridor and she called out: "Ah, Basa-Andrée!"

There is no excellent beauty, Francis Bacon wrote, *that hath not some strangeness in the proportion.* Perhaps, but I'd warrant that Frank never imagined strangeness in every proportion. It was shuffling toward us now in the form of an old and very ugly crone.

"How is the little one?" it—she—rasped in an ancient, rusting voice.

"I think she'll be fine eventually, but I must tend her for now. Basa," she pulled me forward, "this is Christopher Csejthe. He's the one we were sent to recruit."

Basa-Andrée clasped gnarled, lumpy hands together. "Ah! Welcome, honored guest! Please allow me to show you to your quarters." She looked me up and down. "I will draw you a hot bath and see that you are provided with fresh clothing." To Mooncloud: "Leave him to me, dearie. You just run along and I'll see that he's ready for his audience with the Doman."

Mooncloud smiled gratefully. "Go along, Chris; I'll be by to check on you later. You're in good hands, now: Basa-Andrée is one of the chamberlains."

I leaned over and whispered, "She's not human either, is she?"

She shook her head. "*Aguane*."

"Of course. Don't know why I didn't see that immediately."

The old woman cackled as Mooncloud took her leave. "Come with me, dearie. Stefan has decreed that you are to be shown every courtesy." She cackled again as she started off down the corridor. The grasp of her hand was like weathered iron and I tottered behind her, trying to keep up.

My quarters turned out to be a six-room suite that rivaled any hotel I'd ever visited save for the fact that there were no windows and the walls were dressed stone. The aguane showed me through the various rooms, explaining that the kitchenette would be stocked as soon as my dietary needs were understood and as for the closets. . .

Less than two minutes after we had entered the suite, two brownies and a leprechaun (or so Basa-Andrée identified them) had bustled through the door. The tour was sidetracked as they subjected me to a thorough series of measurements and detailed questions pertaining to fashion preferences, fabrics, and which side I "dressed" on. One of the brownies even held up a color chart and pronounced me a "dramatic winter." Then they were bustling back out the door and apologizing that it would be close to an hour before they could return with a complete wardrobe.

"Now," the old crone cackled, "how about a nice, relaxing, hot bath?"

The bathroom was spacious, with a great sunken tub that could comfortably accommodate three with room to spare. As the steaming water neared the top, recessed jets turned on, swirling my bath into a bubbling jacuzzi.

"I've taken the liberty of laying out a variety of toiletries and shaving implements," the old chamberlain said, turning the taps to the off position. "If you have any grooming needs, just utilize the house phone to make your needs known."

"Great." I squinted at the reflective panels of glass. "How about a special mirror that will enable a semi-vampire to shave himself?"

She grinned, displaying teeth that looked like a two-hundred year-old picket fence. "I think we can come up with something that will satisfy. . . ."

I lay back with my eyes closed, letting the heat from the water sink into my cool flesh. It was the first time that I could remember feeling warm in days. Relaxation gave way to sleep and I had a most curious dream.

In this dream I was still lying back in the tub, my arms and legs drifting in the bubbling swirls of heated water. A woman's head poked above the water's frothy surface. "So what would you prefer?" she asked, her green hair swirling about with the currents. "A trim, a full shave, or a compromise where you keep the mustache?"

"Full shave," I murmured, bemused by the turn this dream was taking.

She rose up halfway out of the water to reach for the shaving implements that had been laid out on the side of the tub. Now there was no question that I was dreaming: not only was this green-tressed woman both bare and beautiful, but her lower body seemed to be occupying the same space as my own. Had she been real, I would have felt her weight upon me, legs straddling my sides. Instead, she seemed to have no substance below the waterline: her waist seemed solid enough, but the pale flesh below her navel seemed to bleach toward transparency, her hips disappearing and reappearing in the roiling froth of the water.

An interesting effect, I thought. *Almost as interesting as the effect of her bending over me. . . .*

And then I was distracted by the sensation of cool lather against my hot, sweaty face, surprisingly solid fingers smoothing it down my cheeks, beneath my chin, across my jaw and throat.

The shave was pleasant.

The "aftershave" even more so.

I awoke to the fact that the waterjets had been shut off. I opened my eyes with the memory of the watery barber fresh in my mind. Instead, I was treated to the sight of rheumy, yellow eyes that bulged from an ancient, leathery face: the aguane.

I repressed an impolite scream.

"The Doman sends for ye, lad," she cackled. "I would'na keep himself waiting any longer than necessary." She handed me a large towel and turned to go. At the doorway she paused. "Nice shave." Her mouth stretched into a gap-toothed grin and she disappeared around the corner.

I put a hand to my face: it was true, I was now clean-shaven.

And the closets were now full of clothing, shoes and boots arranged in two military lines across their floor areas.

I dressed in a daze, scarcely aware of my surroundings as I examined the pink patches of new skin on my elbows, hands, and knees. Gone were the oozing wounds from my ungraceful slide on the asphalt from just an hour before.

Gone was the life I had known just four days before.

Less than a week ago I had figured on a short future with long medical bills. Now? Well, dead was dead, but undead? At the very least there did seem to be some physical advantages.

There was a knock at the door as I finished tying my shoes. It was Dr. Mooncloud, who had managed a change of clothes and some fresh makeup.

"How's Lupé?" I asked.

"Fine. She'll be up and around in no time." She offered her arm. "Shall we go? The Doman is having us for dinner."

"An interesting choice of words," I observed as we exited my new quarters.

"Until the Doman makes any decisions concerning your fate," she answered, "the ambiguity is apropos. Don't embarrass me tonight."

"Don't worry," I said. "I'm just *dying* to make a good impression."

Chapter Four

The Doman was not what I expected.

First of all, he wasn't old. Or at least he didn't look old: late twenties to early thirties, to all appearances. Instead of black and swept back from the requisite widow's peak, his hair was brown and wavy and parted on the left. His eyes were grey-blue with flecks of brown—chameleon eyes, but open and friendly at this particular moment. The nose was not the thin blade of flesh I had imagined in a vampire leader: it was long but rounded, rather, with a slightly predatory bent that reminded more of an owl than a hawk. Beneath it, he wore a neatly trimmed mustache—nothing heavy, sinister, or possessing handholds for twirling.

Taken separately, none of his features seemed to suggest inhuman qualities and their sum did nothing to suggest a vampire warlord.

No tuxedo or evening wear here, either: he wore a pair of black slacks and a silk shirt of shimmering purple. The Doman stood just over six feet and had a slender physique that seemed more sinuous than powerful. Stefan Pagelovitch was not a fearsome sight, at all. He seemed pleasant and rather young for such implied responsibility. I tried to imagine him wearing a cape. Failed.

Then we shook hands and I felt the subtle power that radiated from the man as the chilled flesh of fingers and palm enveloped my own.

"Welcome, Mr. Csejthe, and enter. You are my honored guest."

"Thank you, Mr. Pagel—"

"Please: Stefan." The cold grip of the Doman's hand drew me into the room. "It will be so much better if we put aside such formalities. May I call you Christopher?"

I allowed myself to be led toward the table. The room was dark, its only illumination coming from a pair of flickering candelabras on the dining table and the mixture of city lights and moonglow that trickled in from the open terrace on the far wall.

As we were seated, I noticed that there were others in the room, as well. Across the table sat a hirsute, barrel-chested man. He was seated next to a blond woman whose flesh revealed by her décolletage was so pale as to seem an additional source of illumination in the pervading gloom. Both studied me intently as Dr. Mooncloud sat to my right and the Doman took his place at the end of the table, to my left. At the other end of the table sat a man and a woman of incomparable beauty. Dark, lean, with black, curly hair and a clean aquiline profile, he looked like the cover model for countless romance novels. His companion had red hair, blue eyes, and a face so flawless that it—well—defied comparison to anything else. Both embodied the kind of physical perfection that evoked neither lust nor jealousy, so far removed was it from competition or attainment.

Introductions commenced.

The perfect pair were Damien and Deirdre—no last names were offered.

The round, fuzzy guy turned out to be Lupé's brother, Luis. "Can't stay long," he growled, nodding curtly. "I must look in on my sister, again."

The white-on-white blonde in the black dress was introduced as Elizabeth Bachman, " . . . better known to countless viewers as Lilith, TV's late-night scream queen and horror movie hostess," Pagelovitch explained. "Elizabeth has been a Saturday night staple here in

Seattle for the past ten years, but just last year several of the major markets have picked her up in syndication. Perhaps you've heard of her?"

I smiled a cordial smile and shook my head. "I'm afraid I haven't."

"I look somewhat different on television and in all of my public appearances," Bachman said. "I wear a long, black wig and lots of eye makeup." Her voice matched the black velvet of her dress—low, throaty—sounding of whiskey and cigarettes and ten thousand barstools.

"Ah," I said, "sort of a cross between Morticia Addams and Elvira."

Her expression twisted and, for a moment, I was reminded of Kirsten's first taste of sweet and sour sauce.

For a moment. . . .

And then I bundled that memory back into the black trunk of forgetfulness.

Bachman recovered with a smile, saying: "Elvira may call herself the 'Mistress of the Dark,' but I am the Queen of the Damned. And my dresses are more daring. . . ." Her mouth formed a poutish little moue.

"More daring?" I echoed weakly.

"I shall be very happy to prove it to you." She smiled again, showing teeth this time. Some of them were pointed.

"I invited Elizabeth here to meet you, Christopher." The Doman was regarding us over the rim of a crystal goblet. Claret-colored liquid caught the light from the candles and bloodied his face. "I understand you are in broadcasting. I thought Elizabeth would be the ideal person to help you settle into our circle. Her contacts will make it easy to find just the right job." He turned to Bachman. "Perhaps you already have a position in mind, my dear?"

She licked her lips and the smile grew. "Oh, yes, I'm thinking of a position just this very moment. . . ."

"Stefan," Dr. Mooncloud said, "there is something we need to discuss before Mr. Csejthe leaves this room."

"I should think there are a number of things to discuss, Doctor." He took a sip from the goblet. "Just what did you have in mind?"

"Mr. Csejthe's status."

"Status?" Luis Garou was curious.

"According to all we know so far—second-hand lab reports and two days' observation on the road getting here—Mr. Csejthe is in transition. Apparently stuck in mid-transition." She gave the Doman a meaningful look. "Did you know that he entered the premises without invitation or hesitation?"

The room became very still.

"Mr. Csejthe," Pagelovitch was suddenly very attentive, focusing with an intensity that was at odds with his relaxed manner of a few moments before, "did anyone invite you to enter this building?"

I was struck with a sudden case of laryngitis: I shook my head.

Mooncloud cleared her throat. "Neither Lupé or myself had offered the specific invitation, yet, but since we were headed for the door, the implication—"

He cut her off with a gesture. "It would make no difference."

"So, like, everyone—" I had recovered the upper registers of my voice and was still fishing for the lower "—who comes to your—um—nightclub, here, has to have an invitation to get through the door?"

"Not the human clientele," Bachman said. "Only the *wampyr*."

"So I am still human."

Mooncloud steepled her fingers. "But not fully human."

The Doman leaned forward. "The question is: How much?"

Mooncloud shrugged, but an aura of tension fairly crackled about her diminutive shoulders. "You have my initial report based on the blood tests and lab work I intercepted. Mr. Csejthe's appetite for solid food has declined. He's showing an increasing sensitivity to solar radiation. His night vision continues to improve and his strength has already passed human norms for his frame and musculature. While he can still tolerate and even draw nourishment from ordinary food, blood has an increasingly potent and revitalizing effect on his system."

"That's nothing," I said modestly. "You should see me touch my nose with the tip of my tongue."

Deirdre laughed, a short, musical, merry sound. It was also the only sound from that end of the table so far this evening.

"He no longer casts a shadow and his reflection is barely visible in a mirror," Mooncloud continued. "But I would be hard-pressed to classify him as either alive or undead without further lab work." She shot a look at Bachman. "Which I intend to start first thing tomorrow."

The blonde's eyes reflected pinpoints of candle flame as she studied me again. "What fascinating possibilities that raises."

"Precisely my point." Mooncloud turned imploring eyes on the Doman. "We know nothing, yet, of how his condition was contracted or from whom. . . ." Her gaze swept back to the blond woman and hardened. "It's very crucial at this point that his system not be exposed to further contamination."

"Well!" Bachman's outrage seemed more theatrics than true indignity. "I like that! Contamination!"

Pagelovitch nodded slowly. "Perhaps not the most diplomatic of terms, Doctor, but you are correct. His current status must not be violated—for scientific and ethical reasons, as well."

"Ethical?" The word in Bachman's mouth was even more distasteful than "contamination."

I was tired of sitting on the sidelines. "And what does that mean?"

"No doubt you believe the fantasies of pen and film that brand us as creatures of the night—without conscience or scruple," the Doman said. "But we live by a code of necessity and we acknowledge certain responsibilities for what we must do."

"Dr. Mooncloud explained how you're careful to keep your existence a secret," I said, making a cursory effort to keep the irony out of my voice, "and how you've set limits on your population growth in regards to the food supply."

"It's not just a question of available resources nor a desire for safety that drives us to keep our numbers down." Pagelovitch continued calmly. "And we are not always successful in our efforts to do so. The fact is, Christopher, that we do not fully understand how the condition is passed along to some and not to others."

Out of the corner of my eye, I noticed that the redhead had stopped eating and was staring at her plate with an almost stricken expression.

"Why do some humans sicken and die over a long period of time while others expire in a single night?" the Doman was saying. "It is not, I assure you, tied exclusively to blood loss. Why do some find resurrection while still on the coroner's slab while others—in those countries that do not practice embalming—lie in their graves a full month before sundering their coffins to crawl upwards through the dark earth?

"There are many variables that we cannot explain. The good doctor here has hopes that your particular condition may be the key to unlocking some of these many mysteries."

Everyone was staring at me, but I particularly felt the weight of Damien and Deirdre's gaze from the far end of the table.

"And she does not want—" Pagelovitch smiled at Bachman, showing his own pointed teeth "—*contaminated* blood mixing with your own until she knows everything she can learn from its present condition."

"I think I understand the scientific angle here," I said. "But you said there was a moral angle, as well."

"Yes, I was getting to that. The Code of the Grave—" he gave a short, deprecating laugh "—just as there is a Code of the West. We have standards of conduct for our little society of nightdwellers. . . .

"That code places a heavy responsibility upon the hunter. Once I have taken you for sustenance, you become my responsibility until certain conditions are satisfied. If you live, I must see to it that you are unable to betray my existence or the existence of the greater community to which I belong. If you die, I must see to it that your death does not provide the same betrayal through physical evidence. And if you rise from your grave, I must mentor you, bring you into the Community. Or see to it that you are destroyed for the same reasons that I just spoke of."

"The responsibility to the Community," I said.

The Doman nodded. "But not just that. If I am responsible for your infection, I have a moral obligation to you, as well. More so today than a century ago."

I responded with my eyebrows.

"A century ago most victims would end up in a pine box under six feet of earth. While those circumstances might seem daunting to most mortals, it is the egg from which most of us are hatched. We come into our greater strength cracking that wooden shell and clawing our way to the surface. But there are limits to what even augmented strength and iron fingernails can do when locked inside a steel casket and a concrete grave liner. Imagine if you will the fate of a newly resurrected vampire sealed for an eternity in such a prison. It is a horror that might befall any of us and so we are all committed to seeing that it happens to none."

I repressed an unexpected shudder.

"Which brings me back to the point. Although I am not responsible for your present condition, I am responsible for having you brought here. Under those circumstances and, as I am Doman over this demesne, I must assume certain obligations for your welfare. Which brings me to a very important question. Do you wish to join us?"

I cleared my throat. "Uh, as I kept trying to tell Dr. Mooncloud, I was quite happy with the job I had and—"

"No, my friend, you do not understand. Your lot is now cast with us. Even were I to release you from our enclave you would just be killed or acquired by another Doman. As it stands now, you are already being hunted by at least one other enclave. And they want you so badly that they have been careless."

"Three disappearances and a homicide by the time we got to you," Mooncloud said.

"One of the disappearances has since reappeared," Luis amended. "Or at least the body turned up."

"Mutilated and drained of blood," Bachman added. She shook her head and made *tch-tch* noises. "Sloppy."

Pagelovitch scowled. "But at least there were no evident fang marks and the authorities are more inclined to blame Satanic cults than look for evidence of vampires." He shook his head. "Still, through no fault of your own, your existence has already threatened our anonymity. This carelessness worries me. But all that I can do for the moment is deal with your presence here. What I am asking you, here and now, is: Do you wish to complete the Transformation? To become as we are?"

"Stefan! We don't even know if or how that could be accomplished!" Mooncloud protested. "And his value to our research in his current state—"

"I am not asking about possibilities!" the Doman rumbled. "I am questioning his desire. Can the transformation be reversed?"

She shook her head. "Even if such a thing were possible, I wouldn't know how."

Pagelovitch turned back to me. "I speak to you now, ignorant of the scientific principles in this matter. I speak to you, rather, out of moral obligation before you leave this room. I do not know whether your transformation is at a standstill or just progressing very slowly. If progressing, I do not know if we can hinder it further. I do believe that it is within our power to accelerate and complete the Transformation. If that is what you wish. The question is: what do you wish?"

Everyone was still looking at me.

"Well, I don't want to die."

Mouths smiled, teeth glinted, laughter erupted.

"My dear Mr. Csejthe," Bachman said. "If you remain a mere mortal, death is eventually inevitable. As one of us you can cheat death."

"'One short sleep past, we wake eternally,'" the Doman added. "'And Death shall be no more: Death, thou shalt die!'"

I forced a smile. "I think you misappropriate Donne's meaning."

He smiled in return. "A man of letters, Christopher? I thought the last had died out early in this century."

"'The good die first,'" I quoted back, "'And they whose hearts are dry as summer dust / Burn to the socket.'"

"Coleridge?"

"Wordsworth."

He frowned. "Really? I suppose *Lyrical Ballads* . . . ?"

I shook my head. "*The Excursion*. Though I can see your assumption with their collaborative work."

Pagelovitch nodded. "Sam was an acquaintance; I never met Bill. Probably accounts for my neglect . . . but I digress. Elizabeth put it more succinctly than any of the poets: you can cheat death."

I stared past him, at the uncertain darkness outside the window. "'Man comes and tills the field and lies beneath. / And after many a summer dies the swan.'"

He smiled. "If you're citing Tennyson to say that you can only postpone the inevitable, you still beg the question. Who wouldn't bargain for one more summer? Or ten?"

"What price would you pay to live another century?" Bachman chimed in. "Or ten?"

"There are, however, certain tradeoffs," Mooncloud murmured.

"Well, assuming I have any real decision in this process, I'd like to put it off just a little bit longer. I mean there's no hurry, is there?" I was still smiling, but it felt more like a grimace.

The Doman nodded. "Fair enough. Dr. Mooncloud's lab work may help you make a more informed choice when the time comes. In the meantime, I must caution you to share blood with no one." He turned to Bachman. "I trust this is clear?"

She smiled sweetly.

I looked at Mooncloud. "Um, *share* blood?"

"It is part of their vampire lovemaking," Lupé's brother offered with an undertone of distaste. "They sometimes like to bite each other. Suck—"

"Thank you, Luis," Bachman interrupted icily. "I think you forget your place."

Garou scowled but ducked his head submissively. "I must go and see to my sister, now." He pushed back from the table and left the room hurriedly. As he exited two men entered bearing covered trays. Dinner was served.

Mooncloud, Deirdre, and myself were the only ones served solid food, a point the doctor underscored quietly by explaining that once the transformation was finished my digestive system would no longer tolerate anything but blood. "Anything else will make you sick," she said.

"One of the tradeoffs," I observed.

"One. . . ."

After dinner the Doman invited me for a stroll along the castle "battlements." The others were pointedly not invited and said their goodnights as a formality. Obviously, for everyone concerned, the night was yet young.

July in the Pacific Northwest was a bit cooler than in the Midwest and I was surprised to see a light fog hazing the more distant lights of the city.

"A quiet night," Pagelovitch said, leaning out upon one of the upthrust merlons in the crenelated half-wall. "Unlike the New York demesne, where the city's turmoil provides the perfect cover for night predators. I work hard to preserve a peaceful coexistence with the Living in my realm. Do you know how that is done?"

I hazarded a guess: "Blood banks?"

He laughed, the sound of it falling somewhere between polite and weary. "Yes, yes, blood banks. One of the more obvious ploys to serve the needs of the midnight community. Vampire fiction has reduced such stratagems to a clichéd gimmick but it is still a useful and mostly harmless way to attend to our needs."

"You have your own, I take it?"

"Yes, with several outlets. And our personal withdrawals are minimal compared to what is returned to the medical community at large. We are very philanthropic in this area, but—" his smile faded, "that is not what I meant by my question."

"How you rule over a community of vampires?"

He nodded. "Rule is a most apt description. And not just over vampires, Christopher. There are other creatures—perhaps I should say 'beings'—who are assimilated into our community, as well."

"Like the knockers."

"Like the knockers. And the leprechauns. And at least a dozen others—well, you'll be meeting some of them in the days ahead. Their safety and prosperity depends upon the laws that have been set up to govern our community." His voice hardened. "And my ability to enforce them."

"Dr. Mooncloud explained some of that."

He nodded, still looking out over the city. Surveying his domain. "You are my guest—for now. It is my hope that, in time, you will assimilate into our community as a contributing member, whatever your value to our medical and biological research now. But it is essential that you understand this: that I will deal harshly with anyone—*anyone*—who becomes a threat to any portion of our society, here. Do you understand?"

"I think so."

"Then understand that your sworn allegiance means little to me at this particular moment. Your ignorance of us and our ways could make you a greater risk than any desire to do us actual harm. That is why you will not leave this building again until I deem that you are ready."

I didn't like that. But outside of a hot bath and shave there hadn't been anything about the past couple of days that I had particularly liked. "So, I'm a prisoner for now?"

"A guest."

"For how long?"

"As long as it takes." There was a warning edge to his voice.

"'After three days, fish and guests begin to smell,'" I recited.

He raised an eyebrow.

"Dear Abby," I qualified.

He shook his head. "Ben Franklin: Poor Richard's Almanac. And he said 'stink.'"

"Ah. Of course."

"Now we are even."

I hadn't realized that anyone was keeping score. "Not as long as you are making the rules."

Pagelovitch sighed. "This is for your safety as well as ours. I want you to become acquainted with us and our ways while we learn more about you.

"But I must also warn you: the fact that we are a mutually dependent community does not mean that we are all one big happy family. There are those who will use you for a variety of purposes if they see advantage for themselves. Elizabeth is but a mild example of the appetites to be found among us. I have warned her that you are not to be harmed—but that may not stop her from anything that you, yourself, agree to."

"Nice friends."

"That is precisely the point I wish to make, Christopher: we are not all friends. We are allies—which is a different thing altogether.

"Come, let me give you the tour." We followed the parapet around the corner and descended a flight of stairs. "Tell me, are you comfortable so far?"

"The accommodations are excellent."

"I speak of the process of your Becoming. Have you experienced the bloodlust, yet? Taj says that you have not cut the new teeth."

"No fangs, although my appetite has been fluctuating as of late."

He looked at me sideways. "Christopher, there is appetite and then there are *appetites*. You killed a man this evening."

Since it wasn't a question, I felt no obligation to answer.

"Have you killed before?"

We came to a door which he opened, ushering me inside and down a corridor. "Personal question," I said.

"You will be asked a great many personal questions over the next few days. I ask, however, because tonight's impulse—" he gave me another look "—it *was* an impulse?"

"It wasn't premeditated."

"Which brings me to my point. The change is altering the chemical balance of your body. Hormonal changes, mood swings, shifts in brain chemistry—violence will become an increasingly natural response to situations involving stress. The subtler emotions recede. Passion rules—primarily as anger, even hate."

"What about compassion?" I asked suddenly. Thought upon the growing deadness of my heart this past year. "What about sorrow?"

"You are becoming a predator. Compassion will have no place in your altered nature. Sorrow? You will no longer feel emotions in the human spectrum. Your thoughts and feelings are being cleansed of the muddle that mortals are heir to. You shall feel only that which is sharp and keen, a conscience honed from fire and steel."

Perhaps that had already happened. For the past year my closest friends had chided me for not being "in touch with my feelings." Like feelings were something I should want after burying my wife and daughter.

"And then there is the bloodlust," he continued. "And a whole spectrum of appetites and emotions that bridge the gap between the living and the undead." We passed through a small antechamber and then through another doorway into a darkened observation room. A row of glassed windows looked down into the main room of the castle, providing us with an excellent view of the nightclub's inhabitants and their activities.

"Topless dancers," I mused, watching the silent gyrations on the stage below. "I wonder what Bram Stoker would have made of this?"

"Were he astute, he would have remarked on the benefits for the hunter leaving the jungles behind to open his own private game reserve."

"And 'Tits-R-Us' . . . ?" I gestured.

He shrugged. "One of our lures."

I nodded. "The best bait always wriggles on the hook." I could feel the tension building between us but it only inclined me to push a little more. "And is *Fantasies* the slaughterhouse or merely the holding pen?"

"I suppose it is a natural question," he said after a moment's silence, "but I'm beginning to take exception to your tone."

I shrugged. "Must be those mood swings you just warned me about."

"Still, I would remind you of your status as guest here—"

I held up my hand. "Words like 'guest' and 'host' are all very nice," I said, "but hardly appropriate under the present circumstances."

His face tightened. "Perhaps when your transformation

is complete, when your very survival is hostage to blood and secrecy—" He checked himself and visibly relaxed. "But until then you have every reason to be angry and distrustful. Forgive me: I must try to meet my definition of host even if I do not meet yours." He lowered himself into a plush chair situated near one of the windows.

"This castle and its environs serve a variety of functions. Here we provide home and shelter to the society we call the Underworld. Here we transact business that pays for the physical necessities of our community. Two hundred years ago our kind had to live in abandoned buildings and neglected crypts. We could only obtain the necessities of existence through brutality and murder." He gestured toward the darkened room below. "Today we can engage in mutually beneficial commerce with humankind to address our needs. We do not kill unless we are forced to. And we do not take from the unwilling."

"Sounds downright charitable." I lowered myself into the chair across from him.

"We provide services and entertainment for humans. They assume the occasional half-glimpsed oddity on the premises is part of the special effects that we've woven into the ambience and the product. Hence, our name: *Fantasies*. For the entertainment we provide, we acquire currency and resources for our own needs. We provide shelter and such benefits that our people cannot or dare not obtain from the society of humankind.

"One such example is the hospital facility underground where Ms. Garou is now being cared for. In addition to a multifunctional surgery and various treatment rooms, we have a laboratory and research facilities, an extensive library, a gymnasium and pool—"

There was a knock at the door.

"I've summoned one of my assistants to finish your tour, Christopher. I think it's best that I get back to work before the night is too far gone."

That was curious: at no time during our after-dinner stroll had I seen him pick up a phone, use an intercom, or relay a verbal message through a third party. The door opened and a young Asian woman entered.

"Suki, this is the man I told you about," my "host" said. She looked me over and I reciprocated. I would have described her as tiny up until this evening—before I had seen Hinzelmann and the knockers. She was small and delicately formed but still sized and proportioned in the human range. Blue-black hair, sheened like a starling's wing, dropped in a straight flow to her shoulders. She wore a red silk dress with a mandarin collar and a coiled dragon in green embroidery over her left breast. Jade earrings tinkled like emerald wind-chimes as she bowed to me. There was nothing subservient in the act, and her eyes, as they came back up to regard me, betrayed amusement mixed with cool appraisal.

"I'd like you to give Mr. Csejthe the basic tour, make the requisite introductions, and answer all reasonable questions before tucking him in." The Doman turned to me. "I'll catch up to you tomorrow." He extended his hand. "Whether you believe me or not, I do have your best interests in mind as well as our own."

I took his hand and shook it in observance of the social amenities. "Perhaps. But you must understand my need to exercise my own autonomy."

His nod signified acknowledgment of my statement. Not agreement.

Chapter Five

My new tour guide turned to me. "Before we begin, are there any questions that you would like to ask?"

I glanced back down at the stage: new dancers were exchanging places with the others and hardly missing a beat in the music.

Suki smiled. "You're wondering about the dancers," she said. It was not a question.

"I'm curious about the business angle," I clarified.

She just looked at me and smiled.

"Well, the Playboy clubs and their upscale like have long since disappeared from the American landscape. The only places one expects to find topless dancers, these days, is in seedy bars and—"

She held up her hand. "First of all, we do not employ topless dancers."

I glanced back down. "One of us either needs to check our eyesight or our definitions."

She laughed. "Yes, our definitions. *Fantasies* employs exotic dancers." Emphasis on exotic.

"Ah. I see." I smiled. "Topless dancers are bimbos who take off their tops and wiggle. Exotic dancers are artists who engage in interpretive performances involving music, lighting, and costumes—costumes with removable tops."

Suki smiled right back. "An interesting if not entirely original distinction, Mr. Csejthe. But I think you will find that our definition of exotic exceeds your expectations. Come, let us walk while we converse."

I followed her out of the room and down the hall.

"I'm afraid I didn't answer your original question."

"Which was?" I didn't think I had gotten around to actually asking it.

"You were going to ask about the dichotomy of an obviously upscale club like *Fantasies* utilizing low-brow entertainment like topless dancers."

"Exotic," I said.

She hesitated. "What?"

"Exotic dancers."

"Um, yes. Well, to fully answer your question, I'll introduce you to the dancers individually. But a part of the answer lies in the fact that there are still upscale clubs in existence that do cater to a wealthy and hedonistic clientele."

"Private clubs. Exclusive memberships with low profiles."

"You are a quick study, Mr. Csejthe."

"You should see me ride a unicycle."

"What? Oh, I see. I was warned about you."

"And what did they warn you about?"

She merely smiled and kept walking.

We toured the library—three large rooms claiming to hold thirty-five thousand books and a fourth room housing a microfiche viewer, three computer on-line services, and two CD-ROM readers. I looked around carefully, asking pertinent questions about the facilities: if permitted, I would be camping out in here with some regularity.

"How do you get away with it?" I asked as we exited and started down another hallway.

"Get away with what?" She actually batted her eyelashes. "We get away with a great many things: you will have to be more specific."

"Seattle doesn't strike me as being the sort of city that would support your organization."

Once again she cut me off with a simple hand gesture. "First of all, our clientele comes from many places besides Seattle. More than a few are from out of state. Some come from even farther away.

"Secondly, *Fantasies* is not the demesne's only source of income. But I believe you are mainly wondering how we can operate so boldly with minimum scrutiny?"

I nodded.

"There are, of course, feminists and clergy and certain types of politicians, media crusaders, and community leaders who have initially disagreed with the Doman's business philosophies. Stefan makes it a point to always meet with any concerned individuals to try to speedily resolve those concerns."

"And once he has met with these concerned individuals," I extrapolated, "looking deeply into their eyes and explaining how unimportant or misguided their concerns really are—those people leave and forget that they ever had such concerns."

Suki smiled. "As I have said, Mr. Csejthe: a quick study."

We walked on.

The medical facilities were small but quite extensive: small in that they were set up to easily handle up to three or four patients at any one time and extensive in that every aspect of medical need imaginable was provided for. None of the Doman's subjects would ever have to risk exposure by going out for medical, eye or dental care. There was a private pharmacy for in-house prescriptions, therapy rooms, even an MRI unit shared jointly by the medical and research labs. And so on.

"Who pays for all of this?" I asked. "You're not funding this kind of equipment with the kinds of tips that line your dancers' g-strings."

"You'd be surprised at the amount of money that *Fantasies* generates," she said. "But there are other sources of income, as well. The Doman himself has a number of investments that he has managed over several human lifetimes."

At that point we were passing through one of the labs and ran into Dr. Mooncloud.

"Chris! You're just the semi-vampire I've been looking

for. I need to run a few quick tests. Open your mouth."

I looked at Suki. She looked at Mooncloud. "You're the doctor," Suki said.

"Here," Mooncloud said, poking a U-shaped lump of soft plastic in my mouth, "bite down on this and keep your mouth shut until I say otherwise."

I obliged, feeling soft, warm goo mold around my teeth and gums. There was a hard, plastic straw set between the upper and lower impressions that allowed me to breathe normally.

"Now up on the scales; I want another check on your weight and height." The ever-ready clipboard was already in her hands. Next I was de-shirted, affixed with electrodes, and ordered onto a treadmill for a five-minute EKG run. The straw proved a more than adequate airway and the goo, now hardened, didn't come out until I had my shirt back on.

"So what do we know, now, Doc, that we didn't know ten minutes ago?" I asked.

"I'm compiling info for the big picture, Chris; I don't like to jump to conclusions." She studied her clipboard. "But I think it's safe to say that your strength and stamina are still increasing and your sweat glands have either shut down or are becoming unimportant to your body's cooling processes."

"And the goo?"

"Dental molds," Suki said. "I'm sure they'll prove helpful in checking the development of your fangs."

"Or lack thereof," I muttered. "Nice stuff, though: it set in only ten minutes."

"It actually sets in a minute-and-a-half."

"Hmmm," Suki said, "I have a feeling that you'll probably be taking dental impressions on a daily basis, now."

"Maybe hourly," Mooncloud agreed.

They both laughed.

I didn't dignify them with a response. Eventually the amusement subsided and my tour continued.

There was a great deal more room underground, thanks

to the knockers. Suki classified them as mining boggarts from England, Wales, and Scotland, closely related to the gnomes. Emigrating to the Pacific Northwest, they entered into a symbiotic arrangement with the Doman. The diminutive tunnelers had carved an immense space out of the bedrock: additional living space; parking, recreational facilities, including pools, hot tubs, saunas, and a good-sized gym. There was also a dungeon.

Dungeon?

Well, two dungeons, as it turned out. One which served as an extension of the demesne's private law enforcement system. And the other—well, the other was an extension of the services provided by certain rooms upstairs.

Rooms upstairs?

Although Suki's explanation was brief and very generic, I was able to fill in the blanks without too much mental effort: prostitution. With a variety of kinks.

"So you have a pseudo-dungeon for those whose 'fantasies' include a little S-and-M?"

She shook her head. "There is nothing fake about the facilities. One of the strong suits of our operation is the absolute believability of our 'illusions.' "

"And the sex? Is it simulated or real?"

"*Fantasies* provides a number of services to its clientele, services which can always be obtained elsewhere," she said with barely noticeable defensiveness. "The difference is, here, we guarantee safety and satisfaction for all participants, quality service and surroundings, and experiences that exceed anything you would find anywhere else."

An old excuse: if they didn't come here, they'd just go someplace else. And regulated prostitution, at least, has some built-in medical safeguards. But. . .

"Vampire hookers?"

She shook her head. "With a few exceptions, most of our professionals are human."

"And the exceptions?"

"Well, one exception, for example—since we are passing by the dungeon area—involves the CEO for a major conglomerate. He likes to come down here every so often and be whipped until his back bleeds."

I made a face. "He pays you to do that?"

"His fantasy is completed by having one of our pros lick the blood from his wounds."

"Sounds like Liz Bachman."

Suki muttered something low and indistinct that sounded suspiciously like "very quick study," then said more audibly: "Do you see what a perfect exchange of services this is? He even pays an exorbitant amount of money for his fantasy and considers himself very lucky, indeed." She studied my expression. "Can you fault the logic of such a barter?"

"Logic is a piss-poor way of evaluating the worth of human interactions."

"So you question such transactions on the basis of ethical or moral difficulties? No one is really harmed. The act is completely consensual—demanded, in fact, by the client."

"Consensual," I said. "The Kevorkian defense."

"Let's go back upstairs."

I waited until we had ridden the elevator and were wending our way through a chain of offices before returning to the topic.

"And the prostitutes upstairs, the human ones. . ."

She turned to face me, her eyes intent on my face, on my words. She was quick, as well.

" . . . do they know that they're working for the undead?" I finished.

The ensuing silence was as telling as the words she finally uttered.

"The ones who service us do," she said.

A young man of heroic proportions sat on the stage playing a syrinx: a set of multireed panpipes. His only costume was a leather thong that left very little to the imagination. Indeed, his shaggy hair, beard, and considerable body hair provided more coverage than the wispy little bit of leather that was tied about his waist. The portion of his anatomy that drew the eye, however, was his forehead, where two small horns projected through his dangling forelocks. In spite of all this there was something vaguely familiar about the man—if he was, indeed, truly a man in the human sense.

The stage was equally stark, dressed only with the rock that the goatish musician sat upon, a large wicker basket at one end, and a lone tree at the other.

The tree looked natural and realistic—nothing like a prop tree of papier-mâché and silk. Natural until its two major branches began moving in time to the music, that is.

Fascinated, everyone in the main room stared as those two branches twisted and bobbed. *And rippled!* And, as their form flowed and flickered, the silvery bark became pearlescent and they became limbs of a different aspect. The branches became arms, human arms.

Now a face was forming amid the leaves. The trunk began to writhe—bulging here, constricting there, also moving to the rhythm of the music—until it was a human torso. Of feminine aspect.

The remainder of the trunk split to become a pair of shapely legs and suddenly the tree was gone, replaced by a dancing nymph with alabaster skin and green hair. On closer examination, her green "hair" turned out to be green leaves up above and green moss—well—in every other aspect she appeared fully human.

The Panish piper, seemingly oblivious to the transformation occurring behind him, began to turn around. Instantly, the dancing woman turned back into a tree. This was greeted with laughter and applause by the bar's patrons and more than a few whispers of "how'd she do that?"

"Holograms," stated a voice to my left.

I turned and studied the occupants at the next table:

an impossibly young, MBA-type wearing a dark, pin-stripe suit with a red power-tie and an older, rumpled salesman in brown slacks and a beige sports coat with gravy stains on a necktie of indeterminate color.

"They're using some kind of holographic projector," Power-tie was saying. Gravy-stains merely grunted and continued to stare as the piper turned away and the tree became a dancing girl, once more. "I read about stuff like this in *Omni*," Power-tie continued. "They project a three-dimensional image over the dancer to make it look like she's changing into something else." Gravy-stains grunted again and continued to stare at the girl, apparently fascinated by the tree-woman's burl-like formations.

I turned back to Suki. "So, is Junior-Achievement correct?" I nodded at the dancing nymph: "Holograms?" It was the first question I had asked since Suki had dropped her little bombshell nearly a half hour before.

She smirked. "*Fantasies* employs a vast array of special effects and it is against company policy to divulge any of our secrets."

It was a non-answer, but I hardly noticed. My mind was still on the follow-up questions that I hadn't asked, nearly a half-hour before. Like: what kind of "services" do the living perform for the dead? My imagination wisely refused to theorize.

The dance continued with the piper making occasional attempts to look behind him and the dancing woman reverting back to an arboreal state each time.

The next question beckoned: how did the Doman guarantee the secrets of his demesne if these humans were allowed to come and go? The obvious answer was that he couldn't. So, assuming the best—that there wasn't a constant turnover in staff and those who occupied the rooms upstairs were long-term occupants—that still meant the prostitutes had to be virtual prisoners.

With no likely hope of parole.

As I sat there and watched the "entertainment," I found myself getting more and more upset. Or maybe upset wasn't the right word—more like something between agitated and uncomfortable. It was a feeling that was both emotional and physical.

Now the top of the basket popped off and a slender, brown arm rose from the opening like a sinuous snake. The pipe music changed from a pastoral tune to something with a Middle Eastern flavor as a second arm twined the air beside the first. A head appeared. Long, coal-black hair framed a dark face with brown, sensuous features. As she continued to rise from the basket, little details began to catch my attention. Her fingers were tipped with long, clawlike nails. Her eyes were golden and slit-pupiled like those of a cat or snake. She wore nothing but brief wisps of snakeskin. Here and there her dark, lustrous flesh was overlaid with patches of black, brown, and golden scales in banded patterns, most noticeably about her wrists, throat, shoulders, and ribs. As she reached the point where she might have stepped over the basket's brim, the scales returned in greater form, flowing from the hipline to curve across the nether region of her belly like the drooping waistline of an incredibly tight leather dress.

Except it was no dress. As she continued to rise from the basket, the lower portion of her torso eschewed human legs and continued as the trunk of a great serpent.

"Holograms," Power-tie muttered off to my left.

I tore my eyes from the undulating snake-woman and stared at Suki. "A dryad and a nâga." I shook my head. "Makeup, maybe. Contact lenses, possibly. Smoke and mirrors, perhaps. . . ."

She smiled. "Holograms."

"Bullshit. No color smears. No perspective shifts. No diffusion medium. They're real, aren't they?" Even with everything that I'd already seen, I was still resisting a fundamental acceptance of this new twist on reality.

She nodded, her smile broadening.

"Yeah, yeah, don't say it: a quick study." I considered

the piper again. "What about Goat Boy? I don't see anything that couldn't be explained by a little old-fashioned theatrical makeup."

"Damien is only playing the part of the god Pan. We don't have any real satyrs on staff."

I blinked. And looked again. Sure enough, the piper was our handsome dinner companion of a couple of hours before, now made up to look like a mythical faun on steroids.

"So, he's human."

"Was human."

"Vampire?" I asked and then chorused: "A quick study," along with my tour guide.

"I told you that there was a good reason to prefer the term 'exotic' dancer," she added.

"What about Deirdre? Where's she?"

"She's not here," Suki said, looking a little surprised.

"Is she human?"

"Oh, yes." She smiled sadly. "Very."

Surprised me. "Okay, okay." I looked around the bar area, watching the customers stare wide-eyed and open-mouthed. Now I understood how upscale and low-brow could go hand in hand. "The customers all look human."

"Of course they all look human: most of them are. As for the ones that aren't—if they didn't look human they wouldn't be allowed in the bar. Unless they posed as entertainment."

"What about the knockers?"

"We don't serve miners."

I ignored that. "Are we done here?"

She chuckled. "Soon. I think you should watch for a few more minutes, though."

Why not? I had nothing else to do before sunrise. Still, I found the task slightly irritating. I was no voyeur. Even though *Fantasies* had all the trappings of a trendy, upscale nightclub, a part of me felt that I should be wearing a grimy raincoat with the collar turned up.

Watching the undulations of ripe, feminine flesh was unsettling.

Why?

Because these women weren't really human?

Or because it had been a year since I'd had any kind of sex outside of a couple of pathetic wet dreams?

Or both?

I felt myself growing edgy, tense. I found it hard to sit still in my seat. Unaccountably, I was perspiring!

Suki laid her cool hand atop my hot, feverish one. "Now it is time for us to go," she said.

Suki did not speak until we were back at Dr. Mooncloud's lab. It was just as well as it was taking all of my concentration to just put one foot in front of the other. I felt as if I was suffering from the worst case of priapism imaginable and yet there seemed precious little physical evidence to support that belief. Still, my body was throbbing with an overpowering need—a need akin to hunger.

I sat, hunched over in misery on the examining table while Suki and the doctor engaged in a whispered conversation. The next thing I knew there were two needles in my arm, one with blood coming out and the other with something going in. When one ampule was full and the other empty, the needles were removed and I was handed two plastic cups.

"Two urine samples?"

Mooncloud shook her head. "One."

"What's the second cup for?"

She handed me a magazine that proclaimed its devotion to men's issues with photographs primarily devoted to women without clothing.

"Oh."

She pointed me toward the closet-sized restroom on the other side of the examination area. "Don't come out until you have samples of both."

It took awhile: I had to read two articles and the

movie review section while I waited for the urine sample.

"It's getting late," Suki said as I tried to exit the lab without a noticeable limp. It was, in fact, getting on toward sunrise. "I know I promised to introduce you to the dancers, but I'm afraid I'm running short on time."

"It's okay."

"I took the liberty of calling down and telling them you might stop by to say hello. You know where the dressing room is."

Sure.

Like I'm really going to wander in there by myself and say: Howdy, girls; I'm a big fan of nude interpretive dance? By the way, nice buttocks?

Get real.

"I think I'll pass as well," I said, faking a yawn. "I'm pretty bushed."

"Well then, I'll be saying goodnight," she said, offering a polite oriental bow.

I reciprocated, hoping I didn't look as uncomfortable straightening up as I felt. "Goodnight."

"You know the way back to your room?"

I nodded.

"See you tomorrow."

I waved and lurched off down the corridor. Actually I was wide awake and still orbiting a world of hurt. Going to bed was not at the top of my priority list but privacy was.

Back in my room I refilled the tub and turned on the whirlpool jets. It didn't help.

What I more likely needed was a cold shower.

What I ended up settling for was retiring with a copy of Nietzsche's *Ecce Homo* that I had palmed during my tour through the library.

It was a good two hours past sunrise (according to my new, internal clock) before I finally fell asleep in my new bed, in my new room, in my new prison.

Chapter Six

I count backwards and dream of fire.

Then I wake up on ice . . . no. . . .

>*What is it?*

A table. Metal. Cold as ice.

I'm lying down and the metal surface is an efficient heat-sink that sucks all vestiges of warmth from my shoulders, back, buttocks, and legs.

I want to move, to seek warmth and yielding softness, but my body is cold and unresponsive. I am weak and tired and cold . . . so cold!

There are voices nearby. Overlaid by the high-pitched whine of . . . something. . . .

>*What does it sound like?*

Like a dentist's drill. Only not the same. . . .

>*What do you see?*

I force my eyes open and see . . . nothing. Dim whiteness. Something over my face. Damn, I'm cold!

>*Do you know why you're cold?*

Metal table. No clothes. Just a sheet. The sheet is over my face.

>*Can you remove the sheet?*

Cold: getting the shakes. Hands gripping the sides of the table. Can't seem to let go.

Hungry/Thirsty.

Stomach cramping.

Unh. Trying to sit up.

>*Can you do it?*

Yes.

>*What do you see?*

Nothing. Sheet still over my face. Hear better, though.

>*What do you hear?*

The whine has stopped. I hear the voices clearly, now.

>*What are they saying?*

The woman is saying: "Eddie, don't be afraid. They do that sometimes."

The man is saying: "What you mean they do that sometimes?" He sounds upset.

The woman says: "Sometimes a muscle contraction as rigor mortis sets in. Sometimes the differential in air pressure in the lungs: since the air is cooler in the morgue—"

I reach up and pull the sheet from my face. I turn my head and look at a black man wearing coveralls, leaning on a pushbroom. The black man says: "Shit, don't tell me they sometimes do that, too?"

He is talking to a white woman wearing a soiled green surgical smock. She is standing next to another metal table, holding a small, electric circular saw. She drops it and screams.

The man shakes his head and says: "Didn't think so."

The woman is stumbling around the other table, trying to get behind it. And . . . and. . .

>*What? What is it?*

Oh God! Oh Jesus! Oh please!

>*What is it? What do you see?*

Oh shit oh shit oh shi-it!

>*Tell me what you see!*

It's Jenny oh Jesus it's Jenny! And she's all torn up!

>*Goddamn it! I should've seen this coming!*

>*Chris! Listen to me! I'm going to count to three! Do you hear me?*

>*Dammit! Suki, Lupé; help me hold him!*

>*Chris! I'm going to count to three and when I say three, you will wake up! You will be awake and calm and none of this will be anything but a dim memory! You will awake and feel nothing but calm and refreshed! Do you understand?*

Where's Kirsten? Where is my baby? What did they do to my little girl?

>*Chris! I'm counting now! One!*

What is that? Get out of my way! I want to see—

>*Two!*

Oh Jesus! What did they dooooo—

>*THREE*—

I wiped at my eyes. Studied the moisture on my fingertips, the ache down deep inside. "So what happened?" I asked, breaking the strained silence in the examination room. "Did you get anything?"

Dr. Mooncloud shook her head. "I regressed you back to the hospital, a year ago. But it looks like we'll have to go back a little further to get what we need." Her expression was a study in nonchalance. "Sometimes hypnotism dislodges repressed memories after the session is over. Can you remember anything more, now?"

I tried. And for a moment there was . . . something. Then it was gone again.

"I remember crossing the Oklahoma/Kansas border. I remember getting off U.S. 69 and going north on State 7. After that—waking up in the hospital."

Lupé Garou, ensconced in a wheelchair, maneuvered closer. "You remember waking up there?"

I shrugged. "I woke up a lot: I was in and out of consciousness for most of a week." I shook my head. "I'm told the first time I regained consciousness was downstairs in the morgue after mistakenly being pronounced DOA. Someone said I scared the bejezus out of the pathologist and a custodian." Garou, Mooncloud, and my tour guide of the previous night looked distinctly uncomfortable so I tried a smile. "Now that's something I wish I could remember. I'll bet there was a whole lot a' shakin' goin' on!"

Lupé turned away. The expressions on Mooncloud and Suki's faces suggested something uncomfortable. "What?" I asked.

"So," Mooncloud said, consulting her notes, "you were headed north on State 7."

I nodded. "I can remember thinking about stopping for lunch, but we had just passed Scammon."

"Scammon?"

I rubbed my eyes again. "Tiny little town, but they've got this wonderful restaurant called 'Josie's' . . . but I wasn't sure they were open that early in the day. . . ."

"So then you turned east on 103." She was looking at a map of Kansas recently torn from a road atlas and hastily taped to the wall.

I shrugged. "I must have, given that the accident report puts me at the other end. But I don't remember."

"You passed through Weir, Kansas."

"I don't know." An edge had crept into my voice at the mention of Weir. "I must have. But. I. Don't. Remember."

"The accident occurred at the other end of 103 where you were attempting to rejoin US 69 North."

"Yeah. Yeah. That's what the cops told me." I hopped down from the examination table. "But other than what everyone else has said about where I must have been and what I must have done, I remember nothing! Nada! Zilch! Zero! End of report!" I walked up to Dr. Mooncloud, trying to arrange my face into an intimidating glower. "Are we done here?"

She sighed. "So much for feeling calm and refreshed."

"What?"

She snapped the cover down on her clipboard. "Go. But I want you back here in two hours."

"Fine." I stalked out.

Lupé caught up with me at the elevator. "So, where are you going now?"

"Nowhere. Fast."

"My, what a temper we have today." The sarcasm sounded forced.

"You're one to talk."

She grinned unexpectedly. "Speaking of temper, I hear you pulled the Doman's tail last night."

I looked at her. "He has a tail?"

"Figure of speech, Csejthe." The smile transformed her. While her features would never win beauty contests, there was something appealing in the clean, bold lines and planes of her face. "So what's your problem?"

I glared at her, more in annoyance, now, than genuine anger. "If I have to explain it to you—"

"Yeah, yeah; life's a bitch and then you die," she said. "Only you didn't die. Not permanently, anyways, so you got no kick there. No way you could go on living the way you were, so count yourself lucky we rescued your sorry butt from the New York fangs. Now you're here and, as one of the Masters, your life will be gravy. Relax, enjoy; you're at the top of the food chain, now."

"Maybe I don't like having my decisions made for me," I groused. "Maybe I prefer my guest invitations to include voluntary RSVPs. Maybe I want to live my life—or my unlife—free."

The smile turned rueful. "No one really lives free, Csejthe."

"Okay," I said, fighting my own urge to smile, "cheap. I want to live cheap."

"Well, I hope you do not plan any foolishness such as running away. I've retrieved you once. I do not wish to be sent out to hunt your sorry ass again."

"You and me both, Buttercup."

The elevator arrived and we got on. I gave Hinzelmann my floor and the lift started up. Lupé cleared her throat. "I'm headed back to my room to change. Then, down to the pool. Physical therapy." Her smile was fainter this time. "Want to come down and help me into the water?"

I didn't know what had nudged her into the defrost cycle, but I'd be a fool to pass up a potential ally. And any distraction was better than going down to the bar and ogling the dancers again. I nodded: "I'll meet you there in, say, twenty minutes?"

"It's a date."

Now there was an unnerving turn of phrase, I mused, exiting the elevator. I headed down the corridor and turned toward my quarters. Even more unnerving was the sight of Elizabeth Bachman tapping at my door as I rounded the corner.

"Oh, there you are!"

"Here I am," I agreed as she moved aside so I could open the door.

"May I come in?"

"Well, I'm just ducking in to change and then I have to meet someone."

"I won't get in your way. I promise."

Damn straight, I thought, holding the door as she entered. "Make yourself comfortable." I closed the outer door and headed for the bedroom.

"Who are you meeting?" she called from the living room as I rummaged through my dresser for a pair of swimming trunks.

"Ms. Garou." The Doman had been generous in providing for my sartorial needs: I was having to practically burrow through drawers filled with clothing.

"Why?"

The question irritated me. Pushy women irritated me. Of course, everything seemed to be irritating me these days. "We're having an affair."

She seemed to take the jibe seriously. "That's not funny."

"Oh? And why not?" I heard a sound behind me and whirled around. There was a cat lying in the middle of my bed, watching me with wide golden eyes.

"It's unnatural. Do you need any help back there?"

"Not yet," I called back. Now what in the hell would Bachman consider unnatural? Monogamy? The missionary position? "What's unnatural?" I stared back at the cat.

"She's a wolf." Bachman's voice indicated her logic was inescapable.

Except it escaped me for the moment. "And?" The cat was a sable brown shorthair. Burmese, most likely. Except that it had two tails. Non-standard in the Burmese breed. Or any other, for that matter.

"We are the Masters, darling. We command the other creatures of the night. The bat, the rat, the wolf—they are our servants."

Apparently immortality did not guarantee the long perspective on prejudice. "So, is this bigotry based on class distinctions or racial purity?" I walked over to the bed and scratched the cat behind the ears. It purred.

Bachman didn't. "You have much to learn, my dear."

"No doubt we all have." I went to the closet and started through the folded stacks of clothing on the upper shelves.

"I'm sorry, I didn't come here to fight with you," she called in a milder tone of voice.

Yeah? And just what did you come here for? No swimming trunks. I went back to the drawer that held several pairs of shorts to look for a substitute.

"I just want to help you assimilate into our world. And we do need to talk about your occupational situation. . . ."

Ah, yes. How had she put it the night before? My *position. . . .* I selected a likely looking pair of shorts and dropped my pants.

"Oh," she said. "Let me help you!"

I looked up to see her standing in the bedroom doorway. "If you really want to help," I growled, "you can go find me some swimming trunks."

"Swimming—?" This made two times I'd put her off balance in as many minutes.

"I'm going down to the pool and get a little exercise." I stepped into the shorts and tried to pull them up like I wasn't in a frantic hurry.

Her hand came up to her mouth and her eyes

narrowed. Then the cat *merrowed* on the bed behind me and Bachman's eyes shifted, widened, and narrowed again.

"My," she said with a new tone of civility, "what a lovely pussy you have on your bed." She backed through the doorway. "I really must be going. I wouldn't want to make you late for your . . . swim."

And with that, she was gone.

I turned and looked back at the cat. It stretched languidly then lay back down and began licking a forepaw.

Before I left, I rummaged through my newly stocked kitchenette and rewarded it with a saucer of milk.

The pool area was several stories below the street level of Seattle and divided into several pools of varying sizes, including three hot tubs set into the stone floor.

One of the whirlpools was occupied by the drop-dead gorgeous redhead that had sat at the Doman's table with Damien. Strangely, Damien was there with her but, instead of sharing the bubbling hot tub with her, he wore a jogging suit and sat in a deck chair just next to it so they could still be together without actually—well—being together.

I discreetly nodded in their direction. "What's that all about?"

Lupé looked over and smiled a wistful smile. "They're in love." That wasn't what I was asking but she changed the subject as I wheeled her past the deep end of the largest pool. "Tomorrow I'll be out of this thing and walking with a cane."

"Seems a little soon."

She shook her head. "Oh no, not for a lycanthrope. We heal very quickly. And that's certainly handy in both of my professions."

"And what professions are those?"

"Well, the movies, for one. I do freelance stunt work down in Hollywood and on location shoots."

"Really?"

"I've had the training. I'm agile and athletic. And, more importantly, if something goes wrong, I can survive gags that would kill any other normal human being."

"Gags?"

"Industry slang: stunts or special effects involving stunt doubles for the actors."

"Logical. Since you know you've got a better chance of surviving, does it ever make you careless?"

"No. It still hurts if you screw up. And you have to be even more careful lest the hospital X-rays you with a broken neck and then you're up and walking around in a few days. I actually find that, since I know my survival is practically assured under most circumstances, I'm less likely to clutch or suffer a mistiming out of fear."

We reached the shallow end and I set the wheelbrake on her chair.

"And your other job?" I asked as we undid the sashes on our robes.

"Long-range retrieval and enforcement for the Seattle demesne."

She shrugged off her robe and I tried not to stare. Her suit was a white one-piece that contrasted nicely with her dark skin. Although her figure lacked the architectural extremes that the Doman's dancers had displayed the previous night, she had a lean, muscled physique that seemed every bit as distracting.

"Which is a euphemism for what?" My voice hardly squeaked at all.

"Finding people like you and bringing them in." She unlatched the right arm support on her wheelchair and swung it down and out of the way.

"I thought half the uproar was because there are no people like me."

She held up her arms. "I'm beginning to think so, too."

I let that one pass as I bent down and lifted her out of the chair.

This time there was no car crash, no pumping

adrenaline, no gathering crowd to distract me: even with augmented strength, I could tell that Lupé wasn't light. In fact, she was darned heavy for a woman her size. Not that there was anything wrong with her size: I stand six-feet-two in my stocking feet and I've always preferred tall, long-limbed women. Jenny had been the only exception—

"What's wrong?"

I blinked. "What?"

"Am I too heavy? You suddenly looked very unhappy."

"Not unhappy," I lied, "just thoughtful."

"About what?" One brown arm remained around my neck, the other hand turned my face to look at her. "I am too heavy, aren't I? That's what you're thinking about."

"Not too heavy," I said, shrugging my shoulders and rehefting her in my arms. "It's just been a while since I held anyone like this."

"Oh. Oh, I see." Her eyes said that she did, indeed, see. "Well, there's no need for you to pretend chivalrously: I *am* heavier than I look. There's a reason for it."

"Muscle tissue is denser than body fat," I said. "A woman in your shape should weigh more—" I suddenly realized that I was just standing there, holding her in my arms, and making no move toward the pool.

Was it happening again? I was aware of an odd discomfort at her nearness, a physiological response that seemed to be building as I held her in my arms. . . .

But it wasn't quite the same as my reaction to the dancers the night before.

"Nice try, but it's more than a matter of muscle to body fat ratios," she said.

"Okay, I give. What's your secret?"

"Taj says it has something to do with the shapeshifting/mass paradox."

I forced my legs to move and took her over to the shallow end of the pool. "Ah, of course it does." I dipped my toe in the water. It felt warm.

"Yeah? Well, *we* don't understand it as well as *you* pretend to. Vampires and lycanthropes present opposite ends of the same problem: neither group tends to weigh what their body mass would indicate. Weres tend to be heavier than the norm for their size, whether in human or animal form. And our mass seems to shift along with our change in form: we lose it and then regain it inexplicably. Our resident physicist is going nuts trying to figure out how it can be possible without negating half a dozen laws of reality."

A series of half-circle steps descended into the pool and I began wading down into the water. "I take it that vampires tend to weigh less than a human their size should?" She nodded. "And what about mass when they turn into bats?"

She snorted. "Oh, you've been watching too many horror movies. Vampires can't turn into bats!"

"They can't?"

She shook her head.

"Huge, batlike creatures, then?"

She shook her head again.

"Wolves?"

"Nope."

"Mist?"

"Look at me," she warbled, "I'm as helpless as a kitten up a tree. . . ."

Errol Garner was probably spinning in his grave. "No mist, huh?"

"Huh-uh."

"Well, dammit, what can I turn into?"

"You could always walk around the corner and turn into a convenience store or something."

"Bugger. If I can't shapeshift, what's the point of being undead?" I was in up to my waist, now. Reluctantly, I lowered her into the water. "I was really looking forward to being able to fly."

"Oh, you'll be able to do the next best thing," she said. And then ducked beneath the water.

"Next best thing?" I asked when she came back up for air a minute later.

She pulled her hair back into a silky black cable that dribbled water between her shoulderblades. "Did you ever wonder why vampires fancy all those caped outfits?"

"Well—"

"Hang-gliding!" she laughed.

I just looked at her.

"Seriously. A vampire's mass and weight are such that a couple of square yards of fabric, the proper tailoring, and a good breeze occasionally assisted by elevation of a castle parapet or a second story window—well, a lot of folks would swear afterwards that they saw you flying."

"A few might even swear that you turned into a giant batlike creature," I mused.

"I think you get the picture." She submerged again, surfaced by one of the ladders along the side, and began swimming laps back and forth across the width of the pool.

Interesting.

I stood and watched, enjoying the warmth of the water as it swirled around the lower half of my body, enjoying the flash of toned arms and legs cutting the water before me. For a moment I was tempted to join her, to try to match her, lap for lap.

But I was tired. New nightmares seemed to be replacing the old and I hadn't slept soundly in my new bed. The water seemed to sap my strength further, its warmth making me surprisingly drowsy. I moved to the side of the pool and hoisted myself up and out.

The cooler air quickly revived me and I walked down to the diving board at the deep end of the pool. The board was only a couple of meters above the surface of the water, which was just as well, as I hadn't gone off any high-boards since those long-gone college years.

As I climbed the short ladder I looked up and saw

Bachman in the observation gallery, one story up. She smiled so I waved. It wasn't much of a wave, but then it hadn't been much of a smile, either.

Jackknife? Backflip? I walked to the end of the board and decided to make the first dive an ordinary, head-first, try-not-to-miss-the-water affair. After I'd gotten the feel of the board, not to mention my own reflexes, I'd try something fancier.

The board was unresponsive. Or maybe it was my reduced mass that made it seem stiff and unyielding. In any event, I was slightly off balance and I cut the water more like a spatula than a knife. Warmth enveloped me again and I slid down through its enfolding weightiness until I touched bottom.

And there I stayed.

I had always required extra poundage on my weight-belt when I went scuba diving, so I figured my reduced weight and mass would make me even more buoyant now.

I figured wrong.

I reached for the surface, scooping at the water with my hands and kicking off the bottom. I barely moved. This was not good: I hadn't taken a particularly deep breath going in and already my lungs were requesting more air. Panic was kick-starting my adrenal glands and riding them around my body like a couple of circus motorcycles in a round steel cage. I started scrabbling at the water like a marionette on rubber strings.

No good.

Fatigue eventually overpowered my hysteria, bringing the tranquility of exhaustion. Finally, I just stood there on the bottom of the pool, in the middle of the deep end, and looked around.

I could make out a frothy line of churning water off in the murk toward the shallow end. I wondered how long it would take Lupé to notice I was gone.

Think, dammit! My lungs were on fire and my vision was starting to fuzz around the edges.

Walk! I could walk up to the shallow end of the pool! But a few bouncing steps brought me to a steep incline that was too slippery to negotiate. I looked around. It was getting harder to see: the light seemed dimmer, now.

There! Maybe ten feet away. . . .

I turned, angling toward the side of the pool and moving farther into the deep end, again. Walking was difficult: I had to reach out and claw at the water as if tunneling through gelatin and bounce off my toes and the balls of my feet. The result was a slow-motion gait that belonged in an old, fifties, men-on-the-moon sci-fi movie.

Slowly, I turned; step by step, inch by inch. . . .

By the time I reached the side I couldn't see anything at all. I had to feel my way along like a blind man searching for the opening in a wall. Except I wasn't searching for a window or a door.

My chest bucked and heaved, trying to draw air into my aching lungs: despite all conscious resistance, I knew I would be breathing water in less than a minute. Trying to concentrate past the fear, I stood on tiptoes and bounced.

Nothing.

Move down a foot and try again.

Just flat, smooth concrete.

Maybe it's out of reach.

Try again.

Can't even tell if I jumped that time.

Feels like I'm dissolving: legs turning to water.

Hard to keep arms above my head.

Jump.

Something there.

My hand closed on a rung.

I had found the ladder.

As I pulled myself up and out of the water, Elizabeth Bachman leaned down. "Now you know why vampires don't like to cross running water." The brown cat with the two tails was crouched beneath a deck chair some ten feet behind her, watching me with wide, golden eyes. I turned my head and observed Lupé still swimming back and forth across the middle of the pool.

"Thanks . . . for sounding . . . the alarm," I gasped.

She smirked. "I wanted to see if you could make it out on your own."

"And a good . . . thing, too." I used the looping railings on the ladder to pull myself upright. "If you had . . . rescued me . . . I would have . . . been forever . . . in your debt."

It was obvious from the expression on her face that she hadn't thought of that.

I stayed in the pool for a while longer.

My philosophy tends toward the idea of getting right back up on the horse that throws you. But I stayed in the shallow end because my philosophy doesn't include confusing nerve with stupidity.

Besides, I wanted to wait until my legs stopped shaking before trying to walk out in front of Garou and Bachman.

While I experimented with my newfound lack of buoyancy, I watched Damien quit the hot tub area and move to a rack of weights near the far side of the shallow end. He removed his sweats, stripping down to a pair of gym shorts, and started in on a series of stretches and warm-up exercises. It was hard not to stare: Schwarzenegger and Stallone had better physiques, but you could only come to that conclusion after thinking about it for awhile. And, in regards to everything else, the vampire was better looking.

"You continue to surprise me," Lupé said as she steered her wheelchair beside the edge of the pool. "I would've expected you to be the type to stare at Deirdre, instead."

I looked down at my own body. "I think I'm jealous."

"Yeah, me too." She put her hands to her bosom. "He's got more cleavage than I do."

"That," I said, "is a near steal from Groucho Marx."

Her smile turned into a look of confusion. "Gotta go," she said, putting her hands to the secondary wheel rims.

"Hold on, I'll take you back."

"No. I need the exercise." She flexed her arms. "Good for the shoulders and the pecs." She flexed her smile and rolled away with an unseemly degree of haste.

Bachman was already gone, so I climbed out and fetched my towel. Drying off, I wandered over to the weight area.

"You like to lift?" the vampire asked affably as I approached.

I shook my head. "Not as a rule. But now that I'm starting a new life, I probably should be starting some new habits." I looked over various sized weights. "How long does it take to build a body like yours?"

He grinned. "About forty years."

"What?"

He eased the barbell back down to the floor. "I wasn't always into body building. I only started about forty years ago. And then your progress is determined by three things."

"Which are?" I picked up a pair of hand weights that felt light enough for a beginner's workout. I began a set of arm curls.

"Genetic predisposition, the frequency and intensity of your workout routines, and whether you're alive or undead."

"I follow you on the first two," I said. "I'm not sure about the last one."

"Weight training involves increasing muscle mass by breaking it down, first." He slid a couple more metal plates to the ends of his barbell. "You lift weights, which strain the muscle fibers and break them down so that the body replaces them with greater muscle mass.

"But once you become undead," he grunted, hefting the bar up to his chin, "your muscle tissues change, become denser, less susceptible to the breakdown process." The bar rose past his face to its straight-armed zenith above his head. "You can lift greater weights, but your body becomes more resistant to change—even positive change."

As the bar came back down, I counted the weights and did a little simple arithmetic. Damien was cleaning and pressing four hundred pounds.

"Hello, Mr. Csejthe," said a new voice. "How do you like our accommodations?" It was Deirdre, still dripping from the hot tub. Gowned and coiffed the night before, she had been a real head-turner. Up close, wet, and nearly naked in turquoise string bikini, she was devastating. I felt my swimming trunks shrink a bit.

"It's all rather new to me," I stammered.

"Well, the Doman tries to provide us with the best and the people here are very friendly. Aren't they, my love?" She ran a slim hand across Damien's dark jaw as he lowered the weights to the floor.

He grinned and took her hand in his, kissing it.

"I'm going in for about ten minutes of steam and then I'll be ready to go back up," she said. "How about you?"

"I should be done by then."

She smiled and walked away, moving like a twenty-three jewel Swiss watch as she headed toward the steam room.

"I don't wish to contradict her," Damien said fondly, "but to Deirdre, everyone seems friendly."

"I can see why," I said.

"Not just for her looks, but for her personality, as well. 'What is beautiful is good and who is good will soon be beautiful.' "

Damn! He wasn't only good looking and charming, he read Sappho, as well!

And then I noticed that I had miscalculated the numbers on the weights we were using. The dumbbells that I had assumed were merely ten pounds were actually ten kilograms. That meant I was curling close to twenty-five pounds in each hand with no effort. And the plates

I had assumed to weigh four hundred pounds on Damien's barbell were more than double that amount.

I devoutly hoped that he wasn't the jealous type.

Chapter Seven

Three.

I opened my eyes. Looked up at Dr. Mooncloud's face. Pagelovitch was hovering nearby.

"How do you feel?"

"Calm and refreshed," I said. She gave me an odd look and I sat up. "So what did we learn?"

"Nothing, really."

"Dr. Mooncloud regressed you to the last twenty minutes leading up the accident," Pagelovitch elaborated. "We were looking for causal evidence that might link the accident to your condition."

"And?" I looked at Mooncloud who was flipping through her notes and then back at the Doman.

"Nothing evident," he said. "You had a headache. You stopped in Weir for aspirin. Shortly thereafter you fell asleep at the wheel."

"Or passed out." This contribution came from Suki, who had returned to her post by the examination room's door.

"I've got something here. . . ." Mooncloud slipped a finger between two pages and flipped back through the note pad. "A few moments ago you were saying that you wanted to reach Frontenac before sundown, but that it was going to be close."

"Yeah, so?"

"Confirmed by the accident report filed by the county mounties."

"Significance, Doctor?" the Doman coached.

"Well, during our previous session, Mr. Csejthe made a comment about wanting to stop for lunch. . . . Lupé, hand me the map."

Garou, her hair still damp from her swim, maneuvered her chair between us to deliver the Kansas state road map.

"See? Here!" Mooncloud's finger stabbed at the southeast corner. "You would have driven only two more miles, once you passed Scammon, before you had to turn east onto 103. Then, three miles east to hit Weir and another four miles past Weir to hit Highway 69. No more than nine miles to cover from the time you were thinking about stopping for lunch to the time of the accident."

The Doman studied the map. "So?"

"Well, look here," she said. "Frontenac is just twelve miles up the highway from the point of the accident."

"So why would he be worried about beating the sunset?" Pagelovitch concluded.

I considered the numbers. "Somewhere, along that seven mile stretch of 103, I lost several hours. Time I can't account for."

"Perhaps your amnesia is more than a post-traumatic effect of the accident," Mooncloud said. "Perhaps your amnesia was in place before the accident."

"'The Interrupted Journey,'" Suki observed.

"You said something about an old man," the Doman said suddenly.

"I did?"

"No," Mooncloud said. "*You* didn't say it: under hypnosis, you reported that your wife said it." She skimmed a couple of pages of shorthand notes. "Here it is. She said: 'I hope that old man is going to be all right.' Ring any bells?"

Not directly. "No." But suddenly I recalled the white face in the rear window of the antique Duesenberg the night before last. A face that I had never seen before and yet it persisted in my memory like something disturbingly familiar.

It was the face of an old man.

🦇 🦇 🦇

The cat dogged me almost everywhere I went.

I asked around, but no one would admit to owning the creature or knowing who did. It had to be a conspiracy: a cat with two tails doesn't exactly lend itself to anonymity.

"Is it bothering you?" Suki asked on one of the occasions that it wasn't around.

"No, not really," I answered. "Although an animal with two tails is a bit unnerving. And I can't help wondering why it's attached itself to me."

"Maybe it likes you. You look like you'd be a cat person."

"Great," I muttered as she walked away with a faintly catlike stride of her own. "From bat person to cat person."

But, all in all, I didn't really mind that much. Now that I was a freak, myself, it seemed comfortable having another freak around to keep me company. Even if it was only a cat.

If it was only a cat.

If no one was going to tell me, then perhaps I could find out on my own. I popped out of bed the following night, threw on some clothes, poured another saucer of milk for my feline roommate, and headed straight for the Doman's library.

It was already occupied.

Damien looked up from one of the computer consoles tied to outside on-line services. "Chris, what a coincidence! We were just talking about you."

Deirdre poked her head out from behind one of the free-standing bookshelves. "Hello, Chris!"

I smiled. "And why am I so interesting?"

"Well, Deirdre has her own reasons," Damien said, "but, come over here and I'll show you mine." I walked over to the console and he motioned me into a seat. "I've been assigned to monitor the news in your area as a follow-up to your disappearance. The remains found in the fire are assumed to be yours and the case is pretty much closed. But, look here. . . ." He tapped a series of keystrokes and brought another file up on the monitor.

"Deaths and disappearances," he continued, scrolling the text up the screen. "Mysterious deaths and disappearances, that is."

"What about them?"

"I've been checking every police station and newspaper office within ninety miles of your home. I've culled all the funeral notices, accidents, and homicides, eliminating the ones where the witnesses or circumstances identified the assailant or eliminated the supernatural."

"And?"

He held up a hand. "I backtracked to the time your blood samples left the local hospital and were shipped to three independent labs for analysis. Since the New York team showed up at your doorstep the same night ours did, it's a good guess that the initial test results flagged their database simultaneously with ours. There's also the matter of that break-in and homicide at the Joplin hospital. One of your samples was routed there and is now missing."

"I guess as badly as they wanted me, they were more concerned about destroying evidence of my condition," I said.

"Maybe. Except the initial tests had already been run and the break-in and theft would only call more attention to it. They covered that, somewhat, by smashing other samples and scattering files, but your records and sample seem to be the only ones that are actually missing. So, these guys are sloppy. But there is a pattern here that goes beyond mere sloppiness."

"What do you mean?"

"Look. . . ." He brought up another menu on the screen and selected a number. Maps of Kansas, Missouri, Oklahoma, and Arkansas appeared and conjoined. He executed a series of keystrokes and brought the computer's mouse into play: the maps were enlarged until the Kansas/Missouri border took up most of the display. "Here's the hospital break-in where the night nurse was murdered," he said, using the mouse to plant an electronic flag over Joplin, Missouri. "Here, here, and here, are the disappearances that occurred within forty-eight hours of the incident at your radio station."

I remembered the fireball bursting through the roof of the old dormitory. Incident. . . .

Damien was planting electronic flags in the *Marais des Cygnes* Waterfowl refuge in Linn County, another in Garland near the Kansas/Missouri border, and a third in the Prairie State Park north of Mindenmines just over on the Missouri side. "The one in Garland turned up the day after you were picked up."

I grunted. "A missing blood sample is one thing. A corpse missing its own blood volume is another."

"As I said: sloppy. If only that was that the worst of it."

"There's more?"

He nodded. "As I was saying, I've monitored all reported deaths and disappearances since that forty-eight-hour period. There have been four more disappearances and another body since then."

"What? Why?"

"That's what I'd like to know. Ostensibly, New York sent a team to recover you and any evidence that might link you with vampirism. That particular goal and some very unprofessional blunders might explain the first three disappearances and the hospital break-in. Since enforcers characteristically travel in pairs, we assumed the New York team was completely eradicated with your second encounter in the cornfield. Obviously, we were wrong."

A lone flag popped up on the Missouri side, east by southeast of Joplin. "I'm not sure about this one."

"It doesn't fit the pattern?"

He shook his head. "Fellow by the name of Cantrell. Has a ranch over by Aurora, Missouri. Claims Satanists from Arkansas were trying to trespass on his property."

"Um," I said, "Satanists from Arkansas?"

"Said their cars had Arkansas plates."

"Oh," I said. "Of course."

"Said he proselytized them with a shotgun. Sounds like a crackpot."

A memory surfaced and I shook my head. "Harold Cantrell. I know this guy. He was one of our Public Radio subscribers: stable, rock-solid—owns a sizable spread. And while he used to claim Cantrell Ranch was the most lightning-prone acreage in the world, I wouldn't figure him for fringe. But Satanists from Arkansas. . ."

I watched more flags pop up on the map, all on the Kansas side: Arma, Girard, Pittsburg, McCune, Parsons. "More New York enforcers, tells us how. It doesn't tell us why."

"Why what?" Deirdre wanted to know.

Damien leaned back in his chair and stretched. "We know that they know that we have Csejthe. They've already picked up all the existing evidence in the area that might link him with the *wampyr*. The additional disappearances have occurred since then. So why are they still running around Southeast Kansas? What are they looking for?"

I stared at the phosphorescent lines and dots on the CRT. "Dr. Marsh might have some notes—"

"Chris . . . Marsh is dead."

It came to me slowly. "What?" Then I went cold all over. "Dead?"

Damien nodded. "They were very thorough. The Mount Horeb Hospital files are gone. Any notes with your name on them went up in the fire along with Marsh's house. And, of course, the good doctor. It's the one fatality on my list that could be dismissed as an obvious accident."

"It wouldn't be a coincidence," I said, bitterness flooding my mouth like vinegar.

"No, it isn't."

My hands balled into fists. "So, anyone else I know

on your list? Have they tried to silence any of my friends, my coworkers?"

He shook his head. "The rest is puzzling. It's as if they're looking for something else, now. As if they're casting about for a new scent, a new trail." He looked up at me. "You bite anybody on the neck during the last year? Leave your own trail of corpses?"

"That's not funny." I turned and walked to the door. "Not funny at all." I kept going.

Deirdre caught up with me halfway down the hall.

"I want to apologize for Damien," she said, catching my arm and linking it with hers. "He's outlived all of his family, his contemporaries, all of his human friends—"

"What about you?"

"I'm human, so he knows that he will outlive me, as well. He has a different viewpoint on death. He sometimes forgets what it's like to be mortal and attached to other mortals." She squeezed my arm. "Please don't be angry with him."

"I'm not, I guess." It was difficult to be angry when someone like Deirdre was squeezing your arm and gazing up at you imploringly. "Marsh's death is a shock. And I'm furious at the people who did this."

"Let me buy you a drink."

"I'm not really thirsty."

"Neither am I. But I want to talk to you and it just seems easier to observe the social amenities as an icebreaker." Now her arm was locked in mine and she took me in tow.

The night was young and the main room sparsely populated. We ordered drinks and found a distant table next to the wall. I sat with my back to the main stage to avoid distraction and quickly decided that that was a mistake: I needed a distraction from those luminous blue eyes, that perfect face, those curvaceous red lips, her—

"I want to offer myself to you."

I sat there, my train of thought utterly derailed. "Excuse me?" I said after a long pause.

She smiled and leaned toward me. "I'm offering myself to you, night or day, for as long as you can use me. Oh my." Her smile grew deeper. "The expression on your face."

I stared at her. Words wouldn't come.

"Didn't Suki mention anything about this?"

I managed to shake my head—that much I could do.

"I want to help you."

"Help me," I managed further.

"Research," she coached.

"Research. Ah."

"Your presence here is more important than you could possibly appreciate." She put her hand over mine. "But I appreciate the potential you bring. And I want to help tap that potential."

"You do."

She nodded. "So use me."

"Use you," I said.

"I'll do research, run errands, transcribe notes, verify test results."

At that point our drinks arrived, along with my grasp on reality.

"So, you're interested in unlocking the secrets of the vampiric condition," I said, pouring my Perrier over ice.

"Oh, yes!"

I smiled and patted her hand in return. "You and Damien are very much in love, aren't you?"

She nodded and her smile grew into something extraordinary.

"I can see why coming up with a cure for this disease is so important to you."

The smile faltered. "Cure?"

"If Damien could be freed from his curse—"

"Curse?"

"I thought. . ." I stopped. I wasn't sure what I thought anymore.

"Chris, I'm not looking for some magic potion to make Damien mortal, again. I want to be like him."

"Like him?" Great. First I'm echoing her, then she's echoing me, and now I was back to parroting her, again.

"I want to be a vampire."

"Um. Okay. Why?"

"Why?" The question seemed to surprise her. "Power. Immortality—or at least near invulnerability. Eternal youth." She looked down into the mud-red depths of her bloody mary. "And then there's Damien. . . ."

I cleared my throat. "Under these circumstances, I can see how a mixed marriage would be more problematic."

"The Doman has Taj working on too many projects to give your research anywhere near her full time and attention. I've been doing a lot of my own research in the library and on the databases. I thought we might work together, you and I—pool our efforts." She picked up her drink and her gaze wandered off, over my shoulder.

"What about Damien?"

She shrugged. "In a way, he'd be working with us. What he's doing now may coincide with some of the answers that we're looking for. But the Doman's got him busy on other projects, too. We barely see each other some nights." Her eyes came back to my face. "I need something constructive to do."

"Well. . ."

"Say yes. You won't be sorry!"

"Deirdre, I haven't had a chance to figure out where I would really start, what directions to go, what paths to pursue."

"You need to get organized. I can help you right there: I'm a very organized person." Her eyes drifted to the right again. "I think you have an admirer."

"Admirer?" Damn! The sensibility of this conversation had slipped away yet again.

She nodded. "Over there. Near the door to the kitchen. No, don't look!"

"Why not?"

"You'll spook her. She's really staring!"

"Anyone you know?"

She shook her head, raised her drink to her lips and peered over the rim of the glass. "I've never seen her in here, before. Hmmm. She's rather striking. . . ."

"Striking?"

"Attractive . . . but. . . ."

"But?" I sipped my Perrier.

"There's something about her . . . something that's somehow . . . wrong."

"Describe her."

"Tall, maybe five-nine. Slender—no, skinny: almost emaciated."

"The waif look. Very chic."

"Dark eyes, dark hair. Something about the eyes, though. . ."

"What?"

She shook her head. "She's wearing her hair in a French braid."

Sometimes Jenny had worn her hair in a French braid—she knew I liked it that way. . . .

Stop it, I thought.

"She's wearing a white dress with poofy sleeves."

"Poofy sleeves." Jenny had a dress like that. Kept it in a plastic bag at the back of her closet. It was still there—just six or seven months ago—before I had closed her closet door for the last time and promised myself I would only open it again when I was ready to throw everything out or donate—*stop it, stop it!*

Deirdre sipped her drink. "Unusual attire for this time of the year."

I turned and looked. And, of course, because I was thinking about my dead wife, the woman across the room looked just like her for a moment.

The moment stretched endlessly. *The reason the woman across the room looked like Jennifer was because it was Jennifer!*

"She seems to know you," Deirdre said as Jenny crooked her index finger into a "come here" gesture.

I couldn't move.

How?

The answer was quite simple: Jenny hadn't died after all.

You know better.

I never saw her dead.

You were in and out of consciousness for a week. The hospital didn't release you until ten days after the funeral.

Precisely, so how do I know her body lies moldering in a Kansas cemetery?

Your family and hers—made the arrangements, attended the funeral.

Hearsay.

The county coroner—medical documents.

Could have been forged.

To what purpose?

I don't know!

There was only one way to find out: I wrenched myself up and out of my seat, knocking the chair over with a muffled crash. The rest of the room got quiet. Only my wife was moving. Toward the kitchen.

"Jennifer," I croaked. "Jenny!" I stumbled after her. She was through the door before I was halfway across the room. I ran through the kitchen looking this way and that. She was gone.

I grabbed a busboy. "A woman—about this tall—brown hair, white dress—which way did she go?"

He shrugged.

I released him and whirled about: side doors? Left or right would put her into corridors that kept her inside the building. Only the back door was a direct exit to the outside. I ran for it, yanked it open.

Nothing. No one in sight.

A taxi sat, idling, in the service alley, twenty yards away from the rear loading dock. The rear passenger door was open on the side nearest me.

"Jenny?" I called.

I saw a flicker of white in the dark depths of the vehicle's interior.

"Jenny!"

"Chris?" Deirdre's voice behind me.

And Damien's voice: "What is it?"

A white hand at the end of a white, poofy sleeve reached out and grasped the handle on the open cab door.

I moved toward the end of the dock and was caught, pulled back, by clutching hands.

"Let me go," I said. "*Jenny!*"

"Hold him."

"Chris, you can't leave the building!"

"Come back inside."

"Don't let go."

I struggled trying to escape the multitudinous hands and voices. "*Jenny! Wait!*"

The hand pulled the door closed with agonizing slowness. A brief glimpse of her face at the window. The cab was pulling away. In a fit of desperation, I shrugged off two of my handlers, swung my fists, punched and kicked at the flesh that was trying to envelope me. I broke free. Tried to run for the departing vehicle. Made four, maybe five steps before I was tackled, smothered to the ground.

I screamed against the concrete.

The Doman's elbows were planted on the table, his left hand balled into a fist, cupped inside his right. He leaned forward, pressing his knuckles against his lips. "You are sure?"

My own elbows were similarly planted, but I was resting my forehead against the palms of my hands. "It *was* Jenny."

"I don't suppose you carry a photo of your wife in your wallet. It might help Deirdre make a positive ID."

I shook my head. I had taken Jenny's and Kirsten's photos out of my wallet and down from the walls a month after the funeral. Maybe that was a sign of denial. All I knew was that it hurt so much more to open my billfold or look across the room and still see their faces. . . .

Pagelovitch sighed. "Doctor?"

"There are, of course, psychological and stress-related factors that could cause him to imagine that he saw his dead wife—"

"I'm not crazy, I really did see her."

"—so that he might easily see her face and form when no one was there."

"But there was someone there," Deirdre said. "I saw her, too."

"And easier to project her face and presence onto a woman of similar stature and coloring."

Damien entered the room with a file folder.

The Doman raised an eyebrow. "Photographs?"

Damien nodded. "One. Photocopy from a newspaper story—the quality is not that good."

Pagelovitch gestured toward Deirdre. "Show it to her anyway."

I sat up a little straighter. "You have a file on me? On my wife?"

"On you. Any information on your wife is peripheral and, in this case, fortuitous."

Deirdre was shaking her head. "I don't know. It's too fuzzy. Maybe. Maybe not."

"You're not sure?" Clearly, the Doman was unhappy without a clear decision either way.

"I just can't tell."

"Still, it's highly unlikely that your dead wife just turned up here in Seattle."

I scowled at the Doman. "Why not? I just turned up here, in Seattle."

"She was pronounced dead, Christopher—"

"So was I."

"—and buried. You weren't."

"Maybe she was infected the same as me. Maybe

better: maybe she's a full-fledged vampire." A part of my conscious mind was standing back and observing this conversation with a detached sense of horror. Another portion was desperately trying to make Jenny real at any price.

The Doman was relentless: "So, where has she been for the past year?"

"I don't know. Maybe she was trapped in the grave, underneath the ground, in her coffin. Maybe she just got free recently."

"So, why is she with New York?"

"What? New York?"

"We checked all the dispatchers. No cabs were logged in this vicinity during or for an hour either side of this incident. No independent or company taxis in this city match the description of your vehicle.

"Christopher," he continued in a gentler voice, "for some reason New York still wants you. It would be very simple for them to hire a body double to act the part of your departed wife, to lure you outside of our sanctuary."

"With your psychological situation," Mooncloud chimed in, "a little makeup and the right dress would be all that was necessary for the power of suggestion to be complete."

"Perhaps they even went a step or two beyond makeup," the Doman said.

I stared at Pagelovitch. "What do you mean?"

He shrugged. "Perhaps a glamour of some type. . . ."

"Magic? You're telling me they can use magic?"

Looks were exchanged around the room. "Of course not. But if there was another vampire involved. . ."

"A Projective," Mooncloud said. "Some form of mental domination."

"I thought other vampires couldn't come on the premises without a specific invitation to cross the threshold."

His eyes narrowed. "I don't have all the answers, yet." Then his gaze softened. "But that would tend to shoot holes in your theory that your wife had returned as a vampire."

I grasped at my last straw: "Maybe they found some other way to resurrect her."

"Magic? Hocus pocus? Come now," the Doman smiled, showing pointed teeth, "this is reality. . . ."

Chapter Eight

Knowledge is power. So wrote Hobbes in *Leviathan*. In *Of Heresies*, Bacon said: Knowledge itself is power. But perhaps André Gide said it best when he wrote: "*Education, c'est délivrance.*"

If education was, indeed, freedom, the Doman's library was the place to form my escape plan. I began my studies the following evening and, aside from regular evening visits from the two-tailed cat, I worked undisturbed until Saturday night.

"Looking for a cure?"

I glanced up from the tumbledown fortress of books that encompassed me at the library table. "At this point I'd settle for a little sanity."

Taj Mooncloud sorted through the sprawl of volumes that had slid to the far side of the table. "*The Golden Bough*, Crosland's English adaptation of Valeria and Volta's *The Vampire*, a couple of Montague Summers' better known works, *The Natural History of the Vampire* by Masters—my goodness, even a translation of the *Malleus Maleficarum*! You're looking for sanity, here?"

I said nothing and she wandered over to the microfiche reader that I had left on for cross-referencing.

"*Traité sur les Apparitions des Espirits, et sur les Vampires, ou les Revenants de Hongrie, de Moravie—*"

"First edition, Paris, 1746," I appended. "But I'm really more interested in a rather recent work." I lifted the bound manuscript I'd been studying and turned it so she could read: *Vampirism and the Subconscious Mind: The Id Unbound. By Dr. Taj V. Mooncloud, Ph.D., M.D., S.D.*

"I'm impressed: Doctor of Philosophy, Doctor of Medicine. . ." I cocked an eyebrow. "S.D.?"

"Doctor of Shamanism."

"You're joking."

"I never joke," she answered coolly.

"Well." I hefted the book. "I'll bet there're no copies in the Library of Congress."

"No, and more's the pity," she said, pulling up a chair across from me. "Ten years of semicooperative national and worldwide research and we know more about the AIDS virus than ten centuries of scholasticism on the subject of vampirism."

"We still don't have a vaccine for AIDS," I said, unsure of whether I was undermining or underlining her point.

"Bad enough that we can't utilize public facilities, personnel, or funding efforts in our research," she continued, "but it's difficult to secure cooperative information from the other enclaves, as well."

I tapped the manuscript. "You seem to have made some substantial leaps beyond anything else I've read."

"Theoretical leaps. We have a Magnetic Resonance Imaging device, an electron microscope, substantial lab and diagnostic facilities . . . but it's a drop in the bucket compared to the resources we really need—not to mention the statistical base!

"The bulk of the books you have there were first published before the turn of the century, some before the turn of the last century, and more than a few from before even that. They're such a hodgepodge of myth and third-hand stories that you can't be sure of the truth even when they seem to validate your own findings. . . .

"But you," she reached across the table and between two stacks of books to grasp my hand, "may help to change all that!"

"The missing link," I said.

"Oh, don't say it that way! It sounds so—so—"

"Guinea piggish?"

It took her a moment to find her smile. "Exactly."

"Oink, oink," I said.

She tossed my hand back at me. "Guinea pigs don't go 'oink, oink.' "

"I guess someone will need to coach me."

"Obviously, after that stunt you pulled at the pool."

"Ah, which brings me back to my research." I thumped the manuscript back open to my last bookmark. "I need to know all kinds of stuff. About mirrors and garlic and crosses and holy water—"

"You need someone to coach you," she said.

"—and why this stuff works the way it does. I mean, I used to be a great swimmer! What happened to me?" I flipped to the beginning of her manuscript and then back to my last marked passage. "I've skimmed the first part, here, where you venture several theories about the physiological changes that take place in the human body."

"It's really a brief summation of another paper I published earlier."

" 'Published'?"

"Within the underground network that ties all the enclaves together to some degree."

"Yeah, well I noticed that you skipped a lot of the empirical data and just highlighted the conclusions. But it still begs the question on certain aspects of vampiric lore. I see how the physiological changes in body tissues may alter mass, augment strength, prolong longevity . . . but what about holy water, the crucifix, requiring invitations to cross thresholds?"

"Keep reading."

I glanced at the three-inch-thick remainder of unread pages. "I'm in a hurry."

"So am I." She glanced at her watch. "All right. Quick overview. The virus—and immediately we are in the realm of theory, here—the virus seems to enter the cells and combine with the DNA to reprogram the strands of code."

"Like genetic engineering."

"Right. And it produces rapid mutations in the cells and tissues so that entire systems become both more efficient and yet develop built-in redundancies. At the same time these changes create new vulnerabilities, new weaknesses to replace the ones that human flesh is heir to."

"Sunlight," I said. "Garlic."

"Like porphyria," she said.

"Wooden stakes?"

"Wooden stakes, iron lances, silver arrows—it makes no difference as to whether you're alive or undead: one through the heart and you ain't never getting up out of your coffin again."

"Crucifixes?"

"Ah, now here we enter the realm of the subconscious. Are you aware that there are certain codicils to the use of holy relics?"

I nodded. "Basically two that I've run across, so far. One source claims the effectiveness of the crucifix is dependent on the faith of the wielder. Other sources indicate that the cross only works against vampires who were devout Christians in their former life." I cocked an eyebrow. "Which is it?"

Mooncloud shrugged. "We do not know for sure. There is actually enough anecdotal material to support both theories, but we simply have not had enough opportunity to apply rigorous scientific testing. But the common thread that runs through both theories is—"

"Belief," I finished for her.

"Yes. Belief. And it is the same with so-called holy water."

"So what are you saying? That these basic scourges of the undead are psychosomatic at their core?"

"Something like that." She looked around and then got up and walked over to the door. After checking the outer corridor, she closed the door and walked across the room and around the table to sit beside me. "The virus has a variable range of effects on each person who contracts it," she continued in a lowered voice. "And that extends to the mental and emotional adjustments each must make, as well."

"I suppose some have a more difficult time than others?"

"An understatement, Mr. Csejthe. Insanity is the byproduct more often than not. Sometimes quickly. Sometimes a psychosis that grows over the years, the centuries. Sometimes all higher thought processes are lost and the virus reduces its host to a mindless animal. In other cases the madness manifests in subtler and more cunning forms."

"So," I cleared my throat, thinking about my own recent state of mind, "why are some affected and others immune?"

She stared at me for a long and discomforting moment. "You don't understand," she said finally. "The virus affects the brain. *In every case.* The differences only lie in the severity of the psychosis, the amount of time involved in the alteration of the individual's brain chemistry, and how resistant you are to your particular brand of dementia."

"So, you're saying that insanity is inevitable?" I didn't like this at all.

"By your definition? No. But every functioning human being is heir to various mental aberrations—most of us just fall into the so-called normal range. Haven't you heard that there isn't one person who couldn't benefit from a little analysis?

"But the virus does seem to work most frequently in lowering the mental barriers between the conscious and the unconscious areas of what we call the mind. It makes the host more susceptible to certain forms of suggestion, irrational belief systems, perhaps even racial memories."

"So," I steepled my fingers, "if I were a devout Catholic and I woke up in my coffin shortly after my funeral, I would have an incapacitating terror of crucifixes, communion hosts, and holy water?"

She nodded. "The Church has deeply ingrained prejudices concerning vampires and the Powers of Darkness."

"Apparently it works both ways." I thought about the power of the mind over the human body. About how a few, special test subjects under hypnosis would display bruises, cuts, burns, various bodily stigmata produced by a belief in an injury that only existed in their minds. Was it any great leap to imagine a vampire's belief that he couldn't cross another's threshold unless specifically invited to do so?

"What about mirrors?" I asked. "Why don't vampires cast reflections?"

"That's a little more difficult to explain."

"Try."

"I'm not sure you're ready."

"Try anyway."

"Well," she hunched her shoulders. "As I said, the virus affects the brain, alters the brain's chemistry—possibly reconstructing certain neural pathways in the process. This is difficult to prove as there are no remains—ergo, no brain—to dissect following a *wampyr*'s death."

"Cat scans? MRI's?"

She shook her head. "Electromagnetic radiation, whether it's in the visible spectrum or not, is harmful to vampiric flesh. Which reminds me, you should probably avoid using microwave ovens or sitting too close to the TV."

"You're kidding."

She wasn't. "Under these limitations, we can only postulate."

An unpleasant thought occurred: "Or open up a vampire's skull while it is still alive." Or undead. Or whatever.

Mooncloud squirmed. "Vivisection of the undead has been—documented. But, even without such extreme proofs, the evidence of changes to the brain are undeniable."

"So you're saying that the absence of a mirror image is due to the psychosis?"

"No. There are other mental changes, as well." She looked back at the door, again. "Have you ever noticed how the Doman rarely has to summon someone he wants to speak with?"

It took me a moment to understand the question. Then I remembered how Suki had shown up unexpectedly to finish my initial tour of the castle. "Telepathy?"

"Not just telepathy, but other psionic talents as well. You've read about the vampire's ability to cloud men's minds? Or dominate them?"

"So the vampire either consciously or unconsciously blocks the perception of his reflection in the mirror? For himself and anyone else within mental range?"

Mooncloud clapped her hands. "Very good, Mr. Csejthe! I had to explain the concept to Stefan twice before he could grasp the basic theory. You are—"

"If one more person says that I'm a quick study, I'm going to belt them!" I propped up my chin with my right hand. "So, are the vampire's psionic abilities standard equipment or wild card?"

"Wild card. Which brings us back to the conclusion that this is a mutative viral agent. While there is a set range of effects, different hosts manifest different degrees of strengths and weaknesses."

"So why have my mutations stopped?"

"Well, they haven't. Exactly."

I leaned forward. "Well, what have they? Exactly?"

"Well, in some areas, such as strength, reflexes, and the enhanced spectrum of your five senses, the mutation seems to be going forward—although it has slowed recently. In other areas, such as the development of fangs and anticoagulants in your saliva, you don't appear to have even begun the processes. Strange, though—"

"What?"

"You have developed rudimentary clotting sacs. . . ."

"What?"

"They're small sacs that form beneath the tongue that

exude a clotting agent when the vampire is done feeding. It closes the wound and speeds healing."

"How nice."

"Not if you're suckered in by Hollywood's version of the mythos. All those movies where the vampire bites the victim's neck and the victim survives? That's all poppycock. The most potent clotting enzymes won't seal a torn jugular vein in time. A vampire goes for the throat with the intent that his victim not survive. Otherwise, he must feed on the less volatile blood vessels. This would especially be true in your case." She glanced at her watch. "I have a meeting with Stefan."

"Just one more question, Doctor."

"Yes?"

"Why?"

"Why?" she echoed.

"Why? Why am I turning into a vampire and why am I stuck halfway in between?"

She rose from her chair. "That's two questions. And I still don't know the answer to either." She walked around the table and paused by the door. "During our next session, I'll use hypnosis to regress you to the time you passed through Weir. Perhaps the answer lies there."

"Why can't we just do it all at once and get it over with?"

"The Doman insists on being present, now, and he can't make time until tomorrow night."

There was something in her eyes. "And?"

"And your blood pressure goes through the roof every time we approach that period under hypnosis," she said reluctantly. "We're spacing the sessions out to give your body a chance to recover."

She yanked open the door and Elizabeth Bachman practically stumbled into her arms.

"There you are, Chris," Bachman gushed as she pirouetted around Dr. Mooncloud. "I've been looking all over for you!"

"Me?" I looked at Mooncloud who offered a warning glance as she turned and headed out the door.

"You! It's time we checked you out for that position I was thinking of!"

"I thought the Doman was dead set against my leaving the premises," I said as we exited the elevator.

"He doesn't want you leaving the building unescorted," Bachman answered, slipping her arm through mine. "We've made some security arrangements and he's approved them."

"Security arrangements?"

"The Doman believes New York still wants to acquire you, but Damien and I should be more than enough to handle anything unhuman that might come along. And in your enhanced condition as a—what? Semi-vampire?"

I shrugged but silently promised to bite the next person who used that term.

"You should be able to handle anything human, as well." She smiled. "You nearly hospitalized a busboy and two of the cooks the other night. Deirdre is still sporting a shiner and, wonder of wonders, you actually gave Damien a split lip!" She laughed. "I'm sure you can take care of yourself if you're really threatened.

"Besides, since you're here, you no longer pose a threat to the greater Undead community. There's no logical reason to want you dead—no 'un' attached."

"So what do they want?"

"They probably want to recruit you for their own research purposes. Which means they wouldn't want to actually harm you."

"You sound as if you wouldn't mind."

She hugged my arm even tighter. "Oh, I'd mind! I want you all to myself, remember?"

Sigh.

"Anyway, cars come and go from our underground garage all the time. We'll take a limo with tinted glass so no one can see who's inside."

"Won't that arouse suspicions if *Fantasies* is actually staked out?"

"You watch too many cop shows. I use this particular limo every Saturday night."

We arrived at my door. "Should I dress formal or casual?"

"Invite me in and I can help you select your wardrobe."

I smiled and chucked her gently under the chin. "Ah, but then we'd only end up being late, wouldn't we?"

She sighed. "True. Dress casual. I'll meet you in the garage in ten minutes."

Whew. I let myself in as she walked on down the corridor.

My night vision had developed to the point that I almost forgot to turn on the lights. Visual acuity into the infrared and ultraviolet spectra, however, makes for poor color coordination when you're dressing.

I was belting on a pair of tan Dockers when I noticed the piece of paper lying on my bed.

It was folded, with my name written on the outside. Inside was a note, written in a shaky, ballpoint scrawl: I had to decipher as much as read it.

Darling—

It said.

Kirsten and I are alive! There is no time to explain right now! You are in danger!

The people you are with are not your friends! Destroy this note when you have finished reading it! Tell no one that you have further cause to believe I am alive!

You must escape!

I cannot come to you, again; you must come to us! When you do, our friends will help us start a new life!

I love you, darling, and Kirsten misses her Daddy! You must try to get away, soon!

Love,

Jennifer

Below that, in a childish scrawl was:

I love you, Daddy—please come soon!
Love,
Kirsten

I looked around wildly and ran through the rooms, throwing open closet doors as if I might find—what? More messages? Evidence of its authenticity? My dwindling rationality? Only the solidity of the paper in my hand had any palpable reality in this terrible moment.

But the message rang a false note.

I stared at the handwriting, trying to remember if there was anything distinctive about Jenny's style. A year had passed, my memory dimmed, and Kirsten might be a year older in her own still-developing penmanship. . . .

A cold chill had permeated my body and now I felt the first flush of a white-hot core of anger. Jenny never signed her notes to me as "Jennifer." It was always "Jenny" or, more frequently, "Jen." If this was a trick, a false lure, it was unimaginably cruel and sadistic.

If it was, I would find out who—and kill them.

If—

I opened a dresser drawer. I refolded the note and slipped it inside one of the socks at the bottom of the pile.

Destroy the note? *Not bloody likely!*

I dressed in a furor, visions of carnage playing in my head.

If—

But, if it were true, then maybe I was in peril from the people who claimed to protect me. . . .

The Doman had warned me about the bloodlust, the appetite for violence.

He had neglected to mention the paranoia.

I should have expected the first assault.

Damien was up front, driving. Bachman pressed a button and suddenly a tinted glass partition slid up between the front seat and the passenger area where we were sitting.

"I like a little privacy," she said, snuggling next to me.

"Ms. Bachman—"

"Call me Liz." She pouted. "You've probably heard all sorts of nasty little stories about me by now. Well, some of them are true—the best ones, anyway." She smiled. Her teeth were very white, very sharp. "They've probably tried to scare you away from spending time with me because they think I'm a bad influence." She squirmed a little closer, a feat I hadn't thought possible. "Maybe I am. But you strike me as the kind of man who knows his own mind."

I had nothing to say, my mind was still on the note in my room.

And upon the deadness of my own heart.

What if? Jenny and Kirsten were a year dead in my mind, less than six months in my heart. But, searching my feelings, I was troubled to find that resurrecting their bodies might prove easier than resurrecting my feelings. I still missed them. But the passion had evaporated at some point, leaving only a hollow shell of longing. This, more than any other aspect of my transformation so far, marked me for the monster I was becoming.

Bachman leaned into my thoughts, her breath warm upon my neck. I flinched.

"Don't worry, I won't bite—yet," she said. "We'll keep your precious blood pure for awhile longer. But there are other things I can do for you in the meantime. . . ."

"Such as?" I regretted the words even as they were coming out of my mouth.

"Oh . . . well, for instance, you need someone to show you the ropes. I *know* the ropes. I can show you some rope *tricks*, as well. . . ."

She saw the expression of distaste on my face and moved back a bit. "Chris," she said in a more sober voice, "you are coming into a condition of power. It is a power I have, as well. I can teach you how to deal with it, how to wield it. How to profit from it. Your unique status also gives you potentials for power that none of the rest of us have. I can help you exploit it."

"How?"

"You need a friend."

"I thought the Doman and his people are all my friends," I baited.

"You can't be too sure of who your friends really are, my dear Christopher."

Damn straight.

"For example—" she lowered her voice "—Mooncloud and Garou are two that you must be especially careful of."

"Oh?" I lowered my voice to match hers. "Why?"

"The Doman suspects that at least one among us is a warlock."

"Warlock?"

"An oath-breaker, not a male witch."

"I know the etymology of the word. You're saying the Doman suspects a traitor?"

She nodded. "A double agent, possibly working for the New York enclave. And, very possibly, more than one."

"And he suspects Taj and Lupé?"

"He doesn't speak openly of this to anyone. He would be very angry if he discovered that you had been told of this. I'm telling you because I think you have a right to know. I'm telling you because this knowledge may save your life someday. I'm telling you this because, all flirting aside, I want to be your friend. And the day may come when you have to make a split-second decision: if you don't know who your friends are by then, it could be too late!"

"So tell me about Taj and Lupé."

She did.

There wasn't much to tell, all in all.

Just that both Luis and his sister were outsiders and recent additions to the Doman's "family." Both were less than enthusiastic about some of the demesne's policies and Lupé, especially, was considered to be somewhat of a malcontent.

Dr. Mooncloud was not only a medical doctor, she confirmed, but an Amerind shaman or witch doctor, as well. What tribe? Bachman wasn't sure. All existing paperwork and records regarding the good doctor—including her birth certificate and social security number—were not only contradictory but apparent forgeries, as well. And most damning of all: the opportunity to join them as a fellow vampire had been proffered on more than one occasion and Taj Mooncloud had turned them down each time.

By the time we pulled into the TV station parking lot, Liz Bachman had only provided me with rumor and innuendo. But then, hard evidence would have made this conversation moot long before it ever began, anyway.

The tinted glass partition came down as the limousine pulled into a reserved parking slot.

"We weren't tailed," Damien announced, watching me carefully in the rearview mirror. "The coast appears to be clear but I'll walk you to the door, anyway."

"Fine," my companion said. "We can't be too careful these days."

Amen to that.

Elizabeth Bachman reclined on the red velvet couch in a pose reminiscent of Theda Bara's *Salome*. Bara wore surprisingly little in that 1918 film and, in much the same tradition, neither did Bachman.

Her long black gown was ankle-length but slit to the hip and then some, displaying long legs that scissored invitingly. "The neckline" should have been renamed "the waistline" considering where it finally ended up. Bachman's bosom played hide and seek among the thin swatches of fabric as she moved, spending more time seeking than hiding. It was all I could do to keep from calling out: Alley, alley oxen-free-o.

The long black wig covering her blond hair, together with the black dress and Nefertiti eye makeup conspired to imitate Morticia Addams and Elvira, as I had suggested a couple of nights earlier. But only for a moment. Both were caricatures that spoofed that yin and yang gestalt where sex and death meet on common ground.

Elizabeth Bachman was the real thing.

The floor manager cocked his head listening to the voice in his earpiece. "Okay, people: coming out of commercial in three—two—" He mouthed "one" and stabbed a finger at camera two.

"Well, darlings," Bachman cooed, pouting toward the lens of the middle TV camera, "I hope you enjoyed tonight's Creature Classic: *Robot Monster*. If you think it's the worst movie ever committed to film, then you must tune in again, next Friday night, when we scream—I mean, 'screen'—the most horrible horror movie of them all. Yes, maybe you've seen monster movies that left you badly frightened . . . but next week we'll be showing the movie that won the Golden Turkey Award for being frighteningly bad! I'm talking about *Plan 9 From Outer Space*! That's right, the film that was so awful it killed Bela Lugosi! Find out why on the next episode of 'Lilith's Strokes of Midnight.'

"Goodnight, my lovelies!" She blew a kiss. "Sleep tight! Don't let the vampires bite!" She opened her mouth to show her fangs and hissed at the camera. The hiss turned into a sultry laugh and she ran a long, red fingernail down her chest, leaving a small trail of blood between her breasts.

The floor manager drew a finger across his throat indicating the microphones were now dead. "Cue the music," he said and pointed to camera three. The red active light winked on above camera three. "Rolling credits," the floor manager announced. "Fade to black in three—two—*one*! All right, folks; we're clear."

As the cameras were trucked back and the crew began dismantling the set, he turned to Bachman. "Lizzie, the director wants to see you in the booth."

She nodded, pulled the black-tressed wig off, and crooked a finger at me. "Come on, honey. Time to get your foot in the door."

I followed her up a half flight of stairs and over to a small room that housed a switching console and a soundboard. The switcher and the soundman were on their way out as we entered.

The director was a small, snakelike man with receding black hair that looked even less substantial as he wore it slicked back and gathered into a questionable samurai-do. His face was pinched and predatory, and his pencil-thin mustache didn't do anything to detract from the Ratso Rizzo effect.

"Liz, baby!" His voice was friendly and a shade deferential, but his cold and beady eyes gave the lie to his smile and tone. Oily was the operative term here, and this guy would make the *Exxon Valdez* look environmentally safe.

"Jonny, I want you to meet Chris Csejthe," Bachman said, grasping my arm and pulling me forward.

"Gesundheit." Ratty sniggered and offered his hand. I took another step forward, but he turned the gesture into an offhand wave and turned back to Bachman.

"Lizzie, hon; the blood thing was a nice effect—very realistic." His eyes traced the scarlet thread that wended its way down her torso. Just now it was disappearing beneath the nadir of her décolletage.

"Thanks."

"But that's just the problem. . . ." His gaze remained at half-mast. "You know the station manager and the sponsors raise hell when you go too far. You're supposed to get prior approval before you pull any of those kinky special effects." His eyes seemed to be calculating the continuing path of the trickle beneath the black material.

"Now, Jonny," she purred, "you know it's my kinky

special effects that have given this dead-end time slot a higher audience cume than most of your prime time shows. It's what gives me the power to do the show live and the clout to drag all your sorry asses in here at midnight every Friday to assist me." Her voice hardened. "*Assist* me, capeesh?"

Now his eyes were back up where they belonged and her voice and demeanor softened. "I would like you to hire Mr. Csejthe for my crew," she continued.

"*Your* crew?"

Her expression seemed to exert an even greater calming influence on the ratty little man. When he opened his mouth again, his tone was more respectful but he said: "Sweetheart, you know I ain't got any openings at the moment."

Bachman started to speak, hesitated, smiled, and then suggested that I be given an employment form to fill out—just in case.

The little man swallowed and nodded, and in no time we were back in her dressing room where she began removing her makeup.

"It's so hard to get good help these days," she sighed as she traced the black eyeliner with an industrial-sized Q-tip. "Did you see any crew position that you particularly liked?"

I shrugged. "Other than writing scripts, the only job I might be qualified for here would be sound man." I jammed my hands into my pockets and watched her closely. "And that position is already filled."

It was her turn to shrug. "There's always some kind of turnover on the night crew. I wouldn't be surprised if Harry—that's the sound guy—were to just up and take off for parts unknown this very week." She lined up twenty cotton balls next to the cold cream jar and began scrubbing at her shaded eyelids.

I decided that I wouldn't be too surprised if Harry were to suddenly up and disappear, too.

Bachman pouted when I announced that I was going

to wait outside in the limo with Damien; she was just getting ready to change.

It was a short, well-supervised stroll from the backstage door to the parking lot and the waiting limousine where Damien was keeping watch.

If anything, I mused, Damien's real purpose here tonight was probably to insure that *I* didn't try to make a break for it. But, I tried not to think on that. Or on the note I had found in my room this evening. Instead, I intended to enjoy the moment and a hundred feet of outdoor sidewalk with no one breathing down my neck for a change.

I paused as the heavy security door banged shut behind me and savored the night air. But only for a moment: an inversion layer was trapping light wisps of fog close to the ground and, with it, the perfume of a thousand cars, trucks, and busses. Still, it was an outdoorsy smell, and while I took care to breathe less deeply, I still enjoyed the change from the filtered and conditioned air of the Doman's forced hospitality.

As I turned and caught sight of the dark, brooding silhouette of the waiting limo, I caught another scent on the night air. Cigarette smoke. It suddenly occurred to me that, after many years of abstinence, I could take up a long denied and guilty pleasure again with no fear of lung cancer or emphysema.

Suck blood, blow smoke . . . trade-offs.

"Hello, there."

I turned toward the voice and found the source of the cigarette smoke.

A hooker or a stagedoor groupie or maybe both, was loitering just a few yards away, smoking the last of a cigarette. Taking one last drag, she dropped the butt on the sidewalk and ground it out with an ankle-top boot with a three-inch heel.

As she moved toward me I experienced that curious sensation again where time seemed to perceptibly slow and all my senses seemed abnormally heightened.

Although it was still summer and the night had started off balmy, this was the Pacific Northwest and around two-thirty in the morning. The brunette was wearing a black leather jacket, but it gaped open to reveal attire more appropriate for warmer weather or private parties. *Hooker*, I decided as she sashayed toward me in slow motion. She was dressed in biker-chic, wearing a black leather miniskirt that matched her jacket down to the handcuffs-motif and a black, lacy bra that seemed at least one size too small. My skin was prickling now; I felt flushed and feverish.

It was happening again! That same hormonal surging that I had felt the night before last while watching the dancers, was back and steadily building into a tidal wave of hunger. I had never been the kind of man to gawk when an attractive woman walked by, but now I was staring shamelessly. At the swell of lace-capped bosom, at the flash of sleek legs disappearing up into the shadowy hollow of leather, at the twitch of firm abdominals with the winking eye of a navel peeking over the top of the silver-chased belt buckle. Looking at these sliding, shifting, quivering expanses of smooth flesh, I was nearly overwhelmed by the need to touch, to taste. . .

Dear God!

It wasn't *sexual* hunger that was causing my body to ache and burn and throb. It was a hunger for elemental sustenance, pure and simple! I no longer saw an attractive member of the opposite sex coming toward me but food—warm and succulent, firm and tasty.

It was the bloodlust that the Doman had warned me about.

My nostrils flared, picking up the scent of perfume. But underneath I smelled the more compelling aroma of musk and sweat and blood that is the natural fragrance of the body. Saliva began to pool in my mouth.

And then I remembered that I had no fangs. Even if I wanted to give in to the maddening urge to open her throat and drink, I had no means of doing so!

The ache pulsed through my body, ice-picked into my brain. I turned with a sob and ran for the sanctuary of the limousine.

There was a shout behind me. But I was nearly blind and deaf now, all my senses turned inward, focusing on an aching emptiness demanding to be filled. I stumbled against the side of the car and yanked on the passenger door. As the door flew open rough hands grasped my arms and shoulders. I was wrestled away from the car, but not before the dome light came on, illuminating a grisly scene. The rotting remains of a human corpse occupied the driver's seat, held upright by a large wooden stake that transfixed the sternum with the point emerging from the rear of the upholstery.

I managed to shrug off one of my attackers and was just turning my attention to the other two when the hooker in leather stepped up and pushed a potholder for chicken cacciatore in my face.

At least that was my impression just before my head exploded and my eyes turned inside out. Then my legs fell off.

All that I could feel now was the viselike grip of other hands pinning my arms behind me and the hailstorm that had suddenly opened up inside my head.

There was a sensation of movement, though I could not have said whether it was up, down, forward, sideways, or backward. Slowly, my eyes started to pop back into their rightful position and I began to distinguish alternating yellow slashes against a black background. Parking slot lines on blacktop, I decided as we finally reached our destination: another limo on the far side of the parking lot. The trunk lid was popped open and I was heaved up and into the car's cavernous boot. After a lifetime of conventional transportation I was getting two limo rides in one night—how lucky can a guy get?

I moved my head a little, praying that it wouldn't roll off my neck again. Good news: it didn't and, looking down, my legs still appeared to be attached to my body.

I looked back up in time to see the sweep of approaching headlights illuminate the trunk lid.

"Here," said a female voice, "if there's trouble, you know what to do. The Doman says we either bring him in or see to it that Pagelovitch doesn't get him back."

There was trouble: all hell broke loose just ten seconds later. There was screaming. There was yelling. There was the sound of things breaking: metal things, glass things, flesh and bone things.

Then a man was bending over me, a switchblade in his hand. Cleverly, I countered with a forearm block. Stupidly, my arm refused to obey my brain and merely twitched.

Then the man was gone, propelled up and over the trunk lid by a white-gloved hand upon his shoulder.

But not before he had brought the blade around in a sweeping arc, slicing through my throat.

As I was drowning in my own blood, I looked up into an increasingly familiar face just before the darkness rolled up and over my own.

Chapter Nine

"Daddy, look at that smoke!"

I glance in the rearview mirror. "Honey, you need to keep your seat belt on."

"But look, Daddy! I bet there's a fire! Can we go see?"

I keep scanning the road for signs of the outskirts of Weir. Nothing yet. "I thought you were hungry, sweet pea."

"It can't be that far away. Maybe we can go help!"

I look off to the side and, sure enough, there's a column of smoke rising above the fields to the north. "Baby, we're almost to Weir. We can stop and get lunch—why are you giggling?"

"You sounded funny, Dad."

"I did?"

Jenny lays a cool hand on my arm. "You said 'we're almost to *Weir*.' It does sound a bit redundant."

I smile. "It does, doesn't it?"

"Please, Daddy?"

I start looking for a turnoff. "Okay, princess. If we can help, we will. But we won't stop if the fire department's there."

"How come?"

"'Cause we'd just be in the way, then. And we don't want to look like ghouls."

"What are ghouls, Daddy?"

Jenny loosens her seat belt so she can turn to speak to Kirsten. "Ghouls are—

. . . flesh-eating monsters that skulk around cemeteries and rob graves. . . .

"—people who like to be around when bad things

happen to people," Jenny says. "They're not really there to help; they just want to watch other people's suffering and misfortune."

"Like on the news?" my daughter asks.

>*The blood is helping.*

I chuckle despite the odd distraction. "Yes, honey. Like on the news, sometimes."

Jenny cocks an eyebrow. "Sometimes?" she taunts. And grows transparent.

>*He's starting to respond.*

A gravel road appears at the periphery of my vision. I slow and begin the turn.

>*I don't like this.*

The smoke is closer now, rising to veil the sun.

>*If he were completely transformed the wound would have merely inconvenienced him.*

It's getting darker now. And whispering voices are distracting me.

>*If he were completely human it would have killed him.*

The van fades away completely and I am swallowed up in a smokey blackness.

I stayed in darkness a very long time.

During that time sensations returned and, with them, came pain. Then, gradually, the pain began to ease. Became discomfort. Gave way to lassitude. Ennui.

Then discomfort returned: pressure, a weight on my chest. Harder to breathe. My throat began to itch, to tingle. To tickle.

I forced my left eye open. A hill rose before me, brown and blurry. I forced my right eye open. The left eye drooped shut with the shift in my attention. The hill resolved itself into furry haunches.

With a tail.

Two tails.

The cat was lying across my chest, its head nuzzling beneath my chin, and now I could feel the rasp of its tongue licking across my neck.

It was a horrifyingly pleasant sensation.

I turned my head to the left and observed the needles in my arm. The tubes to the needles led up to several packets of blood and a couple of packets of nearly clear liquid. The movement of my head disturbed the cat: it stopped its nuzzling, rising up on its hindquarters to regard me with golden eyes. Then it leapt from my chest to the floor and I heard the whispery sound of its paws as it scurried off, across the floor. A moment later there was the sound of a door and footsteps—human footsteps—coming toward me.

Dr. Mooncloud entered my field of vision, followed by a large, bearded and balding black man. "You're awake," she said.

"Brilliant diagnosis, Doctor," was my intended reply. I opened my mouth, but only a strangled wheeze emerged.

"Don't try to talk," she ordered. "Your vocal cords have been damaged." She turned and gestured toward the black man in the white ducks. "This is Dr. Burton."

Burton smiled and nodded as he made a notation on my clipboard. "Pleased to see you awake." His voice was surprisingly soft.

I made my own mental notation that the good doctor had fangs.

Now the Doman and Suki appeared. "He's awake," Pagelovitch observed.

Mooncloud nodded. "A good sign. But he's not out of the woods, yet."

Lupé and Luis Garou arrived. Lupé was using a cane, now, circling the bed while her brother asked: "Is he awake?"

Lupé took my right hand in hers. "You're awake, I see."

I was surprised that I didn't feel more secure, surrounded as I was by all these brilliant diagnosticians.

The Doman was all business and a little curt. "What can he tell us, Doctor?"

"Nothing, yet. His larynx hasn't had time to heal."

"It's been two days, Doctor."

"I know it's been two days, Stefan," she said. "Considering his stage of transformation, we are doubly lucky that he didn't die immediately and that the blood infusions brought him back."

"But not very far, I see." Elizabeth Bachman was standing in the doorway. "Is he awake?"

I groaned.

"Hush," Mooncloud scolded. "I don't want you doing anything that will interfere with your healing."

"What about a pad?" the Doman asked.

"I'd rather keep the wound uncovered and exposed to the open air."

"Kk," I said, trying to say "cat."

"I meant a pad of paper and a pen or pencil," the Doman said, "so we can ask some questions and he can write the answers."

"You shut up!" Mooncloud said.

Pagelovitch bristled.

"Not you. Him." She pointed at me. "As for the pad, we can try, but I don't want to tire him."

The Doman said something else, but I missed it.

I slipped back into the darkness.

The smoke fills the sky, now, hovering over the farm like an old, mud-spattered shroud. The old farmhouse is still intact though its second story is mostly hidden by thick billows of heavy smoke and flames are starting to show through the windows on the first floor. I look for a place to park the van that won't get us too close and won't get in the way of the fire trucks when they finally do arrive.

"Look, Daddy, there's a man."

I set the parking brake and look around. "Where?"

Kirsten points. "He just went into the barn."

I stumble out of the van and hesitate. *The house or the barn, first? And what if no one has called the fire department? There was no sign of nearby neighbors and townsfolk might assume a farmer was merely burning off part of a field.*

I turn and toss the keys through the window. "Jenny, drive into town or find the nearest phone and make sure the fire department knows about this!"

Kirsten pouts. "I wanta come with you!"

"No," I gesture, half pointing, half waving. "I want you to stay with your mother—help her!"

I turn and run toward the house.

The barn.

As I hesitate I hear the van start down the road behind me.

Come to the barn.

I turn and run toward the barn. But not as quickly as I was running toward the house.

Then I was walking.

I was walking through the desert at night.

It was cold and I was thirsty.

Two yellow moons hung in the night sky

growing

brighter and brighter

chasing the darkness

away

becoming cat's eyes

that watched intently as I struggled

back to consciousness.

The cat merrowed and hopped up on the nightstand to lay across the call button.

Dr. Burton entered the room. "Ah, you're awake."

"Wow," I whispered. "Déjà vu."

"Whispering is fine as long as you don't overdo it."

"What happened?"

"That's what we'd like to ask you. Hold on a moment." While he left the room I had a better opportunity to study my surroundings.

It wasn't so much a room as a cubicle: three of the four walls were tracked curtains, separating my bed from the rest of the infirmary. I checked my left arm. Yep: more tubes and needles bringing me that tick, tick, tick of hemoglobin and plasma. I looked at the cat. "And what do you want?"

It merrowed and began licking a paw while its two tails danced like an animated caduceus.

Burton returned. "The Doman's on his way. How are we doing?" Close up, he looked a bit haggard.

"Well, judging from the way I feel and the way you look, I'd say we're both in trouble."

He smiled. "I've been pulling double duty for the past twenty-four hours."

The Doman came in now. "How is he doing, Gerald?"

Burton gave him a wry look. "Oh, he's definitely feeling better."

"You forgot to observe that I am awake," I said.

"What does that mean?" He addressed the question to Dr. Burton instead of me.

"After-effects of shock and blood loss," was the less than solemn reply.

Lupé limped into the cubicle area. "Hey, you're awake."

"Ah," I sighed, "much better."

"What?"

"Methought I heard a voice cry, 'Sleep no more!' " I rasped.

" 'Macbeth doth murder sleep,' " the Doman murmured.

"I need to reduce his pain medication," the doctor muttered.

The cat merrowed again.

I looked around the room. "So what happened?"

"We were hoping you could tell us," Pagelovitch said.

Burton leaned in. "What do you remember?"

I told them.

It took a while with many sips of water. I had to stop and rest my throat at the point where I was tossed in the trunk of the other limousine.

"Three nights ago," the Doman said, "the bell was rung at the service entrance at about three o'clock in the morning. Someone had driven that limousine to the kitchen loading dock and left it there with the keys in the ignition and the motor running. You were in the backseat, smelling heavily of blood and garlic. . . ."

"The handkerchief they knocked me out with, it was soaked in garlic oil."

"The others were in the trunk."

"Others?"

He nodded. "Three men and a woman."

"Dead?"

"Yes."

"So who drove?"

"That's what we'd like to know. We'd also like to know who administered your first aid."

"First aid?"

"Somebody cut your throat, Christopher. From ear to ear. Were you completely human, you would have been dead in seconds. Were you undead, the wound would have temporarily inconvenienced you. Instead, you fell somewhere in between. When we found you someone had used duct tape to close your throat."

"Duct tape?"

"Not exactly standard treatment, but effective under the circumstances," Burton said.

"Duct tape?"

"And there was blood on your face and in your mouth."

I reached up and felt the line of scar tissue around my neck.

"But it seemed atypical for even a wound such as yours so we took samples and Dr. Mooncloud's analysis determined that the blood wasn't yours."

"Wasn't mine?"

"Most of it, anyway. Do you remember any of this?"

I shook my head. "Duct tape?"

"Is there anything else you can tell us?"

I nodded and told them the last little bit with the exception of seeing the face of the old man. For some reason my mouth wouldn't work when I got to that part.

"It was a mob hit," the Doman said.

I stared at him.

"The New York enclave has mob ties and they've been moving against some of the other demesnes this past year."

"Mob ties?"

"We were able to ID two of the bodies in the trunk. Hitters from New York."

"Hitters?"

"Apparently, they were under orders to bring you back alive, if possible; put you down if they couldn't."

"Put me down?"

"They nailed Damien before you came out. You were already on our doorstep before Elizabeth knew anything was wrong. So the question is: who took down four members of a New York black bag team and saved your life by closing the wound, giving you fresh blood—apparently from one of the assassins while they were still alive—and left you on our doorstep in time for us to pull you through the rest of the way?"

Now I really wanted to tell them about the old man—but, for some reason, I couldn't.

I reached up and felt my throat again. "Duct tape?"

I slept and when I woke again the cat was sleeping on my stomach and Dr. Burton was standing at the end of my bed, checking my chart. The presence of a cat draped across his patient didn't seem to trouble him in the least.

"Where's Dr. Mooncloud?" I croaked.

"Gone." He closed the clipboard and rehung it on the metal footboard.

"Gone?"

He came around to the side of my bed, slipping the ends of his stethoscope in his ears. "A problem came up and the Doman sent her out of town." He pulled the covers back, disturbing the cat. "Which I doubt he would have done if your life was still in any danger." He slipped the stethoscope's metal bell down inside my hospital gown. "Inhale."

"What kind of problem?" I asked after I exhaled again. "Another retrieval?"

Burton shook his head. "I seriously doubt it." He moved the diaphragm. "Breathe in. Nobody briefed me, but it sounded more like a search and destroy mission. Let it out."

"New York, again?"

"Naw. Breathe in. Another rogue surfaced. Happened a couple of days ago and there's already three people dead. The Doman figures the sooner this one's stopped—breathe out—the better, and we don't dare take time for niceties. Sit up."

He helped me bend forward. There was little pain, now, but I was still as weak as a kitten.

The cat looked at me and merrowed.

"Who else went?"

He slid the diaphragm down my back. "Breathe in. She took Garou and Bachman—which reminds me: she left something for you. Let it out. Now cough." He finished the cursory examination by checking my blood pressure and my temperature. "I'd like another blood sample, but after nearly four days of pumping it back into you, you still don't seem to be able to spare any." He handed me a cup and, as I brought it to my lips, I felt a familiar explosion of saliva flood my mouth.

"It's blood!"

He smiled reassuringly. "Think of it as medicine."

"It's not medicine, it's blood!"

"It's what had kept you alive these past four days and I can't guarantee you a full recovery without it!"

"It's not human blood, is it? I told Dr. Mooncloud—and I told the Doman—that I wouldn't ever drink human blood!"

"Come now, Mr Csejthe; don't you think you're being unnecessarily dramatic? You've already ingested human blood: you wouldn't be here now if you hadn't. And what is the difference if your body absorbs it through a needle in your vein or if you take it orally?"

I stared back at him.

"I'll tell you the only real, the only important difference. Your new metabolic structure is able to absorb and utilize it more efficiently when you drink it."

I started to open my mouth, but he walked out of the room. He returned a moment later, saying: "Spare me your superstitious religious dogmas. If you're a Christian, here." He handed me a paperback Bible. "Read the sixth chapter of the Gospel according to St. John. The drinking of blood is at the very heart of the Christian religion."

I could have argued the true use and interpretation of that particular ritual, but I was exhausted.

"Look," he picked up the cup and pushing it into my free hand, "this was contributed willingly. No one died, no one suffered, nothing was taken against anyone's will. This is the pure will of nature, its elixir of life. Think of it as a gift."

In the end it was not his words but my thirst and the craving of my weakened body that convinced me to drink.

"Get some rest now." He took the empty cup from my trembling hand.

"You said Lupé had left something for me," I said as he started to leave.

"What? Oh! Not Ms. Garou. . . ." He opened the drawer in the nightstand and produced a small, wrapped box with an envelope attached. "This is from Ms. Bachman." He pulled the curtains closed as he exited the cubicle.

The cat shifted its position and turned to watch me as I opened the envelope. For a moment I flashed on the note I'd found in my room just hours—no—days ago, now. But the letter inside was in different handwriting with a different message:

Dear Chris,

I am terribly sorry about what has happened. Even though Damien was technically responsible for security that night, I feel that I should have been out there when it happened. Can you ever forgive me?

I tried to donate some of my blood for your recovery but old "Dr. Moony" is still on her kick about not letting you have any nasty ol' vampire blood.

The Doman is sending us out on a mission that should take somewhere between three to six days so I won't be there to help you with any "therapy" (hint, hint). But I have arranged for some special "get well" medicine while I'm gone. The initiation is inevitable so relax and enjoy it! (I certainly would!)

I also got you something that you really need. If it doesn't fit we'll do a new set of molds when I get back. Gotta go, now. Get well soon, and welcome to the family.

Love,

Liz—

P.S. Don't forget what I told you about knowing who your friends are. . . .

The cat was staring at me intently as I refolded the letter and stuffed it back into the envelope. "Parentheses," I said. "Hint, hint," I said. "Well, at least she doesn't dot her i's with little hearts or happy faces."

The cat merrowed.

I tore the wrapping paper off the box and opened it. I pulled Bachman's gift out of the cotton batting and held it up to examine it.

"Well, I'll be damned!" Under the circumstances, I probably was anyway.

Bachman had taken my dental molds and had

someone—someone very good, I had to admit—make a partial plate to match my upper teeth in front. It was designed to fit over my real teeth like a movie appliance—the kind that actors wear when their parts call for a different dental effect from their own.

I could tell that, even with my limited knowledge of the craft, someone had created an artistic masterpiece: up close, the detail was incredibly lifelike and realistic. They looked just like my teeth—except that the two canines or "eye-teeth" were three-quarters of an inch long, slightly curved . . .

. . . and very, very pointed.

The cat got up and walked up my chest for a closer look.

"You want to see? Okay." I checked the appliance thoroughly: it was clean. I eased it up and over my upper, front teeth.

It was a perfect fit. There was a small tube of dental fixative in the box but the appliance fit so well, I didn't seem to need any kind of adhesive.

"What do you think?" I asked the cat. Surprisingly, there was no difficulty or discomfort in talking beyond my already sore throat.

The cat merrowed approvingly.

As I turned to lay the box and envelope on the nightstand I remembered the Bible that now lay in my lap. I hesitated, feeling fatigue drag at my eyelids with leaden curtain-pulls, but curiosity won out for the moment.

I opened it to the fourth gospel and began skimming the sixth chapter. I found the reference beginning with the fifty-third verse:

> *Then Jesus said unto them, Verily, verily, I say unto you, Except ye eat the flesh of the Son of man, and drink his blood, ye have no life in you.*
>
> *Whoso eateth my flesh, and drinketh my blood, hath eternal life; and I will raise him up in the resurrection of the just at the last day.*

For my flesh is meat indeed, and my blood is drink indeed.

He that eateth my flesh, and drinketh my blood, dwelleth in me, and I in him.

As the living Father hath sent me, and I live by the Father; so he that eateth me, even he shall live by me.

This is that bread which came down from heaven; not as your fathers did eat manna, and are dead; he that eateth of this bread shall live forever.

I closed the Bible slowly and pressed the control to lower the upper half of the bed, again. I was tired and confused—

"Oh *thyit!*"

And I had just bitten my tongue with my new teeth.

Chapter Ten

The interior of the barn is dark.

Its only illumination comes from sniglets of sunlight shining through small gaps in the walls and roof, projecting galactic maps on the black, earthen floor. A fresh billow of smoke roils overhead and the galaxy at my feet dims as if swallowed by some vast, dark nebula.

I hesitate on the threshold, my eyes straining to see into the unknown, my nostrils flaring at an unpleasant smell . . . an old smell.

A dead smell—

I came awake quickly for a change.

My watch on the nightstand said that it was 10:53. *A.M. or P.M.?* It was one of those rare occasions that I regretted not switching to digital.

I closed my eyes for a moment and, once again, some arcane sense kicked in, telling me that the sun was up: A.M. Most of the Doman's "people" would be sleeping now with only a skeleton crew on duty.

Now that conjured an interesting image. . . .

I used the bedside control to fold me up to a sitting position. As the cat scrambled to safety, I considered my options. As in Henley's *Invictus*, I had always aspired to be "the master of my fate, the captain of my soul." Lately, I hadn't done much better than "cabin boy." It was time to make some changes.

It was time to take matters into my own hands.

It was time to go to the bathroom before I did anything else.

I tossed the covers aside, swung my legs over the side of the mattress, and was confronted with my first major obstacle: unhooking the Texas-sized catheter.

When it was done I pulled the ruined pillow from my teeth and spat out a mouthful of feathers. A wooden stake through the heart might mean certain death, but now I knew that there were worse things.

I wobbled to my feet and lurched over to the tiny, standing closet for a robe and slippers. Then, more comfortably attired, feeling more alert and less drafty, I shuffled down the empty ward and out into the hallway in search of the bathroom.

Fortunately, it wasn't far and there was no one about to herd me back to bed.

There was a single shower stall and I washed up after I was done. It felt good to be clean again. It felt even better to be up, out of bed, and doing something that wasn't required and monitored by somebody else.

Wiping the condensation from the mirror, I stared at my vague, ghostlike reflection. *Concentrate!* I thought. *I am here! I exist!* As I stood there, leaning over the sink and propping myself up with trembling arms, I force-fed the concept of my corporal reality into my resisting mind.

Slowly, my mirror image took on greater solidity.

I was thinner, now, and there were shadows beneath my eyes. My flesh had a pallid, almost transparent appearance: I looked half dead.

But the scar that circled my throat was already fading. Maybe I was getting better. Or undeader.

I'm ready for my close-up, now, Mr. DeMille.

Another thought occurred.

If the disappearance of my reflection was truly tied to psychological and psionic feedback, why had it started to fade back before I actually knew that I was becoming a vampire? Had my subconscious caught on several weeks before the truth was accepted by my conscious mind? I had a list of questions for Dr. Mooncloud when she got back.

If I was still here. . . .

A wave of vertigo rolled over me and I clutched at the countertop to steady myself. Time to be getting back in bed.

My own bed, I decided.

Except that bed and the suite that I occupied was just as much the Doman's property as the hospital bed I had just vacated. It seemed there was nothing I could truly call my own anymore. Not even my life.

Any question of escape was finally gone. I *would* be leaving. Soon. But first I needed to concentrate on getting well and learning as much as I could about the mutations that were changing me, body and brain. I rebelted my robe and opened the door, deciding that I was going to have to display a more complacent and cooperative attitude until I had what I needed and was ready to leave.

"Ready to leave?" Suki was standing there, outside the bathroom door, with a wheelchair ready and waiting.

"Um," I said.

She took my hand. "It's time to get you back up and on your feet," she said, paradoxically pushing me down into the seat. "Feet up." She adjusted the footrests under my slippers. "Ready?"

"For what?"

"Here we go." She started off down the hall. We went past the hospital area and on down to the elevator.

The doors opened and its diminutive operator leaned forward on his high stool. "Fräulein Suki, Herr Csejthe; *Grüsse*."

"*Guten Tag*, Herr Hinzelmann," Suki said.

"*Guten Morgen*," I muttered.

"*Und wie befinden wir sich?*" the hütchen asked me as he pulled the levers and we started up.

"Well, Hinzie," I groused, "judging by the way I feel and the way you look, I'd say that 'we' are both in trouble."

Suki leaned over and murmured, "Never let a good

line go to waste, do you?" To the old house sprite she said: "Ignore him, Hinzie; he's cranky when he hasn't had enough."

"Enough?" I tried to twist my head to look at her. "Enough what?"

"Er tut mir leid."

"Well, don't be," I said. "It may be true that I am a little—cranky—right now. But I am on the mend." I slumped in the wheelchair. "Thank you for asking."

"Bitte sehr," he said primly. "And you, Fräulein Suki," he continued. "What has you up at this ungodly hour of the morning?"

"Him," she said as the elevator came to a stop. "The Doman said he's taking too long to heal. So, we've decided to kick him out of the hospital, back into his own bed, and go to the next phase of treatment."

"Und wie steht es mit Deirdre?"

"I don't know," she said, helping me maneuver the chair out of the antique lift. "Only time will tell."

"Christopher!" It didn't sound like my name at first; it sounded more like an ancient door on rusty hinges. Then I saw the seamed and wart-riddled features of the house chamberlain. She smiled a terrible smile: while sharks have three rows of teeth, the aguane barely qualified as having one, yet the effect was similar.

"Basa-Andrée," I said, trying to smile back and desperately hoping that she wouldn't try to hug me or wish me a speedy recovery through any other tactile means.

"Good to see ye up and about, lad!" She came toward me, but her attention shifted to Suki. " 'Tis all done, milady; even as himself requested."

"Thank you, Basa," she said. "Is the package in place?"

"I understand that it is on its way."

"Good."

The aguane turned back to me. "Is there anything I can get for you, my boy?"

"Yeah, hang a 'do not disturb' sign on my door for the next forty-eight hours."

"Ah, you're a wonder, laddie-buck," she cackled. " 'tis already a done deal."

Suki wheeled me on down the hall until we came to my door. Basa-Andrée opened it with a key from a prodigious ring and Suki pushed me inside.

Though the lights were off, she easily navigated the chair through the darkened apartment, bringing me into the bedroom. I waved off any assistance as I clambered out of the wheelchair and sat on the edge of the bed.

"Is there anything I can get you?"

I started to say no and send her on her way, but then I remembered my research. "As a matter of fact, there is." I quickly explained my needs in terms of establishing a common database of information. "So, at this point I primarily need a good PC with plenty of hard disk space, a modem, and a good scanner with OCR software."

"I think we can provide you with something in those areas." She sat on the bed, next to me. "Chris. . . ."

"Yes?"

"You—" she hesitated "—you have a lot of anger in you."

A flip response didn't come readily to mind, so I just nodded.

"Terrible things have happened to you. Terrible things have been *done* to you. You have a right to be angry."

No arguments here.

"But you are not alone. Most of us under the Doman's protection are here because terrible things have been done to us, too. We are all prisoners here. We are trapped by the nature of what we have become. And most of us did not ask to become what we are."

And what are we? I wondered.

"We are victims," she said. "Victims who are trying to survive as best we can, without producing more victims in that day-after-day process."

"Practically impossible, isn't it?" I said.

"Yes. Yes, it is. Nature is one vast food chain and life feeds upon life. Here, in the Northwest, the Doman insists that we take nothing except by invitation, use only what we need, and waste nothing. We practice a higher morality than most of the world at large."

"You shear the sheep and spare the lambs," I said.

"We are all sheep," she said, rising, "and all flesh is grass."

"You're mixing your metaphors."

She folded the wheelchair and left it by the doorway. "I know that you are angry. Your body has been violated by changes that you cannot reconcile with the life you knew, the life that society has taught and molded you to live. Now you must face new truths, new laws that the world hides from all but a handful of humanity.

"*We* did not make you this way. *We* did not choose this path for you. *We* cannot help the fact that your body now requires blood for sustenance. But it is an implacable law that Nature assigns to your changed circumstances. Resist it, fight it if you will, but do not blame those of us that share the curse and seek to help you learn the new rules of survival."

I was suddenly ashamed.

"I must sleep now." She smiled from the doorway. "I will see you tonight if you have rested well. In the meantime, try to do those things which will help you to heal. Rest now. And later . . . drink deep."

And she was gone.

I sat there for a while, thinking about what she had said. Constructive anger, properly focused was one thing. Throwing tantrums was something else, again. I would still leave when the opportunity came. But perhaps I did have friends here. Perhaps there were those who did not carry their own motives like a hidden dagger.

But I wouldn't think any more about it, right now.

I untied the robe and dropped it on the floor.

No. I'd think about it tomorrow. . . .

I pulled back the covers and crawled under them.

After all, tomorrow was another day. . . .

I fluffed my pillow with my fist.

. . . or night. . .

I closed my eyes.

. . . and maybe I'd go back to Tara.

"Oh, fiddle-de-dee," I murmured. And fell asleep.

Now the darkness of the barn is merciful.

I can see the cow, lying on its side. See the great gash that has opened up its belly. Slats of dusty sunbeams bisect the spill of entrails, but most of the gore and details are still lost in the darkness.

I hesitate at the edge of a red tidal pool that trickles toward my feet. A hand grasps my arm and I turn to see the silhouette of a man brandishing a bloody knife.

I came awake, gasping for air, my stomach cramping me into a sitting position. In that long moment of leaving the dream behind, I was partially blind, partially deaf: I did not notice movement or sound until a voice spoke.

"You were having a nightmare."

I didn't jump or flinch: nothing was as frightening as that half-buried memory that crept closer and closer each time I closed my eyes.

A woman sat at the edge of my bed. In the darkness I had only her voice and vague outline to serve for clues.

Jennifer?

I looked again, something subtle shifting at the back of my eyes. The bedroom's topography was now evident in patterned greyscale, the furniture layout in dark blue and grey geometric shapes. The woman, herself, flickered like a bright flame: white surrounded by concentric layers of yellow then orange then red in a vague, humanoid shape. I shivered as I realized that my night vision was evolving into an infrared targeting system.

"Who is it?" I asked carefully.

"Deirdre." She reached out and a warm hand caressed my cool, clammy forehead.

Deirdre? "What are you doing here?"

"I am here to take care of you. Think of me as your nurse."

"I don't need a nurse."

"You're still weak and your wound is not entirely healed. The Doman says that this a difficult and dangerous time for you. I want to help."

"I don't need help. I need rest. Why don't you run along and spend your time with—" I caught myself. I was about to say "with Damien" when I remembered that her vampire lover was dead, murdered by the same hitmen who had nearly killed me. "—I'm sorry."

She reached over and switched on the bedside lamp, bumping my vision back into normal mode.

Most so-called redheads actually favor the orange spectrum. Here, hair, lips and nails were the color of blood, deep red and vibrant in hue. Alabaster skin with no visible flaws. China blue eyes, made bluer by the sheen of tears and the shadows of sleepless nights, looked back at me, through me, beyond me.

"He loved me, you know," she said. "He really loved me."

And who could blame him? I thought.

"You're probably thinking that I'm a beautiful woman—why wouldn't he?" she said.

All this and psychic abilities, too.

"Beauty is overrated." She laughed. It was a short, half-hearted thing. "Oh, I know that it's just the sort of thing that beautiful people sometimes say and it sounds incredibly self-centered and boorish. But it is a wall between us. A mask. A façade."

She was rattling. It was obviously an old argument for her and I made no reply: she had an understandable need to talk.

"Give me your foot," she said.

I stared at her. "What?"

"I'm your nurse and this is phase one of your therapy. Besides, it gives me something to do." She gave me a hard look. "I've had nothing to do for four days. I need to do something. Anything." She blinked. "So give me your foot."

I extended my right foot and she took it into her warm grasp. I was reminded again of the widening difference in our body temperatures.

"We live in a world that values beauty, rewards it as if it were a virtue or the product of great labor and achievement. It can be, I suppose," she said, sighing, working her thumbs up the sole of my foot. "But it's mostly the result of good genes."

Her fingers worked their way around and over my instep, moving toward my ankle. There her thumb massaged the outer perimeter, the juncture of the talus and the end of the fibula: my attention began to slide a little.

"Don't get me wrong," she continued, "I'm not whining about what a burden it is to be attractive. I'm just pointing out that a lot of people will treat you like meat or like art or like all their fondest fantasies or the embodiment of their own lack of self-esteem. When you find someone who treats you like a real person, it can be special."

"That's how it was with Damien," I said.

Deirdre nodded. "Here." She pushed on my leg. "Roll over and let me do your back."

"Therapy." I sighed and complied. Maybe she would get to the other foot later.

"He had lived long enough to have gotten past the value systems that most men apply when looking at a woman. He looked at me and saw . . . me. Not just a face or a body. He looked at me as a man and saw more than just sex or a trophy. And he looked at me as a vampire and saw more than just food and drink. He . . . saw . . . me!" Her voice was decidedly unsteady.

A long silence ensued while she worked her hands up and down my spine.

"So, how did you meet?"

"At the library. Late one night, just before closing. I went there by chance that particular night. It turned out that he was there on a regular basis—three or four evenings a week. He said it was a sign: he was reading Keats and looked up and saw me."

" 'Endymion'?" I asked, trying to visualize a vampire with a library card.

"Yes. How did you know?"

> " 'A thing of beauty is a joy forever:
> its loveliness increases; it will never
> pass into nothingness.' "

I nodded into my pillow. "It was a sign."

"Well, I was attracted by his beauty, too. We're all tied to that prejudicial first glance. It's the second look and the third that weighs us and our value systems."

"Was it difficult? Loving someone who was old before you were young and would remain young long after you were old?"

"We never had the time to find out. A few years: what is that in the scheme of human lifetimes, much less those of immortals? He tried to bring me over. . ."

"Over?"

"I asked. I wanted to live forever. Who wouldn't? But it wasn't just selfishness on my part. I wanted *us* to be together. I didn't want him tied to a woman whose body grew older and more infirm as the years passed. And I wanted to share his life, his world. . . ."

"You wanted to become a vampire," I said.

"More for him than for anything else. And he agreed, even knowing it might well mean the end of passion for us."

"The end of passion?"

She worked on my shoulders before answering. "A coldness sets in when you become undead. Not just a coldness of the flesh, though that is particularly evident, but a more subtle coldness, as well. Sexual gratification becomes a pale substitute for the gratification of blood and many male vampires become impotent unless they couple while in the act of feeding. They—male and female—are drawn to us for the warmth of our flesh as well as the nourishment of our blood. It is rare that the *wampyr* experience real passion with one another. Marriages or relationships that predate their transformations rarely survive as anything more than intellectual alliances."

"But Damien was willing to make you into what he had become and risk that." I didn't phrase it as a question.

"He felt it would be best for me, if not for us. He was willing to risk that wonderful intensity that we had found in one another. . . ."

"But he wasn't able to—to—bring you over."

"No.

"We tried everything." I felt the shrug of her shoulders telegraphed through her hands. "For some it is enough to be bitten just once. Others do not change until there have been many feedings. An exchange of blood—once thought to be foolproof in passing the condition—isn't. Damien gave me his blood many times. It came to nothing. The only other possibility was that life was too strong to permit the unlife to take hold: that he would have to drink of me until life was no longer a barrier."

"You would have to die."

"Yes," she said. "And he wouldn't permit that. There was no certainty to the theory and he refused to risk losing me for all time." She gave a short, sharp, bitter laugh. "He was worried about losing me!"

There was nothing I could say that wouldn't sound trite or banal, so I lay there and let her work her fingers up and down my back. Impotence now joined insanity on the list of potential deficits to my transformation. But the skill of her fingers and the weariness of my own not yet recovered body conspired against any further contemplation.

My mind drifted and, to my shame, I dozed.

* * *

"I need your help!" he says.

So focused am I on the bloody knife that he has to repeat himself, shouting the second time.

He tugs on my arm with his other hand and pulls me into the growing puddle of blood. The cow struggles weakly, producing crosscurrents to the feeble tides that are clocked by its failing bovine heart.

There is something else, now; here, in the darkness, beside the dying beast. A dark shape surrounded by a lake of red and the spangled beams of slotted sunlight, huddled in the darkest part of the barn. It shifts and hisses. And smells of woodsmoke and burned pork.

"Take off your shirt and lie down!" the man commands. A beam of sunlight bounces back from the blade of the bloody knife and dazzles me. Though he loosens his grip upon my arm I can no longer see well enough to evade him.

Something shifts on the ground, near my feet, and the cow bellows fearfully.

A miasma of death and terror rises up from the blood, thick and choking. I do not want to be here, to do this thing!

I am afraid for my life! *And for more than my life. . . .*

But gall and bitterness and dread have seized my heart, my mind, my limbs, and I cannot find the ability to do anything beyond what I am told. I do not remember taking off my shirt. I can hardly bear to think about lowering myself into the visceral stew that clots the earth, here. But I am sitting now, staring up at the dark silhouette of the man with the bloody knife. I put my hand out to steady myself and something cold and wet and hungry comes up out of the blood-spattered ground to grasp my arm in an iron grip!

I sobbed and sobbed, trying to purge my heart, my very soul of the sludge of terror and shame. The gory mud of that barn floor still seemed to cling to me here, more than a year later and a half a continent away.

Chilled to the marrow, I clung to the warm softness as if my life depended on it.

But my lungs needed air and, at last, I had to lift my face from the folds of warm terry cloth to catch my breath. I looked up into an angel's face: compassionate blue eyes and perfect features with radiant skin, framed by hair the color of holy fire.

Deirdre.

She was kneeling on the bed, holding me as I wept against her shoulder.

I struggled to compose myself. To pull away. "I'm sorry," I said. "It was just a nightmare."

She refused to release me from her embrace. "Is that what you still think it is? A simple nightmare?"

"I'm okay now," I said, trying to reassure myself more than her.

"You're not okay," she whispered, bringing her cheek to mine. "You've been to the grave and back—not just once, but twice. You've not only lost your own life, but the lives of those you love." Her arms tightened around me. "I want to help. I'm here for you."

I embraced her in return, as much to keep my balance as to reciprocate her kindness. That's when I noticed that she was wearing my robe.

And that someone had replaced the lamplight with candlelight while I slept.

I turned my head to look at her. Her face turned to mine. Our lips met.

We kissed.

I should have enjoyed it. I understood enough about death and loss to know that we sometimes seek oblivion in physical distraction. That we hold back the darkness with life-affirming acts of procreation.

And that, as Harry Chapin used to sing, "loving anyone was a better place to be."

Still. . . "Why?" I asked, as she released my lips.

"We can help each other," she whispered. "Maybe heal each other a little." Her hand came up and caressed my face. "You need me. Need what I can give you. What I can do for you.

"And I need you. I *need* you to *need* me," she continued with a look of desperation. "Let me stay with you. Let me do this for you." She reached down and pulled the sash on the robe. It fell open and I felt my protests die on my lips.

My mind schismed: it had been a year. Jennifer was dead. . . .

Is she?

She must be. The dead don't—

Don't what? Come back? Sunder their graves? Rise from their coffins?

If she's alive, why is she hiding in the shadows? Why doesn't she come to me?

I don't know, the old morality monitor whispered, *but God wouldn't like it.* . . .

The fear, the uncertainty was washed away on a sudden flood of anger.

God lets my wife and little girl die in an awful car crash and spares me so I can slowly turn into a monster: do you think I really give a damn what God likes?

I slid my hands from her arms to her sides, felt the splay of ribs beneath silky muscles, the warmth of human flesh. I opened my mouth to speak and she leaned forward, parting her own lips again: I felt the inquiry of a tongue. The tension building in all of my muscles.

I experienced a curious heat flush throughout my entire body as she fell back and pulled me down with her. Now I was on top, pinning her down to the bed with the weight of my body, my hands grasping her wrists. I stared down at her, taking it all in: the throbbing pulse at the base of her creamy throat, her breasts now slightly flattened and lolling indolently to either side, the rise and fall of her stomach, the warm, firm feel of her flesh, waiting, anticipating. . .

"Love's mysteries in souls do grow," Donne penned in "The Ecstasy," "But yet the body is his book."

Harlequin, take me away.

"Take me," she murmured.

"No." I said it without conviction.

"Don't you want me?"

Oh God, yes! I wanted her like nothing I had ever wanted before. But. . .

"It isn't sex," I said hoarsely.

"I know," she whispered. "Sex is just foreplay for the real thing."

It was a lust worse than concupiscence. It was appetite beyond lust. It was the Hunger.

"Bite me," she commanded.

And I might have. Surrendered right then and there. But: "I can't." I had not grown the necessary fangs. I came up on my knees, gasping for air and for need.

"You can." She sat up and fumbled in the pocket of the robe. "Here." She handed me a familiar box. I opened it and stared at the dental appliance with its gleaming, razor-sharp fangs. "Put it on." She handed a small tube of dental adhesive to me.

It was silly.

It was sick.

"Put it on." Her voice was thick with need. "Now." Her tone, insistent, commanding. Pleading. "Please!"

I was without the will to resist her. I did as she bade me, trying to bury the likeness of other memories—other times, other occasions, when I had to suspend passion and fumble to put something on. . . .

She shrugged the robe from her shoulders and leaned toward me. "Please," she whispered. "I need this as much as you do. More!"

Her hand was behind me head, pulling me down and toward her. Her shoulder rose to meet my lips. "*Bite me!*"

Had I been more experienced, less reluctant, I would have done it quickly. Instead, I opened my mouth as if to kiss the smooth flesh over the trapezius muscle, catching her collarbone with my lower jaw. As I felt the points of the teeth meet the resistance of skin, I hesitated, then brought my arms around her, my right hand cradling the back of her head. She stiffened, tilting her head back as the fangs dimpled her flesh. As the points broke the skin, she sighed. Tilting her head back, as I eased deeper into her shoulder, she shuddered. I could tell now that the slowness of the penetration was more painful, yet she seemed glad of it, welcoming the hurt.

As the blood welled up into my mouth she pushed against me with a languid movement. "Harder," she breathed into my ear. "Suck me. Drink me."

The heat of her flesh was like the sun, warming me, driving the winter from my bones. I could smell her, the perfume of skin and fragrance of perspiration and secret things filled my head like an olfactory intoxicant. The press of her breasts against my chest carried the stroke of each heartbeat into my own flesh with a maddening, rhythmic caress.

And the blood. . .

It filled my mouth like warm, meaty honey. I swallowed and it poured down my throat like boiling wine, sizzling and bubbling and burning a path to my very core. A furnace opened deep within me, filling me with divine brightness.

"Harder," she hissed, clinging to me with a frightening strength. "Bite me again. Harder, deeper."

I pulled back, tearing the wound a little. "I don't want to hurt you!"

"I *want* you to hurt me! I *need* you to hurt me!" She arched her back and pulled my head lower. "Bite me! Here!"

I pressed my face to her glorious flesh; became blind. And obedient.

There were no dreams this time: I slept like the dead. The nightmare came when I finally awoke.

Blood.

I came to myself lying in a pool of red. But there was no barn, no dying beast, no knife-wielding madman. I was in my room, on my bed.

Deirdre was beside me.

She lay in quiet repose, face tranquil, eyes closed, lips locked in a gentle smile. Her ivory skin seemed all the whiter, now, marked with red blooms where she had urged my kisses and surrounded by sheets, stained the color of her lips and hair. One arm was tucked up under the pillow, the other plunged beneath a corner of the bedclothes that lapped at her side like a tide rolling out at sunset.

There had come a moment of lucidity in the midst of the passion, the madness, when I had paused, my mouth dripping, to ask, "Why?"

"I told you that I came to nurse you back to health," she had gasped. And then pulled me back to her breast to do just that.

Perhaps I had known the answer to my question even better than she. But all I could think of was the heat of her flesh, warming me like a hearth fire.

I reached down to cover her the rest of her nakedness, touched her shoulder.

It was cold.

And I knew.

Perhaps I had known in that moment when she first came to me. But I went through the pantomime, anyway: I searched for a pulse at her throat, pulled back eyelids, prodded pressure points. She was cold, lifeless. An empty husk, its former contents drained and flown.

The warmth that she had so recently gifted me was suddenly gone.

As I reached down to reclose her eyes, I tried to recall the passage from *Endymion.*

But all I could remember were the words of Archibald MacLeish:

Beauty is that Medusa's head
which men go armed to seek and sever.
It is most deadly when most dead,
and dead will stare and sting forever.

Chapter Eleven

"You need to sleep."

"I don't want to sleep." I was irritated that I hadn't heard Suki come into the library.

"It's been three days. Abusing yourself like this isn't going to bring her back."

Maybe not, I thought. *But maybe I can hold back the nightmares just a little longer.* "I'll sleep when I'm damn good and ready!"

"It's not your fault," she said. "It was something that she wanted to do and we had given her our blessing. No one thought she'd take it that far."

"We've already had this discussion." I moved the scanner down another page, the LEDs seeming to devour the text in a greenish glow. "By the way, the equipment's great. The optical character recognition software interfaces perfectly with the scanner and the word processing program. And where did you find a notebook computer with a two-gigabyte hard drive?"

She crossed her arms in front of her. "We have our resources and you are avoiding the subject."

"And you are stating the obvious: I already told you that I have no intention of discussing this further. Case closed, thank you again for the equipment, and get out."

She went, slamming the door behind her.

I finished scanning a translation of M. Philip Rohr's 1679 treatise, *Dissertatio de Masticatione Mortuorum,* and set it aside. The stack of tomes left to be scanned was definitely dwindling and I would soon be done with this phase of my research. I opened a copy of Sir

Richard Burton's *Vikran and the Vampire or Tales of Hindu Devilry*. This was an original first edition and I had to be careful of the pages as I began the scanning process anew.

They told me that I was completely healed.

My neck was smooth and unblemished and I felt strength and energy coursing through my body in unprecedented amounts.

Dr. Burton confirmed that I was obscenely healthy—in the physical sense, anyway. He was worried, however, about my unwillingness to sleep or talk about what had happened. After I told him that it was none of his damn business, the Doman paid me a visit.

"I want to show you something," Stefan Pagelovitch said. And, as he looked into my eyes, I felt the full force of his will leeching my resistance. I accompanied him without protest.

We walked down a corridor I had never seen before. It led to the room that served as the morgue. He opened one of the doors set in two of the four walls and pulled out the drawer. There was a plastic body bag on the slablike shelf and he pulled down the zipper. "Come here," he said.

I came and looked. It was the body of the woman who had distracted me in the parking lot a week before. The woman who had provided the switchblade that had opened my throat.

"This the one?"

I nodded, swallowing. The expression on her face suggested that she might have been glad to die.

He opened three more drawers, three more body bags. "Recognize any of these?"

I shook my head. "It was dark." Not that it made a hell of a lot of difference for two of them: the only way anyone was going to identify their remains was with dental records, and that would be a dicey chore, at best.

"A war has begun, I think," he murmured.

"What did this to them?"

"And why were you spared?"

"I lead a charmed life," I said bitterly.

The Doman opened a fifth drawer and pulled out the rolling shelf. "Here." He opened the plastic bag and pulled out an arm. "Look."

I looked from where I stood, too far away to see any real detail.

"Look!" the Doman repeated, commanding me this time.

I shuffled forward on reluctant feet. It was a pale, slender arm. A familiar arm. I did not look down: I did not want to look at the rest of her.

Pagelovitch turned and displayed the wrist. The flesh was torn and gouged in a deep trench from the base of the palm to nearly halfway up the forearm. "The other arm is the same."

I turned away.

"These are not bite wounds," he said, behind me. "You didn't do this to her. She did it to herself."

"I was there," I said, trying to remember, trying to forget.

"She waited until you were asleep and then removed the partial from your mouth and used it to do this to herself. Christopher, it wasn't your fault. She was unstable. After Damien died she didn't want to live. You should be angry that she used you in this way!"

"You're right," I said, turning away. "I am angry."

But it didn't do any good.

I was still being used.

She stood up, clasping her hands together nervously; a thin, wisp of a woman with mouse brown hair, wearing a floral print sackdress.

"My name is Merlene," she said, "and I'm married to a lycanthrope."

The rest of the people in the circle answered in unison: "Hi, Merlene!"

"I guess most of you know me from before," she continued with a wan, twitchy smile. "You were in my first support group back when Howard was bitten and we were trying to adjust to all the changes that were taking place. You all were great. . . ."

"So were you, Merlene!" someone called out from the circle.

She drooped a little less. "It was an adjustment. Actually, the children handled it better than either of us. They thought it was 'cool' that Daddy was a werewolf." She tried a little laugh. It took a little effort.

"I quit coming to group because I thought we had worked everything out. That was two years ago—"

I allowed my mind and my eyes to wander.

Four days had gone by since I had last slept and I had used that time productively: I had typed, scanned, or downloaded all the pertinent materials I could find on the subject of vampires and the occult into my notebook computer. That was the easy part. Now I had to recombine and cross-reference everything into a huge database of information. And then I would begin to cross-correlate to identify consistencies and inconsistencies. And, finally, I would have to separate the wheat from the chaff, the facts from the fiction.

With any luck it would keep me extremely busy for many days to come.

"There was a time when he'd never change voluntarily," Merlene was saying, "only during the full moons, and then he'd stay in the house. But then he started wanting out—just for an hour or so, you understand. I think he was just running around the neighborhood then, working off a little nervous energy. . . ."

As my eyes wandered around the room I was surprised to see another familiar face. Lupé Garou was sitting in on tonight's encounter group session.

She hadn't gone with Mooncloud and Bachman on the Doman's little retrieval mission, after all. Pagelovitch had sent Luis in her place as she was still relying on a cane when they left. Now she seemed to be fully recovered, though we hadn't actually spoken since Deirdre had died in my bed.

Come to think of it, she was the only one who hadn't come around trying to tell me why it wasn't my fault and how I shouldn't feel guilty. At least some people knew how to respect a person's privacy.

" . . . gone all night!" Merlene was clearly upset and the therapist, a tall, rawboned blonde in a tee shirt and sweatpants stood up and put her arm about her. "Now he goes on these weekend camping trips. . . ." She sniffed.

I stared at Lupé until she finally glanced in my direction. I crooked my fingers in a small, unobtrusive wave. She looked away.

" . . . checked his rifle. It hasn't been fired in months! How can you spend every weekend, off in the woods hunting, and not use your rifle even once?"

"Have you confronted him on this issue?" another group member asked.

Merlene's hands were rubbing and clenching each other as if she was auditioning for the part of Lady Macbeth. "He's always dismissing me with comments like: 'What would you know about it?' Or: 'You can't smell a thing with that little bitty nose, so don't be telling me about whether or not this gun's been fired!' "

I looked down at the floor, wishing I'd never agreed to attend these group sessions. At the time it seemed a way to do a little more research and get the Doman and Suki and Dr. Burton off my back.

Someone else asked if Howard had become abusive lately.

"Well, I don't know that it's really abusive," Merlene whined, "but—well—he never likes—normal—sex anymore."

"You know you don't have to talk about this if you don't want to," the group leader murmured. "But it might help if you could be more specific."

"Specific?"

"Like what you mean by abnormal."

"Oh."

I looked at my watch: at least another twenty minutes were left for tonight's session.

"He never wants to do it like we used to," Merlene explained nervously. "Now Howard says it's the missionary position that's unnatural. . . ."

That did it: I was out of here! I tried to ease the folding chair back as I stood, but one of the legs snagged a loose floor tile and it tipped over with a metallic clatter.

Since a quiet, unobtrusive exit was now impossible, I turned and walked briskly toward the door.

" . . . so when the neighbor's dog had puppies. . . ."

As soon as I hit the hallway I began running.

I didn't get far.

The Doman and Suki walked around the corner, coming toward me. Between them was an old man with broad shoulders, skinny arms, and long, disagreeable fingernails. He wore camouflage fatigue pants and an M-65 field jacket with a rust-red beret. On his feet were a pair of iron boots that fairly rang as they strode across the floor.

The Doman frowned as he looked at me and I felt a sudden compulsion to turn around and go back into the therapy session. I reversed my course.

"Ah, Mr. Csejthe," the group leader said as I reentered the room, "since you're already up, why don't you go next?"

I was stuck. Since my escape strategy required a more cooperative demeanor, I couldn't very well refuse.

"My name is Chris," I mumbled, "and I . . . have a drinking problem."

"Hi, Chris," the group chorused.

While I explained just exactly what it was I drank and how I perceived the nature of my problem, I watched Pagelovitch, Suki, and the old man walk around the outside of the circle of chairs and stop to speak quietly with

Lupé. As they spoke, she became visibly upset and, before I knew it, they were escorting her out of the room.

"Yes, Barnabas?" the group leader was saying.

A smallish, fine-boned man wearing a Savile Row suit was on his feet, leaning forward with both hands resting atop a stylish walking cane.

"I'm afraid I don't see the problem, here," he said. "Christopher, you are a vampire and you just admitted that you enjoyed the taste of human blood. So I fail to apprehend your real concern."

"I think Chris's concern," the therapist said, "comes from two issues. One, that he hasn't fully crossed the Rubicon in regards to his transformation. And two, that there are various moral and religious issues in his background that he is having trouble addressing."

"I think I'm hearing a third issue here, as well," said a grey-haired, matronly woman to my left. "I think 'choice' or, rather, the lack of it, is a large part of this young man's problem. You don't like losing that sense of control, do you, hon?"

"Uh, I think self-determination is essential to a life of worth." And one's privacy was something to be guarded from well-intentioned but nosey encounter groups.

"Oh, come now," replied the man with the wolfhead cane, "does anyone here really believe in self-determinism once the strictures of fate and the grave take hold?"

"*Pallida Mors aequo pulsat pede. . . .*" I murmured.

"No, I think there are choices of a sort," somebody else was saying, "but we must acknowledge the limitations on such choices that life—particularly this form of unlife—requires."

A small child said, "I'd say this is primarily a problem of acceptance, wouldn't you, Chris?"

The therapist turned to me. "What do you think, Mr. Csejthe? Can you at least acknowledge that you are irreversibly in the process of transformation and that you must face spending the remainder of your existence as a vampire? Can you accept that your choices will be defined within those parameters?"

Everyone was looking at me with expressions of expectancy.

"At least try to acknowledge the fact of your condition," she prodded. "Admit that you are now defined by a new set of circumstances."

"All right." I cleared my throat and they leaned forward in their chairs.

"I suck, therefore I am."

Obviously, I had a long ways to go on this acceptance thing.

Something was wrong.

More than a week had passed and Dr. Mooncloud, Elizabeth Bachman, and Luis Garou had not returned. Lupé and Suki were nowhere to be found. The Doman was extremely busy and could not be disturbed.

But there were undercurrents that suggested preparations were being made, councils of war held. And, in the meantime, I'd been assigned a babysitter.

I couldn't go anywhere, now, without being accompanied by a great bear of a man, named Ancho. Ancho was big, hairy, and had long, clawlike fingernails. If you looked at him long enough you might begin to suspect that he wasn't quite human.

And, of course, he wasn't.

"Salvani," the aguane replied, when I finally broached the question to her.

"What's a salvani?" My temper had recently improved: Dr. Burton was prescribing some potent sleeping pills that turned my days into dreamless blackouts approximating sleep.

"Perhaps you are more familiar with the term 'vivani'?"

"Of the Four Seasons fame?"

She didn't even blink. "You must be thinking of Frankie Valli. The ones I am speaking of are also called 'pantegani'."

"Doesn't ring any bells." The trick, I figured, was not to blink either.

" 'Bregostani'?"

"About six or seven years ago—maybe."

She peered at me suspiciously. "You met a bregostani six or seven years ago?"

I shrugged. "It was a Hungarian restaurant and they served me a bowl of something that looked like a cross between pasta and borscht. I can't remember just exactly what they called it, but it sounded something like that."

"Ach!" She threw up her hands. "*Non!* The salvani are from the families of the dusky elves and reside in the lower Alps."

"He's a long way from home."

She arched a scabby eyebrow. "Aren't we all, my dear?"

I went back to the library to study. While I had scanned and entered a great deal of reference material into my computer, I had focused on occult matters that dealt directly with lycanthropy and vampirism. I had included references to the more obvious members of the enclave, but it seemed that something new was popping up every day.

Ancho, of course, followed me into the stacks.

"What'cha lookin' for?" he rumbled as I puzzled over where to begin my search.

"Overview material on elves."

"Which kind?"

"That's just it—" I hesitated, caught in the urge of an impending sneeze from all the dust atop the rows of books and piles of manuscripts. After a moment the unfinished sneeze retreated back into the nether regions of my sinuses. "—I don't even know how many kinds there are to begin with."

"Three."

I turned and looked at him. "Three?"

"Yah." He shook his shaggy head up and down.

"Three. Light elves, dark elves, and dusky elves. I'm one of the dusky clan. So's my wife."

"Your wife?"

"Yah: Basa-Andrée."

I started. "The aguane is your wife?"

"Yah. You look surprised."

What should I say? That she's ugly and looks old enough to be your grandmother? "It's just that I'd expect . . . the two of you to look more alike."

He nodded thoughtfully. "Yah. But I think it is good that the aguane look like they do. All salvani I know feel the same. Is not my Basa beautiful?"

"Um," I said, "I've never met a woman with so devastating an appearance."

"Yah," he said and then slapped his knee. "But trouble with being a water elemental is she is so ugly when she is out of the water."

"Um," I said again.

"Bet you had a nice shave, huh?" he said, and then roared (literally) with laughter. "Basa say anytime you want nice bath and shave again, you just call her."

"Um," I said like a broken record. Time to change the subject. I cleared my throat. "Why don't we sit down and you tell me about these three kinds of elves, Ancho."

"Yah, okey."

I led him to the study table and pulled out two chairs.

"Are the light elves the good elves and the dark elves the bad elves?" I asked, flipping open my notebook computer and switching it on.

"Light elves can be good or bad," Ancho said. "Same with dark and dusky clans."

"Then what is the difference?" The prompt came up and I opened my word processing program.

He smiled and his eyes acquired a distant focus. "Light elves are beautiful like butterflies and moonlight. They can change their form and travel through all four dimensions. They spend much time in other worlds and do not become involved in the affairs of this world much, I think."

I was trying to get his answer word for word. As I typed I asked about dark elves.

He rested an elbow on the table and propped his chin in his hand. "They are more like caterpillars than butterflies. Dark elves are creatures of the earth and make their homes under it. The rare ones who live in human places prefer the cellars or a dark corner. If you see one, it will be the colors of the earth: black, brown, grey—maybe red."

"And the dusty elves?"

"Dusky," he corrected. "We are the children of Nature and are bound by Her Laws. Our lives are shaped by our homes: trees, ponds, mountains, rivers, herbs, lakes, glens—"

Out in the hallway a horn began to blare a rhythmic pattern of alarm.

"Fire?" I began closing computer files.

The salvani looked grim as he rose to his feet. "*Non*. Is intruder alert. Come with me."

I had barely parked my hard drive when a great hairy hand closed on my wrist. I had to switch the computer off and lock down the LCD one-handed as he pulled me out of the library and down the corridor. As we neared the elevator there was a curious *chuffing* sound. The lift was coming up to our floor and as the elevator came closer, the *chuffs* grew louder.

"They're on the elevator!" I yelled at my fuzzy bodyguard.

He released my wrist and spun around, looking about wildly. Then, decisively, he ripped back the grillwork that barred the opening to the shaft and braced himself in the entryway. "Run away!" he growled. "Hide yourself! Do not go to your room!"

As the top of the elevator appeared at floor level, the salvani slapped his huge feet on the forward edge of its roof. The motor began to whine as his hands pushed against the top corners of the shaft's entrance and the muscles in his furry arms bunched and corded.

"Go quickly now!" he roared.

The elevator was still ascending, but more slowly now: an inch of the lift was showing above the floor line.

"You cannot help me!" Ancho's massive shoulders were rising up to meet the lintel. As they ground against the top of the doorway, a grinding squeal echoed down the shaft from above: the elevator, showing several inches now, began to shudder and slow even more. "It is you they are looking for! Go! Run and hide yourself!"

The barrel of a silenced gun poked blindly through the widening gap between the floor and the elevator car's ceiling. A second muzzle with a silencer followed the first. I threw myself to the floor as they began chuffing like an all-out race between two steam locomotives: automatic weapons-fire raked the upper walls and ceiling and ricochets whined down the hallway. I rolled to the side, clutching the notebook computer, and then scrambled on hand and knees down the side corridor.

I hit the stairs at the end of the passageway and touched every third step on the way down. I almost passed the landing on my floor before I reconsidered.

Ancho had warned me not to go to my room. But this could be the chance I was waiting for. I already had a knapsack packed and waiting for the right opportunity.

The passages near my room were empty. I crept down the hall and paused outside my door. Listened. I couldn't hear anything stirring inside, so I opened the door and eased into the room. I left the lights off and made a conscious effort to switch to my night vision. Again there was something like an imperceptible click behind my eyeballs and the room resolved into a greyscale matrix. The only color was the warm reddish flicker of my hands at the edge of my vision. Even with excitement, fear, and exertion pumping the adrenaline, my body temperature was now lower than the human norm.

I swept through the rooms, packing another change

of clothes and a few more items in a gym bag and an over-the-shoulder leather carrying case for the computer. While I was in the bathroom packing toiletries, there was a sound from the other room.

I moved silently through the bedroom counting on the darkness to be my marginal advantage. Another quick visual sweep revealed no infrared signatures.

It was time to leave before company arrived.

As I shouldered the carrying case and stooped to pick up the gym bag I was knocked back against the bed. Something was in the room: a dark shape gathered itself and moved toward me again. Oddly, it gave off insufficient heat to register on my perception of the infrared spectra.

I fell back on the bed and brought my leg up as the thing pounced. It landed on my foot and I kicked toward my head, propelling it up and over to crash against the wall above the headboard. Adrenaline exploded in my body and the curious time dilation effect seemed to take hold again; perception and reflexes accelerated.

But instead of slowing down, the dark figure recovered quickly and scrambled to its feet. This time it approached more cautiously and I could distinguish enough of its outline to see that it was human in shape.

But not human enough to radiate body heat in the ninety-degree range.

It struck with inhuman quickness, grabbing my arms. I struggled in an iron grip, making no progress until I tucked my head down and pulled so that its chest butted against the top of my skull. I snapped my head up catching my assailant under the chin. Its head rocked back and the attacker fell away, releasing my arms.

I was probably dealing with another vampire. Since I had not completed the transformation, my opponent was most likely stronger and faster. What had saved me so far was its conceit that humans were easy prey: it hadn't compensated for the fact that I was no longer fully human.

I whirled and felt across the top of the dresser for some kind of weapon. Nothing. I ran into the living room and ran my hands across my desktop. Pens, pencils, a note pad—my fingers curled around a ruler just as a body hurtled into mine from behind, smashing me into the desk. Now *that hurt*!

Blindly, I flung my hand back with the ruler. I was rewarded with the twin sounds of impacted flesh and wood cracking like dry kindling. The blow had all the effect of smacking a rabid pit bull with a flyswatter. As my attacker backhanded me across the room, I grasped the other end of the measuring stick and wrenched it apart: now I had two pieces of wood with jagged, broken ends. I swung the longer piece back in my right hand, hoping that seven-plus inches of a grade school ruler was as effective a stake as any of the standard vampire-killing variety used in the movies.

My opponent saw it coming and closed a slender but powerful hand about my wrist, effectively stopping its forward momentum. I brought up the other piece in desperation: it was barely more than four inches long. The vampire grabbed it with its right hand. Slowly, my wrists were forced together so that they could be pinned with one hand. But as they came into close proximity, one piece of the ruler crossed the other: I saw that I had a second chance.

"In the name of God," I cried, trying to remember the standard cinematic dialog for cruciferous encounters with the undead, "and by the power of His Son, Jesus Christ—" *What came next?* But already I felt a hesitation in the force exerted by my opponent. "—through this cross—" I struggled to hold the two pieces of wood at right angles to each other. "—I adjure you—" *Was* adjure *the right word?* "—begone!" I wasn't too sure about the depth of my belief in a broken ruler at this particular moment, but you work with what you have. "Get thee hence!" I was counting on my assailant's subconscious and Mooncloud's theories that tied vampires and clergy together with Sigmund Freud. "Begone," I said, "foul fiend!" There was less resistance in the vampire's grasp, now. But was that because it believed in the power of Christian symbology? Or was it growing weak from laughter? What else was I supposed to say? I tried reviewing Peter Cushing's Van Helsing to Chris Lee's Dracula. "The power of God commands you!" Olivier's Van Helsing to Frank Langella's portrayal of the count. "The blood of Christ commands you!" Anthony Hopkins to Gary Oldham—but then my train of thought derailed on Hopkin's performance as Hannibal Lector. So much for Coppola's version of *Dracula*.

"Am-scray!" I bellowed, thrusting the makeshift cross at my assailant's face.

Its grip faltered and the makeshift crucifix shot forward, striking shadowy flesh. There was a hissing, sizzling sound that was immediately drowned out by a blood-curdling shriek. The vampire released me, shoving me away, and whirled backward across the room. I raised the broken ruler again, smelling charred wood and burnt pork. The thing flinched away although more than ten feet now separated us. I moved toward it. "Hit the road, Jack," I said.

With an anguished moan it scrambled along the wall and threw open the door to the hall. The intrusion of light momentarily dazzled me and it took a moment to readjust my vision as it fled. It was smaller than my initial impression and wore black from head to toe like some sort of Navy SEAL ninja.

There was no time to congratulate myself on this temporary victory: there was still the matter of automatic weapons to contend with and I doubted that a crucifix—even a real one of cast silver and blessed by the pope—would do much good against such. I ran back into the bedroom and grabbed the computer and my makeshift luggage. I exited my apartment almost as fast as my unfortunate intruder.

And in my haste, I ran the wrong way.

I reached a dead end, but my luck was not entirely wasted: there was a laundry chute built into this particular dead end. A burst of noise from the other end of the hall decided for me then and there: I opened the small trapdoor and dived down the chute.

Luck was with me again: I fell three stories, but there was a huge pile of linens and such at the bottom to break my fall instead of my neck. I scrambled out of the mountain of sheets, pillowcases, and various odds and ends defying quick identification and sprinted through the deserted laundry room.

Listening to the sound of running feet in the corridors one floor above, I descended another level and worked my way through a subterranean passage to the basement of the castle's motor pool. There were a couple of close calls, but each time I ducked back around a corner and hid in the shadows until the voices or footsteps traveled on past.

The garage area was empty when I arrived. There were nearly twenty vehicles parked and waiting and, for a moment, I considered breaking open the key box and making my getaway now. But good sense quickly prevailed. My original plan was to leave when most of the Doman's people were looking the other way. Right now everyone would be on full alert and there was probably a reception committee from New York waiting right outside. No, my best bet was to do as Ancho had advised: hide myself, lie low, and wait for the right opportunity.

The Winnebago that had delivered me was nowhere in evidence, but a bigger motor home was occupying three parallel berths at the back of the garage. I tested the door and found it unlocked: my luck was still holding. I slipped inside, closing and locking the door behind me.

The recreational vehicle was spacious and roomy, basically a remodeled bus. Stowing my gear in a couple of the storage compartments revealed food stocks and supplies loaded and ready. The surprisingly sizable refrigerator held more than perishable foods and beverages; there was an ample supply of blood packets, as well. As I suspected, the bench seats lifted up to reveal sleeping coffins here, too. Not daring to risk any more time out in the open, I climbed into the one closest to the back of the bus and lowered the lid.

Two more hours passed before sleep finally came. Two hours to wonder if Ancho was all right. Two hours to try to guess just what I should do next. And when. . .

And two hours to wonder how I could invoke the talismanic powers of the crucifix when I was in the process of becoming a vampire myself.

Chapter Twelve

The bulwark erected by sleeping pills and exhaustion crumbles and THE BARN returns in full force. But memory falters, staggering like a badly spliced motion picture. Time has passed in this sequence. It's as if missing episodes were run through the projector of my subconscious these past few days while Dr. Burton's prescriptions capped the lens and switched off the lamp.

But now the dream continues, like a horrific home movie full of washouts and jump-cuts—a herky-jerky chain of snippets in which time and events are linked like boxcars on a night train to nowhere.

My arm aches where the needle was gouged, trenching my arm in search of an adequate vein. I keep averting my face away, but my eyes are ever drawn back to the tube carrying my lifeblood away. The cow continues to grunt and huff, sending quivers of distress through the bloody pool that soaks my shirt, permeates my jeans, and fills my shoes. It is a horrific sound that is eclipsed by a more dreadful noise: something else is stirring beside me in this pond of gore.

"Just like 'Nam," the man with the knife is muttering. "Once a corpsman, always a cor—*don't move!*" he screams at me.

I feel life and strength ebbing from my body. It is more than the leeching of my blood. Here, in the darkened portion of the star map that covers the barn floor, a black hole has opened up and I feel as if my very soul is being drawn into a remote and empty universe.

The hand that came out of the bloody stew and

clamped down on my arm is growing stronger. I don't want to see, *I mustn't see,* but my head rolls over anyway.

And I see.

There is a skull surfacing from the visceral swamp, remnants of charred flesh clotting the bone and suggesting what might have been a face before the fire got at it. That tattered charcoal ruin rolls so that its melted features face mine from just a couple of feet away. The nightmare seems complete: it can't be worse than this, there is no imaginable room for greater horror.

And then it opens its eyes and looks at me.

I was dead.

Even as my screams reverberated and died in the narrow confines of the grave, my hands were moving, beating at the walls, the ceiling of my coffin. I was dead and buried. Alone for eternity, smothered in darkness and the memory of something so terrible that I could only peek at it through the fingers of my dreams for a few seconds at a time.

And suddenly, there was light!

I looked up, half-blinded as the lid of my casket swung away, and tried to focus on a blurry face.

Fuzzily, its mouth moved. "It's Chris!" Suki's voice said.

"He's here?" Lupé's voice sounded farther away.

An unfamiliar voice harrumphed: "A stowaway."

And then I heard the whine of tires on pavement beneath me. "Where am I?" I asked groggily.

An old man with a mouthful of snaggled dentatia, wearing a rust-red beret, stepped into view, towering above me.

"Colorado," he said.

So much for a clean getaway.

Although no one seemed to see any need to turn around and take me back, a phone call was made and the Doman informed that I hadn't been abducted after all.

We were on our way to Kansas City, where the rogue vampire had last been sighted. More than sighted, actually: Mooncloud, Bachman, and Luis Garou had run him to ground there. Cornered, he had turned and fought back. Mooncloud had spent the past week in the hospital. The rogue was still loose and running. Lupé's brother and Elizabeth Bachman were dead.

As to the incursion on the Doman's home ground. . .

"Our best guess is another New York hit," Suki said, explaining the little intelligence that had been assembled before they had departed that same day. "They came in and passed through quickly and were gone again without anyone making a positive ID."

"Vampires," the old man said. "They took enough damage t' kill humankinds and still walked oot." The old man's name was Angus, and he wasn't really a man but a dark elf and a "haunt" of one of the lowland castles that bordered England and Scotland. More specifically, he was what was known as a "redcap," the embodiment of ferocious warrior spirits that habitually dyed their hats in their victims' blood.

"Could have been lycanthropes, General." That from a grim-visaged Lupé, who had just traded off the driving chores with Suki.

He shook his head. "Och, not bluidy likely. They'd ha' reverted to natural furms to make their escape."

"Was anybody else hurt?" I asked.

"A few flesh wounds," Suki answered from the front. "Nothing serious. Our folk are naturally resistant to the full effect of gunshot wounds, and these were pros on a specific mission and in a hurry. Once their presence was known and they had little likelihood of success, they blew."

"The worst casualty was Ancho," Lupé said with an uncharacteristic smile. "They nearly had to hospitalize him."

I felt a stab of guilt. "He was protecting me."

"Tell it to Hinzelmann. After the gunmen ran off, the

little hütchen grabbed his cane and started beating the salvani black and blue for breaking his elevator. Poor Ancho would have been better off shot."

Angus wasn't smiling, however. His red eyes glowered at me as he spoke. "Ye say the one that attacked ye in yuir room was a vampire, as well?"

I nodded. "Pretty sure. And, looking back, it was either a slightly built man or more probably a woman, now that I've had time to think about it."

"An inside job," the redcap pronounced.

"What makes you say that?" Lupé wanted to know.

I caught a movement at the corner of my eye and turned to look. Someone had stashed a furry cow at the back of the vehicle where the sleeping area was cordoned off by sets of curtains. I looked back at Angus.

"Because one of them knew where the lad's rooms were. . ." The old goblin scratched his leathery cheek with a long, talonlike fingernail and seemed to take no notice of the beast. " . . . and, as they were vampires from outside the demesne, whoever opened the back door had to invite them to cross the threshold, as well."

I looked again and saw that I was mistaken: it wasn't a shaggy cow. It was a dog the size of a cow. And it was green.

"Do ye ken wha' this means?" the redcap said.

"I have no idea," I murmured, staring at the "dog." It was huge—nearly the size of a two-year-old bullock—and had a tail that had to be at least four feet long that was coiled up on top of its back and hindquarters. Its feet were as big as my own, yet it made no sound as it moved forward a bit more.

Suki finally noticed. "Luath," she commanded, "go lie down." The creature obediently backed up behind the curtains and disappeared.

"It means there's a traitor in the Doman's household," the goblin growled, "an' that traitor could even be one of us on this bus right noo!"

The house was an imposing, multistory affair of stone and brick, replete with garrets, gables, turrets, widow's walks, and a liberal infestation of gingerbreading. Even though the house was well preserved, the lawn neatly mowed, and the shrubbery clipped and groomed, my eyes were drawn to the black, wrought-iron fence adorned with hundreds of twisty points directed toward the night sky.

"You didn't tell me she was staying with the Addams Family," I said.

Lupé ignored me. I had initially chalked it up to distraction over her brother's death. Now I wasn't so sure.

Suki turned to Angus. "Do you mind staying here with Luath, General?"

"Och, I'll keep the *cu sith* company, lass, whilst ye fetch the sawbones."

"There may be a few social amenities to attend to, sir. It might take a while."

"We'll hold the fort."

We exited the bus and I followed Suki up to the front door where Lupé was already waiting.

The doorbell didn't sound like a foghorn, no gargantuan butler answered the door, and the owners didn't look anything like the cartoon creations of Charles Addams. Susan Satterfield was a buxom redhead whose youthful enthusiasm and friendliness belied the fact that she was about to enter her fourth decade. Her husband, Jim, had curly, sandy-colored hair and a laid-back demeanor that was affable in its own way. In fact, he seemed deceptively serious-minded at first.

It didn't take long to discover that they were marvelous hosts, adept at making one feel comfortable and devoid of the need to impress anybody. They were children of the sixties with its inherent values, educated in the seventies, and successful in the eighties; all of which they had retained and brought with them into the nineties with the joie de vivre that comes from being well-centered and unpretentious. And nurtured a wee bit,

Suki explained sotto voce, by having won the state lottery a few years back, as well.

Like the poem "Vagabond House," their home was a three-story treasure trove of antiquities, a museum of knickknacks from around the world, and a gallery of exotica. It was obvious before we reached the end of the hallway that the quick tour would take hours—if we were allowed to ask questions: days.

We entered what would have been the drawing room in another, bygone age and found Dr. Mooncloud.

She sat half-swallowed by an overstuffed armchair with her left leg in a cast and propped on an ancient ottoman of leopard skin and with legs of filigreed jade. Her head was bandaged and one eye still drooped a bit in a lake of purple and red flesh. There was a surprising resemblance to one of the African ceremonial masks that adorned the wall behind her.

She was not alone. A pale man in a dark suit sat in a caneback chair adjacent to hers.

"Lupé! Suki! Chris!" She struggled to rise, but it was clearly a lost battle before it even began. The girls converged, hugged. I hung back and smiled. And wondered.

Wondered about Bachman's and the general's belief that there was a turncoat in the Doman's household. Did that put the finger of suspicion on Lupé since Mooncloud was out of town and essentially out of commission at the time of the raid? Or had she arranged things long distance?

Wondered if they were both guilty but not particularly good at this double agent business as both had suffered heavy losses this past week.

And wondered if this was a good time to make a run for it.

"And you are Mr. Csejthe?" The pale man rose from his chair and extended a hand so white as to be practically indistinguishable from his shirt cuff. "My name is Smirl. Dennis Smirl." His hair was dark, shot with strands of silver, and I figured him for the mid to late forties.

I shook his hand. "I'm Chris Csejthe." I also noticed his impeccable tailoring and how it came surprisingly close to concealing the bulge under his left armpit.

"Mr. Smirl is from Chicago," Mooncloud said. The pale man suddenly had Suki's and Lupé's full attention.

"Perhaps we should all sit down," Susan Satterfield suggested.

"Something to drink?" her husband offered.

It was an interesting collection of stories we had to tell each other.

Smirl explained how the New York enclave had been interfering in Chicago's business dealings these past two years and how there were rumors of a new Doman running affairs in the Big Apple. Lupé followed up with recent attacks on Seattle, and then Mooncloud and I took turns trying to define my part in the current equation. Which brought us around to the Kansas City assignment and why we were all here.

"We tracked it for several days, never quite catching up to it," Mooncloud said. "It's fast. But the reason we were having trouble isolating a pattern and narrowing the search grid turned out to be handlers."

"Handlers?" Smirl asked.

"Black limo and at least three people assisting. New York boys. We also picked up some information on a separate day team operating out of the old HoJo up on the bluff, above the river. Apparently they were investigating the whereabouts of one Victor Wren, but we were spread too thin to check them out beyond that."

I felt a peculiar prickling sensation at the nape of my neck. "Who's Victor Wren?" I whispered.

Mooncloud shrugged.

"Handlers complicate a trackdown," Lupé was saying. "A rogue generally leaves a trail because it's new to the undead lifestyle . . . has no resources. . . ."

"The handlers have been covering the spoor," Mooncloud added. "Eliminating whatever bodies may have accumulated—and, believe me, there will have been bodies with this one."

"What is a rogue doing with handlers?" I wanted to know.

"This one's different." Mooncloud's face looked haunted. "We're not tracking a newly created undead this time. This one has been a vampire for a long time. Maybe a very long time. I think New York provided handlers because this one isn't quite human."

"You sure about the New York connection?" Smirl asked.

Mooncloud nodded. "I recognized my opposite number."

"Dr. Cutler?" Lupé was incredulous. "But he's not a field operative, he's strictly research!"

"Apparently he's doing some field research this time around." Mooncloud shifted her cast to a more comfortable position. "I didn't recognize the other two, but Luis identified them as vampires."

"What happened to my brother?" Lupé's voice was calm but anguish leaked from her eyes.

"It was two nights after we finally tracked them to the old River Quay area. They were using an abandoned warehouse for a nest."

"Certainly fits the New York MO," Smirl murmured.

"Luis had the scent. I was loaded down with the whole AV rig and packing two crossbows, cocked and ready. Ditto for Liz—minus the rig, of course. She was supposed to hang back—wait for my signal. I was waiting for Luis to get in position. Something went wrong. I don't know what she saw from the other side—maybe they were tipped off, heard us or something—but she went crashing in before either of us were ready."

She shook her head. "It was a mess. Cutler's human, so we didn't waste time on him. Luis took down a vampire and I shot another and the rogue."

Suki leaned forward, an expression of uncharacteristic

intensity on her face. "How did you know that it was the rogue?"

"The other two wore suits and—I don't quite know how to say this—*looked* normal. But the other guy . . . whoo! He was a nightmare! Tall, thin, almost spidery—and dressed in black from head to toe. His face was, well, distorted in some odd way. He looked feral—wild, and barely restrained—and, in the brief opportunity I had to observe him, I got this uncanny feeling that his handlers had their hands full."

"But you shot him?" Lupé demanded more than asked.

Mooncloud nodded. "Could have sworn the bolt caught him square in the chest. He went down like he'd been poleaxed. A moment later, he was back on his feet, holding the bloody bolt in his hand. He started for me, but Luis finished the first vampire and intercepted him. The other one had Bachman down. I didn't see her discorporation because he was blocking my view and I was a little distracted at the time, trying to recock the first crossbow. The next thing I knew, he was up and coming at me. Knocked me down before I could get the quarrel in place. If it hadn't been for Luis. . ." She shivered.

"Tell me about Luis—?" Lupé was unwavering in her pursuit of her brother's fate.

"The rogue killed him," Mooncloud said simply. Only there was something that wasn't simple in the way that she said it.

"How?" Lupé was relentless.

"It doesn't matter how. He died bravely. He saved my life. And we must decide how to proceed from here."

"No!" Lupé's fist came down on the chair arm and there was a sharp report as wood cracked from the force of the blow. "I want to know how he was killed! It is not so easy to kill a werewolf and I want to know if they were carrying!"

I looked at Suki.

"Silver bullets," she whispered.

"I don't know," Mooncloud said. By now it was obvious to all of us that she was being evasive.

"Then, how did he die?" The blood from the Latino side of Garou's ancestry was in full evidence now.

"I don't really think that this is a good—"

She was on her feet. "I will look at his body and learn for myself, then!" She turned and took two steps.

Smirl was up and had her by the arm with surprising swiftness and she swung around, growling. The metamorphosis had begun and, as she raked her fingernails across his face, they were already becoming claws. He refused to release her arm, even though the left side of his face was hanging down to his collar in ribbons.

"Ms. Garou," he said quietly, seeming to take no notice that a portion of his jawbone was visible through the spaghetti spill of flesh. Curiously, there was no blood yet. "Dr. Mooncloud has her reasons for sparing you the details."

"I don't want to be spared the details!" she snarled, peach fuzz matting into dense hair along her arms and up her throat. "He was my brother! Do you understand? I have to know! I can't walk away and go on with the rest of my life not knowing!" Her voice became more guttural as her face began to elongate. "I've got to know!"

"Sit down and promise me," Mooncloud demanded, "that you won't try to look at your brother's remains."

"Sit down," Smirl echoed mildly. The muscles in Lupé's captive arm bunched and the shoulder seam parted in her shirt but the man from Chicago refused to relinquish his grip. "You're right: you have a right to know. And so I will tell you. But you will sit down. You will control yourself. And you will have to be content with what she chooses to tell you because you will want to remember your brother the way he was. Not the way he is now."

Slowly, she lowered herself back down into her chair.

As he released her arm, her skin resurfaced amid the dissolving fur and her teeth retracted back into smooth, white uniformity. Smirl reached up, gathering the shredded flesh into his fingers, and pushed it back into the gaping wound in the side of his face. There was still no blood, and the white strips of skin and tissue seemed to melt back into a contiguous whole like a sculpted expanse of pale vanilla pudding starting to set. He sat back down, and it was as if his face had never been touched.

I leaned over and murmured to Suki: "Vampire?"

"No," she whispered, "why do you ask?"

I shrugged. Maybe I'd pursue it later. Maybe I'd decide to forget the whole thing and go get quietly drunk.

"Lupé. . ." Taj Mooncloud took her hands in her own, "there is no way to mince words and still satisfy you on this. The rogue—it tore your brother apart." It was painfully clear that she meant this in the most literal sense.

I got up as Lupé began to cry and wandered to the far side of the room. There were display cases containing shrunken heads, a monkey's paw, a purported unicorn horn, helmets, keys, skulls, charms, amulets, totems, talismans, and other occult and exotic bric-a-brac. There was even an honest-to-God Egyptian mummy.

"Imhotep."

I turned and looked at Jim Satterfield, who was standing at my shoulder. "Excuse me, but you're what?"

He smiled and shrugged. "Im-ho-tep. We named him after the original mummy—the one in the old Boris Karloff flick."

"I thought it was Kharis or something like that."

"Those were the later movies. Kharis and his deathless love for the Princess Anaka. Lon Chaney, Jr. did two or three in the forties, maybe the early fifties, as well. He's remembered for *the Wolf Man* but I think he was an even better Mummy."

What could I say to that? "A boy's best friend," I mused.

"It's authentic," he said, looking as if he should be

wearing a cardigan and smoking a pipe. "We have several consignments of Egyptian antiquities. That bowl right there contains genuine Tanis leaves that we handpicked ourselves in San Al-Hajar Al-Qibliyah, the ancient site of Pi-Ramesse, in the Egyptian delta."

"Tanis leaves?"

"For the elixir of life. You know: three leaves to keep the heart beating, nine for movement—never more than that—and boil them in the sacred urn. . ."

"The sacred urn."

"Right. And over in that display case is the Scroll of Thoth."

"Scroll of Thoth?"

"Containing the magic words that enabled Isis to raise Osiris from the dead."

"Oh, *that* Scroll of Thoth."

"It's an authentic copy. The one next to it is an authentic translation of the text."

"An 'authentic' *copy*?"

He nodded. "Got it from a dealer in Egyptian antiquities."

I squinted at the spidered calligraphy. "Oh, Amon Ra! Oh! God of gods," I read. "Death is but the doorway to new life. We live today, we shall live again. In many forms shall we return. . . ."

"Enough." Taj Mooncloud was suddenly by my side, wobbling on her crutches, one hand grasping my arm.

I looked at her. "What?"

"You don't know what you're messing with. Leave it alone."

I looked at the scroll. I looked back at her.

"It contains Words of Power," she murmured.

I bit back a smile. "For heaven's sake, Taj, it's only a tourist's souvenir," I said in low voice. "There must be thousands of these things sold every year—read by thousands of people."

"Ordinary people," she qualified. "In the hands of a shaman this could be something quite different."

"Oh, and am I a shaman, now?"

"We don't know what you are. You have your own confluence of power. Perhaps you could trigger other Powers. Perhaps not. It is best to err on the side of caution and let sleeping gods lie."

There was no point in arguing. I helped Mooncloud back to her chair. The scroll had to be a second-rate souvenir. Likewise the mummy. Even though it looked genuine, Egypt hadn't permitted the sale or export of its cultural treasures or antiquities for many years. It was highly unlikely that a midwest couple living in the Kansas City suburbs could be harboring a genuine Egyptian mummy. But then I would have calculated higher odds against said couple hosting a werewolf, a semi-vampire, and a Chicago gangster whose real name was probably Gumby, under the same roof.

Behind me I heard Mrs. Satterfield saying: "Are you sure you want to leave so soon? We have extra beds. . . ."

"We're wasting moonlight," Suki said as I turned around.

Mooncloud had just sat down and was once again struggling to leverage herself out of her chair with her crutches. Smirl stood and helped her up. "I appreciate your hospitality and handling the arrangements for Luis's remains. But we dare not let the trail grow colder by another night."

Jim Satterfield nodded. "Is there anything else we can do to help?"

"Cross your fingers," answered Mooncloud.

"Light a candle," Suki added.

Get me outta here, I thought.

We drove to the abandoned warehouse on the riverfront. Smirl followed in a long black limousine. He sat in the back where silhouettes suggested at least one additional passenger. I only caught a glimpse of the driver: it was enough to convince me that I didn't want a closer look.

Smirl's "people" had already tossed the premises so we weren't expecting any additional clues, save one.

"All right, ye great slobberin' beastie," the general was prodding the *cu sith* down the rear steps of the bus, "it's time fur ye to earn yur not so inconsiderable keep."

The *cu sith* yawned, displaying teeth that might have coerced A. Conan Doyle to rename his story "The Chihuahua of the Baskervilles." Mooncloud produced a scrap of black fabric that had been left behind in Luis Garou's grasp.

The redcap held it to the green dog's snout. "Here now, Luath: get the scent, now. Have ye got it, lad?" Luath sneezed and wagged his ropelike tail, causing us all to scatter. "Right, now!" the old haunt shouted. "Hunt, laddie! Bring it to ground!"

The Faerie beast raised its emerald jaws to the sky and made a great baying sound that put city-wide disaster sirens to shame. He followed that with a second that was even louder than the first. I had my hands over my ears before the third bay sounded, but could distinguish no lessening of the volume. I took my hands away from my ears as he lowered his muzzle and could hear the tinkle of broken glass coming from all over the neighborhood.

Then Luath leapt forward, unfolding into a run. He vanished into the darkness of the night.

Suki appeared in the doorway of the bus as we heard the tattoo of massive paws whisper away into the distance. "All aboard or we're gonna lose him!" We all piled into our vehicles. As the bus pulled out again, the limo turned on its lights and followed behind us.

Suki drove, keeping one eye on the CRT display that tracked the homing device in the *cu sith*'s collar. Lupé and the general opened one of the locked closets and were checking out a veritable storehouse of weapons. There were regular crossbows and crossbows with double and triple bow/barrel compositions. There were firearms of more recent design—until you studied them closely and noted deviations in the standard configurations. Some weapons appeared to be the latest in state-of-the-art, while others looked like they'd been ancient before Angle met Saxon.

"The head," the general said, hefting a broad-bladed battle-ax, "a stake through its heart *and* removing its head from its shoulders shuid do the trick."

"We've never had to do that before," Lupé said. "A stake through the heart has always been sufficient."

Mooncloud stared out the window at an unpleasant memory. "I could've sworn I nailed this thing's heart. When it got up, I assumed I'd missed. But if I didn't. . ."

"We could be in a whole lot of trouble," Lupé mused.

"There are myths and stories that suggested other means of disposal," I said.

Mooncloud nodded. "Too bad we can't go back to Seattle and spend a few days in the Doman's library researching this."

"Maybe we don't need to." I got up and retrieved my laptop computer. "I've scanned a number of books and reference articles onto the hard disk. Unfortunately, I've had little time to organize it much less do any actual cross-referencing. It may take awhile to come up with something pertinent."

"Then you'd better get started," Lupé said.

Even with a week's head start, our quarry probably hadn't gone far.

Judging from the trail that the *cu sith* was following, they had spent at least three more days in the Kansas City environs before heading south on Highway 69. Luath circled three different motels between the river and the intersection of 435 and 69 South, indicating our targets had spent time there. Whether they spent more than one day/night cycle in any or all of those places was anyone's guess.

There didn't seem to be much point in spending more time in checking them out: they were already gone and, as Suki had already said, we were wasting moonlight. We left K.C. behind, following the *cu sith*'s collar tracer, and hit pay dirt shortly thereafter.

"Gonna see daylight in a little less than two hours," Suki called from the front of the bus.

I had volunteered to spell someone on the driving chores but was told that my top priority lay with the computer texts and researching alternate dispatching techniques.

Mooncloud laid a hand on my shoulder. "If you've come across anything helpful so far, now would be the time to share it with us."

I scowled at the screen. "The deeper I go, the more complicated it gets. So far, I've identified over thirty different vampire legends from more than a dozen different countries, most requiring different rituals of protection and warding and separate means of extermination."

"Can you isolate any common threads? The next time we run into that thing we need a better plan than the ones we've used in the past."

I opened another file on the computer's display. "See for yourself."

She scanned my short list. "Stake through heart or navel—must be driven with a single blow. Decapitation—consecrated ax or gravedigger's shovel. Complete immolation. Bury face downwards. . ." She shook her head. "The rest are just techniques for warding, delaying, or discouraging vampires."

"You asked for the common antidotes. I'm still compiling data on the more unusual vampire legends."

The general leaned over my shoulder. "Make yur lists, laddie, but I'm bettin' on number two, here." He thumbed the edge of a nasty-looking halberd that seemed to materialize in his hands like magic. "This beastie may not have a heart where we'd expect it, but there's verra little guesswork when it coomes to taking a head from atop its shoulders. It'll no be gettin' oop again once't Axel-Annie, here, has barbered it proper."

"I'm sure you're right, Angus—" Mooncloud stared out the windows at the rushing dark "—but, just the same, I think I'll break out one of the flame-throwers. For luck."

"He's slowing down," Suki called from the front of the bus.

The rest of us crowded forward to watch the blip on the monitor.

Mooncloud frowned at the darkness beyond the reach of the headlights. "What's the map say?"

"We're in Miami County," I said. "Should be Louisburg up ahead."

"What's it like?"

I shrugged. "Don't really know. Small town, maybe a couple thousand residents. I've never spent any time there. Drove through it once."

We turned off on State Route 68 and slowed down as we headed east into Louisburg.

The general leaned toward the screen. "He's stopped."

"About two miles ahead," Lupé said, studying the readouts. "Maybe less."

"Want in a little closer?" Suki asked.

Lupé shook her head and began unbuttoning her shirt. "Give me a minute and then stop the bus." She walked to the back of the bus and behind the curtain, loosening her clothing as she went. A moment later a great grey and black wolf emerged from the sleeping area and trotted up the aisle.

"Be careful," Suki said, pulling the vehicle over to the side of the road. She opened the doors and the wolf leapt to the ground before we had reached a complete stop.

"Get in position, but wait fur us, lass," the general called as she bounded away in the darkness.

"I don't like this," Suki muttered as the bus started back onto the road. "We're cutting this a bit close to sunrise."

"Mayhap. . ." the redcap's hands gripped the back of

the driver's seat, "but I'd rather tackle these beasties noo than try to restrain our Lupé fur another eighteen hours."

An unearthly sound suddenly shattered the silence: Luath had found his prey.

"Ah," I said, "de children of de night! Hear how dey are singing?"

The general snapped out an oath. "Sa much fur the element o' surprise!"

Suki said nothing, pressing her lips together and pressing her foot to the floor. We roared down the road until she reached over and flipped a pair of toggle switches: the engine noise dropped to near imperceptibility. Before I could ask about the muffler system, we were swinging off the road and into the parking lot of a small motel on the outskirts of Louisburg.

The general handed me a machete and then pressed a crossbow into my hands. "Here ye go, laddie; look sharp and don't let the big 'un get away!" He was out the door before Suki had the bus at a full stop. I followed, trying to tuck the machete under my arm while juggling the crossbow and a handful of wooden quarrels. Our driver was right behind me while the engine was still dieseling the last of the carburetor fumes.

Luath was nowhere to be seen, but his foot-wide paw prints were clearly evident where they crossed the dust and gravel parking lot and led right up to the door of one of the units. The door of that particular room was slightly ajar, dim light spilling a wedge out across the weedy doorstep.

"No point in sneaking up noo," the general said, brandishing a wicked-looking halberd. And with that, he charged the partially opened door. Suki and I were hard-pressed to keep up: the redcap was a couple of strides from the door and a good ten feet ahead of us when we heard Lupé call out: "No, General! Don't come in! It's a trap!"

It was too late, of course. Even if he'd had time to

break off his charge I doubt that he'd have chosen to do so. The door slammed open as he burst across the threshold and then the entryway lit up as if a roomful of paparazzi had chosen that very same instant to take flash pictures. The strobe of light was followed by a clap of thunder and smoke hazed the doorway as we came up more cautiously to peer inside.

It looked like any other motel room and, except for the swirl of dissipating smoke, it was cleaner than most. The opposite wall was covered with mirrored tile to create an illusion of depth. When you walked through the door, the first thing you would see (assuming you weren't a vampire) was yourself. The next thing you'd see was scripture—if you walked into this particular room, that is. A message was painted on the mirror in red brush strokes large enough to read from the doorway. It said:

And many of them that sleep in the dust of the earth shall awake, some to everlasting life, and some to shame and everlasting contempt.

—Daniel 12:2

"They were already gone when I got here," Lupé said. She was sitting on the foot of the bed with the cover pulled loose and wrapped about her nakedness.

"When I heard Luath bay I figured the jig was up and came charging in. I only beat you by a minute, at best, and didn't notice the sign until I had reverted and the general came rushing through the door."

Suki sniffed delicately. "They used blood."

Lupé nodded. "They knew that blood would get the general's attention even if the positioning of the message didn't."

"So what happened?" I wanted to know.

"Scripture," Smirl announced from the doorway. "You want to banish a redcap? You read a passage from the Bible to them." He looked at the painted mirror and shook his head in admiration. "Diabolical: tricking a redcap into reading the passage himself!"

I looked around. "So where did he go?"

"Ask Taj," Lupé snapped. "We've got to get out of here right now!"

"Clues?" Smirl asked, looking around the room.

"None. They were expecting us. But I checked, anyway." She began shifting back to wolf form.

"We'd best do as the lady says," Smirl said, backing toward the door. Suki was already outside. "Company will be showing up any minute and we don't want to be here when they arrive." He went with the wolf right behind him. I was the last one out and, as I closed the door behind me, something on the ground caught my eye. I grabbed it and ran for the bus.

Suki already had the bus in motion as I jumped on board and back on the road out of town before I could find a seat. The black limo was nowhere in sight.

"Where?" Suki yelled as she steered a return course toward the highway.

Mooncloud was studying the road map. "If we head back down Highway 69," she said, "we won't hit another town until Pleasanton."

"Time?"

"At least a half hour," I said. "Stay on State 68, past the highway; go another six miles or so and look for an unpaved road going south."

"Where will that take us?"

Mooncloud looked up from the map. "Somerset?"

"Not so much a town as a wide place in the road," I said. "But it will give us a place to park and talk about what we do next."

Suki nodded decisively. "I am going to have to trade off, soon."

Mooncloud picked up the cellular phone and punched in a number. "Dennis? Taj. Where are you?" She listened for a moment. "We're still pulling up our socks, here. Chris has recommended we stop over in a little place called Somerset. West on 68 then south on—damn, the map doesn't even name the road! Can you find it on your map? Good. After I get the kids tucked in, maybe we can find a restaurant and continue our search for the perfect cup of coffee and slice of pie."

As she hung up, Lupé emerged from the back, buttoning her shirt. "Brief me," Mooncloud demanded, shifting her leg to balance the end of the cast on the seat opposite her.

Lupé did and, true to its etymological roots, it was brief. "Nothing to show for it," she summarized, "and we've already had a casualty."

"Two casualties," I said, holding up Luath's collar with the electronic tracer still attached.

"Where did you get that?"

"On the ground, just outside the motel room."

"This is bad," Lupé said, folding up in her seat to rest her chin on her knees. "Now we have no easy way of tracking them."

"Worse than bad," Mooncloud said. "Bad enough that they'd be clever enough to set a trap for a redcap. But to neutralize a *cu sith*. . . ."

I hadn't planned on going to sleep so soon, but the sunrise had a more potent effect on me than I had expected. While it still seemed unlikely to dissolve my flesh and render my skeleton into a vague, chalky outline in ash, I was beset by irritated, itchy skin and a pounding headache. These were relieved as soon as I settled down into the dark, coffinlike compartment in one of the bus's fold-down seats and pulled the lid down to block out the offending solar radiation.

There hadn't been time to sort through all the questions in my mind, much less ask them before hopping into the box. I made a mental list as sleep encroached, planning to corner Mooncloud as soon as the sun went back down. She'd nearly convinced me that vampires could exist in the same physical reality as moonwalks, quantum physics and William F. Buckley. But dark elves and Faerie dogs and gangsters that belonged in a Dick Tracy comic strip?

There was comfort in the thought that maybe I hadn't emerged unscathed from the accident that killed my wife and daughter—that maybe I was still lying in a hospital bed, unconscious and plugged into a variety of tubes and wires and such. That this past year was nothing more than a trauma-induced, brain-damaged delirium.

That's right, Pam, last season was nothing more than a silly old dream; Bobby Ewing is back at Northfork and would you hand me the soap, please?

Sure.

Unfortunately the plots on *Dallas* were more likely than the events of my life these past few months. . . .

The last thing I thought about before drifting into a black, dreamless sleep was the scripture left behind on the motel room mirror.

Surprisingly, I knew the Old Testament passage from my childhood. I had learned it in Sunday School and remembered it long afterward for the verse that followed: *And they that be wise shall shine as the brightness of the firmament; and they that turn many to righteousness, as the stars forever and ever.*

It had once been a comforting thought, a scripture for the times when a young mind turned to thoughts of its own mortality and the endless darkness threatened by the grave. What comfort now for one who, by all religious and secular lore, was considered damned for all eternity?

And they that be wise shall shine. . . .

The darkness embracing my dreamless sleep was blacker than the absence of light, deeper than the confines of my encompassed bed.

Now the shadows cut to the bone.

Chapter Thirteen

I peered at the image that flickered in the RV's tiny bathroom mirror and tried to shave. The lather reflected better than the bleary topography of my face. "I suppose the fact that I still have to do this every few days is a good sign," I muttered.

"Maybe." Garou sat with feet propped across a seat, where she could watch me and still keep an eye on the coffee pot. "But then a corpse's hair and fingernails continue to grow for a while, even after it's been planted six feet under."

"Actually, that's a myth," Mooncloud called from down the aisle. "It's based on old reports of exhumations. Back then they didn't realize that decomposition causes tissues to shrink as they dehydrate, receding from the hair follicles and the base of the nails. It only gave the appearance of growth after interment."

"So I am still alive," I qualified.

"The jury's still out on that," Garou returned.

"And thanks for your support."

"What is it with you?" she growled. "You've got the best of both worlds, right now: near immortality, near invulnerability—and you can still walk around in broad daylight!"

Well, not exactly, but that wasn't the point. "Hey," I said, pointing my razor at her, "you think being undead is so goddamned wonderful, why don't you ask the Doman to bring you over?"

"She is a were," Suki said placidly. "It is not permitted."

"So what's with the attitude? Incisor envy?"

"I wouldn't take it if it was offered," Lupé snarled back.

"Smirl called Chicago, today," Mooncloud said, turning us back to the business at hand. "They're going to send an airplane to help with an aerial search. In the meantime, he's looking for a nearby airport where he can rent a plane and pilot for the next day or so."

"So what do we do in the meantime?" I asked.

Garou shrugged. "Without Luath the only thing we can do is drive through every town and down every back road, ask questions and keep our eyes and ears open."

I frowned into the mirror. "What are they looking for?" My reflection seemed a little slow in frowning back. "I mean, they came down here to find me, discovered that I'd relocated to Seattle, tried to nail me up there—then, all of a sudden, they're back here, still snooping around like they've lost my trail."

"The obvious answer," Garou said, "is that they're not looking for you. They're looking for someone or something else."

"Someone or something connected to you, most likely," Mooncloud added.

"But what? Or who?"

"The same thing we're ultimately looking for, I guess." Mooncloud sounded thoughtful. "What infected you in the first place."

"Shhh!"

We looked at Lupé, who had her head cocked to one side. "Did you hear that?"

I listened. Heard the growl of the RV's motor, the purr of tires over gravel. Nothing more.

"Hear what?" Mooncloud asked.

"Hush!" Lupé turned toward the front of the bus. "Suki, pull over and stop the engine."

A moment later all was silent save for drone of crickets in the fields that surrounded us.

"Listen!" Lupé held up her hand. "There! Did you hear that?"

I looked at Mooncloud. She shrugged.

"It's Luath!" Lupé looked at us. "Can't you hear him? He's still out there!"

I looked up the aisle at Suki. Her shoulders copied Mooncloud's, and she shook her head, as well.

Mooncloud said, "Are you sure?"

Lupé looked at the rest of us. "You don't hear him? I know he's a bit faint—but—" Disappointment crossed her face. "You think I'm imagining it?"

"No." Mooncloud considered. "You hear beyond the human range of audibility in wolf form—maybe you can in human form, as well."

I looked at Lupé. "So where is he?"

She cocked her head again. "I'm not sure. . . ."

Mooncloud and I began opening windows along the sides of the bus.

"Shhh! There! He's sounding . . . that way, I think. . . ." She pointed toward the southeast.

"This should be fun," I murmured as Suki started up the bus and tried to turn around. "Do we stop every five minutes and listen for Luath to bark?"

"No." Lupé began to unbutton her shirt. "Give me one of the walkie-talkies. I'll track him and report our positions back to you."

"You can't carry a walkie-talkie while you're in wolf form."

"Find something to tie it around my neck."

I held up Luath's collar with the transponder still attached. "How about this?"

"Perfect!" Mooncloud took it out of my hands. "We can use this to track you the same way we tracked the *cu sith*." She studied its length, obviously adjusted for a neck that was five times the size of Lupé's. "Hand me one of the combat knives from the weapons locker, will you, dear?"

Five minutes later we were passing the southern end of Somerset, hunting for a side road that would take us back toward the east.

Mooncloud and I were hunched over the monitor, crouched behind the driver's seat. "I think this is going to work," she said.

"Yeah?" I frowned at the phosphorescent blip as it moved across the screen's glowing grid lines. "Well, we've lost the general, Smirl and company are off chasing down an airplane, and we still don't know what happened to Luath. If we find what we're looking for, what makes you think we'll come out any better than last night?"

She gave me a sharp look. "You got any better suggestions?"

I didn't. Something had destroyed my life and my family. Something that was still out there somewhere. If our quarry wasn't responsible, it was a safe bet that they could lead us to it.

"Getting closer! Closing the gap!" Suki called.

"Cut the lights," Mooncloud ordered. "Go to silent running."

It was reminiscent of an old submarine movie: switches were flipped and the engine noise was muted to a murmur. The lights were extinguished and Suki had to depend on her night vision and a faint glimmer of starlight to steer by.

"Getting a return," Mooncloud said.

"What?" Suki was distracted. "There's a campfire out across the field—east. Maybe two to three miles."

"The signal on Lupé's collar is coming back toward us." Mooncloud considered. "Slow down and be ready to stop."

"I see her." The RV stopped and Suki opened the front door.

A moment later Lupé was standing on the steps in human form and breathing hard. My night vision was compensating for the darkness and I tried not to stare.

"Satanists," she said.

"Satanists?" So much for not staring.

She nodded, still trying to catch her breath. "Out in the field, there. Some sort of ceremony. Torches.

Truck. Two, three cars. One of them's the limo we're tracking."

I looked at Mooncloud. "Satanists?"

"Did you ID anyone?" Mooncloud asked.

Lupé shook her head. "Robes with hoods. Everybody covered. Except the altar."

"The altar?" I asked.

"Satanic ceremonies usually require a nude woman to act as the altar," Suki explained.

"Oh." Hell of a recruitment angle.

"Did you see Luath?"

Lupé shook her head. "I could hear him. He sounded strange: faraway and—and—I don't know how to describe it. It was like he had fallen into a hole or something and was running about and barking under the ground. . . ."

"This complicates things," Mooncloud said. "How many of the others?"

"Only saw one perimeter guard. Maybe eight, counting everybody."

"Bad enough risking our own necks," Mooncloud groused, "without having to worry about innocent bystanders."

"Innocent bystanders?"

"Chris," Mooncloud put a hand on my shoulder, "most people who call themselves Satanists are just sad, maladjusted folk who like to dress up in robes and act out silly rituals."

"Sounds like most mainstream religions to me," Suki said.

Mooncloud silenced her with a look. "We're not talking Wicca, here, or Deists or Pagan religions that worship the Lord and Lady. And if these people were true Satanists, we couldn't get this close without Lupé or I knowing it."

"So why would they pretend to be devil worshipers?"

She looked past me, staring at the pinpoint of firelight across the field. "Why do most of us pretend to be what we only seem to be?" She sighed. "While there is the occasional closet sadist who uses Satanism as an excuse to torment and kill animals, most of them are just social outcasts, looking for other misfits who will accept them. Some think it's a private club for kinky sex and others are acting out their dissatisfaction with the religion of their formative years. . . ."

"Most of them," Suki added, "deep down inside, don't believe that they are actually invoking the Powers of Darkness. And the few that really do want to sell their souls to the Devil—well, they know more effective means than acting out symbolic rituals."

"We're here to put down real evil," Mooncloud finished, "not hurt some overgrown children playing dress-up in the dark. . . ."

The first hour was almost exciting: I waited, clutching the general's halberd, crouching in waist-high pasture grass while Suki and Lupé reconnoitered the outer perimeter of the gathering. Both were pros at this, able to move silently through the brush and foliage while I still tended to glide like a drunken rhino. Small wonder I was told to stay back and wait. Though both promised to check in with me from time to time, only Suki made good on her word.

The second hour was a lot less thrilling.

To help pass the time I experimented with my extended senses, counting crickets and determining the gender of toads by their individual voices. And checking the time. I had yet to find a watch whose luminous dial lasted much past sunset but, even though the moon was new, I could clearly see that it was a little before midnight. Comforting to know that for the rest of my un-life I could get by on cheap watches.

By hour three I was trying to tune out the audible and visual spectrums, opting for a zenlike approach to my boring vigil. Which is why I was slow to react to the sound of a footfall behind me: perhaps Lupé was finally making an appearance. More likely that Suki was making a return visit. Lupé had been distant and formal—even a bit frosty, of late. When she wasn't ladling the sarcasm, that is. . . .

I was getting a cramp in my back and, since we were far enough back and into the trees that no one would see us, I straightened up, using the halberd for leverage.

The ache in my lower back exploded into a burst of agony.

I would have cried out, but the breath had already been driven from my lungs. My stomach cramped and, as I pressed a hand to my abdomen, I found something poking through my shirtfront.

Three somethings poking through my shirtfront!

I turned around, feeling a bit woozy and definitely off balance.

It wasn't Suki or Lupé. It was a couple of guys dressed in black robes with their hoods thrown back.

One was big and middle-aged, over six feet tall, with sparse hair and a big, bushy black beard. The other was short and old with greasy, silver-white hair and about three days' worth of stubble on his pinched face.

"What'd you let go a' that pitchfoke for?" the short one said, doing a more than credible imitation of Strother Martin. He raised the shield on the hooded lantern that he was carrying.

"I got 'im, Henry," the big one said. "He oughta be fallin' down now."

"*Hist!* You imbecile! Don't say my real name!"

"Oh. Sorry, 'Asmodeus.' "

"Asmodeus?" I was I was giddy with shock. "And what do they call you?" I asked high pockets.

"Uh, Belial."

Asmodeus tugged on Belial's robe. "Don't talk to him! We're supposed to kill him!"

"Well, I stuck him with the pitchfork, Henry. What else am I supposed to do?"

"Don't call me that, you big, stupid—"

"Boys, boys," I said, trying to keep my voice low: the last thing I wanted to do was bring the rest of the coven running. "I'm really sort of unhappy about this pitch-fork thing—" More than a little unhappy and having no luck in trying to dislodge it by myself. The best I could do was get my left hand behind me to grasp the base of the handle and keep its weight from unbalancing me any further. "—it itches something terrible. Now, if you'll just pull it back out, I might be inclined to let you go without tearing your heads off first!"

"Don't lissen to him," Asmodeus said. "He's about ready to fall over!"

"Now, Henry, do I really look like I'm about to fall over?" Matter of fact, I was, but no point in letting them know it. "Think about it, if I were human, wouldn't a pitchfork through the middle do me right in?"

Belial nodded. Asmodeus just looked like he needed to find an outdoor privy.

"But I'm not human. I should think that was rather obvious. Especially to a couple of experienced Servants of Darkness like yourselves."

"Hey," said Belial, his face lighting up like a two-year-old's at Christmas. "You're a demon, ain'tcha?"

"Bingo." I was getting more than a little woozy.

Asmodeus wasn't convinced. "But them other demons that come through yesterday said we's supposed to kill these folk! Said that Satan commanded it."

"You boys obviously haven't trafficked much with demons." I slid down, onto one knee, no longer able to keep my balance.

"Trafficked?" It was obvious that Belial was totally out of his element now. "Ya mean like drive with 'em?"

"Look, what did these so-called demons promise you in exchange for performing this task?" His expression indicated my wording was too obtuse. "What are you supposed to get for killing us?" Now I was down on both knees.

"Lord Satan is s'posed to raise us up," Henry/Asmodeus preened, "give us power in his kingdom!"

Yeah, that and twenty-five cents will get you half a cup of coffee.

"Exchange?" Belial had finally decoded my previous question. "Them other demons traded Bob Sommer that purty black car for his old chevy van."

Belial's face took on an expression of calculation. "So, if you're a demon, too, what'll you give me if'n I pull out that pitchfoke from your back?"

Your head on a stick, I wanted to scream. Then I saw the grey wolf creeping toward them through the weeds. "See that wolf?" I asked, pointing straight at Lupé. She hesitated, having lost the element of surprise. "To show you that I'm a more powerful demon than the *false* ones who visited you yesterday—"

"Uh, last night," Henry corrected.

"—last night," I continued, feeling some disorientation setting in, "I will invoke the Powers of Darkness and change that beast into a beautiful woman—a—a naked love slave—who will—will—" *where was I going with this?* "serve the one who pulls out this—this—thing." I pointed at the pitchfork with my right hand, starting to slide toward those dark waters of unconsciousness.

"Oh, now what kinda fools d'you take us for—" Belial began.

But Henry poked him with an elbow and said: "Go ahead, demon: show us your stuff."

I looked at the wolf. Who looked back at me. And, for a moment, got the impression that these two fools were the least of my problems. "Okay." I pointed at Lupé and tried to think of something arcane to say. I drew a blank.

"C'mon, mister big mouth demon. Show us your power or we'll show you that we got more farm implements where that pitchfoke come from."

I closed my eyes and tilted my head back, feeling the

handle of the pitchfork bump against the ground behind me. All of my joints were starting to unhinge. "Eenie meenie," I said, "chili beanie; the spirits are about to speak. . . ."

"Are they friendly spirits?" Belial wanted to know.

"Yow!" said Henry.

I opened my eyes and caught the final stage of Lupé's transformation back to human form. *My, my, my. . . .*

"Ooooh!" she cooed, arching her back and running her hands through her long, night-dark hair. Then she smiled a wicked smile and positively sauntered over to where I was standing. "Thou has summoned me, Master?" she exclaimed breathily. Draping herself across my shoulders, she proclaimed: "I am Hell's love slave, here to do thy bidding!" In my ear she whispered, "Are you all right?"

"Do I look all right?" I murmured. "This damn pitchfork is killing me."

"Which of these lusty servants of Satan are you giving me to?" she asked. "Or do you wish for me to serve both?" Sotto voce, she added, "When I get done with you, you may wish the pitchfork *had* killed you."

"No," I answered for our audience's benefit, "I am giving you to the one who draws the pitchfork from my back."

The fight was short and brutal. In less than a minute, Asmodeus was writhing on the ground where he was in an excellent position to look for his teeth. "Gently! Gently!" I coached as Belial planted his foot against my back and started yanking on the pitchfork. "Or no love slave!"

When the deed was finally done, I held myself up off the ground with trembling, rubbery arms, fighting off waves of unconsciousness. Dimly, I heard Belial ask for his reward.

"Come with me," Lupé said, "and I will see that you get all that you deserve."

The bleeding had miraculously stopped and I felt as if my partially transformed body structure had already mended some of the damage. But I was still in a very bad way: the internal repairs were progressing too slowly to get me out of the woods anytime soon. I still fought to retain consciousness.

"Uh, mister demon?"

I looked up, tried to focus my eyes.

It was Asmodeus. Crawling toward me on his hands and knees.

"What do you want, human?" Hard to sound surly when you're getting ready to pass out.

"Um, I was just wondering if there was something I could do to get me one of them love slaves?"

"Love slaves, huh?" I mumbled.

"Y'know, do you some kind of favor or somethin'. Can I get you somethin' you need?"

"Huh. Got any blood?"

"Uh, blood?"

"Yeah, Henry; blood. Red stuff."

"Blood?" His mouth turned up in a terrified grin. "Now, where would I get blood, mister demon, sir?"

"Henry," my words were starting to slur, "you humans are full of it. Blood, that is."

There was a strangled screech from a dark clump of trees behind us.

Henry's eyes grew huge. "What was that?"

"Love-slave passion, no doubt." My chin dropped to my chest. "Tell you what, Henry. I'm fresh outta wolves. But I like you. So I'm gonna make you a special love slave."

"You is?"

"Ri'. But you gotta get 'gredients."

"Tell me what! I get 'um!"

"Gotta catch a skunk."

"Ketch a skunk?"

"Barehanded."

"Barehanded? What if'n it bites me or—you know?"

"Better for the spell," I mumbled. "Gives 'em more—somethin'. Bigger—you know. . ."

"I do?"

I nodded and thought my head would come off. "Then you gotta take it and—and stand in the middle of Highway 69 at high noon—"

"Holding the skunk?"

"Ri'. High above your head."

"In the middle of Highway 69?"

"At high noon. Naked."

"Nekkid?"

"No clothes."

"Anything else?"

The temptation was overwhelming, but I had no energy left. "Go away."

"Go away?"

"Now."

"Yessir. Thank you, mister demon, sir!" He crawled away into the darkness.

Another screech sounded from the trees where Lupé had taken Belial. This time it sounded like Lupé.

I grabbed the halberd and levered myself up from my knees to one shaky leg. The trees around me began dancing the Highland fling. I straightened the other leg into the semblance of a stance and leaned on the ancient weapon, sucking night air and willing the landscape to settle. Then I began lurching toward the trees on rubber legs.

Suki came out of nowhere, passing me on the fly, and crashing into the treeline a good fifteen yards ahead of me.

Now it got really noisy!

I hobbled over and caught the branch of a tree with my free hand just as the bones in my legs turned to jelly. The result was a sort of barber pole effect that left me curled around the trunk like a serpent on a caduceus. Somehow, even twisted up as I was, I had a ringside seat for the show.

Suki had just discharged her crossbow and was fumbling with another wooden quarrel, trying to reload.

Lupé was hunched in midtransformation, the body of Belial, crumpled on the ground, behind her. She reared up on her (hind) legs with her arms crooked before her. While her arms still looked human—albeit rather furry—her hands were another thing altogether. The fingers were blunt and powerful looking, tipped with two-inch claws that curved like rows of small, black scimitars. Her face was neither human nor canine but something of an amalgamation of the two. A mouth full of teeth and then some added to the inhuman effect. She was covered in fur and it was rising in hackles from head to hips.

It was easy to see why.

The creature facing them only appeared to be more human at the first glance. It was tall and thin and more spidery than humanoid. Oh, it had the requisite number of arms and legs and the face contained two eyes, a nose, and a mouth in what should have been the proper places. But there was something wrong with the sum that was more than the individual parts, something deeper than the surface appearance. Something that overshadowed the net effect.

As I said, it was tall: six-six at least, maybe six-eight. And thin—as if someone had taken a man of normal height and stretched him like a piece of warm saltwater taffy. The mouth was also stretched, sideways to an inhuman width, and filled with teeth the way a can of sardines is filled with little fish. Its forehead was deformed, the brow ridges protruding like a neanderthal's and then sweeping up into the hairline like twin v's: it looked a little like one of those alien whatchamacallem's—the Romulans—on *Star Trek*, or Meatloaf in that music video a few years back—the one with the *Beauty and the Beast* motif.

Two crossbow bolts protruded from its blackclad body: one from its back where Suki had undoubtedly loosed her first shot upon her arrival, and a second that had just caught it high in the chest on the left side. Either shot would have killed a human being and should have incapacitated anything else. This thing only looked annoyed.

While Suki was trying to cock her crossbow, Lupé snarled and grasped a small sapling. I say small in relation to the other trees around us: this was a good seven feet in height. She grabbed the trunk just below the midpoint and the muscles in her arms corded, her shoulders bunched. It came out of the ground with a tearing sound and another three feet of tangled roots were added to its overall length.

The creature didn't seem perturbed. Even when Lupé broke the four-inch thick trunk across her knee to make her makeshift weapon more manageable.

>>*KiLl yOu, JaCKelBItCh!*<< The words ice-picked into my mind like stabs of electric current. >>*Kill CAtbITch!*<< The thing glanced over its shoulder. >>*TheN Finish You Off, HalFThiNG!*<< it thought at me.

The words were chilling enough. The mental voice that uttered them was worse. Beyond either were the thought-images that accompanied the telepathic messages, images of pain and carnage that were personalized for each of us.

A surge of adrenaline shocked the strength back into my limbs, the ancient biological failsafe of "fight or flight." I disentangled myself from the tree, recalling the images he had compressed into the thoughtburst blasted at me: pictures of two cemetery plots; of spidery hands digging into the dark, black earth; of Jenny's and Kirsten's coffins being splintered, broken, broached. . . .

"Sonofabitch!" I hissed, hefting the halberd and staggering toward it. It was gathering itself to spring at Lupé while Suki still struggled with the crossbow. It heard my approach and hesitated. My adrenaline rush was good for about five yards, then the physical realities of shock and blood loss kicked in: my legs went from rubber to Silly Putty. My momentum carried me forward for a few more feet and I swung the halberd as I fell. I wasn't sure whether I swept its feet out from under it or if it just stumbled, tripping itself in a little dance of indecision, but the creature followed me to the ground.

>>*kIlL YoU!*<< its mind screamed. >>*tEar YoUr FlEsH!*<<

Then Lupé was standing over us, raising the broken tree trunk above her head. The creature screamed and I echoed with sympathetic pain that rang against my own skull. Then the splintered trunk came down with a horrible crunching sound and the ground shook with the force of the impact.

I rolled away and managed to sit up with the last of my strength. The thing was pegged to the ground, impaled on the shattered tree trunk like a moth on a display pin.

It should have been enough. But the thing writhed and squirmed like a worm on a fishhook. Using the halberd, I pushed myself back up to my knees and hauled the bladed end toward me. Lifting the oddly weighted weapon was almost too much: I nearly swooned but caught myself as the image of Jenny and Kirsten's coffins flickered against the back of my eyeballs once more. The thing turned and looked at me as I brought the ax-blade up.

>>*I HaVe TheM*<< it thought at me. >>*I hAvE ThEM bOTh. I WiLl ShOw YoU WhAT I WilL Do wITh tHem. I WilL ShOW—*<<

But it didn't show me anything. The muscles in my arms turned to water and the blade came down with nothing more than the force of gravity. But it was enough. The axehead sheared through the thing's throat like a gingsu through margarine.

The night became black water and I was slipping beneath its surface.

Death is here and death is there, Shelley wrote, *Death is busy everywhere, / All around, within, beneath, / Above is death—and we are death.*

"Chris!" A hand cradled my chin, lifted my face. I looked up into Suki's face. "How do you feel?"

"Like . . . death. . . ."

"We've got to get him back to the bus." It was Lupé's voice. "We've got to get some whole blood in his system." Hands grasped me under my arms, lifted.

"What about the others?" I mumbled.

"Gone," Suki answered grimly. "Along with two vampire handlers. When the first one went up in smoke the others just scattered. I followed Gruesome here, but I wasn't able to get a good heart shot."

I looked over at the headless thing pinioned by the sapling, but the shadows beneath the trees had swallowed it in a deeper darkness.

"What happened to you?" She flung my arm over her shoulder. Lupé did the same.

"Thespians," I whispered, "outstanding in their field."

"What? What was out, standing in the field?"

"Repertory cast for Steinbeck's 'Mice and Men'. . . ." I murmured. My knees started to buckle and they caught me.

"We'd better hurry," Suki told Lupé. "I'd like to get this thing in a body bag and put it on ice for later study."

"If we don't get some whole blood into Csejthe," I heard Lupé say, "we'll be needing two body bags and twice the ice."

Both women were surprisingly strong: I was totally dead weight now and they were practically carrying me.

Then they dropped me.

Under the circumstances, I could hardly blame them: the creature was moving.

It was still pinned to the ground by the broken tree trunk. But its arms were coming up and a pair of spidery hands grabbed at the wooden beam that transfixed its chest. It pulled and the tree came up out its body with a wet, sucking sound.

"Oh, shit," I said, as it tossed the tree aside and fumbled for its head. It rolled to its feet, clutching its head like a wide receiver looking for open yardage.

>>*KiLL YoU aLl!*<< the creature thought. And then

the misshapen monstrosity was loping away, vanishing into the night's heart of darkness.

"We've got to stop it," Lupé whispered in a shocked voice.

"And how are we going to do that?" Suki asked.

"It's getting away! We've got to—"

"What? Chase it? And then do what if we catch it?" She shook her head. "You put a heart-sized hole right in the middle of that nightmare's chest, Lupé! That tree had to have sundered the spinal cord where it came out! Then we took its head clean off! How you gonna stop a thing that can get up and run away with that kind of damage?" She shook her head again and grabbed my arm. "It's time to get the hell out of here and rethink our plans. And try to keep Einstein here alive, because we're going to need all the help we can get when we catch up with that thing again!"

"Einstein?" I queried as Lupé grabbed my other arm and leg.

"Einstein," she agreed, matching Lupé's sarcasm. They began dragging me back toward the road and the haven of the bus. It would have been better if they had been taller or I had been shorter: my feet dragged the ground and I was losing my shoes.

"What a mess!" Suki's eyes were glistening in the moonlight. "Perimeter guards, everyone armed: it was as if they were expecting us."

"They were," I said, trying to think coherently and get my mouth to cooperate at the same time. "We were set up."

"Is he serious, or is this just more of the same?"

"I'm not sure. The big one put a pitchfork through him and instead of tearing their throats out he was just sitting around and talking to them when I arrived."

"Worries me. The boy just doesn't seem to have the instincts necessary for his new lifestyle."

"Oh, I don't know. He certainly seemed to know what to do with Deirdre. . . ."

"My, my, I think someone has their muzzle out of joint."

"Suki, why don't you just shut up and carry your half—oh, shit!"

"What is it?"

"Isn't that where we left the bus?"

I raised my leaden head and looked where Lupé was pointing. Even though we were some distance away, there was little room for doubt: the bus was on fire.

Chapter Fourteen

"I was just sitting there with my pistol holstered," Mooncloud said, "when they yanked open the door and tossed a couple of Molotov cocktails inside." Equal portions of pain and disgust drew down her mouth and etched new lines in her face. "Never heard them coming."

"Neither did I," I mumbled. No one heard me over the crackling backdrop of the fire.

"By the time I had the fire extinguisher out, they'd thrown three or four more against the outside of the bus. At that point it was a lost cause: all I could do was grab essential items and abandon ship."

"You were lucky," Suki said.

"Yeah, I was lucky." Shimmering light from the burning bus bronzed the bitterness in Mooncloud's face. "I lost our transportation, our equipment, weapons, our medical supplies. I think I rebroke my leg getting out of that firetrap."

"You saved our database," Suki said, brushing off the laptop's carrying case, "and you could have been shot. You could have been killed."

"And richly deserved it," Mooncloud said. "I was careless. I was sloppy—"

"We all were." Lupé finished tying off the makeshift splint around the remains of the cast on Mooncloud's leg. "But this isn't like other retrievals. We've always hunted the newborns: inexperienced, confused, almost always alone. This time we're chasing someone who's had time to acclimate. And he's in the company of professionals.

The people we're hunting are hunters themselves, so maybe we're luckier than we think."

"Lucky. . . ." Mooncloud bowed her head. "Neither Chris nor I are in any condition to travel. The blood supplies, the medical kit, and my other crutch are all burned up. So are Lupé's clothes. In a few hours the sun will be coming up. Suki, you and Chris won't have anyplace to hide, to sleep—"

"We're halfway between Somerset and New Lancaster," she said. "Enough time to reach either at a brisk walk and find some sort of shelter before dawn."

"But not for Chris," Lupé pointed out.

"Hey," I said, finally stirring a bit. "Maybe I've given up on a daytime lifestyle, but I don't think a few hours of sunshine are gonna smoke me."

"Maybe," Mooncloud said, "but we shouldn't take the chance."

"I'm no weenie," I grumbled.

"You're a delirious weenie," Lupé said. "Shut up and let the rational folk make the decisions."

"He's probably right, though," Mooncloud said. "He hasn't progressed much since we brought him in." She turned to me. "You could probably manage a fair amount of daytime, if you were wearing a good sunblock."

"Jeepers, I could start a new trend: vampires with tan lines." I realized I was babbling and shut up.

"Suki, you hit the road now and find a place to hole up for the day," Garou said. "I'll stay here and see that these two find some shade."

Mooncloud produced the cellular phone, the other item she'd managed to grab on the way out. "I called the Doman and he's sending a helicopter and cleanup crew. Trouble is, they won't be here before midmorning. We'll have to cross our fingers that the local constabulary doesn't show up first. A close examination of the fire scene could prove embarrassing."

A cache of ammo in the burning bus suddenly went

off, punctuating her last words with random tracers of sizzling lead. I was already lying down; everyone else threw themselves flat.

"What about our allies from Chicago?" Suki asked once the snap, crackle, and pop became sounds of cooling metal.

"I've tried them repeatedly. They're either out of the car or the phone has been switched off. I'll keep trying, but we can't take any chances. Suki, you hit the road now and we'll meet you back here—mmm, better make that a mile south of here, as soon as you can make it after sunset."

"*I'll* meet you," Lupé amended. "Dr. Mooncloud and Mr. Csejthe are going to be airlifted out of here for medical treatment just as soon as the cavalry arrives."

Suki stood reluctantly. "I don't like leaving you."

"There's no other sensible choice," Mooncloud said. "Take cover and come back tonight."

"All right. Be careful!" She turned to go and took a couple of steps. "Wait. I don't know if this is important, but I noticed that all the vehicles belonging to our little Kansas cabal had Arkansas license plates."

Lupé whistled. "Bubba's a long ways from home."

"Perhaps it's a ruse," Mooncloud pondered as Suki jogged into the darkness, "using false plates to misdirect us. . . ."

"I don't think they're that clever," I said, remembering Rancher Cantrell's tale of midnight trespassers.

"What difference does it make?"

I turned toward Lupé. "It means we're now looking for a Chevy van with Arkansas plates."

"Why?" Mooncloud asked.

"And what are Satanists from Arkansas doing here?" Lupé pondered.

"Don't know what brought them here," I said, trying to lever myself up on one elbow, "but I think they're legit. This part of the country has a history of arcane events—spook lights and hauntings that predate even the white man's arrival here. Maybe they think it's a place of power, a nexus or focal point. . . ."

"Or maybe they just figure they're less likely to have their reputations ruined back home if they're caught out of state," Mooncloud mused.

"Whatever the reason, our quarry apparently ran into this traveling circus last night."

Lupé came over and eased me into a sitting position against a large rock. "Maybe somebody stuck a pitchfork in one of them," I continued. "Somehow, the New York group convinced these jokers that they were demons or minions of Satan, or some sort of folderol, and got some cooperation. First they swapped their limo for somebody's van. Then they told them to be on the lookout for us—promised some sort of reward for killing us. So while we were being oh-so-clever in sneaking up on them, they were already waiting for us."

Lupé's face was skeptical. "They told you all this?"

"They inferred as much."

"Inferred?"

I glared right back at her. "Inferred."

"Great! While they were at it, did they infer what happened to Luath?"

"What happened to Luath?"

"Um, I think," said Mooncloud, "that Lupé just asked that question."

"Hey," I said, "I don't know what happened to Luath. You're the only one who heard him tonight."

"Stop it!" Mooncloud hissed. "Stop it, the both of you!"

We both looked at her. The flicker of firelight made trenches out of the fresh lines in her face.

"We can't afford this. We already have enough problems, enough enemies, without turning on each other. Lupé, I'm surprised at you, baiting Chris when he's in shock."

"Actually, I was baiting him out of it," she said with a half smile. "Got his adrenaline pumping and I do believe he is more alert."

Mooncloud peered at me. "His color is a little better. But he still has a serious need for blood. And we also have to find him some shelter from the sun before it rises. Something better than tree shade, if possible."

"I'll see what I can do," Lupé said, crouching down on all fours. She metamorphosized into wolf form and loped off down the road.

"Strange girl," I murmured.

"She's had a very difficult life."

"I can imagine."

"You can't even begin to imagine," she snapped. "And you're complicating things for her."

"Hey, I didn't ask to be run through with a pitchfork! And it's not my fault the blood supplies got crisped!"

"That's not what I'm talking about!"

"Well, what are you talking about?"

Mooncloud stared at me. "You really don't know, do you?"

I stared back. "What?"

She sighed and settled back against the tree trunk. "Never mind."

"I hardly do, anymore." I lowered my head back to the ground and stared up through the tree branches at the night sky. The stars glistened like chips of crushed ice in the moon's absence. Glowing red embers swarmed in their midst like a host of demonic fireflies. The breeze began to freshen, sweeping the sparks away to the west, along with most of the heat from the smoldering wreckage. My undead flesh, lacking even its basal blood supply, felt the night breeze as a chill wind.

"You're not like other vampires, Chris," Mooncloud said quietly.

"Yeah, no fangs."

"I don't mean in that way. There's a coldness that sets in. . . ."

"I think I'm feeling it right now." I repressed a shiver.

"I don't mean temperature, either."

"Well, I imagine it takes a certain kind of mindset to hunt human beings for food."

She nodded. "That and, as I mentioned before, there are biochemical changes in the brain. I wonder if you'll eventually lose touch with your own humanity as the others have done, take on their arrogance. . . ."

"I don't need anybody else's arrogance; I brought my own, thank you." I thought back to the Doman, Suki, Damien, and Dr. Burton. "But, so far, everyone's been pretty friendly." Not counting New York's involvement. Or Lupé, of late.

"Perhaps you are mistaking curiosity and interest for warmth. Don't get me wrong, Chris; Pagelovitch is a good Doman. Fair, never unnecessarily cruel, and he looks after those he considers his own.

"But you have been treated particularly well because of your intrinsic value on the Underworld market: your condition may be the key that unlocks a number of secrets that have eluded the *wampyr* for centuries.

"It also is a matter of your transition. There is a caste system in which the rules of behavior are very strong and compelling. Mutual respect is *de rigueur* among vampires. But only among their own kind. To the Doman and the other vampires of his demesne, Lupé and I are valued servants, serfs—possessions even. We are not now nor ever can be 'equals.' Vampires are 'the Masters.'"

I remembered Bachman's words in my room just before I got my first swimming lesson as one of the newly undead.

"And it's worse for us than most of the others," she continued. "It's our job as part-time enforcers to go after other members of this Master Race. And put them down, if necessary. You see the problem?"

Yeah, it was starting to come into focus. Given the mindset, Mooncloud and Garou were the equivalent of a couple of uppity niggers to this cold-blooded "Massa" Race. "Is there anything I can do?"

"No. And don't try. You won't make anyone happy and

you'll just get Lupé all the more confused. Was there any sign of Luath while you were out there?"

It took me a moment to mentally shift gears. "No. Why? Do you think Lupé is imagining things?"

"Maybe. But it's more likely that the *cu sith* wasn't fully banished."

"Fully what?"

"He may have only been pushed into an overlapping dimension. Maybe partially phased."

"Partially phased," I said.

"Right. In which case it might be possible that he's still around. In a phased sense, you understand."

"Me? Understand?"

"So it would still be possible to track our quarry as long as Lupé can hear him."

I was tired and cold and even more confused than I had been five minutes before, so I didn't waste my energy trying to point out that we had no weapons, no transportation, and no means of tracking the *cu sith* through the transponder anymore.

"Found something!" Lupé said, loping up out of the darkness. Unnerving enough that we didn't hear her returning, but it always gave me a turn when she spoke while still in wolf form.

"How far?" Mooncloud wanted to know.

"Not far. A short walk." Her muzzle swung over to consider me. "For a healthy man."

"How about if I crawl?" I asked.

"I'll help you." Lupé's shape shifted back along human lines as she came and leaned over me. "Can you sit up?"

I decided I needed proper motivation when I failed at my first attempt. Maybe I'd do better if someone placed a TV remote between my feet. . . .

She hoisted me to my feet on the second attempt and then had to hold onto me to keep me from falling over. "Friends don't let friends walk drunk," I chided.

"Tell the Doman," Lupé told Mooncloud over her shoulder, "that he owes me big time for this."

"Good luck," Taj called as we lurched off down the road.

It was worse than embarrassing, it was humiliating: not just in that I had all the stamina of Raggedy Andy on Percodan, but as lucidity came and went like a bungee jumper, I found myself draped over my human crutch in a variety of positions. Bad enough had she been wearing clothes, but under the present circumstances. . .

When she slapped my face to bring me around, I awoke thinking I had just been called on an "out of bounds" penalty. Slowly I discovered that I was lying down and sitting up at the same time. And that we seemed to be in a tunnel.

"We're in a dry culvert that runs under the road," she said, the corrugated metal tube echoing her words into a distorted booming sound. She put her hand to my forehead. "How do you feel?"

"Thanks for not saying 'we.' " My teeth were starting to chatter.

"You're not running a fever. You're cold. Is that good or bad?"

"Doesn't feel so good. But then again I'm feeling surprisingly well for a guy who got run through with a pitchfork."

She frowned. "Yes, and we have an account to settle on that matter." She reached out and began unfastening the buttons on my shirt. "But for now we'll do what we can about keeping you alive. Let's see if we can get you warmed up." My shirt, still damp but turning crusty with blood, came off, and she used it to sponge the area around my wounds. Then she pulled me against her and down to the ground.

Her skin was covered with short, downy hairs like peach fuzz, and the feel of her was like warm velvet. She wrapped her arms around me and slowly slid her hands up and down my back, trying to pull the chill out of my semidead flesh. The pain receded as I basked in the warmth that poured out of her like secret sunlight.

It wasn't long before I felt a familiar stirring. A hunger was awakening. *Not now*, I thought.

But I needed blood. And that need was inescapable. Undeniable. . . .

Except, as the feeling grew in intensity, it didn't feel like the bloodlust that had become increasingly familiar of late. It was a different kind of hunger, of need.

"Is this helping?" she murmured, her face close to mine.

In response, I touched my lips to hers. She answered in kind. The kiss that followed was long, deep, and more satisfying than anything I could have imagined.

"This is a bad idea," she whispered, finally.

"I'm just full of bad ideas," I whispered back.

She snuggled against me. "Are you warm enough?"

"I'm getting there."

She sighed. "You still need blood."

"It will have to wait."

"You don't have to wait. I can give you some of mine."

I flinched: the thought of taking a little of her blood seemed even worse, now, than what Deirdre had seduced me into doing just days before.

"I can't," I said, falling back on the old standby. "Dr. Mooncloud insists that I have nothing but normal blood. It might contaminate her research—"

She shook her head. "I don't care about research. I care about keeping you alive."

"I don't want your blood."

"You'd drink Deirdre dry but refuse a single swallow from me?" She looked in my eyes and flinched. "I'm sorry. I know that wasn't your fault." Claws extended from her fingertips. "We can argue about this later." She drew a single claw across the inside of her hand. Blood began to gather in her cupped palm. "You've got to have something." She raised her hand to my lips. "Drink."

"If you take even one swallow," said a new voice, "then I shall be forced to kill you both!"

I looked over and, at the opening of the culvert, I saw a familiar face.

The face of Death.

I swooned.

"Chris, what happened? Are you all right?"

"Daddy, Daddy, what happened to your shirt?"

I look down and eventually realize that my shirt is half on, half off and soaked with a witch's brew of blood, water, and mud.

"What happened to him?"

"Don't rightly know, ma'am," the fire chief is telling my wife. "My guess is he got a lungful of smoke, staggered into the barn, and collapsed. We found him there and the paramedics have been looking him over.

"Hey, Jim!" He motions to one of the firemen who was holding a breathing mask over my face when I woke up.

"We gave him oxygen," Jim explains as the chief moves off to direct cleanup efforts, "but he's still pale and shocky. Take him straight to a doctor or the emergency room and have him looked at."

"What about that bandage on his arm?" Jenny wants to know.

"Well now, ma'am, I was about to ask you the same thing. That's not our handiwork; he had it on when we found him."

"Well, he didn't have it an hour ago." She looks at me.

"I—I don't remember," I say. It is something that I will say for the rest of her life.

"Will you help me get him into our van?" she asks the paramedic. "I'll take him straight to the nearest doctor."

"I can walk," I say. When I prove that I can, I'm even more surprised than they are.

"Daddy, are you going to go to the hospital?" Kirsten asks as her mother eases the van around in a slow, tight turn.

"No, honey, we're going to go straight home so I can rest."

Jennifer gives me the Look. "We are taking you to a doctor."

"Seriously, Jen; I am feeling better!" And I am. The farther away we get from the fire and the creepy old barn, the better (safer) I feel. "In fact, I'm ready to drive now."

"Don't be silly."

We are back on 103 now, and the town of Weir is just ahead. "Tell you what, though," I say, spotting an IGA Food Mart up ahead, "I could use a couple of Tylenol. Why don't we stop here? It'll only take a moment."

My wife is a woman completely devoid of guile. More surprising: after nine years of marriage, she still doesn't expect it from me. When she comes back out with the tiny sack, I am sitting behind the steering wheel with the driver's door locked. Kirsten laughs delightedly at Jennifer's scowl. "Daddy tricked you, Mommy! Now he gets to drive!"

"I don't think you're funny," she says, climbing into the passenger seat.

"Oh, lighten up, Jen," I say, pulling us back out onto 103. We head east.

"You're a macho pig just trying to prove how tough you are." The words are not devoid of affection as she says it.

"Not only that," I say, "but a penny-pinching tightwad who doesn't believe in wasting ninety bucks and another hour in a waiting room with two-year-old magazines just so a doctor can tell me to take some Tylenol and go home and lie down."

Outside the town limits, I bring the van up to fifty-five miles per hour and set the cruise control. "See?" I raise my knees to the steering wheel. "Nothing to do but steer. And I can do that with one hand. With one finger."

"My, my, aren't we feeling better?" She smirks, but there is genuine concern in my wife's eyes. I'll always remember those eyes, just that way. Wide, cornflower blue—they have a way of shining in a very special way when she looks (looked) at me. "Now, maybe you can tell me what happened to you back there in that barn?"

"Wh-what?" I feel an unexpected wave of dizziness.

"I hope that old man is going to be all right."

My heart lurches in my chest. "Old . . . man . . . ?"

"Can't you remember anything?"

Don't want to!

"The barn?" The periphery of my vision is clouding, growing dark. My foot dances for the brake, finds only the accelerator. A red tide washes over my thoughts.

"Slow down, Chris; we're coming up on the highway."

Can't see it! I'm groping in darkness for the cruise control release, for the brake. The steering wheel slips out of my hands.

And I remember—for just one moment—the horror that was waiting for me in the barn. A horror that I thought could not be surpassed and still survived.

And then I know that there are worse things than the horror in the barn.

They are unfolding even now as the sound of the tractor-trailer's airhorn drowns out Kirsten's screams. . . .

I remember, now.

And, with the memory, I opened my eyes and looked at his face.

It was an old face, ancient, in fact. But not infirm or beset by any of the weakness or dissolution that one associates with the aging process. It was a strong face, whole, unmarked by scars or wounds where the flesh had once been burned away from the bone.

It was the face that had looked out the rear window of a black and white, 1931 Duesenberg the night I arrived at the Doman's castle in Seattle. It was the face that looked down upon my death throes in the trunk of a limousine belonging to an assassination team from New York. It was the face that waited at the end of that dark culvert I had last found myself in that had spoken just before I passed out.

And it was the face that had surfaced from the bloody stew, locked away in my nightmare pit of forbidden dreams.

It spoke now.

It said: "Good evening, Mr. Csejthe." My name rolled oddly off of his tongue. "I trust you are feeling better?"

I wasn't feeling better. I was feeling stronger. There was a difference. It wasn't easy tearing my eyes away from his, but I felt the needle in my arm and I needed to look: five plastic packets of whole blood were suspended on a telescoping pole beside my bed. All were feeding directly into my arm.

My eyes returned to that ancient face, to the man standing at the foot of my bed. There was something in his eyes, in his bearing, in the all but visible aura that seemed to surround him that suggested this was a man used to meek subservience and unaccustomed to insolence.

"I've had Monday mornings that were worse," I answered for just that very reason.

He smiled. His lips were cruel—a phrase I'd never expected to encounter outside of a bad romance novel and yet no other description came close. His smile was not a particularly comforting expression.

"I'm afraid you have the advantage of me, sir." I was never one to be content with tugging on Superman's cape when I could spit into the wind, too.

His smile grew broader, revealing the sharpest set of canines I had seen on a vampire yet. "Forgive me, I have been unaccountably rude. I am," he said, executing a slight bow, "Vladimir Drakul Bassarab the Fifth."

"Count Dracula," I said.

He clicked his heels. "At your service."

Chapter Fifteen

"You're the monster in the barn?" Lupé squeezed my hand protectively as she sat next to my motel room bed.

"It was an old farmhouse," Dracula said, continuing his story from the chair on the other side of my bed. "The fire department decided the fire was caused by a short in the electrical wiring. Victor was in town at the time. I, of course, was in my coffin, sleeping. By the time the smoke had reached the basement and penetrated my sleeping chamber, there was no way out except through solid walls of flame. I summoned Victor, but I could not wait for his arrival.

"I was badly burned in passing through the flames. I made it outside under my own power. There, my charred flesh was further consumed by the sunlight that my kind seeks so assiduously to avoid."

"According to Bram Stoker," I said, "you were able to go about during the daytime with no difficulties save that your powers were somewhat diminished."

"Bah! That hack? And whom else do you count upon for your research, Mr. Csejthe? Hollywood? Ellstree Studios? Anne Rice?" The outburst seemed more theatrics than actual temper and he returned to his account as if uninterrupted. "I collapsed just outside the barn moments before Victor arrived."

"The New York team was asking questions about a Victor Wren," Lupé murmured.

"Victor is my servitor and liegeman. He has been with me for many years and I have owed my life to him on more than one occasion." He glanced at an ornate pocket watch. "I wonder what is keeping him."

"So, you summoned Chris to the barn when he arrived," Lupé persisted, "and took some of his blood to stay alive?"

"I was fortunate: I was too far in extremis to take nourishment for myself," he said. "Mr. Csejthe came along at just the right moment. Victor was a medical corpsman in Vietnam and, fortunately, was able to jury-rig the necessary materials for a blood transfusion."

"*Un*fortunately," Mooncloud said from the suddenly open doorway, "it was sloppy." It was getting all too easy for anyone to sneak up on me. "In the process, Chris was partially infected."

"Sorry we're late," Wren said, coming in behind her. "We were delayed en route to the hospital. Traffic was backed up on 69 for miles in both directions. Some old guy was standing out in the middle of the highway, naked as a jaybird, and holding a skunk over his head." He shook his head. "You wouldn't believe what happened next. . . ."

Out of my nightmares and in the light of day, Wren was neither formidable or frightening. Of medium height, he had fair skin and long, carrot-colored hair worn in a ponytail that hung halfway down his back. He looked thirty-something, but a tour in 'Nam meant another decade at the least. Good genes? Or something beyond human norms?

"What do you mean 'partially infected'?" Lupé asked as Mooncloud swung across the room on new crutches.

"Well, we know that Chris is stuck in midtransition. That certain parts of the metamorphosis haven't even begun yet—most noticeably, the development and extended growth of a new set of upper incisors." She lowered herself into a chair and propped her leg, in its new cast, on the edge of my bed. "I've been working on this theory for awhile now, but I can only prove about half of it. For the rest?" She shrugged. "I'd need to get both of you into the government biocontainment labs at USAMRIID. So, I can only tell you what makes sense based on the evidence."

Dracula—or Bassarab—signaled for her to continue.

"We've pretty well established that we're dealing with a mutative virus with recombinant effects on human RNA and DNA. We know that, though there is a baseline effect, the actual range of mutations varies from one individual to the next."

I interrupted: "So there's something in my genetic makeup that is resisting or suppressing a portion of the virus?"

Mooncloud shook her head. "I don't think so. No. Based on the circumstances of your infection, I believe the incompleteness of your transformation is due to the fact that you were not fully infected to begin with."

"Oh," I mused, "kind of like being a little bit pregnant."

"Excuse me, Doctor," our host said, "but, over the centuries, I have taken an interest in diseases of the blood. And, while I do not have a medical degree, I have more than a layman's acquaintance with the subject of viruses." He leaned forward, his face a dissertation on intensity. "One is either infected with a virus or not. A virus may be carried in a dormant phase for months or even years. The effects can be somewhat localized, or the severity of the infection can be graded on some sort of scale . . . but it would be incorrect to say that only part of the virus was at work here."

"Except that it *is* true," Mooncloud insisted, "*if* the vampiric condition is the result of a combinant super-virus."

"Super-virus?" someone said. Maybe it was me.

"A virus that is the 'offspring,' " she explained, "of two separate but combinant viruses."

"Wait a minute," I said. "You're saying that the vampire virus is actually the product of two separate viruses—and that these two viruses combine to change the host body to undead status?"

"Ah, a quick study, Mr. Csejthe." Bassarab steepled his fingers and turned back to Mooncloud. "So, you are suggesting that he received *one* of the two combinant strains through the transfusion. But not the other?"

She nodded.

I waved my arms, nearly dislodging my own IV's. "Wait a minute, wait a minute, here! I don't know a virus from a bacterium but I think I know enough about transfusions. As the donor, *I* might infect the count—"

"Prince," Bassarab corrected.

"What?"

"I was never a 'count,'" he elaborated, "but in the fevered imaginings of hack writers!"

"—but *he* shouldn't be able to infect me," I concluded with an apologetic nod to our rescuer.

"It was a messy business," Wren confessed with apparent discomfort.

"Aside from that," his "master" added, "vampire blood has some very unusual properties."

"That's true," Mooncloud seconded. "I've seen tainted blood cultures actually move toward untainted cultures on the same microscope slide—the platelets actually seeming to home in on whole, red cells."

"But are we talking about two separate viruses that work in concert, or two phases of the same virus as it mutates?" I asked.

"The first," Mooncloud said, "I think.

"You see, there are four basic effects of viral infection at the cellular level. Some viruses are *endosymbionts*, existing in a dormant state in the host cells. Some are *cytopathic*, killing the cells outright. *Hyperplastic* viruses act similarly, but they stimulate the host cells to divide before killing them. And then we have the *transformative* or mutative viruses that stimulate cells to divide in the same manner as hyperplastic viruses but, instead of killing the cells, they recombine with the cells' RNA and/or DNA to produce mutations in cellular growth and reproduction.

"While the final virus is a *transformative* virus, the two component viruses that combine to produce it are *hyperplastic* in nature. They survive only a short time outside of a vampiric host as they tend to destroy their host cells and eliminate their own habitat.

"Virus A, let's call it, infects the cells in the bloodstream and as those cells are killed off, they must be replaced with fresh host cells. This is one of the reasons that the transformed body of the vampire requires fresh blood regularly: infusions of living, uninfected, host cells for the virus.

"Virus B," she continued, growing excited as the pieces of evidence were finally falling into place, "is more theoretical as I have never been able to turn up cellular evidence in the lab. I always assumed that it was carried in the bloodstream like Virus A and that the lack of cellular evidence was due to an extremely accelerated gestation cycle: it reverted it to endosymbiotic status, making it impossible to find a few days or even hours after the initial infection.

"That's where I went wrong."

"And how is that, Doctor?" Our host seemed quite intrigued.

"Once Virus A and Virus B combine, they cease to exist within the bloodstream as separate entities. Virus A eventually returns in its separate form but not Virus B. When the super-virus enters its gestation cycle, it produces a new generation of 'A' and 'B' viruses—like a bisexual organism spewing out both eggs and sperm. Virus A settles into the bloodstream, but Virus B goes elsewhere to roost and wait."

"Where?" I demanded, getting a little fed up with her use of dramatic hesitation.

"The saliva?" Lupé guessed.

Mooncloud nodded.

"It's that simple?" I asked, shaking my head. "Because I wasn't bitten but came in contact with infected blood, I'm half a vampire? Then how come—"

"How come there aren't other instances of Virus A being transferred in the same way?" Mooncloud smiled. "It's theoretically possible. But stored blood would be much less likely to host the virus for any extended period of time. And transfusions with vampires, I suspect, are rare indeed."

I tried to image an occasion where a vampire would offer to donate blood. Failed.

Bassarab frowned. "But I have heard of viruses surviving for hundreds, even thousands of years—"

"*Some* viruses, sir. But the apparent difficulties of creating new vampires—even after repeated exchanges of blood and saliva—suggests that this virus is much less hardy than the host body that is its undead carrier."

"You are speaking of theories here, Doctor," Bassarab reminded her.

"True. But it fits all of the known data and answers a number of questions."

"But," he stroked his chin and turned to look at me, "in theory, then, I should be able to complete Mr. Csejthe's metamorphosis by biting him, now."

"Now hold on here," I said, easing back against the headboard.

"Only with your permission, of course," he added with a smile.

"Theoretically, yes. . . ." Mooncloud turned and looked at me with a speculative look that gave me chills.

"It would certainly go a long way toward proving your theory," Bassarab said.

"Yes. . ."

"No!" Lupé snarled. The hair on her forearms was standing up, and she was positively bristling.

"My, my, I am impressed," Bassarab remarked mildly. "Even though you are not fully transformed, you command great loyalty in your servitors."

"Mr. Csejthe has no servitors here," Mooncloud said icily.

He smiled. "You are joking. You would have me

believe—what?—that *you* are in charge of this mission?"

I leaned over and murmured to Lupé: "Define this for me—are we witnessing an exhibition of misogyny, racism, or some kind of multispecies/class superiority prejudice thing?"

She still bristled, but I saw the hint of a smile and a little of the tension seemed to ease from her trembling frame.

There was more of a smile on Dr. Mooncloud's face as she steepled her fingers and bit back. "Mr. Bassarab—or Vlad Tepes or Count Dracula or whoever you claim to be—I think the fact that we are allies," she smiled more broadly, "and you are certainly in need of allies these days, entitles us to a little more courtesy on your part."

While all of this was going on I was shaking off my emotional lethargy. My black pit of forgetfulness was unsealed now, and ugly memories were starting to crawl out.

"Allies? How dare you!" Bassarab was standing now, his long, pale features white with anger. "I am the Drakul, *Voivode* of Walachia and Warlord of the Transylvanian Unity! It was I who time and time again beat back the numberless hordes of Mongols, Turks, and Hungarians, winning victory after victory against insurmountable odds! My name is synonymous with terror, I have outlived my foes and their progeny even unto their great-great-grandchildren! I wield powers and forces that are unknown and unthinkable to mere mortals! I am deathless! To my enemies I am Death!"

"And yet," Mooncloud interrupted, "you are on the run from a carful of thugs."

"I have my reasons for my present actions. I owe you no explanations. I owe you nothing—except for Mr. Csejthe, whose blood-bond—"

"You owe me my wife and my little girl, you son-of-a-bitch!" I was halfway across the length of the bed of a sudden, IVs popping from my arm and whipping about the room. "I want them back! I want my life back!"

Lupé caught me, held me back. Had I not already been seriously weakened, even her lycanthropic strength would not have been able to restrain me.

"But you can't!" I panted. "They're dead and there's nothing you can do to bring them back!" I strained against Lupé's grasp. "So what good is your fucking blood bond to me . . . or. . ." To my own horror I sagged in her arms and began to weep.

The old vampire seemed to rise off the floor, spreading his cape wide like the unfolding wings of a great, ancient bat. "As Warlord I slew tens of thousands of my people's enemies. As *voivode* of the unliving and, later, as Doman of the New York demesne, I personally took hundreds more, thousands through the actions of those whom I made dark immortals. Blood is spilled, Mr. Csejthe, among the innocent as well as the guilty. I cannot feel an obligation to a victim each time I must feed. I owe nothing to any mortal, save Victor here, and he is well compensated for his service.

"But you and I, Christopher Csejthe, share a blood-bond for our life-forces have been mingled. And, according to the code that our society has adopted from necessity, I must take responsibility for you until such time that you are fully assimilated.

"And I am sorry for the loss of your wife and child: it was needless and served no purpose."

"But that happened after the blood-bond was forged," Mooncloud pounced, "so you are not without responsibility in the matter!"

Bassarab turned on her with a scowl. "Will you play the barracks lawyer with me, Doctor? Very well, let us split hairs and strain at gnats! If Mr. Csejthe is not truly *wampyr*, not fully undead, is the blood-bond fully in effect? If he is still mortal, then I owe him nothing and may do with him as pleases me!"

"Yeah?" I struggled to get past Lupé's arms and my

tears and was only half successful. "Come on! Float your candy-vampire-ass over here and take your best shot! We'll settle all debts right here and now!"

"Shut! Up!" Mooncloud yelled at me. "It was an accident, Chris! There is nothing that any of us here can do that will bring them back! And you!" she continued, rounding on Bassarab. "If you would pretend to be Vlad Drakul Bassarab, called Dracula, it would serve your little masquerade to remember than the *Voivode* of Walachia was a man of honor! Further victimizing this man will not serve his memory or help your cause! What we must do, here and now, is forge an alliance that will prove mutually beneficial, insure our mutual victory, and bring death and vengeance down upon our enemies! To accomplish that we must begin with a truce and a modicum of mutual respect!"

Bassarab lowered himself back into his chair. He still glowered as he turned to Dr. Mooncloud, but his lips twitched as if fighting a smile and there was a suspicion of respect in his voice as he spoke.

"Perhaps I was wrong about you, madam. I begin to believe that you may indeed be *voivode* and warlord in your own demesne."

Fifteen hours later we were back in Kansas City buying a new Ford Bronco. With cash.

"Who's Salmon P. Chase?" Lupé asked as she slid behind the steering wheel.

"Who?" I mumbled groggily. The infusion of blood by IV had helped a great deal, but I needed a good day's sleep. It was now eleven A.M. and my biological clock was insisting that it was hours past my bedtime.

"Salmon P. Chase. He wasn't a president. All the others were presidents."

I pushed the felt-brimmed fedora up off my face and adjusted my wraparound sunglasses against the glare of the midday sun outside the Bronco's tinted windows. "What are you talking about?"

"These bills. . . ." She fanned the thick stack of grey-green paper at me.

"Federal reserve notes," I corrected, "not 'bills.' "

"Look here," she continued, pulling individual notes from the stack. "William McKinley on the five-hundred-dollar bill, Grover Cleveland on the thousand. . ."

I yawned. Felt my incisors to see if they'd grown. Nada.

" . . . and here's James Madison on the five-thousand. All presidents."

"Ben Franklin's on the hundred-dollar bill," I said, studying my indistinct reflection in the vanity mirror on the passenger-side visor. Picture Indiana Jones trying to pose as a Secret Service agent. "He's not a president." The sunblock I had slathered on felt like ancient cold cream gone bad and starting to curdle. But . . . so far, so good: I hadn't burst into flame or started crumbling to dust, yet.

"Franklin I know," she retorted. "But this guy on the ten-thousand-dollar bill I never heard of." She turned the key in the ignition and the Bronco's engine growled into a purring idle.

Dr. Mooncloud tapped on my window and I lowered the glass. "Here's a list of the sporting goods dealers that carry crossbows," she said, handing me a list. "Victor and I have the other half of the list, and we'll meet you back at the motel as soon as we're done." She glanced over her shoulder. "Have you tried to call the Doman, yet?"

Lupé nodded. "Twice. Every time I get within ten feet of a telephone, I want to throw up!"

"Mental domination. It's like a post-hypnotic suggestion."

"Damn vampires and their mind control!" Lupé patted my hand. "Present company excepted."

"Well," Mooncloud said, "if you can think of anything else that will help, get it. Any questions?"

"Yeah," I said, jerking my thumb, "Lupé wants to know who Salmon P. Chase was."

The doctor frowned quizzically. "He was a lawyer, politician, and an antislavery leader before the American Civil War—three-term senator, governor of Ohio. Tried to win the Republican candidacy for president twice, and the Democratic candidacy once. He served as Secretary of the Treasury on Lincoln's war cabinet. He was instrumental in establishing a system of national banks that could issue notes as legal tender. Ended up being the fifth—no—sixth chief justice of the Supreme Court." She smiled. "Anything else?"

I shook my head. "Let's get this done so we can get back and get a little shut-eye."

She nodded and headed back over to the Duesenberg where Wren was waiting.

"Still seems a funny choice for a picture on the ten-thousand-dollar bill," Lupé muttered as she shifted gears and headed toward the lot's exit.

"She left out the part about him running against Lincoln," I said, leaning my seat back into a thirty-degree incline and pulling my hat back down over my face. "He put his own face on most of the denominations and the ten-thousand-dollar note as a campaign gimmick. The ten thousand is the sole survivor."

"How—"

"I watch a lot of *Jeopardy*."

"*Jeopardy*?"

"Call me old-fashioned and Trebek is fine, but he's not Art Fleming."

"I hate you now." I couldn't see her smile but I could hear it in her voice. "So, do you think he's legit?"

"Alex Trebek?" I grunted.

"Count Dracula. You know: Mr. Death to his many friends and admirers."

"Hmmp. For a servitor, you seem to be lacking the appropriately reverent tone in discussing a member of the Master Race. Particularly the Grand Prince of said race, himself."

"If himself he actually is."

"Does it really matter?"

"Well, it is a pretty incredible story: Dracula as head of the New York demesne. . . ."

In addition to claiming that he was *the* Count—excuse me, *Prince*—Dracula, our host had told us that he had ruled the New York demesne for over a century. Eventually, he explained, he had grown tired of the responsibilities: the intrigues, plots, the infighting. One of the factions had become involved with organized crime, opening a Pandora's box that even the self-styled Prince of Darkness found distasteful. There had been attempts on his life (or unlife, if you prefer) even by his own kind—the ancient tradition of advancement by assassination.

There had finally come a day, he'd explained, when he had grown weary of the games and decided to live free, once more.

Of course, one doesn't "retire" from a vampire enclave any more than one retires from certain covert governmental agencies or the Mafia. Especially if you are *the* Vlad Dracula.

"And so I had to disappear," he'd told me on the long, night drive back up to Kansas City. "I planned it very carefully, liquidating selected assets that had been accumulated over the centuries, preparing a dozen different safe-houses with sheltered networks of investments and income, hoarding equipment and supplies, building false identities and essentially creating a secret demesne for myself that would be as invisible to the other underground enclaves as they were to the world of mortals.

"And so, I reasoned, where would one look for the *Voivode* of Walachia, the Prince of Darkness, the king of the *wampyr*? London? Paris? Monaco? One of the world's great cities with a never-ending night life and millions of human cattle to hunt and hide among?

"Ah. Maybe someday. . . .

"But for awhile—and what are a few years when one has lived for centuries, may live for millennia?—it made sense to lie low and regroup where no one would think to look for the legendary Dracula.

"Kansas."

Now one might think that Count Dracula would stand out in the cornfields of Kansas like Liberace at a black tie and tails affair.

Especially since Liberace is no longer among the living.

But as Blowfeld once said to 007: "If I destroy Kansas, Mr. Bond, it will be two years before the rest of the world would notice that it's missing."

Well, it's not really quite that bad: hardly anyone really believes that Eisenhower is still president and a few of us have heard rumors that we might be putting a man into space almost any year now. But Kansas still provides the opportunity to drop out of the cultural and social mainstream if one so wishes, and neighbors tend to mind their own business. There are farmhouses adrift on vast tracts of fenced land where God-knows-what has gone on for generations. Don't get me wrong; Kansas is full of good-hearted, friendly, and even wonderfully wise and talented folk. . .

. . . but there are certain lonely dirt roads that you should hope to never run across by day and God help you should you run out of gas by night. The southeast corner of the Sunflower State has more than its share of tales murmured around campfires at night—stories of drifters and hitchhikers and pits and hungers and abandoned houses that weren't quite empty. . . . Away from the gatherings in the cities and towns, a man's privacy is respected and certainly never challenged without risk.

Bassarab had chosen carefully. And it had almost worked.

But some ancient wiring in an old Kansas farmhouse had nearly done what time and armies and assassins could not. And, even though he had survived the fire, there was something in the aftermath—a fireman's story, a hospital record, a police report, a newspaper article—that had been enough to flag the hunters back in New York. The privacy screen of eighty acres of fenced pasture land had failed.

When Mooncloud and Garou had turned up in Pittsburg, Kansas, it was to rope a stray and solve a medical mystery. New York's retrieval team had had a different agenda: I was their best clue to finding Dracula.

But now the hunters had become the hunted.

"Yes," I said to Lupé, "I think he actually is who he claims to be." I smiled, picking up the huge roll of bills from between the seats. "But, as I was saying before, it really wouldn't matter. He's providing us with everything we need to finish this mission and he solved the big mystery about my own circumstances and condition." I looked out the window. "And maybe given me a few ideas of my own. . . ."

The crossbows were easy.

We found a dealer who carried the Barnett International line from England. We started with six Trident models with single-hand pistol grips. Their forty-five-pound draw had an effective range of forty-five feet and would hurl a bolt approximately one hundred and twenty-two feet per second.

We then selected four Ranger models with a one-hundred-fifty-pound draw and a bolt speed of two-hundred and thirty feet per second.

Lupé was comparing the Desert Storm model for its additional ten yards of range and ten feet per second bolt speed when I noticed a unique-looking rifle with a spear protruding from the muzzle.

"It's an Air Bow," the dealer explained, noting my interest. "Uses liquid carbon dioxide or compressed air as a propellant and has a muzzle velocity of two-hundred and twenty FPS. There's a fishing attachment that puts fifty feet of seventy-pound braided line onto a barrel-mounting reel and attaches to a special fishing arrow.

And you can get a twelve-gram quick-change unit that will give you extra shots and make changing your propellant bottles quick and easy."

"I'll take the rifle and the quick-change unit," I said, "but I don't think I'll need the fishing stuff." I tried to imagine reeling in a vampire once I had nailed him. Ugh.

"As you wish. Is there anything else I can help you with?"

I nodded. "I notice all bolts and quarrels are primarily aluminum or plastic. Do you have any wooden ones?"

"A few. But I think you'll find the aluminum ones perform just as well and hold up a lot better—especially with repeated use out in the field."

"Oh," I said casually, Lupé watching me like a hawk, "I prefer wood. Especially ash, if you have any."

He shook his head. "No ash. But I can call a couple of places in town that specialize for archery tournaments."

While he did that, I picked out a couple of Splatmaster Rapide Semi-Automatic paint pistols, a Spartan Paintball rifle, twelve tubes of paintballs, and five dozen CO2 cartridges. "What do you think you're doing?" Lupé hissed as I dumped our additional purchases on the counter.

"Trust me," I said, as the shopkeeper came back with an address.

"They may be able to help you with ash dowels for your bolts," he said. "Will there be anything else?"

"Well, we'd like carrying cases and four belt-mounted quivers. . . ."

Lupé grinned wolfishly and leaned across the counter. "And we'd like all of these outfitted with your best hunting scopes."

Two hours later we were ready to head south, loaded down with two additional compound bows, seventy-three ash dowels, six fletching kits, five hypodermic syringes, four bottles of solvent, two bicycle tire repair kits, five knapsacks, four handbags, and two dozen small glass bottles.

"Pull over," I said.

Lupé looked up at the cathedral as she parked at the curb. "You don't need to do this," she said. "Taj already has it on her list."

"I want to try something and if it works, we're going to need more." I opened the door and stepped out onto the curb. "This shouldn't take long."

The sunlight seemed to hit me with a palpable force and I felt vaguely nauseated as I climbed the stone-blocked steps that stretched across the front of the church. At the top I hesitated, realizing that I hadn't really spent enough time thinking this one out.

For openers: did the "welcome" sign constitute an invitation to cross the threshold, to enter? Of course it did—but in terms of a personal invitation? To a vampire? Or half a vampire? Maybe a halfway invitation was sufficient for a halfway undead person.

Or did I really require an invitation at all?

What would Freud say?

Never mind that: what would the pope say?

I took a deep breath and reached for the door. My real discomfort in entering, I decided, had nothing to do with vampire lore and possibly being in a state of damnation. It had to do with the simple fact that I was Protestant.

Though I had certain Catholic friends who would delight in pointing out that there is no real difference between being damned for eternity or being Protestant, my main concern was that I didn't know my way around a Catholic church. Fortunately, the object of my quest was not far from the entryway: the marble font containing water consecrated for ceremonial use.

It should have been easy: the coast was clear, no one was around. But now it occurred to me that there was no way for me to dip the bottles into the basin of holy water without getting my fingers wet. And I hadn't thought to buy gloves.

I am not Catholic, so holy water is not part of my

belief system, I told myself. *Furthermore, I am a rational man: I know that there is no scientific principle to support holy water having any different qualities than regular water. I know that it cannot harm me. . . .*

Yeah, right, answered the other half of the Csejthe stream-of-consciousness debate team, *just like you rationally know that vampires don't exist.*

But there's a scientific principle involved in creating vampires. . . .

Maybe, but can you explain werewolves, Binky?

This was getting me nowhere. Very gingerly, I dipped the tip of my little finger into the basin of holy water. No pain, no smoke, no bubbling froth, no dissolving flesh.

As quickly as I could, I filled four bottles and made my escape.

"Now where?" Lupé asked as I climbed back into the passenger seat.

"Another Catholic church," I said, swapping full bottles for empties. "I figure we'll need to hit five more cathedrals or kidnap a priest."

"Wonderful."

As we spent the next hour collecting *aqua sacra,* I was troubled by the question of why it didn't affect me. Was it because I wasn't a believing, practicing member of the Catholic faith? Or because I was not yet fully transformed into an undead creature and wholly damned? Perhaps it was because, as a rational man, I was immune to the superstitious influence and power of my subconscious mind?

Or maybe this stuff just wasn't all it was cracked up to be. . . .

Chapter Sixteen

"What is that?" Mooncloud had opened the motel room door and maneuvered two crutch-steps into the room when she noticed that I was pointing an odd-looking handgun at her.

"It's a Splatmaster Rapide Semi-Automatic paint pistol," I answered, studying her through the weapon's three-power, cross-haired scope. "It's used in war games and fires paintballs for marking hits on human targets."

"I know what it's used for," she snapped, standing perfectly still. "Why are you pointing it at me?"

"This is a test," I answered. "This is only a test. . . ." I pulled the trigger. *Pffthok:* the paintball left a ragged wet mark on her slacks, just above her right knee.

"What did you do that f—" She stopped in midroar and reexamined the stain. "It's not paint."

I shook my head. "It's water."

"Water?"

"Tap water."

"Tap water?"

"For the test." I holstered the pistol and sat back down in front of the cluttered desk. "It's very simple, though a bit time consuming. I took a paintball and used a syringe to suck out all of the paint. Then I used another syringe to inject the tap water. Finally, I used a wee bit of sealant to plug the leak and—*voilà*!"

"And, instead of tap water," she guessed, "you plan to reload your paintballs with holy water." Her smile fell a little short of amazed admiration, but she said, "How clever you are, my dear Christopher. Excuse me while

I get a towel." She turned on her crutches and went back outside.

"I don't think that was such a good idea," Lupé remarked from the bed. "Nor very sporting considering her broken leg."

"Aah, it was good for her. . . ." I picked up a virgin paintball and inserted the hypodermic needle. "The doc needs a little loosening up. And she can hardly argue with the effectiveness of my little demonstration." The door opened behind me. "Right, Doc?"

"Granted, it's a novel approach," I heard her say as I excavated the paint from the plastic spheroid. "But one should always apply the KISS criteria when attempting any approach to a problem."

"Kiss?" Lupé wanted to know.

"Yeah, K-I-S-S," I said, squirting the paint back out of the syringe and into the plastic lined wastebasket. "It stands for 'Keep It Simple, Stupid.'"

"You said it," Lupé laughed, "not me."

I looked up and saw Mooncloud's reflection in the mirror that hung above my desk. She was leaning on the armrests of her crutches and brandishing a toy rifle outfitted with green and yellow plastic tanks and a tangle of connecting tubes.

"The Super Hoser Ten-Thousand-S," Mooncloud explained, "has a full tank capacity of nearly four-and-one-half gallons. It can shoot a continuous stream of water nearly forty feet for a duration of eight seconds per burst."

"Where did you get that?" I asked, turning very slowly and trying not to make any sudden moves.

"Kiddie Kastle. There was a sale on all squirt guns and water pistols." She smiled and slide-cocked the damn thing. "This is a test," she said.

I dived out the chair, rolled once, and then threw my superhuman reflexes into jumping up and running for the bathroom.

I almost made it.

* * *

Bassarab's timely rescue and financial backing had given us a momentary shot of confidence. False confidence, perhaps, as one of our foes had survived staking and decapitation: all our high-tech firepower might not mean a thing when our paths crossed again. After loading a dozen paintballs with holy water, I pulled out my laptop computer.

The database on vampire legends was growing and the list of remedies becoming more complex and contradictory. Still, there was something that tugged at the back of my mind—some foreign bit of fable that resonated to our most recent encounter.

I finally found it under the Malaysian grouping. "Here we go," I announced. Mooncloud came over and adjusted the screen for a better look.

"What's it say?" Garou asked from the chair she had aligned with the failing air conditioner.

"According to this," Mooncloud said, "there are a number of Malayan legends and stories that tie in to the vampire mythos. You've isolated seven different manifestations: the *polong*, *bâjang*, *pëlësit*, *langsuir*, *mati-anak* or *pontianak*, and the *pênanggalan*."

"That's it," I said, "the last one."

She studied the information. "The *pênanggalan's* head separates from its body and goes flying off in search of its prey. After it feeds its head returns to its body before sunrise."

"Sounds like our boy."

She scrolled down the text and frowned. "Maybe not. Look here: the head leaves the body voluntarily and strands of guts and entrails dangle down from its neck while it flies about. Don't remember voluntary and I don't remember guts."

"Maybe."

She hit the PAGE DOWN key then scrolled backwards a half screen. "Here's more. *Pênanggalans* are always female, never male."

"Who knows what gender this thing is."

"And, finally, the biggest telling difference: the *pênanggalan's* body remains inert."

"Inert?"

"Inanimate—totally helpless—until the head returns to rejoin the body at the neck. We saw this thing running away with its head tucked under its arm."

"Well, if it's not a *pênanggalan*, then what is it?"

She shrugged.

"Look, up until now I've bought into this RNA/DNA, Virus A-Virus B, and Recombinant Virus C crap. But no amount of medical biobabble can explain a thing that can get its head chopped off and then gallop off like some refugee from a Washington Irving story!"

"Yet, you have seen it and you do know that it exists," she snapped back. "So, like it or not, you've got to deal with its existence!"

"And find a way to kill it," Lupé added.

"If it can be killed."

"Oh, it can be killed."

I looked at Lupé. "You're so sure?"

"We'll run down the list. If necessary," she bared her teeth, "we'll experiment."

I sighed and pressed a sequence of keystrokes. "Okay, from the top. We start with Albania and the *sampiro*. The approved method of disposal: a stake through the heart."

"Next," Garou called from her chair.

"Ashantiland," I read. "Species: *asanbosam*. Method of disposal: unknown."

"Unknown? You're sure?"

"Hey, I've had just enough time to scratch the surface, here. Check back with me after six months of intensive research and I might have a few more answers. Which brings us to the Austrian *vampyre*. My notes indicate that we must read scripture while destroying all images or portraits of that thing and be sure to use pentagrams in the process."

"What does that mean?" Mooncloud pondered.

"Sounds like we should take some Polaroids the next time we run into that creepy bastard," Garou said.

"And pentagrams?"

I shrugged. "I'm the novice here. I just transcribe the information. I leave analysis to the people with actual field experience."

"Next."

"Bavaria: *nachtzehrer*. Place coin in mouth, decapitate with ax."

"The coin sounds like a modification of old burial practices," Mooncloud said. "I doubt if it would have made any difference."

"Which brings us to Bohemia and the *ogoljen*. Best bet: bury at crossroads."

"*Real* practical," Garou mused. "I can just see the two of us holding that thing down while you rent a jackhammer and tear up the intersection at First and Main. Next."

"British Columbia: the *kwakiytl*. Means of disposal: any."

"Obviously not our man."

I paged down. "Two different species from Brazil: the *jaracaca* and the *lobishomen*. Both fit in the unknown category. Two more from Bulgaria: the *krvoijac* and the *obours*. To dispose of the first you must chain it to its grave with wild roses—"

"Ah, days of vine and roses. . . ."

I ignored Garou and continued: "The second requires witchcraft, burning, or bottling."

"Bottling?"

"Highly unlikely, totally impractical, and I'll explain later if you insist," Mooncloud said. "Keep going, Chris."

"Well, that throws out the *polong* of Malaysia, as well: my notes say it must be caught in bottle of special dimensions."

Garou muttered something that sounded suspiciously like, "I'd rather have a bottle in front of me than a frontal lobotomy." I kept going.

"China: the *p'o*. Lightning strike or burn the body to ashes."

"He didn't look Chinese," Garou offered.

"Chinese vampires are actually demons and don't resemble anything human in the least," Mooncloud explained. "Next to a *p'o*, our boy looks like Norman Normal."

"Crete: *kathakano*. Boil head in vinegar."

"Gee," Garou said, "I wish we'd known that the night before last."

"Denmark," I continued, "the *mara*. Use knife blade which has been blessed and/or consecrated."

"Maybe we should check this thing's passport."

"Maybe you should take this business a little more seriously," Mooncloud admonished.

I looked up and saw the color drain from Lupé's face. "You think I don't want this thing dead?" she said through clenched teeth. "Come up with a plan and I'll carry it out." She got up and walked to the door. "This thing tore Luis apart and I've sworn a blood oath to kill it! I'm not afraid to die trying, if that's what it takes! Perhaps it is the rest of you who should be taking this a little more seriously!" She walked out and slammed the door.

Mooncloud looked at the ground. I stared down at the LCD display. After awhile I began reading again.

"Greece: the *brukulaco*. Cut off the head and burn it. Also native to Greece, the *vrykolakas*. Celebration of mass followed by disinterment—remove heart and burn with incense, fill mouth with holy water."

Mooncloud made no reply, so I kept going. "Germany: *drakul*. Place coin in mouth, cut name from shirt, break corpse's neck, pin to ground with stake, burn body to ashes."

Still no response.

"Grenada: the *loogaroo*. Method of disposal: unknown. Guinea: the *owenga*—also unknown."

Mooncloud finally spoke. "How many on your list are unknowns when it comes to disposal?"

"Let me resort." I pressed keys and a new list appeared:

Species/(Country)	*Method of Disposal*
Otgiruru (Hereros Land)	Unknown
Baital-Pachisi (India)	Unknown
Bhût (India)	Unknown
Hánh Sàburo (India)	Unknown
Hánt-Pare (India)	Unknown
Hántu-Dor Dong (India)	Unknown
Jigar-Khor (India)	Unknown
Mah'ânah (India)	Unknown
Pênangal (India)	Unknown
Pisâchâs (India)	Unknown
Rákshasa (India)	Unknown
Vetala (India)	Unknown
Civateteo (Mexico)	Unknown
Bruxsa (Portugal)	Unknown
Baobhan Sith (Scotland)	Unknown
Vampiro (Spain)	Unknown

Mooncloud whistled as she followed the rising list. "If our quarry is any of these, we're screwed. What's left?"

I did a quick count. "Twenty-seven, counting the *pênanggalan*. But I think we can also eliminate the *mau mau* of Kenya, the *ramanga* of Madagascar, the *pëlësit* of Malaysia, and the *moroii* of Rumania—apparently they can be dealt with as if they were ordinary human beings." I squinted at the display. "Although it is recommended that the *pëlësit* be buried with a cat when the process is concluded."

"How many left on the list require incineration?"

I rekeyed the list into another subfile.

Species/(Country)	*Method of Disposal*
Pamgri (Hungary)	Burn body to ashes

Vampir (Magyar)	Stake through heart, burn body
Romanati (Rumania)	Body removed to remote place, hacked into pieces and cast in fire where every piece of flesh and bone must be incinerated
Vieszcy (Russia)	Destruction by fire or execution with a gravedigger's shovel
Vlkoslak (Serbia)	Cut off toes, drive nail through neck. Burn body to ashes

"Fire sounds like our best bet but I noticed a couple of variations on the stake method. How many other listings suggest some form of nailing or impaling?"

I opened and processed another subfile.

Species/(Country)	*Method of Disposal*
Oupire (Hungary)	Iron bar through heart, decapitate with ax
Vampir (Hungary)	Stake through heart, nail through temples
Vryolakas (Macedonia)	Pour boiling oil on, drive nail through navel
Pênanggalan (Malaysia)	Impale head on Jenyu leaves, destroy body or keep head and body separate for 24 hours
Strigoiul (Rumania)	Remove heart, cut in two; garlic in mouth, nail in head
Zârne ti (Rumania)	Iron forks driven through the heart,

	eyes, and breast of an exhumed female vampire; grave considerably deepened and corpse buried face downwards
Upierczi (Russia)	Appear from noon to midnight only; oaken stake through the heart with just one blow; exorcism

"All right, what's left?"

"Mostly preventative burial measures." I opened another subfile.

Species/(Country)	*Method of Disposal*
Dearg-dul (Ireland)	Pile stones on grave
Langsuir (Malaysia)	Hair and nails must be cut short and clippings stuffed into hole in back of neck
Mati-Anak or *Pontianak* (Malaysia)	Put hen's egg under each armpit, needle in palm of hand, glass beads in mouth, use charm
Upier (Poland)	Bury face downwards with willow crosses under chin, armpits, and chest; decapitate, mix blood with flour to make bread that frees victims once eaten
Gierach (Prussia)	Put poppy seeds in grave
Neuntoter (Saxony)	Bury with lemon in mouth

"Sounds like immolation is our best bet. Anything left?"

I scanned the remaining notations.

Species/(Country)	*Method of Disposal*
Mulé (Gypsy)	Ambush with thorns and gun
Bâjang (Malaysia)	Drowning
Vârcolac (Rumania)	Breaking the thread they climb on to banish them to another part of the sky
Vampyre (Yugoslavia)	Rituals performed by *dhampir*

"*Dhampir*," I mused. "I wonder what a *dhampir* is and if we could get in touch with one?"

"Unlikely," Bassarab answered, giving us a start. "The *dhampir* is the son of a vampire. I know of only three who still might be living and none of them reside in this hemisphere, much less this country."

I eyed the door behind him, wanting to ask how he'd managed to enter without our noticing. I imagined mist pouring through a keyhole and decided not to raise the question.

"The sun is down." Bassarab unlocked the door and opened it with a flourish: it squeaked noticeably. "It is time to travel."

A quiet, smooth ride is the last thing one expects from an automobile over sixty years old. But Bassarab's '31 Duesenberg glided over the uncertain surface of US 69 like a ghost, the silken response of suspension and the purr of the antique V-12 motor giving the lie to the speedometer's insistence that we were topping eighty miles an hour.

Even more hair-raising was the fact that we were

doing this in complete darkness: it was a moonless night with nothing but empty fields to either side of the highway and the only light emanating from the car were the tiny LEDs indicating that the radar detector was on and sweeping the road ahead for county mounties.

Lupé, following behind in the Ford Bronco, had also extinguished her headlights, but where she had the advantage of night vision similar to my own, Victor had to wear a light-amplification device that looked like a cross between a starlight scope and virtual reality headgear. It was not a reassuring sight and I made sure my seat belt was securely buckled.

We had just passed *La Cygnes* Lake and off to our left was *Marais des Cygnes* Massacre Park, commemorating the mass murder of Free-staters by Confederate sympathizers. A few miles ahead, just past Pleasanton, would be the Mine Creek battlefield. A land rich in the heritage of violence. I thought about the bloody footnote we were about to contribute to that history and tried not to feel overweening pride.

"What the hell am I doing here?" I whispered.

Bassarab stared straight ahead, his face cloaked in shadow. "You are fighting back. As every man must who would rule those about him."

"I don't have the slightest interest in ruling anyone," I said.

"Then you will be ruled. A man either rules those about him or they, in turn, will rule him."

"I don't believe that."

"Then you are a fool. A man may hold another's fate in his own grasp and then grant the other the 'gift' of choice. But he must first have mastery if he is to have his own freedom."

"'He is weakened by every recruit to his banner,'" I murmured; "'Is not a man better than a town?'"

"Your Emerson had the truth of it. His essay on self-reliance would have served me well when I was *Voivode* of Walachia."

"But is a prince and warlord really free of obligation?" I asked. "As a ruler, isn't there a plethora of responsibilities to those you rule?"

He bowed his head. The silence was so long that I felt the question had been dismissed. And then he spoke.

"I was born in an uncivilized time, in a primitive province, and raised to the throne under savage circumstances. By modern standards my people were barbarians. We were civilized only by comparisons to those who wished to enslave us. There was only one way to resist the armies and provinces that surrounded and outnumbered and sought to master us; we had to conquer such barbarians by becoming even more barbaric than they."

He raised his head and looked at me. "And it worked. Time and again we turned back the invaders with inferior forces. Armies that should have overwhelmed us, engulfed us, slaughtered us to a man—fled, Mr. Csejthe! Turned tail and ran! Killed each other to get away! And do you know why?"

"They feared you," I said.

"Feared me? My own people feared me and I was their protector! What the Turks and Mongols felt at the mere mention of my name was beyond terror! For many, beyond sanity: the rumor of my arrival was enough to cause husbands to slay their wives, mothers their children, warriors to cut their own throats! Only death offered mercy and true safety from the unspeakable cruelties of the Devil's own son!

"My hands," he said, lifting them like black claws in the darkness, "were stained with the blood of hundreds, thousands of acts of unnecessary cruelty! Unnecessary except that it put overwhelming forces to rout and saved my country when nothing else could!

"All of the unspeakable tortures and deaths by impalement, all these horrors committed while I was still a mere mortal, heir to the life and frailties of flesh and blood, were for my people. Do you think I burned my own people alive for my own enjoyment? Do you believe that I erected a forest of bodies on stakes and poles to win the admiration of anyone? My most loyal officers, even my own family, plotted against me even while I was staining my hands and my very soul to preserve them against enemies who could not otherwise be defeated!

"So do not presume to question whether I understand the responsibilities of a ruler! I know better than any man what obligations, what debts crouch in the dark nights of the heart like deranged and leprous beggars!"

"And . . . New York?" I prompted when the silence had grown long, again.

"I was the fool then," he answered bitterly. "I had been a prince. I thought to be one again. But with the passing of the centuries I had forgotten the responsibilities of sovereignty and remembered only the glory. And with the passing of time, the world had changed, and I had changed, as well.

"But not in the same directions. . . .

"Savagery remains, Mr. Csejthe. But it is a subtle, artful savagery now. The barbarians at the gate wear three-piece suits and sport fifty-dollar manicures. Warlords no longer defend countries and provinces but little plots of land designated as 'turf.' Their kingdoms have boundaries and borders that run down the middle of neighborhood streets and cut through the centers of playgrounds, parking lots, and old tenement buildings. Tribute is paid in pharmaceuticals and stolen goods.

"And honor . . . bah!"

"What about honor?" I asked.

"The strong will ever prey upon the weak," he answered quietly. "But there are those who cannot drink from the well without poisoning it for others. Who cannot take their needful prey without savaging half the flock and scattering the rest. When one is *voivode*, he cultivates his allies and makes war upon his enemies. He does not confuse the two. He demands tribute from those he conquers but does not destroy his own possessions once they are in his hands. . . ." He stared out the window.

I cleared my throat. "Speaking of allies, why won't you let us contact the Doman of Seattle?"

"He is not my ally."

"But I don't believe Pagelovitch is your enemy, either. And since New York seems to be your mutual enemy, isn't that grounds for an alliance?"

He brooded over that. "I have my reasons," he said finally.

"But couldn't you let Dr. Mooncloud telephone, just to let him know that we're all right?"

He shook his head.

"He wouldn't have to know anything about you or where we are. Just a simple message saying we're alive and well. How could—"

"No! As I said, I have my reasons."

"And I have my concerns."

"Your only concern, right now, should be about what you are here to do."

"Yeah? Well, why don't you make it easy on me: just what am I here to do?"

He stared at me. "My mistake was walking away without cutting off the head of the serpent that had plotted to take my place. I had assumed they would leave me alone once I had left New York for them to squabble over as they saw fit. I had forgotten that your enemies are not only whom you say they are, but whom *they* say they are, as well."

"And my enemies?"

"Whom do you say they are?" he asked mildly.

"Why should I have enemies? I've done nothing to anyone."

"Mortal men are your enemies: they'll hunt you down and dissect you if they think your body holds the secret of eternal life. The *wampyr* are your enemy: they'll hunt you down and destroy you if they think your existence poses a threat to their own secret existence. The Doman of Seattle will add you to his stable of kept creatures. The Doman of New York will take you apart to learn your secrets and hope that you can tell them where to find me. If you would live free, then all of these are your enemies."

"Swell." We were past the town of Prescott and nearing Fulton; Fort Scott was maybe ten or fifteen minutes ahead. "So, if they're all my enemies, I'm back to my original question: what am I doing here?"

Dracula turned and, as he looked at me, I felt a palpable force flow emanating from his eyes. "Serve me in this task and I will reward you with what you want most."

"And what is that?" I asked, fighting to keep my will independent from any external control.

"Your freedom. The opportunity to live your life on your own terms."

"Why?"

"Why do I do this? Because of the blood-bond. Because we both want the same thing."

"No, I mean: why does Dracula need the help of anyone else, particularly a man who is not fully *wampyr*?"

Before he could answer, the CB radio mounted under the Duesenberg's dashboard crackled to life.

"Breaker eleven, breaker eleven," Lupé's voice announced, *"this is the wolf calling the bat. You got your ears on, good buddy?"*

Bassarab scowled and Wren reached over for the mike with an ill-disguised smirk. "This is the bat, pretty mama; come back."

"He's sounding," she answered, barely waiting for the invitation to talk. *"I can hear him—faint, but up ahead!"*

"Who's sounding?" Bassarab wanted to know. Victor relayed the question into the microphone.

"Luath!" she cried, the volume of her voice distorting the words. *"He's still on the trail! And I can still hear him!"*

I looked at Bassarab. "The *cu sith*," I said.

Bassarab nodded, a thoughtful expression on his long, ancient face. "To answer your last question," he said slowly, "I need you because I suspect that the task before us will be more difficult than Dr. Mooncloud and her associate may imagine. That, to achieve our goals, both of us will have to die. . . ."

A sign flashed past, proclaiming Fort Scott was just another five miles up the road.

"My God," I whispered, "it's the old Tremont House."

The building was located at the corner of State and Wall Streets, at the north end of town and just a mile from the historic landmark that gave the town of Fort Scott its name. Three stories high, it had a mustard-colored, stucco-over-brick exterior that looked younger and newer under the actinic wash of the streetlamps. Closer inspection revealed that it had been closed up for a long time. The boards over the windows and across the doors looked as old and weathered as the wood frames they were nailed across.

Over its one-hundred-and-twenty-some year history it had served the city as a grand hotel and housed a variety of businesses, including the Eagles Lodge, the People's College, and a Greyhound bus depot. According to local rumor it had even been a bordello back in the sixties.

Now it was daynest for the undead.

We parked at the end of the block and gazed back up the hill. "So, what's the plan?" I asked as we huddled between the Bronco and the Duesenberg.

Everyone looked at me.

"Well, do we go in and get them or wait for them to come out?" This wasn't really such a stupid question, was it?

"I will need a closer look," Bassarab announced abruptly. He pulled at his black duster, wrapping the long coat around himself like a cape, and strode up the street.

"A reconnoiter is definitely called for," Lupé agreed, and began disrobing. A moment later a large, grey canine form was loping toward the hillside nest in Bassarab's wake.

Mooncloud crutched over to me while Wren opened the rear boot on the Duesenberg. She whispered: "I don't like this."

"Hey," I said, "we're about to attack a bunch of immortal creatures who can't be killed or even hurt in most of the conventional ways, who are superhumanly strong and highly motivated to kill and hurt us back—what's not to like?"

"I'm talking about Bassarab," she hissed, pulling on my arm. We moved away from Wren as he began unloading equipment.

"What are you complaining about? I'm the one who had to ride with him."

She pulled me farther away. "This mission is possibly the most difficult and dangerous one I've ever undertaken and that was before these guys—" she jerked her head toward the antique auto "—came along and complicated everything."

"As I remember it, we'd lost our transportation, our weapons, our equipment, supplies, and pretty much our self-respect before these guys came along. I should think you would feel a little more gratitude, Doctor."

She turned away, her arms stiff against the metal tubing of the crutches, and grunted. "He won't permit us to contact Stefan. He insists that we do things his way. And he won't discuss strategy with us until the last minute. And maybe not even then." She turned back to me. "I don't trust him, Chris. Even if he is who he says he is. Maybe I trust him even less if he is the real Dracula." She grasped my arm. "I've sworn my allegiance to Pagelovitch—no one else. And the Doman has always allowed me to run my missions my way. I won't take responsibility for the lives at risk, otherwise." She glanced back at Wren. "So if and when push comes to shove, you're gonna have to decide."

"Decide what?"

"Whether you take orders from him or from me. If I give the signal, Lupé will neutralize Wren and I'll take down Bassarab myself. I hope I can count on you."

"To take orders from you?"

She looked at my face and was not reassured. "You'd side with him?"

"What if I side with me?" I asked quietly. "What if I decide to follow some orders of my own?"

"Chris, he's the one responsible for your condition! Directly or indirectly, he's the cause of your wife and daughter's deaths!"

"You're missing the point." Now it was my turn to steer her a few feet farther from the Wren. "That day I drove through Weir and saw a column of smoke—well, it was the last day that my life was my own. I was *summoned* into that barn. And ever since that moment, I've been sleepwalking through an ongoing nightmare."

"We've tried to help—"

"Oh, yeah!" I snapped. "I was abducted, kept under house arrest, and basically told how my life was going to be from now on!"

"I thought you understood the reasons for—"

"Your reasons," I said harshly, "not mine. I'm not ungrateful and I do understand the necessities as you and the others saw them. But I'm through taking orders. From now on, I'll cooperate when it's the obvious and meaningful thing to do." I curled my fingers into a fist. "But it's my life," I said, thumping my chest. "Such as it is. And it's long past time for me to start taking responsibility for it again."

The gesture was obviously meant to be conciliatory. But, as she laid her hand upon my arm, I felt a surge of resentment. "We need you, Chris. And you need us." A sense of manipulation there. "Think of the research—"

"Since you are so fond of research, Doctor, let's try something right now. Look in my eyes."

"What?" She looked up at me, startled but unafraid.

"I'm a member of the Master Race now. Maybe a half-breed bastard by analogy, but definitely something beyond human." I smiled, feeling hollow. I looked into her eyes, forbidding her to look away. "You, Taj, are merely human."

A puzzled frown tugged at her lips and forehead. "Why are you talking this way?"

I swallowed, the taste of ashes was in my mouth. "Kiss my feet."

"What?"

"It's very simple, Doctor: I want you to get down on your knees and kiss my feet."

The frown was fully formed, but her eyes were still clear. "And why should I do such a thing?"

"Why? Because I command you," I said in a reasonable tone. And all the while forced the image of her compliance to the forefront of my thoughts. "You will obey me because I wish it. Because your will is no longer yours, but mine."

"I-I don't understand. . . ." Now there were clouds gathering in her eyes. She trembled a bit.

"It's not important that you understand, Taj. It's only important that you obey me. Kiss my feet."

"I don't want to." Her voice was shaky and her eyes were starting to unfocus.

"It doesn't matter what you want, my dear. It only matters what I want." I pushed at the image in my mind, made the mental image of Mooncloud drop to her knees. "Get down on the sidewalk and kiss my feet."

The woman in front of me slid the crosspieces from under her arms and, gripping the stems of the crutches, lowered herself to one knee. "No," she whispered.

"Yes." I pushed the mental image further, felt the bile rise in my throat. "Do it!"

The other knee came down. "Please," she whispered. The crutches clattered to the ground on each side of her.

"I can make you do it," I said. "You can't resist my will."

"Please. . . ." She was swaying on her knees and

suddenly fell forward, arms rigid and hands splayed, catching herself before her face landed on the sidewalk.

"Taj," I said, speaking gently but holding the command in unyielding mental subjugation, "say 'uncle.'"

"It's the virus," she grunted through clenched teeth. "It's already begun to affect your mind—your personality—"

That wasn't the reason I was doing it, but I released her, anyway.

"You bastard!" she said, red-faced and struggling to pull herself back up on her crutches. "What the hell did you do to me?"

"Research, Doctor. Vampires are supposed to have the power to cloud men's minds, to dominate another's will. To bind mental slaves and hold them in thrall. I wanted to see if I could do it. I think I can." I easily intercepted the slap aimed for my face, held her wrist in my grasp. "Do you agree or do I need to repeat the experiment and carry it out to an undeniable conclusion?"

"Yes, damn you!" Her eyes were no longer clouded; the fear was gone, replaced by anger.

"Hell of thing, research," I remarked, still holding her wrist in my grasp. "And a hell of thing when people can control you, make your decisions for you." I released her wrist. "Well, what have we learned here, Doctor? I've learned that my brain chemistry is, indeed, changing. What have you learned?" I turned and walked back toward the Duesenberg.

"I thought we were friends, Csejthe," she called to my back.

I stopped. "I thought we were friends, too," I said quietly. "But tonight I realized that you would still be my keeper." I walked on over to the Duesenberg and found Bassarab already returned and in conversation with his chauffeur.

"Problem?" he asked as I approached.

"Nothing I can't handle," I said. "Didn't notice your return."

He shrugged dismissively. "Didn't want you to." He looked about. "Where is the lycanthrope?"

My turn to shrug. "I don't know, I'm not her keeper." My temper was short tonight.

"You need to remedy that."

And getting shorter. But before I could open my mouth, Lupé trotted up.

"Black limo and tan Chevy van parked on the side street to the west. Arkansas plates on the van." The wolf paused, lifting her hind leg to scratch at something behind her ear. "No loose boards on the ground level. Try checking the fire escape."

"And only one is presently home," Bassarab added. "The rats say that he may be sleeping. I think that we can take this one easily enough and then await the return of the others." He buckled on a belt and scabbard. A richly ornamented sword hilt protruded from the wooden sheath. "Come. Let us hasten before the others return."

I hoisted a miniature flamethrower up and onto my back while Victor helped fasten the shoulder harness across my chest. Burning—burning should work. Of course, so should decapitation and a stake through the heart. So buckling on a web-belt with twin holsters was not really a matter of overkill: the two Splatmaster Rapide Semi-Automatic paint pistols that I slid into their leather scabbards were a logical if less than reassuring precaution under the circumstances. When I looked up, Mooncloud was cocking her second crossbow and Wren was loading the airbow with a fresh CO_2 cartridge. A barbed spear with an ash shaft was just showing at the barrel's opening, already locked into firing position. Over his shoulder was a bag filled with wooden stakes. Lupé was going empty-handed as she hadn't any. Hands, that is: she had elected to remain in wolf form.

"Follow me and move quietly," Bassarab ordered. "I will go in first, followed by Victor, and then Mr. Csejthe. Doctor, your crutches will be a liability in close quarters.

You will remain outside to help the wolf-bitch guard the outer perimeter."

Lupé growled softly.

"Rats, huh?" I said as we started down the street toward the ancient structure. "The rats told you how many people are in the building and what they're doing?"

Bassarab nodded.

"Telepathy, right?"

Bassarab nodded again.

"Boy am I just brimming with confidence, now."

"And why is that?" Lupé rumbled.

"Because," I murmured, "they always say: 'It's not just *what* you know but *who* you know that counts.'"

"Mr. Csejthe. . ." Bassarab remarked.

"Yes?"

" . . . shut up."

Chapter Seventeen

I saw Michael Jordan once. It was at a Bulls game in Chicago—back during his first basketball career when he could defy gravity like nothing I'd ever seen.

But tonight that memory was fully eclipsed and I had seats up front and center court.

Air Dracula.

The old man took two brisk steps and flung himself into the night sky. The fire escape was at least twelve feet above the broken sidewalk and he caught the top railing coming down. That was the first miracle. The second was that it didn't come crashing down: the rusted out remains of iron grillwork hung lopsidedly from the second story and its drop-down ladder had long since dropped down and disappeared. Silently, he scrambled over and into the boxy metal basket like some great condor returned to its stony nest. Then he locked his feet through gaps in the ironwork and hung downward, extending his hands to us.

I boosted Wren up to where his master could pull him the rest of the way and then made my own leap. I made it without too much effort, the major difference being that I had to grab hold on the way up instead of down. I guess I wasn't thinking my "happy thought."

The window was open, but the old man hesitated. He looked back at us. "One of you will have to go in first," he said softly.

I looked at Wren. "Nerves?" I murmured.

"He's a vampire," Wren whispered. "He has to be invited across the threshold."

Oh. "Then who invited the Brady Bunch inside when they got here?"

"Vampires don't need invitations into empty and abandoned buildings." He nodded toward the dark interior with his head. "But now that they're here, it's no longer empty and abandoned."

Dracula gestured toward the dark depths on the other side of the casement: "Mr. Csejthe, under the circumstances, I suggest we stake first and ask questions later."

Wren went in first, extended the invitation to Bassarab, and I followed close behind after shuffling my feet and fighting a strong urge to guard the window from the outside. Was it because I was coming close to requiring my own invitation? Or simply that common sense and basic survival instincts were pointing me in the opposite direction?

Mercury-vapor streetlamps glared through the second-story windows, throwing blue-white swatches of dazzling light across the empty room. My night vision couldn't compensate for vast differences in light and darkness every few feet, and I had to grope in the wake of my companions. I hoped the blind weren't leading the blind.

We passed through a doorway and into a trash-littered hall that ran the length of the building, punctuated by doors on either side. I reached out to try one and the old man stopped me with a gesture.

"My sources tell me there is only one and that he is on the floor above us."

Rats.

We moved on down the hallway and found the stairs going up. As I grasped the banister railing with my left hand, I drew one of the Splatmaster Rapide paint pistols with my right. We started up the stairs.

Bassarab's feet seemed to drift above the step surfaces as he ascended. Wren placed his feet at the very edge of the treads and used the railing to take more of his weight. Although I tried to step lightly, I planted my foot in the middle of a tread.

It squeaked.

Wren looked back at me and mouthed a four-letter word. Bassarab sailed up the stairway like a runaway balloon and disappeared into the dark at the top of the stairs.

A series of bumps and thumps ensued from the third floor. No point in being quiet, now: as we thundered (and squeaked) up the rest of the stairs, a squalling sound erupted and then bubbled away.

"A stake, Victor!" Bassarab commanded as we erupted onto the third floor. A prone body squirmed beneath his right foot, its heels slamming against the blood-slimed floor, making thudding and spatting noises.

Victor started forward, pulling a sharpened dowel from his satchel. He slipped at the edge of the growing pool of blood, his feet flying out from under him like some madcap comedy involving a banana peel. He fell flat on his back, shaking the floor and rattling the windows. The bag full of stakes went flying like a great canvas milkweed pod spilling wooden spores.

Now I caught sight of the head. It lay some four feet beyond the squirming body, connected to that spreading crimson tide by its own burgundy estuary. Its angle was such that I couldn't see if its eyes were open or closed, but I couldn't shake the feeling that it retained some horrible imitation of life tied to the severed body that writhed under Bassarab's foot.

"Csejthe! Damn you, man! Come here and help me!"

Victor was still stunned and woozy, trying to get up on hands and knees but unsure of his directions: left, right, up, down? Holstering the Splatmaster, I retrieved one of the scattered stakes and stepped carefully toward the grisly tableau, not wanting to slip. Not really wanting to go forward.

"Here, man; plant it here." He withdrew his sword from the corpse's side, where it had pinned it to the floor, and pointed to the center of its chest.

"Why isn't it dead?" I moaned, falling to my knees

beside the decapitated vampire and positioning the stake over its sternum. *One unkillable vampire was bad enough. . . .*

"It probably is," Bassarab said. "But *wampyr* are like psychic lawyers. If there is a metaphysical loophole, they will find and exploit it. There is safety in following the old traditions to the very letter.

"Drive it home!"

I leaned on the wooden shaft. This wasn't like sliding a thin sliver of metal into soft, yielding flesh. I had to punch a blunt wedge of wood through the bone that conjoined the ribcage over the heart. That took considerable force. I had the physical strength to do it. The mental and emotional strength were something else altogether.

"Hurry!" I could feel Bassarab's eyes boring mental holes through the back of my brainpan, trying to overshadow my will with his.

I added more weight to the stave, but it wasn't sufficient to break through the sternum. I looked back at Victor. "I need the mallet!"

Then the corpse grabbed me, its cold and bloody hands tearing at my arm and side. It was the best motivation I could have asked for: I swung the stake up and back and then smashed it down, burying it in the thing's chest. The headless vampire went rigid, trembling like a plucked string. And then it burst like a meaty bubble, heaving steaming entrails and gobbets of flesh in all directions.

"Jesus!" I cried, causing Bassarab to flinch. "What happened to smoke and ashes?"

Bassarab scowled, trying to regain his composure. "It has been a long time."

"What?" I stood up, wiping the gore from my face and eyes. "It's been a long time since you had one blow up on you?"

"A couple of centuries ago," he said, leaning upon his greatsword, "I fought against an Egyptian sorcerer. He had a small army of cutthroats and brigands. A few were mercenaries, most held in thrall that they might willingly die at his behest. He had some art: many fought like demons and more than a few had to be killed twice. Several, three times."

I suddenly noticed that while Bassarab's clothing was still beslimed with blood, his face and hands were clean and dry. I imagined skin pores like hungry little mouths and repressed a shiver.

"They were *wampyr*. But unlike any that I have seen before or since. Until tonight."

"Then, the other. . ."

He shook his head. "From your descriptions, that one. . . ." He shook his head again. "I do not know: perhaps it cannot be killed."

"I don't believe that," I said, echoing Lupé's sentiments. "Everything can be killed—somehow—in some way."

"Ah, you are so sure." Bassarab sighed. His sword was as inexplicably clean and dry as his skin. "A month ago you were so sure that there were no such things as vampires."

My face spasmed into a frown. "Let's look around for clues or something so we do a little better than guessing in the dark."

We tossed the place but came up with next to nothing: a couple of sleeping bags, a set of car keys, a Kansas map, and a small, leather journal. The journal was probably full of clues but the handwriting was a crabbed script in an unknown language. "Not French, Spanish, German, or Latin," I said, handing the notebook to Bassarab.

"Not Rumanian," he mused, flipping pages, "or Russian, or anything Central European."

"A code?"

He shook his head. "Would still be recognizable as some language character set."

"Arabic?" Wren asked, looking at the writing over Bassarab's shoulder.

"Maybe. Could be Middle Eastern. . . ."

I peered at the twisty script. "Turkish?"

"Bah. I do not know. That was a long time ago. When the others return, I will . . ." he smiled " . . . make one of them read it for us."

"You do that." I palmed the keys. "I'm going downstairs to kick some tires." As I turned toward the stairs, a dog barked down the street.

"Someone is coming."

I frowned. "A telepathic dog, right?"

"No. It is the bark of a wolf. Garou."

"Time to rock and roll," Wren said, shoving stakes back into his bag.

I drew both Splatmasters, cocked them. "Time to bite the hand that bleeds us."

"Bah! You young people!" Bassarab made a face as he led us back down to the second floor. "You watch too many movies."

We didn't move quickly enough: company was coming through the fire escape window as we reached the second floor. Even as Bassarab closed the distance with inhuman quickness, I was firing both CO_2 pistols. It was the monster that Lupé had driven the tree trunk through. One of the projectiles caught it in the side, splashing holy water.

It stopped, clutching at its ribs where the black material was soaked. The expression on its face was not one of pain or fear, however, but one of puzzlement and uncertainty.

Then it straightened, raised its hand to its face and licked the moisture from its fingers with an inhuman smile. The process of elimination, I thought, and felt my bowels turn to water.

I dropped the useless Splatmasters back into their holsters and tried to light the nozzle of my flamethrower. The igniter didn't immediately spark. That gave it time to take two steps forward and one step back as Victor's airbow planted a barbed shaft in the middle of the creature's chest. It started to pull on the stake and then noticed Bassarab.

>>*AhH, TePEsH, I HaVE fOUnd yOU. . . .* <<

The thoughts uncoiled in my mind like insolent serpents.

>>*ArE yOu noT tIRed Of ruNniNg?*<<

"Bey the Jackal," Bassarab spat. "Now, Bey the Lackey. Are you not tired of running errands for others?" He stepped in, swinging. Perhaps it was because he had the look of an old man and the monster hadn't anticipated his inhuman speed: the sword came up and around; the creature had barely enough time to throw up a hand to block the deadly arc. Fingers flew like an explosion of pink maggots as the blade skimmed along the top of its palm.

>>*BEy THe DeAThLeSS*<<

it mocked, seemingly oblivious to the mutilation. >>*Or hAVe YoU FOrGOtTeN?*<<

"Tonight the hunter is become the hunted!" The blade flashed again, but this time the thing Bassarab called Bey was ready. It clapped its palms to either side of the blade with inhuman speed. Twisted. Bassarab turned his sword in the same direction before his opponent could use his momentum against him.

>>*HoW WilL tHESe Few mIsFIts gIve yOU adVaN-TagE wHen wHOLe ArMIes faIlEd YOu cEntuRIEs AgO?*<<

"Stand still and find out," the old vampire taunted back.

And then I had a clear shot. I pressed the trigger on the wand's pistol grip and doused the creature with an arc of flame. Fire raced across the air between us as if running up and over an invisible arched bridge, and then fanned out across the monster's body.

The thing shrieked like a maiden aunt who had just caught sight of a peeping tom. And then it lurched at me, lumbering across the room like Johnny Storm on Thorazine. I stumbled backwards, still pumping liquid napalm at it. Instead of deterring it, the fuel only served to make it more dangerous as it trudged toward me.

I suddenly found myself backed into a corner, walls wedging my shoulders into zero maneuverability. I slapped the quick-release catch on my chest harness and shrugged off the fuel tanks as it closed within four feet. Then Bassarab swept up from behind and whirled the great sword blade: the creature's blazing cranium toppled from its fiery shoulders like a broken matchhead. I rolled along the wall as its legs staggered and momentum carried it toward the corner and crashing down upon my abandoned flamethrower.

It was a good time to leave.

Unfortunately there were a couple of vampires between us and the exit, with more coming in through the fire-escape window.

Fortunately, these were your garden-variety vampires: wooden stakes and holy water—even fired by Splatmaster Rapides—took their toll. I effectively blinded three with headshots while Wren moved in to deliver the *coup de grâce*.

I missed my fourth shot.

Elizabeth Bachman hesitated on the threshold, considered the carnage unfolding before her, and didn't find the odds to her liking. She seemed remarkably solid for one presumed to be discorporated and, as recognition lit my eyes, hers widened as well: she looked at me and hissed, showing inch-long incisors, and then moved backward through the window. That's when I missed my fourth shot. And I didn't just miss: the projectile burst against the ceiling a good three feet short of the window and a couple more to the left.

I fired a second time as she rolled backwards through the casement and down onto the fire escape, but my aim was even worse. My hands were shaking as I started across the room. There was a shout from Bassarab and I looked back in time to see the back half of the room ablaze. Something stirred in its flickering, crimson depths.

Something man-shaped but lacking a head.

I wanted to stay, but there was nothing more that I

could do. The remaining fuel in the flamethrower's tanks would be nearing the combustion point at the center of the inferno. And I had bigger fish to fry.

She was already on the ground by the time I was out on the fire escape. Lupé moved to intercept her and Bachman dealt the werewolf a backhanded blow that slammed her into a light pole and rattled the mercury vapor bulb into stuttering darkness. Then she ran toward the limo.

I vaulted the iron railing, dropping ten feet to the ground and landing rather gracelessly on my right ankle: I went sprawling. It felt like I'd stepped on a flare gun: a burst of white-hot pain shot through my foot, ricocheted up my leg, and exploded in my knee. I wasn't quite sure whether the sound I'd heard as I landed was the *snap* of bone or merely the *pop* of overextended cartilage. It was obvious, however, that I wasn't going to catch Bachman on foot.

I wasn't the only one drawing that conclusion. Lupé had spun about and was loping toward the Bronco. Mooncloud was there, ahead of her, sliding behind the steering wheel. As Bachman gunned the limo's motor and peeled away from the curb, Lupé was leaping through the Bronco's passenger window, already sliding through the first stages of transmogrification toward human form.

A moment later I was standing alone, watching twin plumes of exhaust line the street toward the highway. Then I remembered the car keys I had pocketed, upstairs, just minutes before, and a Chevy van with Arkansas plates parked just across the street.

There was a bang like God's own starter pistol and battering rams of flame smashed out all the windows on the second floor. Great: now every cop in the city would be here inside of five minutes. Time to make like a mule train and haul ass.

I took a step and pain blossomed in my ankle like a fiery flower, rolled up my leg like a serrated yo-yo. So what. Even if it was broken, it couldn't be that bad—not to a man who had awakened to a new life on an autopsy table, whose throat had been cut from ear to ear and "lived" to tell about it.

I fished the keys from my pocket and began hobbling toward the van.

The Chevy drove like it was on autopilot, gliding over the highway like a hockey puck slapped-shot toward a shadowy goal. I stretched both legs over to the passenger side of the floor, relying on the cruise control to handle the accelerator. The brakes I trusted to fate.

What was I doing? There was no hope of my catching up to Bachman or Garou. And even if I did, what could I hope to accomplish with only one good leg to maneuver on? So, what was I doing?

Going home.

I felt curiously light-headed. Going home?

Back to the house.

The house? But why?

Someone's waiting for you.

Someone— Bachman?

Come and see—

And then I was bumping over railroad tracks, announcing that Pittsburg was just ahead. I swung my legs back over and nearly missed the brakes in time to cut left on Atkinson Road. Another left turn and I was on Hugh, headed back north, just three blocks from. . .

. . . home. . . .

I cut the lights, shifted into neutral, and killed the engine: two blocks, now.

One block.

A right onto Cedar Crest and barely rolling. The van glided over to curb in front of my house and stopped as if docked by remote control. Houston, do you copy: the vampire has landed.

Now what?

Go inside.

I opened the door, jumped as the ignition buzzer sounded. Palmed the keys and eased myself out and down, onto the pavement. Pain sank its razored teeth into my ankle as I brought my left foot down, but it wasn't quite as bad as before. Either my tolerance was increasing, or my altered genetics had vastly accelerated the healing process. Even so, I wasn't going to be running the four-forty before sunrise.

I limped around the van and into the front yard. There was a snapping sound to my right and I whirled, only to be confronted with the wind-whipped remnants of yellow, crime-scene tape that struggled to free itself from the evergreen bush where it was anchored. "CENE—DO NOT CROSS POLICE CRIME SCE" it warned, flinging itself toward my face.

I had been told I was presumed dead in the explosion and fire that swept through the radio station on the night of my abduction. So why had my house become a crime scene in the interim? And if the police had been to my house and I was presumed dead—or even if I wasn't—wouldn't it now be locked up tighter than a drum? I patted my pockets: no house keys. I hadn't expected to end up here when I had fled the Doman's castle just a few days before.

Then I saw the light.

A dim glow from the back bedroom on the second floor illumined the glass in the first two front windows on the left. A shadow climbed across the hallway ceiling like Jeff Goldblum in *The Fly*.

Somebody'd been sleeping in my bed.

The police tape snapped at my head as if trying to regain my attention. Do not cross. . . .

Yeah, right: like I'm gonna climb back in the van and go running back to my two best buddies, Bassarab—assuming he was still alive—and Pagelovitch.

I stumbled across the lawn, humming "Tie a Yellow Ribbon" under my breath.

Chapter Eighteen

The door was unlocked.

The door was even a quarter of an inch ajar.

I hated this stuff in the movies: teenagers, abandoned house, stalked by a crazed killer. Not that I objected to Freddy or Jason or Michael killing the couples who slipped off to have illicit sex—*that* sent a high moral message to all the hormone-crazed kids in the audience. Nope, it was the Stupidity Factor that made me crazy.

You know how it goes: trail of blood leads down into the cellar and someone with a death wish always seems to volunteer to go down alone to see what caused it: this is how Mother Nature purges excess stupidity from the gene pool. Another body turns up and everybody decides to split up and go out alone into the dark to see if they can find clues. Uh-huh. At this point I toss my popcorn and start rooting for the homicidal maniac.

So, why was I acting like one of those stupid twits and entering an abandoned house that wasn't quite as empty as it was supposed to be?

Because I was a badass vampire with an attitude and without a hell of a lot left to lose. I drew both Splatmasters and pushed the door back with my toe. "Honey," I murmured, "I'm home."

The stairs inside the entryway went in both directions: one set led down to the rec room, the garage, and the room I had used as my sleeping chamber this past year; the other flight, up to the kitchen, living room, and hallway. Up above, an uncertain light magnified shadows at the top of the stairs. Below, there was nothing but darkness. I hoped.

I reached out and flipped the light switch. Nothing. The power would have been shut off, of course. The glow from the end of the hallway wavered as a breeze sighed through the open door and wandered through the house. Candles? More likely the kerosene lamp on the dresser in the master bedroom.

A shadow reared from the floor, grew against the hallway wall to a monstrous size and shape. A voice spoke.

"Daddy! You came back!"

The silhouette at the top of the stairs was scarcely four feet tall, contrasting the distorted shadow it threw up the wall and across the ceiling.

The weakness in my ankle transferred to my knees. "K-Kirsten?" The glow behind her lit her hair in a pale nimbus of light. The face at its center remained in shadow like an inky Rorschach blot.

"Daddy. I missed you."

The voice was strange, scratchy. It didn't sound like Kirsten. But, after a year, I wasn't sure I remembered what Kirsten sounded like. Wasn't sure of a lot of things.

"Mommy's gone," she said.

Of course she was.

"I know, honey," I whispered. I lowered the Splatmasters back to their holsters. One missed, slipped from my nerveless fingers, and fell to the floor with a clatter. I ignored it. I only had eyes for that shadowy face surrounded by a flickering halo of light. The rest of my body had grown distant, remote; a fuzzy lethargy extended its buzzing feelers into my head, my thoughts.

"But she'll be back," the apparition continued.

And then it became clear, the thought rising in my mind like the sun over a darkened plain, driving away the shadows of doubt.

I had survived death and so had my wife and daughter!

To hell with Pagelovitch! The confusion was only in

the details, there was no other answer: they were infected the same as I! Jennifer and Kirsten were alive and, as the thought sank more deeply into my awareness, I felt a mantle of guilt lift from my shoulders. It was only now that I realized how heavily it had pressed down upon my soul.

"Daddy, I want a hug."

I lurched forward, stumbled on the second step and clambered up toward my daughter on hands and knees. At the top of the stairs she leaned over me, wrapped her arms around my neck, pressed her face to my cheek. I shivered as cold lips moved across the side of my face, moved down to where my jaw folded into my neck. I drew a deep and ragged breath.

And nearly gagged.

Garbage, came the far away thought as I closed my eyes. *The food has gone bad in the refrigerator, the pantry. . . .*

Lips parted and I felt the hard, sharp edge of teeth against my flesh. I jerked back. Clapped a hand to my neck.

Nothing.

No blood.

No wound.

Nothing but gooseflesh and paranoia.

Kirsten's shadowy lips curved into a smile. "What's the matter, Daddy?"

My head ached. "Nothing, princess. I'm just surprised to see you, that's all. Where have you been all this time?"

"Here." Her face was still in shadow and now she was backing into the darker recesses of the kitchen, abandoning the uncertain glow from the hallway. "Mommy thought you might come back here and told me to wait for you."

"I see." I didn't. Not at all. "And where is—Mommy—now?"

"She's out getting some food." Her voice—only it wasn't her voice, not the voice that belonged to my little girl a year ago—turned whiny and petulant. "I'm hungry."

"You're hungry?" I was trying to think, but my mind fought me every step of the way.

"I don't want to wait, Daddy. Can I have something now?"

Maybe the accident had damaged her vocal chords. Maybe. . . "Something?" I echoed.

"Something to eat."

Maybe. . . "Maybe we should wait for—for your mother to come back, first."

I caught the shake of her head in the darker depths of the kitchen, even though my night vision was failing to draw an infrared signature from her small body. "Just one of the cold things, okay? It doesn't have to be alive."

"What?" I fumbled at the switches at the top of the stairs. Nothing. My only light source was in the back bedroom at the other end of the hall.

"Just one little piece, Daddy. Alright?"

I shuffled sideways, clutching at the doorframe to the kitchen. "I don't . . ." I suddenly noticed that, as Kirsten moved away, the ripe, unpleasant odor had retreated with her. " . . . know. . . ."

There was a sound. It took a moment to identify it: the refrigerator door being opened. No little light came on. The darkness remained unbroken. But then the stench rolled over me like a wave of effluvium. There was a reek like the wind from a slaughterhouse and it drove me back down the hallway and into the master bedroom.

The kerosene lamp sat upon the dresser, the mirror behind it amplifying the meager flame that tipped its flat cloth wick. I snatched it up and cast about wildly. A month after the funeral I had moved my clothes out and made my bed downstairs. Though I had rarely entered the room since then, I still knew its topography intimately: something had violated this space, something nested here. I turned up the flame until it climbed a third of the glass chimney's height and dribbled smoke at the ceiling.

And then I stood there.

I did not want to go back down the hall.

I did not want to go into the kitchen.

I did not want to open up the darkness and look at my daughter's face.

At what unholy larder was kept in that long-dead icebox.

So I stood there, trembling, in a faint circle of light. As long as I did not look, it was still possible that my daughter was infected like me.

Was still human. Like me.

"Chris." Another voice. Also alien.

I turned and nearly dropped the lamp.

She stood in the hallway, where the pale lamplight seemed to barely touch her and then slid away into the darkness. "Jenny," I said.

"Darling." Her voice was as alien as Kirsten's. "I've missed you."

Neither of us moved for a moment.

In the uncertain lamplight she looked much as she always had. Except thinner. And dark circles under her eyes.

And something was wrong with her mouth.

She moved, turning her head as if reading my thoughts. Came into the room and veered to her left. Orbited a quarter circle, crossing to the bed.

"I've missed you," she said again. "Did you miss me?"

Yes, I thought.

"I can't hear your answer, Chris. Did you forget me while we were apart?" She sat down on the rumpled bed.

I opened my mouth, tried to say no. No sound would come.

"Maybe you got distracted. Maybe there's someone else, now. Is there, baby? Did you find somebody—some *body*—to take my place?" She slid across the rumpled sheets, moving to the center of the mattress and leaning back against the headboard. Her voice took on an edge: "Maybe that werewolf bitch?"

I closed my mouth. There could be no answers where this conversation was heading.

"You like to do it doggie-style, Chris?" The edge in her voice turned and each word was like a hammer blow. "Are you into bestiality?"

I just stood there, immobile except for a tremor that was starting to work its way up my leg.

She laughed suddenly and yellow teeth flashed in her mouth. "It's all right, darling. 'Till death us do part.' Remember? So I can't really blame you: you can cop on the technicality."

"I—I thought you were gone," I whispered. "Forever."

"We're ba-ack," she sing-songed. "So, what do you say, honey? Can we be one happy family, again?" Her eyes caught the flame from the lamp and reflected it back as yellow pinpoints. "Or are you going to play doghouse with that Canadian huskie?"

It wasn't Jenny's voice. And I couldn't believe they were Jenny's words. The only real evidence I had before me was Jenny's body.

And there was something wrong with it—something beyond its painfully gaunt appearance—that I couldn't quite put my finger on.

"What about my body?" she asked, squirming in a nest of tangled sheets. "Did you miss it?" She reached up and unfastened the button at her throat. "I can do it doggie-style, too." Another button. "You like animals? I can be an animal. Remember?" A third button and her shirt began to open. "Only I've gotten better this past year. I can be a real animal, now." The forth button and the front of her shirt gaped, a breast emerged like a sly predator. She cupped it in her hand. "Remember this? Remember how good it could be?"

But I wasn't looking at her breast. I was looking at the black, ropey scars that ran from her shoulders to her chest, where they joined in a rough and lumpy "Y" and continued down her stomach to disappear beneath her jeans.

Autopsy incisions.

I stepped back. Took another step. Kept backing up. Into the hall.

"Darling," I heard her say, "whatever happened to 'for better or for worse'?"

I tripped, stumbled. Looked down at the body lying in the hallway like a bloody speed bump, and lost my footing altogether. The lamp slipped out of my grasp, rebounded off the wall, and crashed against the opposite baseboard. Blue flames washed across the floor, became yellow tapestries that fluttered up the walls. I scooted backwards, slapping at the fiery tongues that flagged from my sleeve, my pants, my shoe. The body at my feet lay half-in, half-out of the spreading flames. An older male—fifty, maybe sixty years old—it hadn't been lying there when I first came it. Hadn't died there, either: even though his throat was practically nonexistent, there was very little blood on the carpet.

Mommy's out getting some food. . . .

Kirsten.

I rolled over and crawled back toward the kitchen.

"Kirsten, where are you?"

No answer. The flames were following me back up the hallway, providing better illumination. Now I could see the outline of the icebox, its door still ajar. Masking the charnelhouse reek was the growing smell of burning hair and roasting flesh. I started to crawl onto the linoleum and nearly fell on my face as my hands slid through something thick and wet and viscous.

"Kirsten!" I screamed. There was no response, and now the flames were lapping at my feet and blistering the wall next to the stairway.

She was surely gone, more out of harm's way than I was. I turned and threw myself down the stairs. The ceiling overhead rippled and turned orange. Smoke flowed down the stairway, impelled by a sudden downdraft. I grabbed at the doorknob, twisted, pulled. The door was locked.

I fumbled with the turnset on the knob. No good: the door was secured with a double-keyed, sliding bolt. I turned and stumbled down the half-flight of steps leading to the lower level of the house.

The door to the garage was on my left at the bottom of the stairs. It opened easily.

I entered the garage and closed the door behind me. That cut off the smoke-filtered glow of the spreading flames up above. I took a step and banged my shin on something solid. *Hold on,* I told myself: *Think!*

Flashlight.

I fumbled along the wall and found the flashlight we'd always kept plugged in, next to the door, for emergencies. There hadn't been any. Until now.

I didn't know how long the power had been cut off but the batteries still held enough of a charge. The beam cut a swath of visibility through the smoky darkness.

A black car . . . sedan . . . no. . .

Station wagon . . . no. . .

A *hearse*. . . took up most of the space.

There was barely enough room for the two coffins, resting on pairs of sawhorses at the back of the garage. And a small table, the workbench, actually, set with unlit candles, a crucible, and another bowl—half filled with long, narrow leaves—some scrolls, an ankh. . .

Scrolls?

Detail was uncertain at this distance, in this light, but the text looked familiar. Before I could move closer something slammed against the door behind me. The knob rattled. but the door remained closed: out of habit, I had locked it behind me.

"Kirsten?" I called.

No response.

"Jenny?"

There was a low growl on the other side of the wood.

I tried to picture the sound coming from a human throat.

Couldn't.

The door began to shudder under repeated impacts. Smoke drifted down from the ceiling turning the flashlight beam into a Jedi lightsaber.

Time to leave.

I edged around the hearse. The garage door was locked and the mechanism was out of reach, nearly flush with the car's rear end. Behind me I heard the sound of splintering wood. It was inspiring: I tore the metal tie-rods loose from their moorings and then punched a hole in one of the wooden panels with my fist. The garage door made protesting sounds, but it went up without any further hesitation. Smoke rushed out into the night air and I followed along behind.

The windows of the van reflected the red and yellow flicker of what used to be the second story of my home. I hesitated, thinking of Kirsten, and then ran for the van. It was too late, now.

Too late by at least a year.

Chapter Nineteen

In my dreams the rabbi tells us to roll away the stone. We uncover the hollow carved into the hillside.

"Lazarus, come forth!" he says.

The sloping ground opens and a figure, wrapped in grave clothes and spiced linen bindings, emerges.

"Loose him and uncover his face."

I do as the rabbi bids. I step forward and tug the linen napkin from his face.

Only it is her face.

Jennifer's clear, clean features gaze back at me.

I turn, but the rabbi is gone. The burial place is swept away in a tide of sand. The hill is now a pyramid and I hold in my hands not a linen napkin but a golden mask wearing a serpent crown.

"Unbind me," she says. And her mouth is . . . right. Her teeth are white, her eyes bright and unshadowed, the hollows are gone from her cheeks.

"Free me," she says

I search the bindings in vain: there are no knots or loose ends to unravel.

"You will need help," she says. "Ask Thoth."

Hurry, Daddy!

I bolted awake at the sound of Kirsten's voice echoing from inside the tomb.

I stared up at the night sky, at Bassarab's face hovering overhead.

Felt the grassy mound of earth against my back, turned my head and saw dozens of other landscaped hillocks, each with its own stone or marker to give it a pretense of individuality.

"An interesting place to take a nap," he said. "Perhaps you are changing more than you realize." He sat on my wife's headstone, leaning over to observe me like some great, dark vulture. "It will be dawn, soon."

I turned my head to the east, finally noticed the colorshift of night sky from black to deep cerulean at the horizon. "It was the only place I could think of to go to," I croaked, my throat gone rusty with ground vapors and dew. "I must have fallen asleep."

"Perhaps. Perhaps you even dreamed."

I sat up with an ache-induced groan. *We are such things as dreams are made of*, I thought.

"And our little life is rounded with a sleep," Bassarab said. "But did you truly dream? Or did you make contact?"

"Contact?" Annoyance pushed the grogginess from my head.

"What did your wife tell you?"

I struggled to my feet. "She seemed to think I had been unfaithful to her this past year." I tested my legs: they didn't seem entirely trustworthy.

"I asked what your wife told you. I was not speaking of the thing that nests in her remains. Dance at the masquerade, if you will, but do not be taken in by the costumes."

I glared at him. "What do you know about my wife? Or my daughter, for that matter?"

"I know that they could not be undead," he said gently. "They were not infected with vampire blood as you were. What infested your house was only an illusion, a pantomime of shadows." He sighed, looking strangely human for a moment. "Your wife and daughter are gone, Christopher."

"You don't know how much that comforts me."

"I am glad."

My hands balled into fists and then reluctantly relaxed:

how does one explain irony to someone who's been around about five hundred years longer than you?

"How did you find me?"

"It is the blood-bond. Your blood calls to me; if I concentrate, I can hear it singing from many miles away."

"How poetic," Mooncloud interrupted. She was making her way toward us through the maze of grave markers. "Lupé and I had to follow the fire trucks to his house and then guess where he'd go next." She gave him a look. "I can hear your blood singing," she mimicked. "Oh, *please*."

"How clever of you," Bassarab said sourly. "Where is Garou?"

"Back at the car. Dressing."

"And your quarry?"

"Got away. How about the creature?"

Bassarab scowled. "The same: got away."

"Whoa, whoa, whoa; hold on a moment!" I reached out and grabbed the lapels of his scorched greatcoat. "It couldn't have survived that inferno!"

"Christopher," Bassarab's voice was flecked with traces of defeat and resignation, "you cannot kill something that is already dead."

I stared at him. Something stirred at the back of my brain, just below the surface of my mind. "Can you be killed?" I asked finally.

After an even longer pause, he nodded.

"Then it—that thing—can also be killed."

The old vampire shook his head. "I said that you cannot kill something that is already dead. I am undead. There is a difference."

"Yeah?" A red light began to bloom behind my eyes. "Well, what exactly is that difference?" For a moment I thought the sun was bursting over the inky horizon—but it was still dark all around us: the terrible, burning brilliance searing into my brain was something worse. "You son-of-a-bitch!" I cried, remembering, "you *know* that thing! You *spoke* to it!" The burning brightness intensified, blinding me. "You called it by *name*!"

"Kadeth Bey."

"You set us up!" I roared, lifting him off the ground and shaking him like an unrepentant doll.

"No! I want him dead as much as you do!"

"*Liar!*" I flung him backwards and a tombstone, fifteen feet away, toppled over backwards in breaking his fall.

"New York is using him," Bassarab panted, "to track me—"

"I know that!" I yelled. "I'm not stupid! Time after time I've been the fall guy for you, but *no more*! And you don't want him as dead as I do! You can't!"

"Christopher, even a man who is five centuries undead doesn't want to die."

I reached down and wrenched up the headstone from my wife's grave. "But maybe it will find you and you'll die anyway! And then what?" I panted, raising the massive granite block over my head. "It'll be over! You'll be dead! Like you were meant to be—five hundred years ago! Like all men are meant to be at the end of their allotted time!" I took a step toward him, arms and legs thrumming with the strain. "No one will dig you up! No one will want you coming back! You can rest!"

I turned and flung the headstone at the iron fence a couple of plots away. The monument took out ten feet of iron fusillades with their concrete anchors and posts. "You can rest—" I fell to my knees "—under the cool green grass and have peace," I sobbed. "But not my little girl. Not my Jenny."

"It's not them anymore. They're not—"

"Shut up," I screamed, "*shut up!*"

Off in the distance a siren wailed, echoing the sound of my pain.

"I have," I panted, "every reason in the world to save that thing the trouble and kill you now."

"He's not your enemy, Chris," Mooncloud said softly, "Kadeth Bey is."

I looked up at her. "This isn't about friends or

enemies, anymore. The one thing that you and Dracula here have taught me these past few weeks is that one controls or is controlled. One dominates or is dominated. In the end it's results that count. Not feelings.

"And now we've gone too far beyond who started what and whose fault lies where. That thing—Bey—dug them up! Dragged my baby and my wife back up out of the ground." I slammed my fist against the earth between my knees. "Violated them to get to me! To get to him! And it still has them! It *still . . . has . . . them. . . .*"

"We've got to destroy it," Bassarab said, climbing to his feet. "I had hoped you might succeed where I had always failed. You must understand that we both want the same thing—"

"*No!*" I said, climbing to my feet. "You don't seem to get it, do you? This thing has my family and it will do anything, *anything* to bring you down. If I can find a way to destroy this thing, I will. But if I can't, I'll set Jenny and Kirsten free the only other way I know how." I stabbed a shaking finger at him. "It won't need them if you're dead. So you'd better pray I can figure out how to kill something that's already dead. You can stake your un-life on that!"

Red and blue lights strobed the early morning mist at the cemetery gate. A side searchlight cut the predawn twilight and circled us in a porthole of light. "Don't anybody move," admonished an amplified voice from the speaker mounted on the roof of the squad car.

There's nothing happening here, I thought furiously. *Go away!*

The searchlight remained on. But now it passed over us and on as the police car continued up and around the circular road. By the time it had circled back out the gate, we were climbing into the Duesenberg.

"His name was Kadeth Bey and he was an Egyptian sorcerer," Bassarab said. He frowned at the glow of daylight that framed the shades drawn down over another motel room's windows. "I really know little more than that."

"How did you meet?" Garou asked.

"The Turks brought him late to our conflict. That was back in the—let's see—fifteenth century. I had, of course, developed my own reputation as a master of the black arts by then. The Ottoman Empire was losing battles that it should have won without effort. They were frustrated and demoralized. The sultan had exhausted his reserve of holy men in trying to counter the demonic forces I brought to the conflict. When they proved ineffective, it was decided that perhaps they should counter with an unholy man, instead."

"Bey," I said.

He nodded. "The little I know was difficult to come by. And it has done me little good through the long centuries up to this very day."

"Perhaps your information is less than reliable."

"It was reliable." His gaze turned reflective. "At great cost to my own troops I was able to capture two of his acolytes. I was exceedingly careful in my questioning—more so than usual: the long stake loosens most tongues even before the process is begun. Toward the end, all falsehood is stripped away. They confess, not to me, but to the God they are about to face, to whom they must commend their souls. No, Csejthe, these men spoke the truth as they knew it."

"And what truth was that?" Mooncloud persisted.

"That Kadeth Bey was both vampire and necromancer. That he was a high priest of the Egyptian god Set and became a vampire *after* his death by means of sorcery. That he was entombed as a royal high priest in the Egyptian manner, hence your problem of driving a stake through his black heart."

I snapped my fingers. "Egyptian burial. The organs are removed and placed in separate burial urns when the body is prepared for mummification."

Bassarab nodded. "Canopic jars."

"So what do we do?" Garou asked. "Find his jar and slam a stake down inside? There must be hundreds of those things in Egypt, alone, not to mention museum exhibits throughout the rest of the world."

"Anything else?" I asked Bassarab.

"Leaves. Bey was always preparing potions involving leaves that he had to have brought back from the valley of the Nile. About the only thing I could do to thwart him back then was ambush the returning trains of packmules and squeeze his supplies to a minimum." He paused, ruminating. "That's about it."

"Tanis leaves," Mooncloud said.

"What?"

"It sounds just like those old mummy movies that the Satterfields were talking about."

I remembered now. "Right. They had some at their house, in fact.

"Tanis leaves," Garou said.

"Yes."

"No," she corrected, "you said tan*is* leaves. In the movies they're called tan*na* leaves."

We all looked at her.

Bassarab cleared his throat. "Is there a point?"

Garou shrugged. "My mother always said that the Devil is in the details."

"Hollywood," Bassarab muttered.

I leaned back in my chair and stared up at water-stained ceiling tiles that might have been white back in the 1940s. Back when the old black-and-white Universal horror movies were being shot on Tinseltown's back lots. "She's right," I said. "Maybe this particular detail isn't significant. But we can't discount any potential piece of information at this point. And an inconsistency could be a red flag."

"Oh, well, if it's inconsistencies you want," Garou said, "there's a rather largish one at the beginning of *The Mummy* series."

Mooncloud gave her a look. "I had no idea you were such an old movie buff."

"When you're on call for the graveyard shift, cable doesn't exactly offer a smorgasbord of culture."

I cleared my throat. "I believe we were discussing inconsistencies."

"Oh, right. Boris Karloff played the first mummy. Then it was mostly Lon Chaney, Jr. though there were two or three others."

"Christopher Lee, as I recall," Mooncloud mused.

"Now there was an actor. . . ." Bassarab rested his chin on folded hands. "I did not mind so much when I was portrayed by the likes of him. And Langella, of course."

"And Lugosi?" I murmured.

"Bah! That dwarf?"

"Lee came later," Garou continued, "during the Hammer Films era. I'm talking about the old Universal classics."

"Jack Palance?" I whispered.

Bassarab looked at me.

"Dan Curtis production back in the seventies. Two-part made-for-TV movie."

"Hmmmm." Bassarab looked thoughtful.

"In the original *Mummy*, Karloff utilized the Scroll of Thoth to raise the dead," Garou elaborated. "The tanna leaves angle didn't show up until Chaney was gimping around in three-thousand-year-old duct tape after Princess Ananka's reincarnation."

"Two different mythologies," Mooncloud observed. "But could both hold a portion of the truth?"

Bassarab roused from his reverie. "You are not serious."

"Yeah," I echoed. "Vampires, werewolves, three-thousand-year-old dead guys still walking around—get serious!"

He scowled at me. "There must be better sources of information."

"Find me one." Then I told them about what I had seen in my garage before escaping the fire.

"So, he's using both the tanna leaves and the Scroll of Thoth," Garou said when I was done.

"Tanis leaves," I corrected.

"No," said Bassarab simultaneously.

I turned to him. "You're starting to sound like a broken record."

"No," Bassarab insisted. "Bey would not use scrolls or anything else involving the god Thoth."

"He's right," Mooncloud said. "If Bey is a disciple of Set, he dabbles in black magic. Thoth, in many ways, was Set's nemesis."

"Thoth," I said, "Thoth. . . ." The name resonated in my mind like a half-remembered melody. "Tell me more about this Thoth."

Mooncloud looked thoughtful. "My Egyptian mythology is a little rusty. As I remember it, Set murdered his brother Osiris. Thoth gave power to the goddess Isis to resurrect her husband. Out of that process, the Egyptians say, the process of embalming was handed down to mortals."

"And the Scroll of Thoth," Garou said, "is what was used in the first Mummy movie to animate Boris Karloff. The tanna leaves came later, during the Lon Chaney, Jr. series."

"Your friends back in Kansas City," I said to Mooncloud, "they have a Scroll of Thoth."

She smiled. "An authentic copy."

"This is madness," Bassarab muttered.

"And tanis leaves," I concluded, pulling a cellular phone out of my backpack.

"Where did you get that?" Bassarab wanted to know.

"Kansas City during our recent shopping spree." I turned to Mooncloud. "The Satterfield's number?" I asked.

"I forbid it," he said as Mooncloud gave me the information.

As I started punching in the area code I could feel the old vampire's mind force enveloping me like a musty shroud. "When I'm done I'll need Smirl's number so we can arrange some fast transportation."

"You will put the phone down," Bassarab ordered. His mental domination intensified. "I command you!"

The color drained from Mooncloud's face.

Garou's eyes were filled with pain.

I was getting seriously pissed off.

"I command—"

"Hey, Vladamir," I said, "bite me." The phone began to ring at the other end of the connection.

The hat, sunglasses, and sunblock were less effective now and, during the drive to the airport, I drifted through that no man's land between pain and discomfort.

I welcomed the burning lancets of sunlight pricking my skin, loose photons seeming to turn the air noxious as I breathed it in. I was tired and it slapped away my lethargy, I was thirsty and it offered preeminent diversion. I was moving out onto thin ice and I would need my wits about me for the next forty-eight hours.

Smirl was waiting at the Pittsburg field with a plane and a pilot. I got out of the car and waited for Mooncloud. She had removed the keys from the ignition and unbuckled her seat belt, but remained seated behind the steering wheel.

She looked up at me with a stricken expression. "I can't."

I stared back, puzzled. "You can't what?"

"Get out of the car. He won't let me."

"What?"

"Bassarab."

It took me a moment. I had developed my own vampiric immunity to Bassarab's mental domination, but Mooncloud was still human and susceptible. "Posthypnotic suggestion," I asked, "or is he using some kind of telepathic remote control?"

She shook her head. "I don't know."

"Well, how about this?" I opened the driver's door. "I command you to get out of the car and follow me." She sat, unmoving, and I pushed a bit with my mind. She clutched at her head and moaned.

"Never mind," I said, relenting. "Stay here and help Lupé keep the trail warm. I'll be back tonight."

"The Doman isn't going to like this," she said.

"Tough. Under the circumstances, Stefan Pagelovitch is the least of my worries. And if the plan fails, I'll be beyond caring."

A fool's plan. . . . The words whispered at the back of my mind like a serpent sliding beneath dry leaves.

Lie still in your coffin, old man, and keep your thoughts to yourself. You've had five hundred years to deal with Kadeth Bey. Your continuing impotence in this matter should curb the tongue of your mind as well as the one in your mouth.

"Are you all right?" Mooncloud asked.

I looked at her.

"You look a little unsteady on your feet."

"A headache," I said. "Nothing more." *And I plan to be rid of it permanently in just a short while.*

Bassarab, if he was still listening, made no reply.

"I'd better get going."

She reached out and put her hand on my arm. "You're going to need something very soon. . . ."

I turned and walked through the gate and out onto the field.

The tiny Kansas airport wasn't much more than a main building with a two story tower and a couple of runways. A half dozen hangars and metal sheds, a couple of fuel depots, and a chainlink fence completed the layout. Although the sun was still up, it was after six P.M. and the nominal staff had left for the day. Local traffic tended to be light, mostly Cessna 100 series and Pipers with an occasional Beechcraft thrown in. Regional flights usually diverted over to Joplin, where they were better able to accommodate charters and median jets.

Large commercial carriers gave both airports a wide berth.

"You it?" Smirl asked, as I walked briskly toward the plane.

"Yeah. Let's move." While I didn't necessarily think the old vampire would sabotage our takeoff, I was in a hurry to put a little more distance between us while he was still preoccupied with Dr. Mooncloud. Five minutes later we were off the ground and headed north, toward Kansas City.

Smirl had provided us with a Beechcraft Baron, a plush, prestigious, and very expensive twin-prop that made me wonder about the Chicago demesne's resources. What was more important, however, was that the Baron had an average cruising speed of two hundred miles per hour. The clock was ticking and I didn't want to see the sun come up again before my errand was through.

"I got the stuff you asked for," Smirl said. He pulled a leather valise out from under his seat and unzipped it. Reaching in, he extracted a vest of meshed nylon covered with canvas pouches that were all interconnected with insulated wire. "Special Ops, ALICE-type vest with twenty-eight bricks of high propellant C-4 Plastique in canvas utility pouches with wireless system primers tied to a single circuit." He eyed me as he held out the vest. "You ever work with this stuff?"

"Years ago, in the service."

"What were you? Special Forces?"

I stopped examining the wire leads and stared at him. "Do my military records say anything about Special Forces?"

"No . . . but your service records are unusually vague in some areas. And your shopping list—"

"Weekend warrior stuff, I assure you," I said. And then I reassured him some more with a little mental push.

As I refolded the vest he produced a small black box with a hinged cover. "Remote detonator. Range of at least five hundred meters if you've got clear line-of-sight."

"Range isn't going to be a problem," I murmured as he flipped the lid open.

There were four toggle switches arranged in pairs. He pointed to the top two switches. "Two separate circuits if you want a backup charge. The top switch arms the circuit." He moved his finger. "The switch beneath it detonates the charge. You want the vest wired to the left pair or the right?"

I reached out and took the small plastic case into my hand. I closed my eyes and ran my thumb across the switches, trying to imagine the easiest configuration under the most difficult of circumstances. "The right pair, I guess," I said, opening my eyes. As I did, a sable-brown cat with two tails appeared from beneath a seat at the back of the plane. It ambled up the aisle and jumped into my lap.

"Where did you get the cat?"

"She insisted on coming along," he answered. As if that was any kind of an answer at all.

I was feeling more than a little disoriented from the combination of sun, Bassarab's interference, and the sudden change in altitude as I exchanged the vest and detonator for a flashlight with a black, insulated exterior and a ringed spring-clip at the butt end. "Browning submersible Sabrelight," he said. "Looks pretty much like an ordinary flashlight, but it has a xenon high-intensity lamp with four hundred percent more candlepower. They're used by U.S. Army Special Forces counterinsurgency strike teams. I got you two, just in case, with three sets of spare batteries, each."

The cat formed a furry doughnut in my lap as Smirl took the flashlight back and placed a wooden box in my hands. I opened it and considered the oversized handgun nestled in the green felt interior.

"Dartmaster CO_2 tranquilizer gun with twelve hypo-darts and two spare gas cartridges," he catalogued.

"Modifications: Tasco Propoint PDP4 electronic sight, ALS MiniAimer laser sight, Hogue grip."

"Perfect."

"Something you didn't ask for." He exchanged the boxed weapon for a miniheadset and mike wired to a belt/pocket battery clip. "Tracker hands-free comm set. VOX circuitry for voice activation. Two-channel, military issue."

"Anything else?" I asked as he repackaged the various items and arranged them in his valise.

"I still don't understand how you're going to get him to put on the vest."

"I don't need Kadeth Bey to wear the vest for the desired effect. I just need him to stand close to me while I'm wearing it."

He drew back. Perhaps he even blanched: it's hard to tell with a complexion like Casper the friendly ghost.

"Now, what about the books?"

He fished a sack out from behind his seat, obviously uncomfortable with the turn the conversation had taken. "Explosives and guns—easy stuff. Books are a little different."

He pulled six books from the sack and handed them to me. I shuffled through the stack: a glossily pictured text on ancient Egypt, two reference books on general mythology, *Brewer's Dictionary of Phrase and Fable*, and two volumes from Frazier's original *Golden Bough* that looked like they might have been from a first edition collection. I turned them over and considered the numbers inked across the bottom of the spines. "These are library books."

"I went to three bookstores and nobody had anything like what you wanted. I was running low on time and the library was a safe bet."

I turned the books back over. "Three of these are from the reference section. How did you get permission to check them out?"

"Check them out?"

I sighed and opened the first. "I'm going to read, now. When we get to Kansas City, I expect to be done and I expect you to return these to the library and put them back on the shelves exactly where you found them."

"You're fixing to blow yourself up, but you're worried about overdue books at the library?"

The cat looked up at me.

"The C-4 is Plan B. I'm still working on Plan A."

"I hope it's a little less fatal than Plan B."

"'Fatal,'" I said, "is one thing." I turned and stared out the window at cooling twilight. "'Permanent' is quite another."

It was quiet for the remainder of the flight.

Chapter Twenty

"Well, of course, the popular mythologies have Thoth as nothing more than vizier to Osiris and his kingdom," Jim Satterfield said. He consulted the crabbed script on the papyrus and counted nine leaves into the boiling water.

"Nine going to be enough?" I asked.

"That's what the formula calls for."

"An authentic copy of the formula?"

He shrugged. "Maybe some Egyptian street vendor copied it off one of the old late-night movies. Maybe some Hollywood scriptwriter made it up straight out of his imagination and Sir Thomas Johnstone Lipton's *Recipe Book*. Maybe the only power you can count on is the power of urban myth and the cybernetics of superstition."

"But maybe, just maybe," I said, taking a large wooden spoon and stirring the mixture, "the movie script did manage to take its cues from actual legend."

Susan Satterfield entered the kitchen, surveyed our efforts and reached between us to adjust the burner on the stove top. "Why do men always suppose the only way to cook something is maximum flame? You're supposed to boil it until the leaves dissolve; that means medium heat. Otherwise the water will evaporate before the leaves do."

Her husband smiled. "It's genetics, hon. Goes way back to our forebears living in caves and hunting mastodons. A nice big fire, the bigger the better."

"How many leaves?" she asked.

"Nine for a full range of motion."

"Universal-Lon Chaney, Jr. or Hammer-Chris Lee?"

"Um, Universal—if I remember correctly. Three to keep its heart beating and nine for the mummy to rise and walk. And something about the cycle of each full moon."

"Wait a minute," I protested. "How can the potion keep a mummy's heart beating when the heart is removed during the embalming process?"

"The heart wasn't always removed," Jim answered. "And sometimes it was removed and then replaced during the embalming process."

"Egyptian embalming techniques evolved and changed with time and class differences," his wife added, rummaging in the pantry and emerging with a bottle of wine. "The processes you're probably familiar with are the royal ceremonies practiced during the New Kingdom period, between 1738 and 1102 B.C. Herodotus gave a detailed description of the technique back in the fifth century B.C., including the use of canopic jars for the various organs to be stored outside the body."

"But all of that's moot in regards to your question," Jim said. "In the movies, the mummy was Kharis, who, as high priest, was entombed alive for his violation of sacred taboos. So his heart was never removed in the first place."

"But did he die?"

They both looked at me.

"I mean, did the tanna leaves bring him back to life? Or did he remain in some form of suspended animation during his burial and never taste of true death in the first place?"

They both looked at each other. Then back at me.

"I mean, will this stuff work on something that is already dead? Or only on something that never died to begin with?"

"Something that never died to begin with?" Susan asked slowly.

I nodded.

"Well," Jim mused, "I suppose that would depend on just exactly which it was and what effect you wanted."

"Something that is supposedly dead and still walking around," I said. "Something that is not alive by the prevailing definitions."

"Yet, not undead in the vampiric sense?" Susan qualified, working a corkscrew into the mouth of the wine bottle.

I nodded.

"And the desired effect?" Jim asked.

"To make it alive once more."

Now neither of them would look at me. Or at each other. After a long silence Susan cleared her throat. "We, um, understand that you lost your wife and daughter last year."

My throat felt like it needed clearing as well. I nodded.

"This, uh, potion," Jim said, "assuming Hollywood tapped into an arcane truth and actually got it right. . ."

"Which is highly unlikely," Susan interjected. The cork came free with an audible pop.

". . . well, at best, it was only supposed to restore a semblance of life, of animation."

"Three leaves to keep the heart beating," I said. "Nine to grant the power of movement. Semblance of life? What if we used more leaves?"

"Not recommended." Jim Satterfield pulled his pipe from his pocket. "I can't recall the specific warnings from the movies but it was assumed that adding more than nine leaves to the potion was dangerous."

"Why?"

"I don't remember." He unfolded a penknife and began scraping at the bowl of his pipe. "Maybe it made Kharis too powerful. Or maybe it would destroy him." He looked at his wife. "You going to pour that?"

"I'm letting it breathe."

"Oh."

"Or maybe it would make him too human and therefore beyond the control of his master," I said, reaching for the bowl and dumping the remaining leaves into the bubbling pot on the stove.

"Maybe," Jim conceded. "But if you were wanting to bring someone back from the dead—someone you really cared about—you'd be a lot better off using the Scroll of Thoth."

"Why?"

"Stronger magic, I guess. Not to mention the theological angle. You familiar with the Osirian myths?"

I nodded. My little study session on the flight up had covered the basics. According to mythology, Osiris was the grandson of Ra, the chief of the Egyptian gods. Since the Big O was a real peacenik and didn't believe in violence of any sort, he was an easy target for his brother Set. In a fit of jealousy, Set killed him—twice, according to some versions of the legend—and the final time he hacked Osiris into fourteen different pieces. Although Isis, who was Osiris' wife, and Thoth, his grand vizier, were able to resurrect him, he decided to go with the momentum and become ruler of the Egyptian underworld.

"So," I said, after repeating the basic outline, "Osiris is now the god of the Underworld and Thoth, in some aspects of their theology, serves as the gatekeeper between life and death."

He rapped the bowl of his pipe against the counter as Susan produced three wineglasses from a side cupboard. "Mmmm. A bit of an oversimplification, but the interpretation holds."

"So, let me ask you a hypothetical question," I said as he swept the detritus of ancient tobacco into the wastebasket. "Let's say that there was a high priest of Set. And this necromancer was using tanna leaves to animate dead bodies. But these dead bodies are not really alive—just . . . animated. Could the Scroll of Thoth be used to restore these dead bodies to life? To real life? Not just animated corpses?"

Susan hesitated in her pouring to cock a coppery eyebrow. "Hypothetically?"

I stared back. "Of course."

Her husband began packing his pipe with fresh tobacco. "Hypothetically . . . it might. Or it might merely negate the animating effects of the tanna or tanis leaves. On the other hand, it could destroy those same corpses as they are ensorceled by Set or his magicians: the power of Thoth is antithetical to the influences of Set."

I nodded. "Set was an enemy of Thoth and his master."

"Well, of course there's that. After Osiris went to rule in the Underworld, Thoth served Isis and her son Horus. He intervened to save Osiris's child on several occasions, including attempted assassinations by Set's minions. Later he served as judge between Horus and Set when they were brought before the tribunal of gods. The fact that he ruled in favor of Horus and against Set cemented their enmity."

"So, if an Egyptian necromancer were an acolyte of Set," I asked, "he wouldn't be too inclined to use the Scroll of Thoth in his incantations?"

"Good God, no. Set is the very incarnation of Evil, the god of opposition to all things good. Thoth is the god who supposedly invented all the arts and sciences: arithmetic, surveying, geometry, astronomy, soothsaying, magic, medicine, surgery, music, drawing, and above all, writing. As the inventor of hieroglyphs, he was named 'Lord of Holy Words.' As first of the magicians he was often called 'the Elder.' "

"But that's just one version of the old boy's credentials," Susan said, handing my glass to me. "According to the theologians at Hermopolis, Thoth was the true universal Demiurge, the Divine Ibis who had hatched the world-egg at Hermopolis Magna. They believed that the work of creation was accomplished by the sound of his voice alone." She handed a glass to her husband and then raised her own. "The Books of the Pyramids are a bit ambiguous about his pedigree, as well. . . ."

The Burmese with the bifurcated tail jumped up on the counter and sniffed the air adjacent to the open bottle. I set my glass by her and tipped it just enough to bring the wine within reach. The cat lapped delicately at the lip of the glass and purred, twin tails twining and untwining in rhythmic contentment.

"Sometimes he's listed as the oldest son of Ra, other times he's the child of Geb and Nut, the brother of Isis, Set and Nephthys. . ."

"But normally," her husband concluded, "he's merely friend and not member to the Osirian family. But, by any account, Thoth was a heavy mana-dude."

"Good," I said. I looked down at the blushing contents of my wineglass. I was thirsty. But not for wine.

"I'm not sure we answered your question," Susan said.

"I'm not sure you can."

"Well, if there is anything we can do in addition to the tanis leaves," Jim said, "don't hesitate to ask."

"Okay," I said. "I'd like to borrow your Scroll of Thoth."

Ahhh, Csejthe, you return. . . .

I had been staring into the inky blackness that seemed to stretch into infinity. Now my eyes refocused, expecting to see Dracula floating just outside the Beechcraft's wing window.

But it was only his voice fluttering in the back of my head.

Did you find what you need?

Maybe (I thought back at him.) I sent a mental picture of vest loaded with pockets of C-4 explosives.

This is your plan?

This is my fail-safe.

Fail-safe?

I'll be wearing this stuff the next time I go toe-to-toe with Kadeth Bey.

The Devil! You are serious?

As a heart attack. But the plastique is Plan B.

Plan B?

Just in case Plan A doesn't work.

Plan A?

And I want you right beside me.

For this Plan A of yours?

That's right.

So what is it you need for me to do?

Nothing. Just hang. I want you close to me.

For Plan A?

You could say that.

Then tell me of your plan.

No.

Then how can I help you with your Plan A?

You can't.

I do not understand.

I want you close to me just in case Plan A fails.

But if Plan A fails. . . .

Plan B (I thought), and sent him a mental picture of the probable explosion.

He left me alone for a while and I turned my attention back to the night sky.

It calls to you, he whispered, finally.

What? Art there old mole? "Hic et ubique" and get thee to a nunnery.

You are drawn to the darkness.

Not the darkness, old man, but the emptiness.

The emptiness?

The sky. It's empty, you know.

He had no immediate response.

When I was a child I used to lie on the ground and stare up at the sky, I mused. I used to believe that Heaven was an actual place. That it lay just beyond those distant blue curtains that shrouded it from earthbound, human eyes.

Now, looking up at the stars, I know better. The sky is an empty place. And except for a pittance of cosmic matter, the emptiness just goes on and on in all directions. Forever and ever. Amen.

It is true, Bassarab answered. *When the sun goes down and the light withdraws from the world, one can see things more clearly.*

I don't (I thought bitterly). I don't see clearly, at all. . . .

"Headache?" Smirl asked, breaking through my meditation.

I shook my head. "Just thinking."

"About life and death?" He smiled at the look on my face. "No, not telepathic: those of us who dwell beyond the boundaries of humankind think about it, too. Why not? You humans all do. You create religions and philosophies to sculpt sense out of chaos and promise something better on the other side of the dark. We have no theology that grants us eternal souls, existence beyond the grave. So we clutch at the edge of the cemetery gate and refuse to go gently into that good night. We are the embodiment of that rage at the dying of the light."

"So what do you believe?" I asked. "That you simply cease to be?"

He nodded over steepled fingers. "Do the complex array of memories, perceptions, emotions, distinctive selfness that each of us perceive as 'I' come undone and sift away into oblivion—irretrievable, nonexistent, forever lost?"

"Dust in the wind," I murmured, staring into the darkness, the emptiness outside my window.

And, when we are gone, our consciousness flown, are there other minds, other—things—waiting in the darkness, waiting to take up residency? Move into an abandoned body before it loses its viability?

What are you trying to say, old serpent?

That reality is not a one-way street. That, if there are

spirits that grow ancient and strong in the cold and darkness, might not other souls grow great and powerful in the nurturing light?

Voivode and Poet, Vladimir? What would you know about the light?

You are young, Csejthe. Come back and prattle your philosophies to me when you have the experience of five centuries.

"Some of us do terrible things," Smirl mused. "And we suffer terrible things to be done to us. All because undeath seems better than death final and irrevocable."

The plane tilted, making a leisurely turn in the dark emptiness. "We're here," he said. And looked at me.

Pay attention, my dear Christopher: the game is about to be taken to a new level.

Smirl looked away. Looked back at me. There was something in his eyes—something I wasn't sure I liked. "May I ask you a personal question?" he asked.

"I guess so."

"What would make you happy?"

I stared at him. "Happy?"

"Happy. Assuming you successfully eliminate Kadeth Bey and survive the process."

I hadn't really thought much about happiness, lately. "Peace on earth," I tried, "goodwill toward men and women."

He grimaced.

"Loose shoes, a significant relationship, and a comfortable bed?"

"Seriously."

"Seriously?"

He nodded.

"I don't know." I did know. I wanted my life back. I wanted to erase this past year.

"You want your life back," he said.

"What would be the point of wishing?" My voice sounded steady enough.

"Precisely. So, beyond that, what do you want? Realistically?"

"Control."

"Control?"

"Of my life. What's left of it, anyway. Since that day in the barn, I've been a dupe or a pawn or a trophy for somebody or something. I want to be left alone." Bassarab's words came back to me: *serve or be served.*

Smirl shook his head. "You gotta know that's as unlikely as the first. Even if you were just another ordinary vampire, they wouldn't allow you to run rogue."

Just another ordinary vampire. . . .

"So, the point is," he continued, "which demesne are you going to be happiest with?"

The cat stirred in my lap, cocked its head, and regarded Smirl warily.

"Given the situation with New York, I'm sure you don't want to even consider one of their offers. And nothing against our allies in Seattle, but the message I'm getting here is that they're cramping your style."

The cat made a rumbling sound in her throat. It wasn't a purr.

"Now, Chicago, on the other hand, has enough territory and opportunities that a man of your needs and resources—"

The cat hissed and Smirl seemed to suddenly remember its presence. "Anyway," he mumbled, "the Doman of Chicago has authorized me to offer you an invitation and," he eyed the cat warily, "it wouldn't be fair to you to not enumerate all of your options." He cleared his throat. "That's all. You make up your own mind."

The darkness was suddenly perforated by a double row of runway lights below us.

"Gone," Lupé said.

"Gone," I said.

"But not far."

"Not far," I said.

"Apparently they were using the old hospital complex for a daynest."

"What? The remains of the old Mount Horeb Hospital out by Atkinson Road?"

Lupé nodded. "They vacated early, last night. Headed south. I think they've retreated to Weir—possibly to Bassarab's farm. I didn't want to get too close: the terrain is so open out there, they'd likely see me coming long before I could get a glimpse of them."

I nodded. Yawned. Glanced at my watch: a little less than two hours before sunrise. "Okay. I gotta get some sleep and I imagine you do, too. Let's get an early start this evening and I'll have more to tell you then."

As I shifted my weight on the bed, my canvas valise toppled over and spilled three old wine bottles that had been recorked and then stoppered with wax.

"Not more holy water," Mooncloud said as I righted the bottles, checked the seals for leaks, and returned them to the bag.

"Not," I agreed. I handed her the Satterfield's copy of the Scroll of Thoth. "You once told me that this contains Words of Power—your caps. What does that mean?"

She unrolled the papyrus and considered the writing. Then she looked at me. "If you're looking to bring your wife and daughter back—"

"Will it bring the dead back to life? Yes or no, Doctor?"

"I'd rather discuss the ramifications—"

"No ramifications. No moral issues. As I said last night, we are past such philosophical meanderings. Before I take this plan, this crusade, a step further, I need to know what will and will not work. The road to this point has been littered with half-truths and lies and I will not go forward without knowing the truth."

"The truth," she said. And cleared her throat. "The truth is . . . I simply don't know."

I waited.

"Yes, there are Words of Power here. And, yes, change would likely be wrought upon dead tissue were these words invoked. But what kind of change?"

"So these are the words which Thoth spoke to raise Osiris from the dead?"

"Maybe. Probably. Who knows? Yes, there is power here. As a shaman I can tell you that powers invoked are designed to return a dead body to some semblance of the living state. But I can't tell you anything regarding the degree or quality." She reached out and grasped my arm. "And even should the body grow warm and its heart begin to beat once more, I can't tell you that the forces invoked by these words could accomplish the rest: could seek out that soul which had departed and return it to its former shell. I can't tell you that. No one can."

I raised my hand. "It is enough if you promise me that you can read the words and make dead flesh a living body once again."

She looked down. "I don't know that I can promise that."

"You don't know that you *can*? Or only that you *will*?" I reached out and cupped her chin with my hand. Raised her face and studied her moist eyes. "Taj," I said gently, "I need your trust in this. Trust me that I will do the right thing with this."

"Then trust me, too," she answered. "Tell me your plan so I can best help you."

I looked away. "I can't."

She caught my chin with her hand, turned my face back to hers. "Can't," she asked pointedly, "or won't?"

"Both, actually," I said. "I won't because we are plotting against creatures that are inherently telepathic. They have been one step ahead of us throughout this entire pursuit. The more each of you knows about the final plan, the greater the likelihood that a stray thought will be overheard. The greater the chance someone will unwittingly betray all of us."

And I "couldn't" because I still had to arrange a betrayal.

"Oh! Amon Ra," moaned a voice in the darkness.
"Oh!" echoed the sepulchral sound.
"God of Gods," it sighed in the blackness.
"Death is but the doorway to new life," the voice intoned, seeming to come from the earth itself.
"We live today. . . ." The hair on the back of my own neck was starting to rise. "We shall live again. . . ."
Cold, clammy hands clutched at me and—
I awoke to the sound of thunder and the rattle of rain against my motel room window. I rolled over and pulled my watch from the nightstand: 1:22 P.M. Outside it was dark.
I closed my eyes but sleep would not come. Perhaps I was feeling a little ambivalent about putting out the welcome mat.
I got up and began dressing. The cat merrowed from the foot of the bed and I found myself the object of its unblinking stare.
"What are you looking at?"
The cat merrowed again.
"I'm going out to the lobby for a paper." I pulled on a pair of cheap running shoes and Velcroed them snugly. "Don't wait up," I said, going to the door and palming my room key. "And don't use my toothbrush while I'm gone."
Locking the door behind me, I moved down the hallway, thinking furiously. First, I needed a taxi: the Chevy van was too hot to be driving about in broad daylight—even if it wasn't exactly daylight, now. Which was why I was going out, now. Which was why I needed an umbrella, first.
And then a taxi.
The motel lobby was devoid of pay or courtesy phones. I turned to the desk clerk, a plump, middle-aged woman with a greying beehive hairdo. She was lowering

the receiver back into the cradle of the multiline at the back of the counter. "I was going to call a cab for you," she said, "but there's already one waiting outside."

Sure enough, a taxi crouched just beyond the glass door wrapped in gauzy curtains of rain. I looked around the lobby but no one else was in sight. I wondered how soon the real fare would show up and if they'd be inclined to share. Unless things had substantially changed since my departure, there was only one taxicab servicing Pittsburg and Frontenac combined.

I looked back at the desk clerk. *I still need an umbrella*, I thought.

"Here," she said, reaching under the counter, "you'll be needing an umbrella."

Interesting: unconscious domination coupled with telepathy. That thought was chased from my mind as I took the umbrella and moved toward the door. There was something else, now—something like an invisible force, an airy riptide that pulled me toward the hunched vehicle. As if the car were a domelit magnet and I was an iron filing with legs.

Get in.

The thought reverberated in my mind, but it didn't originate there.

Get in. Take a ride.

Why the hell not?

I opened the umbrella and pushed out into the rain. As I opened the back door of the cab a sodden brown mass of fur splashed past my feet and catapulted into the backseat. Twin tails attempted to wring each other dry.

"Hey," said the cabbie as I slid in next to the cat, "no animals without a carrier!"

"Don't mind the cat," I said, trying to reclose the umbrella and the passenger door simultaneously.

"I don't mind the cat," the driver said.

"She won't be any trouble." I hoped.

"Won't be any trouble," the driver said.

The cat seemed oblivious to the exchange, giving

Chapter Twenty-One

Atkinson Road ran a portion of the boundary line that separated northernmost Pittsburg from southernmost Frontenac. There, girdled by three vacant lots, a pond, and a building that once served as the old student nurses' dormitory, stood the vacant shell of the original Mount Horeb Hospital. It was abandoned and bricked up when the "new" hospital had opened on the south side of town some decades past.

Although I gave no destination, offered no directions, the cab pulled over onto the muddy, rutted path that parted the weeds between us and the ancient, three-story brick edifice. Vacant-eyed, he half-turned in his seat. "Jeez, mister," he asked through slack lips, "you sure you wanna go here?"

I looked up at the weathered brick walls. Unlike the old Tremont Hotel, these windows had long outlived their plywood barriers and had finally been mortared shut. And now the mortar was crumbling with age. I thought about the labyrinth of rooms and corridors and operating theaters inside that had been evacuated before I was even born.

And so Childe Roland to the dark tower came. . . .

A moment later we were sheltering under my borrowed umbrella as the taxi plowed twin trails of mud in its wake. "I still say you should've stayed in the room," I said as the cat looked up at me and merrowed piteously. "No, I'm not going to carry you. You chose to come along on your own, so you can just hoof it, the same as me."

Come. . . .

The cat stiffened, its tails forming twin exclamation points.

"So, you felt it, too," I murmured.

Come inside. Come out of the rain. . . .

The cat yowled and took off after the cab like . . . well . . . a cat out of hell.

"Wuss," I said as it streaked off, a brown blur melting into the grey mists behind me.

Come. . . .

"Okay, okay; keep your cape on." I turned back toward the old hospital complex and began picking my way through a minefield of mud puddles.

A mental voice has no tone or timbre in the way that speech does when produced from human vocal chords. Even so, there was no mistaking the signature of this summoning: Elizabeth Bachman was putting out the welcome mat.

I could turn back even now. At least that's what I was telling myself. The possibility remained that any willpower I felt was an illusion itself.

But I moved toward the daynest. The plan was not complete: even now it might go one of three ways. Within the hour the final course would be set and the plan locked in. The important thing was to not die prematurely: I had to rescue what remained of my wife and daughter, first.

And then all bets were off.

Climb . . . came the thought as I reached the side of the building.

Of course. With the windows and doors mortared shut. . . . I laid the umbrella on the ground. Then I thrust my fingertips into the slotted spaces between the bricks over my head. Red chips and grey powder sifted down as I pulled myself up. Bricks fractured and mortar crumbled as each new handhold pitted transformed flesh against ancient masonry. I scaled the three stories effortlessly, like a human fly. Or bat. Or some*thing*. . . .

Once on the roof the way in was obvious: an access hatch jutted from the flat, tarpapered surface and had been capped with a metal trapdoor. Superhuman strength had wrenched the cover free of its latching mechanism and curled it backward like so much tin foil. No attempt had been made to bend the metal back into a semblance of its original shape: a reminder that these people were careless and sloppy.

But still dangerous.

Come down . . . come inside. . . .

I started across the roof but never made it to the trapdoor. The tar paper sagged beneath my feet and tore like soggy cardboard. I fell ten feet, passing through the remains of a secondary ceiling and landing on a sodden mass of debris on the floor of the third story. The room was empty save for the rusted, skeletal remains of an old metal bed frame. I stood up and allowed the dribbling waterfall that followed me down from the roof to wash the grit and detritus from my already rain-drenched clothing.

"Christopher. . . ."

I scrambled down off of the mound of trash and stumbled to the door.

"Christopher. . . ." No mindspeech, now, but an actual voice drifting up from the depths below.

My night vision was compensating for the narrow cone of uncertain light filtering down from the hole in the ceiling and roof. But, as I moved out into the hall and approached the stairway, the visual greyscale faded to near-black. For the moment, there was only my own, cooler-than-human body heat to provide illumination in the infrared spectrum. The only other source of light was an occasional crack or chink in the mortar of the outer walls and rain-swollen clouds had already turned day into the equivalent of night.

"Fie, foh, fum," I whispered, and groped my way down the stairs. My feet shuffled through patches of loose debris, fallen plaster, and ceiling tiles. And what felt like the desiccated remains of small animals—perhaps birds, perhaps rats. . . .

As I reached the first floor I could see a faint gleam of light another level below. I completed the turn with my hand firmly coupled to the bannister railing and stepped down into the depths. Now I was descending into the basement, below the surface of the earth. Though a vague promise of illumination flickered somewhere below, I felt the darkness pressing in more forcefully now.

I reached the bottom of the stairs and stumbled as my foot sought another step down where no more steps remained. To my left the darkness was cleft by a shimmering thread of gold, a thread which trembled, then exploded with a metallic groan into supernova brilliance. There was no time to shield my eyes: I was dazzled into temporary blindness.

My hands remained outstretched before me as if to ward off the light and the vague shapes that moved within its painful depths. Unseen fingers curled around mine. I was pulled toward the light.

I did not resist: I could not fight what I could not see, and more importantly, I had come to cut a deal.

To arrange a betrayal.

And when the blinding glare had finally diminished, shattered, and fled back to the hundreds of candlewicks that crowned the waxen obelisks scattered about the old boiler room, I looked into the scarred face of Elizabeth Bachman and made my mouth smile.

A wooden ruler, broken in two, and held so that both pieces intersected to suggest a Christian symbol—the triumph of light over darkness.

The potency of belief.

Cool, dry wood, fleetingly touched to the skin and yet the ruin of her face could not have been equaled by burning firebrands in that same amount of time.

The wound began at the left corner of her mouth and

angled just beyond the edge of her eye, where it made inroads into the hair at her temple. Bisecting this was another trenched burn that continued on the perpendicular and on down toward her neck. And it wasn't the wealed scar tissue in shiny hues of white, pink, purple, or grey. It was black. Charred flesh that refused even the semblance of a healing. There was no half-hearted, plastic compromise of cicatrix here nor even the more severe keloid deformity that one would expect as the aftermath of a severe burn. Just a hideous crucifix of blackened flesh scooped from the side of her face as if seared by intense heat only moments before.

And, like the wound, itself, the pain hadn't diminished with the passage of time. She teetered on the brink of madness with the unrelieved agony of it.

Undead flesh did not heal like living tissue; it required infusions of living blood to regenerate and knit. Yet the blood she had taken since I had branded her had failed to erase the mark or lessen her pain.

The potency of belief. . . .

Elizabeth Bachman now believed she could only be healed by the blood of the one who had wounded her. By the blood of one who was neither living nor dead. Nor undead. By the same blood that transcended such distinctions.

Blood, *she* believed, that must be offered willingly.

Not that she wouldn't try to take it by force, *I* believed, if it was denied her.

"So I have a bargaining chip," I said, as my own superhuman hearing picked up the sound of feet shuffling down the stairs behind us. Dead feet.

"A bargain?" Her mouth twisted and spasmed. "You did this to me and you speak of bargains! You *owe* me!" she screeched.

A jittery madness seemed to fog the air and I felt my composure slip a couple of notches. "Owe you?" I inquired softly. "I think *not*.

"The Doman of Seattle may owe you: repayment for

your betrayal. What do I owe you? Repayment for violating my family's graves? For working unnatural sorceries with their remains? Tormenting me with false hope?" My own voice was growing shrill. "Tell me what I owe you for that. For stalking and hunting me, driving me from my home, and preferring me dead if I did not ally myself to New York?"

"I was your friend!" she protested, trembling. "If I served the Doman of New York instead of Pagelovitch, that was no concern of yours. You, yourself, said that you owed him no allegiance. And during that time I was looking out for your best interests—"

"*I* look out for my best interests!" I snarled. "My mistake was ever in letting *anyone* decide *anything* for *me*. Well, no longer! I have learned to put my faith in no allegiance and you, among my many teachers, have tutored me best!

"But—" I hauled myself back from the edge of high melodrama "—I *will* bargain with you so that we both might have what we want," I concluded in a more reasonable voice.

She stared at me, her body quivering like the plucked string of a musical instrument.

"Your terms?" she whispered.

"First, call off your lackeys. I heard them on the stairs a few moments ago and I know that they have just come through the door behind me. If they take another step toward me, I shall leave this place and your bargain is flown."

Her eyes narrowed. "I summoned you here. I could summon you again."

I picked up a fat candle and hurled it at her. "I heard your call, and I came of my own free will because I wish to make you an offer. *Of my own free will.* That's the power in my blood. But if you continue to annoy me, I will be done with you and take my business to others who will treat me with respect."

She hesitated.

Call them off! my mind thundered.

She was visibly shaken. She gestured and I felt those behind me back out into the corridor. "You have changed."

"You don't know how much."

"What do you want?"

"Where is Kadeth Bey? Where is the Egyptian sorcerer?"

"Not here."

"Where?"

"Why should I tell you?" she growled. But I had already plucked the answer from her mind: *In Weir, lying in the ground beneath Bassarab's barn. Slowly regenerating his shriveled flesh and laying darker plans for the future. . . .*

Some twenty minutes to the southwest by car.

"I don't want him eavesdropping on this conversation. So, I'll tell you what I want." I turned and pointed at the grotesque forms of my wife and daughter adrift in the darkness just beyond the doorway. "I want them. I want them put to rest eternally." I turned back to face Bachman before their appearance could unnerve me. "And I want Kadeth Bey."

"You want Bey? Why?"

"So that once they are laid to rest, he can never disturb them again."

She shook her head slowly. "My Doman would never—"

"*To hell with your Doman!* He can't heal you or you wouldn't be suffering now! *I can,*" I said harshly. "So think about that but don't take too long! What does New York care about Kadeth Bey? He's dangerous, barely under your control, and he's messy. The only reason you suffer his existence is to serve as your hunting hound in tracking Dracula."

"Then you understand why I cannot bargain the Doman's best hope in running the Dark Prince to ground."

"I'll give you Dracula," I said.

"What? How?"

I smiled a painful smile. "You didn't originate the role of Judas, my dear. What makes you think you have a monopoly on it, now?"

"You'd give him to us? But we thought—"

"I told you that I have no allegiances," I said. "None. It's true that I have found those I travel with useful for a time. But that time is all but done. And Dracula? He's the reason my family is lost to me and I'm trapped between the living and the dead."

Bachman's eyes clouded as she weighed her choices.

"Here is my bargain," I continued. "I will give you the Prince of Walachia. Then you will no longer need Bey. Lay my family to rest and I will bring you Dracula. Do with him as you will and then destroy Bey. And I will be content."

Her face became a twisted mask of cunning. "You say you do not trust me. How do you know I will keep my part of the bargain and destroy the sorcerer once you have delivered the *voivode* into our hands?"

"Because when the deeds are done—and only after I know that Bey is utterly destroyed—I will give you what you want."

"Your blood," she whispered. And licked her lips. "How much?"

"As much as you require."

The right side of her mouth turned down. The distorted flesh of her face kept the left corner of her mouth twisted upwards in a contorted grimace. "Like you, I am not so trusting of bargains where I have no guarantees. What is my guarantee that you will give me of your blood once Bey is destroyed?"

"Hey, babe; you said the blood should be given willingly. You gotta exhibit some trust at some point."

"Nice kitty," croaked a voice from behind me.

I turned and saw Kirsten's small form emerging from the darkness by the stairs with her arms wrapped around a cat. A sable brown cat with two tails. The cat struggled in her embrace, but Kirsten's child-sized arms held it with more than human strength. A brown paw reached up and claws raked her throat. Three of the scratches, though deep, didn't bleed. Something oozed from the fourth claw mark, but then retracted after a brief inspection of its surroundings.

"Why, Chris," Bachman cooed, "all this talk of bargains and trust—and then you bring this creature along to spy on us?"

My mouth was suddenly dry as I looked back at her. "It followed me."

"Well, we can't very well have it going back and telling the others about our little bargain, can we?" She gestured and Jennifer—or, rather, the thing that still wore Jenny's form—extracted the cat from Kirsten's embrace and carried the hissing and spitting animal toward us. I stepped back as it was handed to Bachman.

The cat went still in her grasp as she raised it at arm's length. "My, my, my; what a naughty little pussy! Yes, you are! Yes, you are!" With inhuman speed she shifted her grasp so that one hand had the animal by the neck and the other closed around the base of both tails. Then she brought her knee up and the animal down in swift and simultaneous motions. There was an audible crunch and the cat fell to the floor like a dead thing.

Only it wasn't quite dead. Eyes glazed, it pawed feebly at the floor with its front paws and coughed blood from its nose and mouth. Its torso was bent at an unnatural angle and its hind legs flopped like boneless things, nearly indistinguishable from its twin tails. Bachman had broken the animal's back.

The cat twitched and shuddered and then stopped moving, its eyes focused on eternity in a half-lidded stare.

"It's dead," Kirsten rasped. "Can I play with it now?"

"She's not dead," Bachman said. "At least not yet. She's a lot harder to kill than that." The vampire gave me an appraising look. "I must say, you're a cooler customer than I thought. Back at Pagelovitch's castle I believed—but then I guess your bargain is the real thing, no? You really do have no allegiances, do you?"

I looked down at the twitching form of the broken cat and tried to hide the anger and the horror I felt. What I needed to accomplish here was far more important than the suffering of some dumb beast. And yet. . .

"Wanna play, wanna play," the Kirsten-thing was whining. "Hungry, Mama. Huunnngrrry!"

"I must confess," I said suddenly, "that I am not without some affection for the creature. And when this is done and I leave the others, I had thought. . ." What had I thought? I had to say something convincing before Bachman turned it over to the demon child that ranted behind me. " . . . to take her with me. To keep her as a pet. . . ." My voice trailed off at the expression on Bachman's face.

"Judas wept, Chris! Your ambition knows no bounds!" She shook her head. "When this is done, come back with me to New York, and our Doman will give you a dozen like her."

"Perhaps. Perhaps I will come to New York when this is all over. I would very much like to meet your Doman."

"And *she* would like to meet you," Bachman said, her lips twisting in the travesty of a smile.

"But before we lay any plans regarding future relationships, let's see if we can work things out in the here and now." The Kirsten-thing was edging closer, and I moved between her and the cat. "You wanted your guarantee, so how about this: when I have given you Dracula and you have given me Bey's destruction, then I will offer you the blood you need in exchange for—" I was about to say "the cat" but something whispered in my mind that I mustn't "—her."

Bachman looked dubious. "I think she will hate you for what you do here, tonight. I think she would rather die."

"You let me worry about that. Now, where shall we make the exchange?"

"Why not here?"

I looked around. "When?"

"How soon can you deliver Bassarab in a tractable state?"

"How soon can you dig up Bey and be ready to pull his plug?"

She stared at me and I could feel mental fingertips scrabbling at the latches of my skull.

"Tomorrow night," she said finally.

I shook my head. "You want Bassarab tractable? It has to be during the day."

"Daylight gives your side the advantage."

"It'll just be the two of us. The others will be left out of it."

"And how will you accomplish that?"

My smile had no humor behind it. "I'm running the show now. Not everyone knows that, yet, but they will by tonight." A thought occurred and my smile turned into a frown. "There may be a problem getting Bassarab's coffin up and onto the roof."

"There is another way in." Bachman picked up a candle from one of the dusty workbenches and motioned for me to follow. "There is an underground service tunnel," she said as I stepped carefully around the twitching cat. "It connects the basement with the remains of the old physical plant to the northeast." A row of boards, standing on end, leaned against the far wall. Bachman pulled them aside to reveal a stone-flagged arch compassing a closer darkness that stank of mold and cobwebs and sour earth. "There's a ladder at the other end that goes up and comes out where the generators used to be. An old sheet of plywood camouflages the opening and keeps the rain out."

"What's the distance?"

"From here to the other end? Maybe thirty or forty yards. Perhaps you should ask Kirsten: she spends hours back in there. It's her favorite place." Her smile turned into a scowl as she looked back over my shoulder. "Get back!" she shrieked. "Get away from her!"

I turned and saw the Kirsten-thing and Jenny-thing step back from where the cat laid.

"Go through the service tunnel," she ordered. "There are plenty of fat, juicy rats there. Hunt until you are full and do not return until I call for you." We moved to let them pass and she turned back to me. "Shall I call the cab for you?"

"No, thanks," I said, "I'll flag down my own ride back."

She reached out and touched my throat, slid her finger down my chest. "I still want to be your friend, Chris. And I will be pretty again, soon." I stepped back so that her hand fell away. "And I will be very grateful for the healing of your blood. Certainly more grateful than she will be," Bachman said, gesturing toward the cat.

I turned toward the stairs—as far as the service tunnel was concerned, two was company and I wasn't about to turn it into a crowd. As I moved to step carefully around the cat, the universe suddenly did a corner-turn on its axis and everything was suddenly changed. . . .

The puddle of blood had grown and so had the body. Suki lay, twisted on her side, eyes glazed, blood leaking from her mouth and nose. She twitched. But only the upper half of her body moved.

How long I stood there, I could not tell. It was Bachman's voice that broke the spell, reminding me of where I was, that moments were passing. "Chris?" Her voice was touched with amusement and surprise. "Chris? Oh my. You didn't know, did you? You really didn't know!" She laughed. "Oh, this makes me feel much better about our bargain! For a while I thought you might be keeping secrets from me. But you, poor baby, you are the one who's still in the dark."

I turned, wanting to do terrible things, but icy will managed a feeble grip on my sanity and held its ground. "The bargain still holds, Elizabeth."

"Now that you know, darling, wouldn't you rather I remove this complication from the equation?"

I pointed a finger of stone at her. "The bargain still holds. She is your guarantee of the blood given willingly." And then I turned and ran for the stairs.

My control held through the long ascent to the roof and my skittering descent of the outside wall. Splashing through puddles and mud mired weeds, I was nearly across the field and back to Atkinson Road when I finally fell to my knees and began to vomit.

Chapter Twenty-Two

Perhaps there was a God.

And maybe He did answer prayer: the sun was starting to break through the clouds as I sent my ride on his way with no memory of his hitchhiker. I glanced at my watch: 4:11—maybe another three and a half hours before sundown. Nearly four hours before Bachman could leave her daynest and drive to Weir to collect Kadeth Bey.

It was a boon and blessing, but it might not be enough. I had to trust that Bachman would take her two creatures with her rather than trust them alone with Suki. And I had to hope my basic plan would tolerate some improvisations as I went along. There was still much to do, and I was too tired and thirsty to think clearly.

Smirl's eyes were muddy from lack of sleep and the mental compulsion to meet me as he opened the door and let me into his room.

"How much C-4 can we remove from the vest and still guarantee Bey's destruction?" I asked as he closed the door behind me.

"Proximity?" He pulled the valise from the closet and sat on the bed.

"Same as before: five feet or less."

"Close enough to shake hands."

I nodded. *Or take him by the throat.*

"If he were human, a couple of bricks would be more than enough."

"But he's not," I said. "We've been over this before."

"And I told you that you could use a third of what's

wired into that vest and there still wouldn't be enough remains for DNA testing."

"I need to be sure, Dennis: I don't want him coming back after this." I considered. "You said the remote had two circuits. Do you have a second detonator? And the material to arm a second charge?"

"Yes. But the only plastique I have is what is already wired in the vest."

"Half," I decided. "You said a third would be more than sufficient for taking out Bey. So take half from the vest and prepare a second circuit."

"I may need more wire. What kind of a charge do you want and how long before you need it?"

"Four hours," I said. "It's got to be ready in four hours."

Going back to my own room was like entering a fairy tale—specifically, "Goldilocks and the Three Bears."

Someone was sleeping in my bed.

Well, not sleeping exactly. And it wasn't Goldilocks.

"Where have you been?" Lupé asked, bare shoulders emerging from under the covers.

"I've been to London to look at the queen."

A slow smile spread across her mouth. "Pussycat, pussycat, what did you there?"

"I hunted the rat that hides under her chair."

"Really?" she asked, sitting up. The covers drooped and I was treated to the sight of more than bare shoulders. "You found her? Where? She returned to the daynest?"

I hesitated. Locked the door. And then nodded. "Don't!" I said sharply as she started to move. "Go there now and you might—I say *might*—have a chance at Bachman. But not much of a chance and Kadeth Bey will escape us for good. Give me twelve hours. By sunrise tomorrow morning, everything and everyone should come together. Please. That way we can both take our revenge. Trust me."

"I do," she said, eyes glistening, "I trust you more than anyone I know."

Her words and the look in her eyes brought back Mooncloud's warning of a few days before: *She has no one, now, Chris. Human companionship is out of the question. To her undead masters she is nothing more than a subservient species. And if she tried to rejoin her own kind, the taint of the Nosferatu would cling to her like a shroud.*

And what about me? Was I really human anymore? The societies of Pagelovitch and the other demesnes were anathema to me, as well, so weren't we really two of a kind?

"What are you doing in my bed?"

"Waiting for you."

"Why?" I felt myself on a mental tightrope, trying to stay focused on the equation of betrayal and revenge I had set in motion this day. I was tired, thirsty, and my head throbbed from the glow of sunlight that was leaking around the motel room curtains.

"You know why. Why do you pretend to ask?"

I didn't need any additional distractions: the next several hours were going to be complicated enough.

"Or maybe I was wrong," she continued. "I thought you—that maybe we—" She looked down suddenly. "What am I," she whispered, "to you?"

"An ally," I said. "A friend. . . ." A chess piece?

"Am I woman, as well? Or am I some kind of creature—a thing—that looks like a woman?"

You like to do it doggie-style, Chris? You like animals? But the memory of Jenny's yellow, predatory gaze faded as I looked at Lupé and saw the moisture brimming below her warm brown eyes.

"No," I said. "You're not a thing. You're not a creature. You are the most human person I've known since my wife and daughter died."

"Then, is that the problem? Your wife? You're still in love with your wife."

"My wife," I said harshly, "is dead. She has been dead for more than a year. The past is dead and buried." My lips curled as those last words escaped my mouth. "Dead, anyway. And after tomorrow—I hope—permanently buried."

"But you're thinking of trying to bring her back. The Scroll of Thoth—"

"Even supposing it were possible—something has taken their place. I don't know that they could come back now. And if they could—" my voice suddenly broke "—I don't know if they should."

She was out of the bed, then, and taking me by the hands, leading me back to it. She sat on the edge of the mattress and began unbuttoning my shirt. "You're tired."

"Yes."

"You're thirsty."

"Yes. . . ."

"Too much to do," she said. "Too many thoughts of death." The belt was next. "Let it all go for a few hours. Rest."

I felt numb and detached, but not totally passive; I stepped out of my pants and shoes, undressed the rest of the way and moved onto the bed as she slid over to make room. "Three hours," I mumbled. "Wake me at sunset. . . ." I closed my eyes.

I felt her roll over on her side, felt slim fingers at my temples pushing at the tension that had accumulated there over the long hours, days, weeks.

"You'll need strength for tonight," she whispered.

"Mmm," I said. And promptly fell asleep.

"Oh!" moans a voice in the darkness.

"Amon Ra," it sighs in the blackness.

"Oh!" echoes the sepulchral sound.

"God of Gods," the voice intones, booming in the tomblike stillness.

"Death is but the doorway to new life. . . ." The hair on the back of my neck starts to rise.

"We live today. . . ."

The power begins to gather.

" . . . we shall live again. . . ."

Death hisses at me—

" . . . in many forms shall we return. . . ."

Reaches for me—

"Oh, mighty one. . ."

There is a sound of thunder and raw earth fills my mouth as I try to scream—

Awake—

"Shhh." Slender hands caressed my face, stroked my forehead. "Shhhh."

I opened my eyes and looked at Lupé. She knelt, straddling me. The room had grown darker and infrared overlay of my night vision made her appear to glow, golden brown skin seemingly lit from within. My vision clarified as sleep receded and I could see the tiny hairs that fuzzed her arms and legs and belly and coalesced into a downy trail that led southward from the dark pit of her navel.

Then I saw the knife. She lifted the golden blade, saying, "This is my body." She opened a vein in her arm. "This is my blood. . . ." She leaned down and pressed the wound to my lips, pressed her flesh to mine.

We filled one another.

Oh!

In the dream I am running at tremendous speeds.

Amon Ra. . . .

I am a human express train barreling through a kaleidoscopic wind tunnel of lights and sounds and smells—especially smells! A profusion of scents batters my nostrils, ricochets through my sinuses, explodes inside my skull.

Oh!

It is distraction to the point of disorientation and I do not notice the sounds at my back until I have been running for quite some time. The sound of wolves, howling. Gathering.

Hunting.

Pursuing.

God of gods. . . .

My feet are invisible, the rolling ground is a blur beneath me. New awareness: I am running uphill. And the ground seems nearer my face than it should! Behind me the howls rise in an unholy chorus.

Death is but the doorway to new life. . . .

And death waits ahead, up the trail. Bassarab rises from a jumble of rocks. Spreads his cape with his arms like a giant bat flexing its wings. "So!" he says. "You have broken the Law! You have defied the Covenant! Even after my warnings. . . ." He gazes down at me like a stern falcon: disapproval before the kill.

"Now you must run!"

We live today. . . .

"Until today you were the secret they coveted, a prize to be won. But now you are become the secret that the vampire lords must keep hidden from even their own kind. A secret they must destroy to keep to themselves." He hunches in upon himself.

. . . we shall live again. . . .

"So you must run in earnest, now," he growls, changing. His skin bursts open in silent explosions of dark fur. His face lengthens and his mouth sprouts twin rows of triangular teeth. He falls forward and his limbs shorten to bring him forward and parallel to the hardscrabble ground.

Now his height matches mine.

I look down and consider my forelegs. Lift a paw and examine the tufts of fur between my toe pads.

. . . in many forms shall we return. . . .

"Now, run, little one! For the blood-bond, I will show you where and how you may hide. But it must be your cunning that breaks the trail from your pursuers!"

Oh, mighty one. . . .

He leaps forward and I follow quickly. The sound of the pack at our backs raises hackles of fur from my shoulders to my tail. . . .

* * *

I had fallen asleep in Lupé's arms. I woke up, not on the bed but crouched on the floor of another room. Bassarab stood over me, his expression unreadable.

"What happened? Where am I?"

"My room," he said, handing me a blanket to cover myself with.

"How did I get here?"

"You traveled the path of your dream."

"I was walking in my sleep?" The thought of involuntary sleepwalking was bad enough. Wandering about the corridors of a public motel, starkers, worse.

"You did not walk. You came as the mist."

"Missed?" I was still in a fog. "Wait a minute. What are you telling me, here? That I came in like the fog? On little cat feet?"

"In a manner of speaking."

"Really? You're saying I turned into a bunch of mist—like in the movies—and flowed under the doors?"

"No." He sat on the bed and looked tired. "I'm not saying that."

"So what are you saying?" I stood, wrapping the blanket about me Indian-style. "Are we talking teleportation, here? Telekinesis? Stuff like that?"

He nodded—reluctantly, I thought. "Something like that."

I gave a low whistle. "How come nobody told me that this was part of the process?"

"Because it isn't. Part of 'the process,' that is. It only happens to a select few."

"How?"

He just looked at me.

"Lupé's blood," I answered for him. "When you first revealed yourself, you told us that the blood of the *wampyr* and the lycanthrope must never mingle. That it was the law and the penalty for breaking that law was death."

No response beyond the single nod of his head.

I shook my head in turn. "It can't be that simple. If all it took was a little of her blood to give me this power, then vampires would be biting werewolves at every opportunity, law or no law."

"It isn't that simple," he agreed.

"Of course not; I just said that. So what's the rest of it?"

Bassarab contemplated the worn carpet at his feet. After a protracted silence he sighed and finally spoke. "The part that should immediately concern you is this: once the others know that you've acquired the power of a Doman, they'll see you as an even greater threat. They will hunt you down and destroy you. Not for the sake of superstition—but because the law was conceived to keep others from becoming rivals to their power. And because you are not fully *wampyr*, but straddle the worlds of the living and the undead, you may be even more powerful than they imagine."

"But I'm not a threat! I don't want what they have!"

"Look at me!" Bassarab's eyes seemed to smolder deep in his skull. "I turned my back on them all. Bequeathed them nearly all of the wealth and power that I had amassed over the long centuries. Said, 'Here, take it and leave me in peace. In solitude.' Were they grateful for my abdication? A larger selection of the spoils?

"No! They have hunted me and hounded me! The very demesne I fathered recruited that corruption Kadeth Bey. Turned him loose like an unholy hound to sniff out my trail and destroy anything that might have ties to me!

"They know I will keep their secret. Most owe their success, their very existence, to me. So what mercy and consideration do you expect from these undead masters who have decreed the law and its penalty for all of their own kind?"

"One thing at a time," I answered him. "If I survive this night, then I'll worry about tomorrow and next week and next year."

His thin lips curled in a humorless smile. "That is precisely what must not happen," he said. "You must not survive this night. . . ."

Nor must you, I thought, matching my smile to his.

I had to walk back to my room with the blanket draped about me like a vastly oversized toga: try as I might, I was unable to return to my room by the so-called dreampath. Bassarab refused to discuss the matter further. Time was short, he said, and we would continue that particular conversation after Kadeth Bey was utterly and irrevocably destroyed. If either of us survived, that is.

So we discussed the Plan. And before we were done, we not only knew that we would both have to die, but we also knew when and how, as well.

The sun was already down before I could join Smirl in the drainage ditch that ran along Atkinson Road. The runoff from the storm churned around his boots as he crouched against the angled embankment and studied the ruins of the old hospital and the field around it through a pair of Brunton infrared binoculars.

"You're late," he said as I slid down into the water beside him. Unlike Smirl, I wore tennis shoes, and the icy water leeched the feeling from my lower legs in seconds.

"Any movement?"

"They left ten minutes ago." He capped the field glasses and scrambled up and onto the shoulder of the road.

I looked down to where my shins disappeared into the roiling water and my jeans were wicking the water up toward my knees. Then I looked up at Smirl's waterproof Magnums that were already beading dry. "How many?" I grunted, climbing back up to join him. Water dribbled from my laced eyelets as we walked across the road.

"Three. Just as you said."

"That should be it, but I'm going inside to make sure."

He reached inside his trenchcoat and produced two Tracker headsets, handing me one. "How much time do we have?"

"Minimum of forty-five minutes," I said, adjusting the earpiece and microphone arm. "Maybe two hours at the other end." I clipped the control box and battery pack to my belt. "Assuming they don't change their minds on the way over and come back without picking up Bey."

"Then we'd best hurry," Smirl murmured, his voice crackling in my earpiece.

I nodded and jammed my fingers into the old hospital's ancient mortar. I began climbing.

The tunnel would have been easier and my wet tennis shoes made this ascent harder than the last. But it would have been entirely too logical for Bachman to booby-trap the passage against my premature return, and the fewer who knew about the back door, the better.

This time I managed to cross to the trapdoor without punching any new holes in the roof. I slid down the steel access ladder, unclipped the Sabrelight from my belt, and switched it on. I worked my way down the stairs, making a cursory sweep of all the rooms on each floor before descending to the next level. I found nothing of import: trash, broken plaster, and archeological evidence of furniture from the premodern era.

The only significant finds were the dead rats.

I'd seen dead mice before: you don't grow up in the country, with a cat, without experiencing a parade of feline gifts on your doorstep.

But rats are a good deal larger. And these particular rodents had been gutted so that little remained but their furry rinds. Some had their heads bitten off; others, their legs torn out. I tried to not speculate whether that had happened while they were still alive. About the kind of hungers at work here.

And then I was down in the basement and easing my way into the furnace room.

It was darker now. The myriad candles had burned

lower and many had gone out, reduced to shapeless puddles of wax, dark smears marking the grave of each wick. The area seemed deserted. Nothing stirred. No one was in sight.

Then I heard breathing.

Gasps, actually; sharp intakes of breath, followed by explosive exhalations. A sigh. A sob. Soft, slithery sounds.

I moved to where I had last seen Suki. She was gone. A smeary trail of blood led away from the area where she had been dropped. I followed it. Found her trying to wedge herself beneath one of the workbenches. She had used the failing strength in her arms and shoulders to pull herself across the concrete floor, leaving a spoor of blood and displaced debris in her wake. Now she was propped up on her forearm and using a piece of scrap lumber in her other hand, trying to push her unresponsive legs between the heavy wooden supports of the bench and toward the rear wall. Before it disappeared into the dark, dusty depths, I noticed small, bloody wounds on the back of her left leg.

Bite marks.

Larger than a cat's, lacking the elongated pattern of a canine muzzle.

Smaller than a human adult's bite radius. . .

"Oh, dear God," I whispered.

Suki stopped pushing and tried to look up. As she twisted around, her eyes rolled up in the back of her head and she passed out.

I reached down and gently extracted her from beneath the workbench. And then, because there was no other way and time was running out, I lifted her in my arms. She groaned but didn't wake or stop breathing. I was counting on her inhuman physiology keeping her alive despite the damage that would accrue in moving her. I turned around and started toward the stairs.

Smirl was standing in the doorway, holding a cordless, electric drill. "Is this smart?"

"Smart?" I echoed.

"Removing her as a hostage from the equation," he said quietly. "Will it put you in a stronger negotiating position? Or will the others call the whole thing off when they return and find her gone?"

"I can't leave her here."

He stared at me. "No, I don't suppose you could." He replaced the drill in the valise and walked around the room, studying it from the floor up. Finally he sighed and slipped a Glock 19 auto pistol out of the shoulder holster under his coat. "If you'll give me a few more minutes, I have some things I need you to carry back to the motel for me."

He slipped out of his trenchcoat, folded it neatly, and slid it into the valise. Then he sat down and began tugging at his left boot.

It was midnight when I finished the last of my errands and returned to my room. My clothes were stiff with drying blood and clotted here and there with masonry dust from a bricked-up window I had kicked out in the back of the old hospital, on the first floor. Though I had done a fair job of restacking the bricks, there was no chance they'd pass muster in the light of day. I had to hope that darkness and other distractions would camouflage my makeshift exit until it was too late.

I stripped off my clothes and cranked the hot water in the shower up into the lobster zone. I stood under the scalding spray until the water heater recycled and the temperature began to drop. My skin steamed as I toweled off, but inside my chest was a coldness that continued to grow. That felt as if it would never be warm again.

I lay on the bed and tried to relax. I couldn't.

I closed my eyes and tried to find my way onto the dreampath. I couldn't.

Thought about Suki and tried to feel reassured about the way I had left her.

I couldn't.

I lay there, as the hours passed, ignoring Lupé's occasional, tentative knock at my locked door, and thought about monsters and fear and death.

Of how my greatest fear was of what I was becoming.

And the madness that seemed to be creeping closer.

"Rise and shine, sleepyhead," Jenny whispered.

I was tired. My eyes didn't want to open.

"Come on, Chris, it's sunup." Her hand grasped my shoulder, shook it. "If you don't get up, you know what I'll do!" she teased.

"Nooo," I finally moaned. "You're cruel woman. . . ." But I knew I had to get up: I couldn't let her—

My eyes snapped open and I grabbed for her wrist. She wasn't there, of course. I was alone in an empty room. Sometime during the wee hours, I had drifted off to sleep only to be roused from my dreams by yet another dream.

I rolled out of bed and began dressing. My tennis shoes were still damp: there was no help for it but to pull them on over dry socks. I buckled on a Bianchi shoulder rig, but discovered the Dartmaster pistol didn't sit the holster properly. I pulled the harness off and rummaged through Smirl's valise for something more suitable. The best I could come up with was his trenchcoat. A bit loose, but the pockets were large and serviceable.

I sorted through the hypodermic darts, loading one into the gun, placing two more in my shirt pocket, and dropping the rest into the left coat pocket. Then I shrugged into the coat, hoping Smirl wouldn't mind, and dropped the Dartmaster and the extra CO_2 cartridge into the right pocket. Then I clipped the radio set to my belt and adjusted the headset so that the microphone and earpiece were positioned properly. The detonator was next, and I used four rubber bands to hold it snug against my left wrist.

Special Forces. . . . I smiled grimly. *All that training, largely gone to waste these many years. If the major could only see me now. . . .*

Last of all, I considered the piece of papyrus on the floor by my bed. I had dropped it there when I had dozed off, trying to memorize the text.

"O! Amon Ra, oh!" I murmured, picking up the paper and folding it into the front pocket of my jeans. I picked up the pocketed vest, now devoid of half of its volatile adornment. "God of gods. . . ." I picked up the Sabrelight on the dresser as I crossed the room. I reached down and twisted the doorknob. "Death is but the doorway. . . ."

I walked out the door.

Chapter Twenty-Three

I knocked on the door to Bassarab's room just as Mooncloud and Garou rounded the corner and started down the hallway.

Wren opened it after a moment with an expression of mild surprise. "Too late," he yawned, "he's already asleep."

"Good." I pushed Wren back into the room and crossed the threshold.

"I didn't invite you in," he said, half-puzzled, half-annoyed. His eyes widened when he saw the gun in my hand. "Hey, there's no need for that."

"I'm afraid there is," I said, hearing the others pause at the open doorway. "Lupé, shut the door."

I heard them enter behind me and, as the door clicked shut, I pulled the trigger.

"Ow—shit!" he said as the dart caught him in the shoulder. Garou grabbed my arm as Wren pulled the projectile out of his flesh and looked up at me, his face a mask of disbelief.

"Too late." I pulled my arm free and tucked the gun back into my coat pocket. "The tranquilizer is already in your bloodstream. It's extremely fast-acting, I'm told."

It would seem I was told correctly: he took a couple of uncertain steps toward me and then seemed to misplace his equilibrium entirely. He staggered, sank to his knees, and then keeled over onto his left side.

"You probably won't lose consciousness entirely," I said, picking him up and depositing him on the bed, "but you won't be able to move about under your own power for the better part of the next hour or so."

"Are you mad?" Mooncloud wanted to know.

"What is the problem, Doctor? It wasn't very long ago that you wanted my allegiance in just such a betrayal. Now I'm doing your work for you."

"Wha—yoo—wan?" Wren slurred, head lolling on the pillow.

"Your master and I have a little business to conduct," I answered. "He may prove somewhat reluctant and I would prefer to not have to address your reluctance, as well. You should spend the next hour contemplating a career move. I think you're about to become unemployed."

The packing case that served as Bassarab's daybed was under a blanket and pushed up against the inside wall, blocking the closet. I yanked the blanket aside and opened the valise.

"I think it's time you filled us in on the rest of your plan," Mooncloud said, a touch of fear tingeing her voice.

I shook out the pocketed vest containing the plastique charges. "As I said before, Doctor, the less you know the safer we all will be. It's time to choose: you can follow my orders, or return to your room now."

"What if I change my mind halfway through?"

"I can command your obedience," I said, giving her a mental push. "Remember?"

Her mouth tightened. "Tell me what to do."

"Pull the shades."

She did, the room darkened, and Garou switched on a lamp in the corner.

"Help me get this open." They both came over and lifted the lid while I knelt by the midpoint of the camouflaged coffin.

Just like some Hollywood cliché, Bassarab lay in repose, flat on his back, with his arms folded across his chest so that his fingertips were pointed toward opposite shoulders. His eyes were closed, his face a study in hardened wax.

"Now what?" Lupé wanted to know.

"Help me sit him up."

"*What?*" they both chorused in shocked whispers.

"Help me sit him up!" I tugged on his arms. At the last minute they joined in and we managed to bend the old vampire at the waist until we bore a passing resemblance to the historical tableaux on Mount Suribachi. "Now we have to dress for success." I unfolded an arm and slid it through the appropriate opening in the vest.

"Pretty flexible for a sleeping vampire," Garou grunted. "They're usually pretty rigid when we pop them during the day." She had to change her grip as I brought the vest around and behind. "Of course, once the stake goes in, they're total *stiffs*."

Mooncloud didn't smile at the pun. "We've never dealt with anyone half as old. And since we stake them as soon as we open the coffin, we really don't know how much handling it would take to actually wake one."

"Or how much talking," Bassarab said, just as I got his other arm though and pulled the vest closed across his chest. The vampire's eye were open now, and I slapped the Velcro closures shut. "What are you doing, Christopher?"

Mooncloud and Garou, staggered back, clutching their heads; I suffered no personal discomfort. I held the remote detonator up before his eyes and sent him a mental picture of just what he was wearing and what I would do if he didn't cooperate. Then, for the benefit of Mooncloud and Garou, I explained it again, out loud.

His lip curled. "You can't be serious."

"On the contrary," I replied, "I've never been more serious in my life."

"And you'd detonate these explosives, knowing that you will be killed, as well?"

"If you'll recall, Vladamir, the original plan was for me to wear the vest. I've already died once and I figure the odds are against my seeing the sun set this evening. My only concern is that there are two people I'd like to take with me when I go."

"You blame me for your family's deaths," he said. "This is your revenge."

"I want Bey," I said. "He's the one who dug them up. He's the one using them now. You're my ticket to his destruction. I'd rather have Bey, but I'll settle for you if you don't cooperate."

He considered my words and then glanced at Mooncloud and Garou. "Perhaps you are willing to sacrifice yourself. But am I to believe that you would blow up your friends, too?"

I smiled. "Have you forgotten so quickly? I have no 'friends.' Only allies. You taught me that." I turned to Mooncloud and Garou. "What do you say, ladies? Would I blow you up, too?"

Garou's face was coarse with impending change: she nodded slowly. Mooncloud's features were ashen. "I do believe you would," she murmured.

"So, it's settled," I said, pushing him back down into the long packing crate. "Cooperate and this might all work out so that we are both rid of Kadeth Bey. Mess with me, and we'll all go find out what God really looks like."

He made no reply and I slammed the lid shut.

Garou and I wrestled the packing crate down the hall and out the side entrance while Mooncloud drove the Bronco around to meet us. Even after dropping the tailgate and the rear seats, we had to shift the box in diagonally, letting a good foot and a half hang off the rear end. I crawled in with it to stabilize the load while Garou rode up front with Mooncloud. No one spoke during the short drive. Mooncloud kept glancing in the rearview mirror at the detonator strapped to my wrist. Garou sat in stony silence, glaring out the window as if some sort of meaning might be found in the passing scenery.

We drove to Atkinson and then followed the rutted

path across the field. "Around to the back," I said as we approached the old hospital building. "Stop here."

You couldn't miss it in the light of day: the bricks had been replaced in the southeast window, but now they were a jumbled stack instead of the uniform wall of the day before. Anyone coming up from the basement after sunrise would notice in an instant. Perhaps they noticed last night.

Perhaps they noticed Suki. . . .

While Garou and I wrestled the packing crate out, Mooncloud adjusted her transceiver headset and turned it on. "Now what?" she asked, as we set Bassarab's transport on the ground, next to the building. "Do we knock?"

"Yeah," I said, picking up a melon-sized chunk of concrete. I hurled it through the old casement and the brick façade exploded inward. "Knock-knock."

The three of us lifted the crate over the tumbled sill and shoved it toward the shadows inside.

"Now what?" Mooncloud repeated, dusting off her hands.

"It's very simple, Doctor," I said, pulling the Dartmaster out of my pocket. I shot Garou in the thigh. "You are going to assist Lupé over to the Bronco while she can still walk, get in, and drive to the far side of the field where you will wait for further instructions."

"You bastard!" Garou cried, yanking the dart out of her leg. "Why?"

"It's a cleaner equation if you're not part of the math. Better move toward the Bronco: I calculated a more potent dose to compensate for your lycanthropy."

She started to stagger and Mooncloud moved in to provide support. "Let me put her in the Bronco and then come with you."

"There's no need for either of you to go where I'm going," I said with a half smile. I turned and pulled myself up and through the ragged opening. Then I turned back and flashed the remote, strapped just below my left hand. "Remember, the far side of the field, and don't come any closer until this deal is done." I switched on my own headset. "Adios."

Garou was definitely getting wobbly. As Mooncloud attempted to shepherd her toward the vehicle, I broke open the Dartmaster and removed the CO_2 cartridge. I didn't know how close the test firings coupled with the two shots I'd used on Wren and Garou had come to exhausting the charge, but I wasn't going downstairs without a fresh load of propellant. I changed cartridges and tossed the extra dart I had readied for Garou just in case the first dosage had been insufficient. I reached into my other pocket and loaded one of the special darts I had prepared for Kadeth Bey.

And then I kicked open the lid to Bassarab's box.

"You are a dead man," he hissed.

"You have a knack for stating the obvious." I repocketed the dart gun and gestured with the detonator. "Get up."

He moved sluggishly, except where the wedge of sunlight through the broken wall threatened to touch him. I slipped the detonator off my wrist and used the rubber bands to refasten it to the Sabrelight while he reached into the crate. He shook out the black duster that served him as a nineteenth century substitute for an eighteenth-century cape.

As he opened the lining in the back of the garment, I wondered how he would upgrade his wardrobe for the next century. Nehru jacket? Probably not as handy for hang-gliding nor for concealing weapons like the Mossberg 9200 shotgun he was sliding into the opening that would drape between his shoulder blades.

"This is madness!" he protested as he donned the coat and adjusted the shoulders against the awkward weight down the middle of his back. "How do you expect to pull this off?"

I repressed the urge to say, "That's for me to know and you to find out." Instead I countered with a question of my own: "How come you didn't travel the dreampath the day your house burned down?"

"What?"

"You were already burned by the fire. Why did you subject yourself to further damage from the sun when you could have transported yourself by traveling this so-called dreampath?"

He scowled and studied the wedge of sunlight spilling through the shattered wall, a reminder that all of his escape routes were cut off. "It is not so easy. I was disoriented from the smoke, the heat. And the sun was up: I have never traveled a dreampath during the day. I'm not sure that it can be done.

"To travel the dreampaths, you must relax, clear your mind. You must focus your mind on a specific destination or you may become lost in between."

"And where's that?"

He shrugged, moving closer to the inner door that opened on the central hallway. "Limbo. Between dimensions."

"Like being banished?" I was remembering Luath and the general.

"Very like. Perhaps worse."

"But the first time I did it, I ended up in your room, and I wasn't focusing on a destination at all."

"That was my doing. I sensed your movement within the dreamplane. I intercepted you to keep you from becoming lost in between."

"So, what happens the next time I dream? What if you're not around to reel me back in?"

"This is not to become a problem."

"Yeah? And why not?"

"Because," he said, "very soon we shall both be dead."

"Oh, yeah," I said, "I forgot."

He eased the door open and peered into the darkness of the corridor. "However," he said after a long moment, "if you and I were to both survive this—"

"We're speaking hypothetically here, of course. . . ."

"Of course."

"Thought so."

"If we were to survive, I would probably find the time to coach you through a couple of controlled dream-walks—"

"I can't believe you two are bickering about this," Mooncloud's voice crackled in my earpiece, *"while Bey and Bachman are probably waiting right around the corner."*

"I was wondering when you were going to join us, Doctor. How's Lupé?"

"Still conscious, but unable to do anything beyond cursing your name. If they don't kill you, there's a very good chance that she will, once the tranquilizer wears off."

"Don't worry about us, Doctor: Bachman is already expecting us, and we're making enough noise to let them know we're not trying to sneak up on them."

"Perhaps we should not keep them waiting," Bassarab said, reaching the junction of the hallway and the stair-well.

"Okay, Doc, close your mike and listen closely: I can't afford any distractions once the negotiations begin. If everything blows up in our faces, I want you to get over to Mount Horeb Hospital as fast as you can. There's someone you'll need to see in Fifth-floor-Psych, room 512. You got that?"

"Room 512, Mount Horeb Hospital, Fifth-floor-Psych. Who and why?"

"I'll explain later. Just remember and get there as fast as you can after this is over. Bye, Doc." I looked over at my hostage. "Ready?"

He readjusted his duster, nodded, and started down the stairs. I followed a few steps behind.

They were waiting for us in the furnace room, Bey and Bachman, insolently at ease and seated upon a jumble of crates like moldering royalty in an Egyptian tomb. Only a bare dozen candles were lit, shifting the clumps of darkness around us like stray cattle from a shadowy herd of the damned.

Bey was a mess. His skin was black and shriveled from his torching at the Tremont, here and there, portions of ruined flesh had flaked away to reveal smooth, albeit grey, skin beneath. Bey the Deathless was on the mend.

Bachman, however, wasn't. And her anticipation of my promised blood had her even edgier and jumpier than I had seen her last.

>>*So, dRAcUl*<< Bey projected, the skin at the corners of his mouth cracking and splitting as his mouth twitched, >>*yOu HAvE cOMe tO tHrOW yOUrSeLf UpoN oUr mERcY*<<

"Your mercy, Bey?" Bassarab spat a gob of scarlet on the floor, at his feet. "Not bloody likely!"

I cleared my throat. "Perhaps you should explain our working arrangement."

Bassarab parted his greatcoat to reveal the vest. "This yearling has managed to entrap me with this garment containing a large concentration of high explosives. If he pushes a button, the plastique charges in this vest will detonate." He smiled and his teeth seemed sharper than I had ever seen them before. "The result for you, Bey, will be no simple decapitation: I doubt that all the king's horses and all the king's men would ever be able to put Bey the Jackal together again."

It was hard to tell from the charred ruin of the sorcerer's face if he was discomfited by this revelation, but his ectomorphic form shifted on the crates like an alert cobra's. >>*WhY iS He sO aNXiOuS To dIe? AnD, FOr tHAt maTTEr, hOw Is iT tHAt yOu ARe sO cALM aNd cOoPErAtIVe?*<<

The old vampire shrugged. "As for Csejthe, he is nearly mad with Christian guilt over his own damnation. Your violation of his family has pushed him over the edge. He is more than ready to die if it will destroy you and return his wife and daughter to their eternal rest. As for me? What choice do I have? He tells me that, if I cooperate in the bargaining here, I may live past another sunset."

>>*BaRgAInINg?*<< Bey’s eyes narrowed and piece of crusted ear dropped off to reveal a smooth, grey lobe. >>*I wAs TOlD yOU WErE sURrEnDErINg yoURsElF tO rETuRn wITh Us TO nEW YoRk.*<<

Bassarab’s smile became a smirk. “Uncoerced compliance? The centuries have petrified your brain if you believe that I would give myself up without a fight. No, the bargain I refer to is between my captor and your keeper,” he said, nodding to Bachman.

Bey looked at Bachman. >>*WhaT iS He bABbLiNG aBOuT?*<<

But Elizabeth was staring at me. More specifically, she was staring at the detonator in my hand. “Your promise,” she whispered. “What about your blood?”

“I expect it will be literally vaporized along with the rest of us. Let me spell it out for all of you,” I announced, switching on the Sabrelight and pointing it at the ceiling. “I am not a happy guy. And, unless I get a whole lot happier in the next few minutes, I am going to turn this little basement tête-á-tête into a real open house.”

>>*YoUng oNe*<< Bey crooned, >>*aRe yOu rEAlLy sO wILlINg tO dIe?*<<

“The way I figure it, asshole,” I growled, “is with you finally gone, my family can rest in peace. I’ll be very happy to send Dracula to Hell as he’s the one who made me what I am. If it wasn’t for him, my wife and my little girl would still be alive.”

“And what of me?” Bachman’s voice was hushed and harsh with fear and need. “What of our bargain—the promise of your blood freely given?”

I flashed the light in her face, blinding her for the moment. “You traitorous bitch! You betray your friends and lure them to their deaths and you have the nerve to speak to me of promises and bargains? You just sit there for now and don’t say shit unless I ask you a question!

“Now,” I continued, trying to control the trembling in my voice and my hands, “I am even more unhappy than I was when I walked through the door a few moments ago." I still held the remote and flashlight in my left hand. I slid my right hand into my coat pocket and pulled out the Dartmaster. I pointed it at the Egyptian sorcerer. "Where is my family?"

He looked at the pistol. >>*WHat Is tHAt? A gUn? WhAT cAn yOU hOpe tO aCcoMpLisH wITh a guN tHaT YoU coUlD nOT Do wIth SWoRd, fLAme-ThROwEr, aNd sTAkE?*<<

I answered by shooting him in the chest.

He didn't even flinch. He looked down at the dart protruding from his shirt in mild surprise. With deliberate slowness, he pulled it from his flesh. I fumbled the Dartmaster's chamber open and inserted another dart as he examined the spent projectile. "I'm going to ask you again, where is my family?"

>>*HOw fASclnAtINg.*<< He turned it over and over in his spidery hands. >>*It iS bOTh a DaRt AnD a tINy sYRinGe. ThEy UsE thIs fOR tRANqUiLiZINg aNi-MALs, dOn'T tHEy?*<< He looked up. >>*Is THat wHAt yOu'RE tRYiNg tO Do? PuT mE to sLEeP?*<<

I shot him in the belly this time. "I said, where is my family? What have you done with them?"

>>*YoU mUSt rEaLIze tHaT tRaNQuIliZeRS, dRUgS, Or eVEn pOIsOns wILl hAve nO moRe efFeCT thAn sTAKinG, bEheAdINg, oR bUrnIng.*<< He pulled out the second dart and sniffed the needled tip. >>*YoU'vE alReaDy tRIed YoUr sO-caLlEd hOly wATer aNd yOu kNOw hOW eFfEcTiVe tHAt tUrNEd oUt To bE.*<<

I had fumbled through another reload and shot him again. This time I almost missed, barely managing to tag him in the arm. "I'm running out of patience, Bey! I want to see my family! I want to see you exorcise them with my own eyes!" I broke open the chamber and fumbled for another dart.

>>*ThEy aRe aWAy,*<< Bey said with enhanced nonchalance. >>*ShaLl I gO GEt tHEm aNd bRInG thEm To yOu?*<<

"I'm sure," I said, "that you can do that from right here, without moving a muscle." I glanced over at Bachman. "Where's Suki?"

"I'm here," came a hoarse cry from the back of the room.

"You surprised me," Bachman said, ignoring my directive to only answer direct questions. "I expected you to come to her rescue while we were gone, last night. Your humanity is slipping, indeed."

"Are you all right?" I called.

"She crawled under a workbench and hasn't spoken or moved in hours." Bachman tried to make her ruined mouth smile. "Don't worry: I kept your family away from her."

A hot flare of anger erupted behind my eyes and I brought the Dartmaster around and shot Bey again. "I'm waiting!" I screamed at him. "Get them back here now!"

He smiled and pulled the dart loose. >>*ThEy aRe tOo fAR aWaY. EvEN iF tHey cOUld ReSpoNd tO my cAlL, It mIgHt bE aN hOur bEfoRe thEy wOUld gEt hErE.*<<

I fumbled another dart into the chamber. "Vlad, go over there and get Suki out from under that workbench." I swung the Sabrelight's beam back into Bachman's face. "You—go help him."

>>*WhY dO yOu kEEp sHoOtINg yOUr sIlLy lItTle DaRTs At mE?*<< Bey asked mildly as the vampires moved to the back of the room. >>*YoU mUSt rEaLiZe tHAt yOu cAN't kILl a MaN wHo Is aLreADy dEaD, aNd tHEsE lITtLe sTInGs dO nOt eVEn qUAlIfY aS a mINoR aNnoYaNCe.*<<

"Then grin and bear it, you son-of-a-bitch. It makes me happy, and as long as I'm happy, I'm not pressing the button." I swung the beam so that I could see the workbench. An arm came out from beneath the bench and Bassarab stepped back so that Bachman would have to take the extended hand.

A crate creaked as Bey shifted his weight, and I turned and shot him in the face. "Don't move, goddammit!" I fumbled for another dart as I swung the light back to the workbench. Bachman was bent down, pulling, and Suki's face appeared in the circle of light. Her shoulders emerged. Then her other arm. She was holding something in her other hand: a Glock 19 auto pistol. The gun barrel came up with inhuman speed and came to rest just above the bridge of Elizabeth Bachman's nose. The impact of the hollow-point bullet took the top of her head off, scooping out the brainpan, and hurled her body halfway across the room where it impacted with the remains on an old boiler tank.

Her body started decomposing even before it finished slumping to the floor.

Distracted, I didn't see the monstrous forms of my wife and daughter until they were well out of the shadows and hurtling across the room. They descended on me, shrieking like the fire alarms of Hell. The Glock fired a quick succession of shots at the thing that looked like Kirsten and the impact of the bullets jerked it backwards as if it were executing a quick, spastic moonwalk. The creature wearing my wife's body was upon me before Bassarab could bring the shotgun out and around. I staggered, off balance, and the remote went flying out of my hand, the Sabrelight spinning its light-show trajectory like some kind of deranged UFO.

>>*YoUr fAMiLy iS hERe, CsEJtHe,*<< Bey taunted. >>*ArE yOu nOt hAPpY tO sEe tHEm?*<<

I cursed him then. Called him every vile name and used every epithet I'd ever heard or imagined as I slapped away the hands that had once caressed me and used my fists upon the face that had once meant more than life, itself, to me. Tears came, hot and blinding, as I split the lips that had kissed mine a lifetime ago.

Then a hand grabbed my wrist from behind. I shook it loose, but another hand grasped my shoulder and an arm fell across my throat. A multiplicity of hands fell on me, then, clutching and grasping. A smell like sour earth and long-dead rot washed over me, and my gag reflex took over in a shuddering succession of dry heaves. The Dartmaster was pulled from my grasp, and when my eyes could focus again, I could see others in the room.

Others like Jenny and Kirsten. Only not so well preserved or presentable. Bey had looted the local cemeteries for reinforcements, and now a shambling phalanx of corpses formed a ring about the necromancer. Dozens of hands and arms, inhumanly strong despite their putrescent flesh and denuded bone, held Bassarab and myself immobile as Bey retrieved the remote detonator.

He turned and walked over to Suki, bent down, and pulled the now-empty Glock from her hand. >>*AnD wHeRE dID yOU fINd tHIs, My pReTTy?*<< He turned the weapon over in his hand and then tossed it across the room. One of the corpses swayed "to" when he should have gone "fro" and the handgun struck him in the face. Half of his jawbone, including his chin, clattered to the floor along with the Glock.

>>*BAcHmAn tOLd mE YoU wErE tOO wEaK to cAUSe AnY tRoUBlE,*<< Bey continued, reaching down and grasping the Asian girl by the throat. >>*I gUEsS tHaT'S tHe lASt mIsTAkE sHe'Ll eVer mAkE.*<< He chuckled and lifted Suki up, off the floor by her neck.

She made a choking sound and grasped at Bey as he lifted her into the air, but his reach was longer than hers.

"Now you're the one making a mistake," I said.

>>*ReALlY?*<< Bey smirked. >>*HEr GuN iS eMPty aNd hEr bACk Is StiLL bRoKEn. I aM gOiNg To kILl hEr nOW. I'm gOInG tO LeT yOu wATcH. WaTCh AnD thiNk aBOuT whAt I'M gOIng tO dO tO eACh oF yOu wHEn iT's yOUr tURn.*<<

"I still say you're making a mistake," I said. And then Suki's right foot flashed up between Kadeth Bey's legs. He gave a screeching sort of grunt and bent forward, releasing his captive. It was too late: as she dropped, Suki's left foot came up and nailed his groin a second time, completing a double scissors-kick.

As he rolled away, still curled around his unexpected agony, several more corpses shuffled forward. "Now would be a good time, I think," Suki said in a surprisingly deep voice.

I nodded and bowed my head, still straining against the clammy hands that held me in death's cold embrace. "O," I said, "Amon Ra, oh!" My voice seemed suddenly louder, echoing through the basement as if whispered in an empty sepulcher.

"God of Gods," I intoned, my voice taking on strength and timbre, booming down the access tunnel across the room.

"Death is but the doorway to new life. . . ." The hair on the back of my own neck was starting to rise as I spoke the words and felt the power starting to gather.

Bey recognized the text from the Scroll of Thoth: >>*BlASpHeMy!*<<

"We live today, we shall live again. . . ."

>>*SiLeNCe!*<<

" . . . in many forms shall we return. . . ."

He uncurled himself and turned toward me.

"Oh, Mighty One. . . ."

He moved stiffly, uncomfortably. But it was more than the discomfort of a kick to the groin that slowed him now. Decapitated, impaled, flame-broiled, sliced and diced, Kadeth Bey had been discomforted, but hadn't actually experienced true pain for thousands of years.

Until now.

And as I spoke the Words and the potion spread through his body, the pain began to spread, as well. >>*KiLl yOu ALl!*<< he thought venomously. >>*DoN't uNdERstAnD! CaN'T huRt Me! cAn'T kIll mE!*<< He was growing disoriented as nerve endings came to life, sending long-forgotten sensations to his ancient brain.

As his attention faltered his necrotic army relaxed their grip and we shrugged ourselves free.

"Oh, I understand all right," I said, having completed the incantation. "And thank you for explaining it so succinctly the last time we met." I switched off my light and the few sputtering candles that remained did little to hold back the darkness.

"Do you see?" Bassarab asked. "It has begun."

It took me a moment longer to clear my vision: after-images bruised my retinas in yellows and purples and blues. But beyond the fading aurora borealis a different candle flame flickered, caught hold and grew in intensity, forming an orange nimbus about a swelling, yellow core.

>>*WhAT's HaPPEnIng? WhAT HaVE yOu dOnE?*<<

"The only thing I could do, under the circumstances," I answered. "As you have already said, we cannot kill something that is already dead. So, I have utilized forces antithetical to yours to perform a resurrection. Thanks to the Scroll of Thoth and hypodermic darts filled with tanna leaf extract, Kadeth Bey: this is your life!"

>>*WhAT? WhY?*<<

"Oscar Wilde said it best, I think," Bassarab growled, stepping forward. He slide-cocked the Mossberg as the orange began to shed a red aura, the orange turning yellow, the yellow core turning white. "'And the wild regrets and the bloody sweats / None knew so well as I. . . .'" He raised the shotgun to his shoulder. "' . . . For he who lives more lives than one / More deaths than one must die.'"

>>*I dONoT UnDErStANd!*<<

"You are no longer the walking dead," I said. "Now you are alive. And, now that you are alive—you can finally be killed."

He reached toward me and Bassarab swung the shotgun around. "Down!" he commanded.

I ducked as a hand clutched at my shirt from behind. The Mossberg roared, peppering me with stray pellets, and the grip on my shirt disappeared along with a sizable swatch of fabric. I hit the ground and rolled, turning over to look behind me. *Jennifer*— I closed my eyes and thought of death.

"Release her, Bey!" Bassarab's voice seemed to come from far away. "It was blasphemy before, but every second of false life now is an abomination! Let her go!"

>>Or wHaT? YOu'Ll kIll mE?<<

"That won't be necessary," I heard myself say.

"It won't?" Bassarab's voice was incredulous.

I tried rising to my hands and knees. "As part of the embalming process, he had his heart removed and preserved in a canopic jar. Isn't that right, Bey?"

He hissed but made no reply.

I climbed shakily to my feet, careful not to look back at the trembling, twitching, headless thing that once had been my wife. "As the tanna leaf extract spreads through your system, it's turning everything back on and starting everything back up. You're becoming human, again, Bey. Your body will once more be subject to the laws that govern flesh and blood. I think you'll find it's important to have your heart in the right place."

He clutched his chest and the detonator tumbled from his trembling fingers. He sank to his knees, his mouth forming a gigantic "O" of pain.

As I reached down and retrieved the remote, Bassarab stepped forward and placed the shotgun muzzle to Bey's head.

"That isn't necessary," I said, bringing the Sabrelight to bear on them both. "He can't survive with a hole in the middle of his chest."

"I want to make sure."

"So do I. But think of the irony of Kadeth Bey being the agent of his own death."

"Fuck irony," Bassarab said. He pulled the trigger.

The roar of the Mossberg gave way to a collective sigh and whisper as the ring of cadavers collapsed around us like unstrung marionettes. That sign, alone, was more reassuring than the incomplete corpse of the necromancer himself.

Still, I had to walk over and kick at the more substantial portions of his remains. I could hardly see, and it was awhile before I realized that it was because I was weeping again. But I didn't stop right away: I had to make sure.

No one else moved. No one else spoke until Mooncloud's voice crackled in my headset: *"Is it over?"*

"Almost," I said, moving the beam of my flashlight until it picked up Jenny's foot protruding from a mound of human debris. The foot no longer twitched or shook.

I opened the case of the remote control. "Dennis, get out of here."

Suki took one step forward, her face congealing with masculine features. "That's not necessary," she said with Smirl's voice as I pulled out the telescoping antenna. "Bey's dead."

"So am I," I whispered, the basement amplifying my words like a microphone. "So are the *wampyr*. So you see," I said, looking over at Bassarab, "I have to make sure."

"There are better ways of making sure." Suki's bosom flattened out and sprouted chest hair. Her hair retracted, became wiry and shot with grey.

I shook my head. "Doctor, Mr. Smirl will be joining you momentarily. As soon as he does, I suggest you provide him with the clothing I stashed in the spare wheel compartment. Then you need to get to the hospital, post haste, and get Suki out of room 512."

"What is Suki doing in the hospital?"

"She has a broken back and internal injuries, Doctor. I slipped her past security and put her on the Psych floor where the overnight staff is stretched thin and a little more isolated than the other floors. I left instructions with the charge nurse to give her whole blood and keep her room dark. I don't know how much that's helped, but by now the night-shift has gone off duty. It's just a matter of time before the day-shift finds discrepancies between their floor records and Admissions." I looked at Smirl, who now only showed vague vestiges of Suki's topography. "Time to go."

"Why don't we all go?" he asked.

I shook my head. "I have to make sure." I pushed him toward the door with my mind.

"A rendezvous with Death?" Mooncloud asked as Smirl headed up the stairs. *"At some disputed barricade?"*

"You're quoting Seeger, Doctor. I'm thinking of Swinburne."

"Swinburne?"

"Algernon Charles Swinburne." I flipped a switch arming one of the detonator circuits. "He wrote: 'From too much love of living, / From hope and fear set free. . . .'" I turned off the flashlight. Only two guttering candles remained to light the scene. "' . . . We thank with brief thanksgiving / Whatever gods there be. . . .'"

Bassarab stared at the remote, seemingly transfixed; he made no move to escape. "' . . . That no life lives forever. . . .'" My hands began to shake and my voice broke. "' . . . That dead men rise up never. . . .'"

It was time to make an ending.

"' . . . That even the weariest river / Winds somewhere safe to sea.'"

I pressed the switch that blew Christopher Csejthe and Vladimir Drakul Bassarab V out of existence.

Chapter Twenty-Four

It is said that when you die you see a light in the darkness, that you are drawn toward the light. Nothing is said about the smell of brick dust and scorched concrete and liquid copper roiling in your nostrils.

It is also said that there are beings waiting in the light to greet you—angels or loved ones that have gone on before. No one ever suggested that you might look upon eternity and see Vlad the Impaler reaching out his hand to you.

I blinked, trying to clear my vision. It slowly became obvious that I wasn't dead, yet.

Bassarab helped me sit up and then moved the Sabrelight's beam about to reveal the damage done.

The plastique that Smirl had planted between the first and second floors had brought the entire building down on top of us. That I had counted on: it was part of the plan.

I had also figured on the building's collapse sealing off the stairwell with a rockslide of shattered concrete and brick. With the basement buried under the collapse of the upper three stories, I had counted on the access tunnel being our secret escape route. But, as the flashlight beam picked out the spill of earth, rock, and ancient brick spilling from the tunnel's maw, I realized that all exits were lost. I might just as well have triggered the detonator for the vest and saved us both a long, slow, lingering death.

I lifted a leaden arm and checked my watch. 3:49 in the P.M.: I had been unconscious for hours. As I digested this piece of information I noticed something else: it was as quiet as a tomb.

Or perhaps not. Bassarab had ahold of my arm and was making strange mouthy expressions at me: he was speaking, maybe even shouting, but I couldn't hear a thing. I put a hand to my right ear, felt something sticky. Bassarab moved the flashlight so I could see my fingers more clearly. My ears were bleeding. So was my nose. Although the ceiling above us had held, the concussive shockwave from the blast had slammed into the basement like an invisible battering ram.

I lay back down and closed my eyes. Bruised and bleeding and stone-cold deaf, I probably had internal injuries that would have killed me had I been human. Might kill me, yet: I wondered how long it took a semi-vampire to die of dehydration. Perhaps Bassarab would solve my problem by finishing the task he'd started in his barn, nearly a year before.

I dozed.

Dreamed of Jenny and Kirsten and happier times. The nightmares didn't come this time.

I awoke to Bassarab shaking my shoulder.

"What?" I asked, my voice now sounding muffled and faraway.

He gestured, pointed at a narrow fissure in the debris choking the access tunnel and then beckoned for me to follow him. With that, he bowed his head, crossed his arms across his chest, and began to fade. As his body became less distinct, it lost form all together and dispersed as a kind of mist. I picked up my Sabrelight and tracked the now tenuous nimbus of vapor as it floated into the passageway and faded from sight.

I glanced at my watch: after ten P.M., now. The old vampire had escaped by traveling the dreampath.

I closed my eyes and tried to focus on the outside.

Tried to imagine the far end of the tunnel where it came up and out in the remains of the pump station.

Tried to image myself outside.

Tried to project. . .

A hand fell on my shoulder. I looked up at Bassarab who had returned for me.

He gestured.

I gestured.

Together we pantomimed our way through a discussion of what we already knew: my first dreamwalk had been a fluke and I didn't know how to repeat the process. Although they seemed to be healing, my ears were still nonfunctional and, with my head still buzzing from the blast, I couldn't "hear" Bassarab's mindspeech. He couldn't guide me onto the path much less help me off again.

I waved him away. Maybe if I slept, healed a bit. . .

He gestured that he couldn't wait. The sun would return in a few short hours and he had to find Wren. Tell him that the plan had worked. For the most part. I switched off the Sabrelight and he left, signing that he would return.

Sure.

Less than a week before, when we had discussed faking our deaths, Bassarab had promised me wealth undreamed of, a new identity, and a life of ease. Ease, particularly, in the sense that once we were believed to be truly dead, undead hitmen and shapeshifting assassins would stop complicating our existence. We would no longer have the resources of several vampire enclaves scouring the country for us.

Not that I really cared.

I had finally figured that my chances of nailing Bey were next to zip unless I was standing face-to-face with him when I pushed the button. The only reason for adding an escape clause to the plot was to guarantee Bassarab's cooperation.

And it had worked to that degree: Bassarab had cooperated. And now he was escaping.

But I didn't mind, really. All that really mattered was putting an end to the ancient necromancer and giving my family final peace. Now that it was accomplished, I could let go of everything else. I would be joining them soon.

Bassarab wouldn't be coming back. With me dead and buried, his existence was secure. I was an amateur at living this half-life and would eventually make a mistake that would betray my own existence and, therefore, his, as well.

All in all, I felt something akin to contentment. It didn't matter whether I had actually ended my mortal life on the muddy floor of an old barn, in a tangle of twisted metal at a Kansas intersection, or hooked up to life-support equipment in a hospital emergency room: I had lived my life. Maybe it wasn't the biblical three score and ten, but who said life was fair? I certainly knew better by now.

I lay on the cold, hard floor of the tunnel and waited for a final ending.

Slept again. . . .

Chris.

I awoke to a new dream: the voice of my wife, calling to me.

Outside the sun was setting again. I could feel that another day had passed.

I looked up and there she was.

Jennifer sat above me, lotus fashion, floating in midair. *Darling,* she said, *it's time for you to go.*

"I'm already gone," I mumbled, unwilling to invest myself in one more hurtful illusion.

You mustn't think that way.

"How do you know what I've been thinking?" I asked awkwardly. Dimly I registered that I could hear her voice clearly while my own words were still a bit muffled.

Chris, I've always been able to tell what you've been thinking. She smiled—a little wistfully, I thought. *I'm worried about you.*

"About me? You're dead."

And you're not. She shook her finger at me. *Not yet. And there's no need for you to hurry the process.*

She glowed with a faint, bluish white light: cold and fluorescent, not the red-orange-yellow spectrum of body heat and life force. And I could not only see the details of her face but the details of the brick spill behind it.

I picked up the Sabrelight, but my thumb hesitated on the switch: I feared she would dissolve like so much gossamer if I switched it on.

Still—

"You're not real," I said sadly.

What is real? she asked rhetorically.

"There's no such things as ghosts."

Nor vampires, nor werewolves. . . .

"That's an easy argument that you could use to justify anything. But I know you're not real."

What is real? she asked again.

I shook my head, felt my ears pop as I worked my jaw. "I was warned early on: the virus that creates the vampiric condition also affects the brain—eventually causes madness. You are nothing more than a hallucination."

An undigested bit of beef, a blot of mustard, she retorted, *a crumb of cheese, a fragment of an underdone potato.*

"A clever comeback, but you make my point. You never did have a head for quotations—even something as mainstream as Dickens. You are merely an early warning system for full-blown dementia."

You silver-tongued charmer; you always did know how to sweet-talk a lady.

"You're not there."

Okay. She unfolded her lotus and floated down to sit by me. *If I'm a manifestation of your own mind, then make me disappear.*

"Disappear?" I was surprised, wondering why I hadn't thought of that. But then, according to my theory, I just had. . . .

She reached around to place her hands on my shoulders. I could almost feel her massaging the tension out of my stiffened muscles. *You don't want me to go,* she crooned. *After all this time, now that the barrier is finally down: I show up for real and you want to send me back to oblivion?*

"You're not real," I whispered.

What is real? she asked again.

"Jennifer—what happened to Kirsten?"

She went into the Light, *Chris. She went a long time ago.*

I felt tears gathering. "Why didn't you?"

I've been worried about you. I couldn't leave until I knew you'd be all right. Let me help you focus.

"You're not real!" I yelled. "Go away!"

She began to cry. *It's hard enough being dead! I don't need you yelling at me and saying I'm not real on top of everything else!*

I found myself stammering an apology. "I—I'm sorry, Jen. I-I'm having a rough time, myself, right now."

Poor baby. She wiped at ectoplasmic tears with noncorporeal fingers. *I came here to help and all I did was get you all distracted.* She tried to touch my face and her thumb went through my nose. *You must concentrate.*

"What?"

Chris, your only way out is to travel the dreampath. And you can't do that unless you focus your mind completely.

"I don't know how."

I'll help you.

"How?"

Close your eyes.

I closed them.

Now, press the heels of your palms against your eyelids. Push.

"A blot of mustard," I muttered.

None of that. Now, as soon as you begin to feel a

pleasant buzz, I want you to expand the feeling outward so that it fills the space around you.

"A pleasant buzz?"

Wait for it.

"Turn on, tune in, drop out?"

In a sense. When it comes, you want to imagine everything around you as being fuzzy, losing its form. We're going to disconnect you from this reality before we try to focus on your destination.

"Sounds dangerous."

I'll be with you every step of the way.

"Not the most reassuring line seeing as how you're dead."

At least you're not accusing me of being unreal.

"Don't know what's real anymore: everything is starting to get fuzzy."

Good. Embrace the nothingness. Push everything else away.

"I'm pushing."

Push harder.

"Pushing. I'm pushing!"

And breathe! Don't forget to breathe!

"What is this, the Lamaze approach to teleportation?"

You never listened to me when I was alive and now you won't listen to me when I'm dead! Her voice was growing fainter.

"Wait a minute; come back here!"

Don't open your eyes.

"Well, don't leave me here."

How can I leave you if I'm not real? If I'm only a projection of your own subconscious?

"This is just the sort of argument I would have with myself."

Fine! Have it with yourself: I am leaving!

"No, you're not! You're my occipital delusion and you're not leaving until I'm ready to imagine it!"

Make me, fang-boy.

I lunged for her. Felt my ears pop. And then my head.

Felt a cool breeze stirring my hair, brushing my face and hands.

Opened my eyes.

I was outside. A mound of rubble some forty yards away marked the collapse of the old hospital. Flashing yellow lights atop highway barriers strobed the darkness, marking the perimeter of the tumbled ruin.

I looked around. "Jennifer?"

She was gone. As if she had never been in the first place. Of course.

Now what?

Walk back to the motel?

Find a phone and call the Doman to come and get me?

Stick out my thumb and try to hitchhike before the sun came up and after me?

As if in answer, a pair of headlights at the other end of the field flashed on and then off again. Red-in-violet parking lights blinked back on and an engine growled to life. Darkness moved within darkness and a vague shape gleamed in starlight. Then a wink of chrome as an automobile took form. A 1950 Mercury Club Coupe—younger sibling to the '49 model James Dean drove in *Rebel Without A Cause*—rolled toward me. Long, low, incredibly sleek, it had a chopped roofline, narrow windows, and frenched headlights. Darker than black, it was the color of a tar pit at midnight. Only the running lights and a silver chasing of chrome gave it any definable form in the darkness.

I forgot to breathe until it stopped a scant three feet away.

A tinted window slid down. Victor Wren looked out and up at me. "He said you would get out."

I looked at him. "Where is he?"

"Busy. Making sure you—and he—both get a head start. When the time is right and the coast is clear, he'll find you."

I nodded. "What about Suki?"

"She'll make it. She's already on the road to recovery." He opened the door and stepped out.

"And the others?"

"Also gone. Half the town came running when the building blew. It'll take weeks and heavy equipment to excavate down to the basement—if that's what the town fathers eventually decide to do. The consensus has both of you dead. Smirl didn't mention the second set of charges, so I don't know what he really thinks. Pagelovitch called his people home. Smirl flew back to Chicago. They let me keep the Duesenberg."

"Where's Bassarab?"

He smiled. "Waiting in the shadows somewhere. We figure someone's going to be watching me for awhile."

"Where will you go?"

"Home." He smiled and handed the ignition keys to me. "A little present from the boss."

"It's beautiful."

He nodded appreciatively. "Not all of it's vintage antique. You'll find out when you open her up out on the highway." He kicked a tire. "It should get you home."

"Home?"

"Wherever you choose. As long as you stay away from the enclaves. Papers are in the glove compartment. Along with an atlas showing all the known demesnes, marked and labeled. Also an envelope with new identity papers, documents, letters of introduction, credit cards, bank accounts. I hope you don't mind."

"Mind?"

"The name. New identity, new name. We were in a hurry and the boss seems to have developed a sense of humor of late." He smiled. "Serves you right for shooting me with that dart gun. I hear it made Lupé toss her cookies."

"Her dart was loaded with something a little stronger than sterile water. By the way: nice acting job."

"Thanks." He gestured to the rear of the interior. "Your knapsack and computer are in the backseat, along with three suitcases filled with cash. I didn't get an exact count, but it's in the neighborhood of five million dollars. Instructions are included to keep you clear of the IRS and any other banking procedures that might compromise your anonymity."

I stood there, staring at the car, at nothing, at something too complex to decipher yet.

"You really should get going: the local authorities have a lot of questions for anyone 'just passing through' of late."

I opened the door and slid behind the wheel. The front seat felt like a comfortable old sofa. "Can I give you a lift?"

He shook his head. "It's a beautiful night for a walk. I think I'll just stretch my legs a bit."

I closed the door and he leaned down to the window. "Thought about where you might go?"

I shrugged. "Maybe Louisiana."

"Stay away from New Orleans, if you do."

"Enclave?"

He nodded. "With literary pretensions." He reached through the window to shake my hand. "Good luck. After this all dies down, they may forget about me. Then, maybe, my master will take me back."

"Is that what you want?"

He smiled. "I've worked my share of jobs. As employers go, I've had worse."

I turned the ignition and the motor purred to life. "One more question," I said. "You've seen a lot of things: vampires, werewolves. . ."

He nodded. "Categories don't come easy."

"What about ghosts?"

He shook his head. "There ain't no such thing."

"You're sure?"

"Positive. Have it on the best authority." He stepped back. "Take care now. Don't let the sun shine on your parade."

There was nothing more to say. I put the Merc into

gear and headed back to I-69. I turned north at the light, planning a quick good-bye and then a one-eighty run south.

I was turning into the cemetery when I heard the catches pop on one of the suitcases.

Wow! We're rich! Jenny's voice said.

I rolled to a stop and looked around. "Where are you?"

Right next to you. Though I'm kind of twisted around and hanging over the seat, right now.

"I don't see you."

I'm invisible.

"Yeah, right."

The suitcase behind us relatched itself with a double snap and her voice turned petulant. *Don't start with that "I'm not real," stuff again.* The dark glass of the passenger window slid down. *What are we doing here? Oh. I see. You came to say good-bye, didn't you?*

I nodded, in spite of the fact it was a conversation I was having with myself.

That's so sweet! But it's also rather silly, darling. After all, Kirsten and I are buried under what's left of the old Mount Horeb Hospital building. There's nothing here but two headstones marking two empty graves.

I bowed my head against the steering wheel.

And one helluva big dog!

It took a moment to register. The "dog" was in motion as my head came up, running straight for the car.

Now why, Jenny was saying, *would a dog chase a car that wasn't even moving?*

"It's not a dog," I said, groping for the button that locked all the doors. There was no such thing in a 1950 Mercury coupe, even one that had been customized in the nineties.

With the window down it was a useless gesture anyway: the wolf leapt, scrambling over the door panel, landing on the passenger seat with its front paws in my lap.

Oof, said my wife's ghost. *I'd better get in the backseat. Nice doggy.*

A moment later the "nice doggy" was gone and Lupé Garou was sitting beside me with one hand grasping my arm and the other gripping my leg.

"Don't you ever, *ever* do that again!" she hissed through clenched teeth.

My goodness, Chris: she's naked!

"Uh," I said, "do what? Shoot you with a tranquilizer gun?"

But very pretty. In an understated sort of way.

"Shoot me with a tranquilizer gun! Not trust me with the truth! Make me think you were dead!" Her eyes were wet and furious. "All of it!"

I take it that the two of you are involved—to some degree?

"I'm sorry," I said. I seemed to be apologizing a lot for a guy who was supposed to be dead.

Not that I mind, you understand. You really do need someone to look after you.

"Well," she sniffed, rolling up the window on her side, "don't ever do any of those things again. Now, let's get going."

I don't mind sharing you now. Death is really very liberating—emotionally, that is.

"Going?"

You learn to let go of so many things—

"The sun is going to be coming up in a few hours. You'll need a place to sleep."

What about her?

"Um," I said. "What about you?"

"I'll need a place to sleep, too," Lupé said. "I haven't had a moment's rest since the old hospital blew up. Let's go."

She seems very practical. I like that. You need a practical woman. I was always very practical—

"No, you weren't," I murmured.

"Excuse me?"

"Nothing. Never mind."

I put the car back in gear and drove the circular road

back out and onto the highway. "Would you turn the heater on?" Lupé asked as I swung right and onto the bypass that arced around Pittsburg to the west. "It's a little cool."

Of course she was: she wasn't wearing any clothes.

As I reached for the heater knob, my wife's voice piped up from the backseat: *Honey, aren't you going to introduce us?*

I gripped the steering wheel a little tighter and cleared my throat. "So," I asked, "how did you know that I wasn't really dead?"

"Ah," Lupé answered, doing a fair imitation of Bassarab's accent, "the blood-bond! It called to me!"

I had to laugh. "Really."

"You're a survivor, Chris. You don't give up easily. And . . . I didn't want to believe that you were really gone."

This is really rude, Christopher; conversing as if I weren't here with the two of you.

"So, now what?" I asked. "Do we drive back to Seattle? Or do you need to call the Doman to arrange for a pickup?"

"Neither. I quit. Told Taj to hand in my resignation for me."

"Will they consider you 'rogue'?"

"Probably."

"So, they'll be looking for you. May even suspect that I might still be alive, as well."

She shrugged shapely shoulders. "Relationships always complicate things. You gotta expect a certain number of problems."

Chris—

"Hush!" I snapped.

"What?"

"Not you."

"I don't understand."

I sighed. "My wife's ghost is in the backseat."

Lupé turned around to look.

Pleased to meet you, Jenny said.

"Not really," I explained. "I'm just imagining that I hear her voice. Talking to me. The dementia phase of the virus seems to be advancing."

"So," Lupé considered, "she's not really back there."

I am, too!

"Of course not," I said. "You don't hear her voice, do you?"

Lupé shook her head. "But you do?"

"Just call me Cosmo Topper."

If I'm not real, then how can I do this? The glove compartment opened by itself and a large manilla envelope floated into view.

"If she's not really in the car with us," Lupé asked, wide-eyed, "then how do you explain the floating envelope?"

Precisely, Jenny said primly. A piece of paper emerged from the envelope and unfolded in midair.

"One of the by-products of my altered brain chemistry is certain telekinetic abilities," I answered, trying to keep my eyes on the road and steer. "If I can transport my body along the dreampaths, I can certainly float some pieces of paper without tweaking any conscious brain cells."

"So you're saying your dementia is not only providing auditory hallucinations," Lupé said, "but causing your subconscious to manifest certain psychic episodes, as well."

I nodded, only half-listening to her words. "What are you doing?" I demanded.

Checking on your new identity. The end opened and a piece of paper floated out. *Oh my.* She started to laugh.

"What's so funny?"

"May I see?" Lupé asked.

Your new identity. Jenny turned the paper so Lupé could see, too.

"What?"

As of now your last name is "Haim," Jenny announced.

"Haim," Lupé murmured. "What an odd name. Wonder what nationality that might be."

Celtic, Jenny replied with a giggle.

"Celtic?" I asked. "What makes you think it would be Celtic?"

Lupé began to giggle as well. "Because your first name is now Samuel." On the last word both of their giggles bubbled over.

"What's so funny about Samuel?" It took me a moment: "Samuel Haim—*Sam* Haim?" I wasn't laughing.

Oh, darling; it could be worse. They could have made your new name Hal O. Ween.

"I'm still not laughing." I pulled up to the four-way stop where 160 split off to the west and 57/171 angled off to the east and then a long curve around to the south.

Lupé kept twisting around to look behind her. "You know, you've got me half-convinced that your wife's ghost is here with us, after all."

Admit it, babe. You're not fully convinced that I'm nothing more than a subconscious manifestation of your deteriorating psyche.

"You're not real," I insisted as my foot danced from brake to clutch and I torqued the steering wheel.

"Are you really so sure about that?" Lupé asked with a smile. "After all, it wasn't that long ago that you didn't think vampires or werewolves—"

"You're not real, either," I announced as the envelope floated back into the glove compartment and closed with a snap. To close off any further conversation, I reached over and switched on the radio.

An oldies station was playing the last few bars of "Earth Angel." There was a disembodied chuckle behind me and Lupé was grinning wolfishly.

"I don't find any of this particularly funny."

Hey, Jenny's voice murmured in my ear, *didn't anybody ever tell you: dying is easy; comedy is hard.*

I stomped on the accelerator as the radio segued into a new selection.

It was "The Monster Mash."